THE JOURNEY HOME

A "FORGOTTEN FLOWERS" NOVEL

MICHAEL J. SULLIVAN

Publish Authority - Offices in
Newport Beach, CA & Roswell, GA USA

The Library of Congress Cataloging-in-Publication Data is available.

Cover design lead: Raeghan Rebstock
Editor: Gordon Jackson

www.PublishAuthority.com

As our time on earth draws to an end, we will be fortunate to have our memories though they too have an expiration date. We will become less important to loved ones who will be consumed with the complexities of guiding lives yet to be lived, of dreams yet to be achieved. We will also be fortunate to have those willing to be both friend and companion, individuals who will see that our lives retain some semblance of dignity and respect. To those caregivers of the elderly who are victims of longevity, and seemingly unimportant to all, I thank you from the bottom of my heart.

PROLOGUE

I n *Forgotten Flowers*, Michael J. Sullivan first introduces us to Daniel Kilgore, a man seeking answers for his wife Vivian's fading memory by working at Magnolia Gardens, an expensive assisted living facility in Charleston, South Carolina. There he meets Dr. Jane Lincoln, a research scientist who provides Daniel with a horrible prognosis concerning Vivian's condition. In time, she also presents the possibility of second love. Each struggle with their own past as their feelings for each other escalate. We meet Madeline Orsini, the retiring executive director of Magnolia Gardens, who has convinced Jane Lincoln to take her position as the new executive director. Madeline devoted over twenty-five years to caring for an elderly population with fading memories of lives well lived. Having never married and with no children, she also has memories of a life that could have been.

Read *Forgotten Flowers* and prepare yourself for the emotional and tragic saga of these characters in *The Journey Home*.

1

MADELINE'S NEW HORIZON

With the door ajar, Samantha felt no need to knock. The entrance to the director's office was customarily left open. She nudged the door open with her foot as her arms were encumbered with several cardboard boxes. Madeline had made the announcement to the staff several weeks ago that she was retiring, but still, the sight of her office now nearly bare of her personal belongings startled the young girl.

Seeing Jane Kilgore sitting at Madeline's desk, she asked, "Madeline's not here?" as she set the boxes down on the oak conference table.

There was no immediate response from Jane, who was preoccupied with reviewing several binders full of state and federal regulations relating to the operation of an assisted living facility. She had been asked by the Board of Directors to consider staying on as the temporary Executive Director until a search committee could find a permanent replacement. Her frustration with a workload with which she had no prior experience caused her to bristle at Samantha's question. Without even looking up, she snapped, "No, she's taking a walk around the facility. Kind of her last farewell."

Samantha was taken back a bit by the abruptness of Jane's answer, as she was accustomed to Madeline's more caring and endearing personality. Wanting to give Jane the benefit of the doubt, Samantha thought maybe she hadn't gotten rid of that "I'm the professor, you're the student" sternness she maintained when she was teaching at the College of Charleston.

Samantha did not take kindly to being talked to in such a condescending manner, but she decided to respond with honey and not vinegar.

"That doesn't make sense to me, Jane. After all, the Board of Directors is allowing her to stay in one of the independent living cottages. It's not like she's moving away."

Realizing Samantha did not fully comprehend the effect retirement had on Madeline, Jane felt guilty for her curt response. She rose slowly from behind Madeline's desk and walked over to the double French doors. She opened them and gazed out over the landscape; the expansive patio with its neatly arranged tables and chairs, the pristine green lawn leading down to the duck pond, and those magnificent Magnolia trees with the God-sent shade they provided.

"All this is no longer her charge. She's touring the facility, taking time to converse with the residents. Giving this all up had not been an easy decision for her to make. She wants to ensure the residents understand that she is not departing for some lofty position or abandoning them. After so many years, her emotions are deeply invested in this place. I suppose you could call it sort of her last hurrah."

Samantha took off her glasses and massaged her temples. She had no difficulty comprehending this not particularly complex situation, but emotional acceptance was another thing altogether. Madeline had been a role model and mother figure as few others could have provided. Her departure from the directorship was going to create a void in Samantha's life.

"I guess I hadn't thought about it that way. Just knowing she's still here doesn't change much in my mind. She'll still be the boss. She taught me everything of real value in terms of elder care. I will never forget that!"

Jane was quite taken with the sincerity expressed in Samantha's words. Now more than ever before, Jane fully understood the value of this woman in terms of her professionalism and role as a compassionate caregiver.

"She is something of a legend around here, and I intend to keep it that way," pronounced Lincoln.

"Have you made a decision on Madeline's offer?" asked Lincoln, aware that Orsini had offered the position of Director of Volunteer Services to Samantha.

In the five years Samantha had been at Magnolia Gardens, she had finished her BA in Gerontology at The College of Charleston and an MA in Public Health Administration. The change from leisure pants, t-shirts supporting any number of ecological causes, and a baseball cap, to pants suits, business dresses and the occasional pair of slacks with complementary cotton tops, were signs of her new sense of professionalism. Her husband, Mike, had finished his degree in Criminology and had joined the Charleston Police Department. Magnolia Gardens was every bit a part of Samantha's fabric as it was for Orsini. Samantha's grandmother, Sandra, had passed away here. With her relationships with the residents and staff so ingrained in her, Samantha couldn't imagine being anywhere else.

"Yes, and I'm humbled by the confidence Madeline has placed in me. I won't disappoint her," responded Samantha.

Jane smiled at this last remark. She would have continued the conversation if not for the deliberate movement of the woman walking up the pathway from the pond to the patio that caught her eye. Orsini didn't move with her normal swift gait. The cast on her right foot was the result of a fall while jogging that resulted in a broken ankle. Still, Madeline Orsini had not lost her eye for fashion. Stylish tan slacks complemented her sleeveless cotton blue blouse. Gold triangle earrings hung from both ears. From the pond to the patio, the path had several flattened areas with benches for residents and visitors to use as resting places. Orsini took advantage of each spot to sit and pause, perhaps giving a thought to a lifetime of memories at this locale.

"I see Madeline returning now," Lincoln said, as she watched Orsini thoughtfully plan each step with the aid of her cane.

Now giving Madeline her full attention, Lincoln called out her name. Waving back in response, Madeline acknowledged the call and headed to the opened doors of her office. Once there, she rested in her old leather chair, more fatigued than she realized. An annoying fly, who took advantage of the open office doors, landed on Madeline's desk and did not seem the slightest bit alarmed by Madeline's swishing of a file over its location.

"I certainly need to build up my endurance," said Orsini, "if I expect to move around like I used to."

There was a dogged determination in her voice that brought smiles to the faces of Samantha and Jane. Madeline's physical appearance belied her chronological age of sixty. Other than a generous smattering of gray throughout her auburn hair, Orsino looked twenty years younger. Her complexion retained its perpetual golden tan. Hazel eyes still shimmered when she spoke, and but for a few extra pounds, her figure still caught the eyes of admiring males.

Rejuvenated, Madeline rose from the chair and slowly walked to the worktable where she had arranged her personal belongings. She carefully, almost meticulously, placed each item in the reinforced moving box which proudly displayed the mover's name on all sides.

"Did you ever think this day would come?" asked Lincoln, as she watched Madeline begin placing her personal belongings into a cardboard box.

Madeline said nothing. She was lost in the memories that each item held. The cameo broach with the image of a Magnolia tree etched on it was a gift from the Johnson family for the years of devoted service the staff had given their mother, Estelle. Orsini teared up a bit as she gazed at the crystal platter from Samantha and Mike Callahan engraved with the words, "You have been a mother, a mentor, and a friend." With each item placed in the box came a reminiscent smile and a tear. Using her cane for balance, Madeline walked slowly to her favorite chair, a high back ergonomically designed armchair made of the softest Moroccan leather. It was a bit ostentatious for her personal taste, but it was a gift from the Board of Directors in sympathy for her injury, and Madeline felt compelled to use it lest she offend someone's sensibilities. In time, she became very fond of the chair. Its adjustable back lent itself to the most enjoyable power naps when Madeline found herself working long hours.

She leaned back in the chair and slowly swiveled left and then right, taking in every detail of her office; the crown molding gilded with interwoven sprigs of bougainvillea, the built-in mahogany bookcase along one wall with its doors of mosaic cut glass, and her favorite, a painting of the driveway leading up to Magnolia Gardens. The artist, a son of one of the Gardens' oldest residents, painted it as a gesture of gratitude for the love and kindness extended to his mother. He captured in exquisite detail the blossoming Magnolia tree with its white blossoms salting the ground below its branches. The stately white columns bordering the entrance were suggestive of an old plantation, and the sabal palmetto palms seemed three dimensional with each spiked leaf distinctly growing out from its base.

Jane rested on the edge of the oak conference table, her hands braced on the edge, not wanting to interfere with Madeline's moment.

She sat forward in her chair. Her thoughts became words.

"No job lasts forever. I knew someday this would have to end. But Magnolia Gardens has been my home for nearly twenty-five years. In that time, I've witnessed countless families bring their loved ones here because they knew they would be treated with compassion and care."

Madeline's heightened emotion alerted Jane to the cathartic episode about to occur. Samantha sensed the two women needed to be left alone.

"I think I'll be on my way. Call me if you need anything."

She politely backed out of the office.

"Jane, I've watched our residents fall victim to the ravages of dementia and Alzheimer's. Minds once vibrant and alive with memories of the past, now couldn't recognize their own children. Mercifully, in the advanced stages of that horrible disease, they were not aware of the need to be washed, dressed, and fed. And the staff, Madeline, I've nurtured a generation of young caregivers to value the residents and the lives they led. In moments when others would turn away, they've tended to the most personal needs of our residents with the utmost dignity and respect."

Moistened eyes could not hold back the watershed of emotion brought on by Madeline's memories. The years of watching the lives of her residents play out to the end of their time had taken a toll on Madeline.

In keeping with her professional philosophy, Madeline had moved much of her own furniture into her spacious one-bedroom suite. Her queen-sized bed with its matching Cherry wood armoire fit comfortably in the bedroom. Madeline loved the en suite off the master bedroom, taking special delight in its sunroof. The kitchen was spacious and provided a sizable dining area which her custom-made mahogany table for eight had no problem filling. She was particularly fond of a small alcove that opened to a private patio. It would become her reading room. It took several weeks of arranging and rearranging furniture and hanging pictures before Madeline felt a sense of home. When she finally did, a sensation of contentment settled over her. For years the busyness of her career consumed much of her mental energy. But now, barely a month into retirement, she began to have second doubts.

My God! These residents have been my family and the staff like my children. You don't leave family and children, do you? Why couldn't I stay on just a little longer? After all, my mind still works. What difference does it make if I need a cane to walk?

Her heart said one thing, but Orsini's mind was more pragmatic. The auto accident had left her with a broken back and unable to spend hours on her feet or at her desk. Her mobility impairment slowed her ability to move through the facility to a snail's pace. Her mind knew what her heart struggled to accept. It was time to move on, like it or not

One night, feeling rather melancholy for no apparent reason, Madeline set her teapot on the stove. She then went to her bedroom closet and retrieved a small cherry wood box from the top shelf. The evening warmth from that hot summer day caused Madeline to leave the door to the patio partially open. She poured herself a cup of hot water and placed a bag of her favorite Macha in it to steep. She set her cup of brewing tea on a small Victorian lamp stand next to her chair. Nestling into the overstuffed chair, she cradled the small box in her lap. There was no need to open it. She knew its contents: letters, dozens of them. She knew what each one said, line by line, word by word. Her hand formed a fist. As it began to open, her heart began to ache at the emerging memories her mind was no longer able to fend off. In the palm of her hand was a gold Seal Challenge Coin engraved with the words, "The only easy day was yesterday." The color was now faded: its lettering worn from decades of fingers pressing against them. Her lamentation echoed through the stillness of the summer night, "Eddie, my love, my love."

2

JANE'S REVELATION

Daniel finished seasoning the tri-tip roasts, then deftly hung them over the coals in his smoker.

"Forty-five minutes to an epicurean delight," said an unabashedly smug Daniel Kilgore to a smiling Mike Callahan.

Jane had invited Sam and Mike over for what had become a monthly BBQ get together. Sam and Jane took these gatherings as an opportunity to talk about what they wanted to accomplish at the Gardens, expanded services for the residents, greater community exposure, and the most intriguing one for Jane, expanding the list of family visitors. Jane had become fascinated with genealogy and had constructed a family tree for one of the residents, Leticia Lamberson, Letty as she was referred to by the staff. Letty Lamberson walked with the use of a cane, but that did not dissuade her from maintaining a near-perfect posture. Her head was held high. Her shoulders square. Hazel eyes that focused on you when you talked. All these were reminiscent of a generation when a women's appearance was thought to reflect her social standing. Letty's hair had long ago turned snowy white, and thanks to a stylist from the salon, Letty's hair resembled that of Mae West. When coming out of the salon, Letty was sometimes seen coming down the hallway with that famous Mae West swagger.

Maybe it was genes, maybe it was the cosmetic creams she had used all her life, but Letty maintained a smooth complexion despite those aging lines brought on by her near seventy years. Through Letty's own recollection, information from her family, and some online research, Jane had been able to trace the Lamberson family back to the Revolutionary War period. It was an amazing tool to present to her and her family members when they came to visit. Jane watched from afar the day Letty's daughter, Margaret, and her granddaughter, Carrie, came to visit.

~

"I'M HERE TO SEE MY MOTHER, LETTY LAMBERSON," MARGARET TOLD THE receptionist.

"She's out on the patio. She's been expecting you."

Letty was seated at a table near the gate leading off the patio and down to the duck pond.

"Mom, you look great!" smiled her daughter, who was so grateful for the care she was receiving at the Gardens.

"Flattery will get you a hug," smiled Letty, as she stood up to greet her daughter and granddaughter. "I've got something to show you. Have a seat."

Carrie pulled her chair close to the table, eager to see the awaiting surprise. Letty held up a large white poster board labeled, "The Lamberson Family Tree," smiling with pride.

"Jane has been working with me to construct my family tree. This goes back nearly four generations of my family."

"Grammy, I didn't know you were related to General Pershing! He's a really famous World War I general" gushed the gleeful teenager who was hugely interested in history, something of an anomaly for a thirteen-year-old.

Margaret Lamberson, Letty's daughter, sat in awe of the famous and infamous relatives hanging from the branches of the tree.

"I can't believe our family is related to John Wilkes Booth, Mom."

"Your father's side of the family," chided Letty.

～

JANE CHUCKLED AT THE MEMORY OF THAT MEETING. MIKE AND DANIEL were much less profound. They preferred debating the finer points of the spread offense and what it would take for the Carolina Panthers to make it to the Super Bowl.

Jane and Sam had labored to create a beautiful platter of finger food to snack on before dinner. Much to their dismay, the boy's favorite was a container of store-bought guacamole dip and chips. Daniel poured the chilled Bogle Chardonnay into four glasses. Mike raised his glass.

"To us and those who want to be like us, damn few."

Jane looked askance at him.

"It's a Marine thing, Jane. Ignore him," said Samantha, who had long ago gotten used to the plethora of mumbled, nearly unintelligible Marine Corps expressions uttered by her husband.

"Is this Directorship thing really a temporary thing or is the Board going to make it permanent?" asked Mike, who was inquiring more for his wife's benefit than his.

Daniel smiled as if he would approve either way. His neutrality belied the way he really felt. He kind of liked their life the way it was. Jane had cut back her teaching load to half-time. Daniel still spent time at the Gardens. If Samantha would accept Madeline's offer to become the new Director of Volunteer Services, he'd had even more time to spend with Jane.

"I got the feeling Madeline pretty much told them she wanted me as her replacement," said a humbled Jane.

"Speaking of Madeline," Mike asked. "It was family that brought Sam and me to Charleston and the Gardens, and it was a sense of family that led Daniel to become involved with the residents. What do we know about Madeline's family? Did she ever marry? Did she ever have children? What about parents, brothers or sisters? If you think about it, the woman is a mystery, even to those closest to her."

"My, aren't we the inquisitive one, Mr. Holmes," quipped Sam, as she tipped glasses with her husband.

Mike's queries gave Daniel pause to think.

"Come to think of it, I've never heard Madeline speak of any family members, and certainly she never talked about ever being married or having children."

"Kind of odd, don't you think?" replied Mike.

No one responded as each was lost in their own thoughts of conjecture.

∾

THE CONJECTURE ABOUT THE PRODUCTIVENESS OF CONSTRUCTING A FAMILY tree for the residents continued to plague Danial through the night and into the next day. The next evening as he helped Jane prepare dinner, he asked, "Do you really think this family tree thing is going to help?"

He was relegated to making the salad. Daniel stood at the counter, his back to Jane, carefully slicing a red onion and some cherry tomatoes. His focused attention and deliberate knife strokes indicated his frustration that her plan would result in any benefit. His skepticism seemed well deserved. After all, many of the residents even in the independent living wing had trouble remembering things, much less some extended family member in their family tree they probably never met during their lifetime. Jane ignored his question as she tended to the crown rack of lamb searing in a cast iron skillet. There was a decided edginess to his voice when he repeated his question.

"Well, do you?"

With the crown rack of lamb at its desired degree of sear, Jane sprinkled some chopped garlic on top with a couple of sprigs of Rosemary and placed the skillet in the oven. A noticeable slamming of the oven door caused Daniel to turn around. He now wished he hadn't been so terse. Jane turned and walked over to him. His apprehension would prove to be unnecessary. What he thought was going to be a chastisement for his lack of confidence in Jane's newest twist of therapy, instead turned out to be an outburst of newfound excitement on Jane's part.

"Sorry, I didn't mean to slam the oven door. That hinge spring is really strong."

She took a sip of wine from her glass.

"That lamb will take about twenty minutes. Let's sit outside," she said.

The enthusiasm in her voice eased his trepidation. Sitting on the log swing on the front porch, both took a moment to enjoy the olio of sweet aromas of the blossoming fruits trees in the front yard. Jane curled one leg under the other and turned to Daniel.

"You know Ira and Selma Levinson?" she asked. "They live in the independent living facility."

"God, how could anyone forget Ira. Put ten people together, and Ira had his audience to perform his old stand-up routines from the Catskills. I'll bet whenever he opens the refrigerator door, the light is his signal to begin a monologue."

Jane laughed. Daniel was right. Ira Levinson was the resident comedian whose infectious personality and exaggerated Yiddish accent brought laughter even when it was not intended.

"Theirs was the second family tree I ever did. I was able to trace their lineage back to the early 1900s when a Lewis Levinson migrated to this country from Poland. Tragically, after World War II, there were gaps I was never able to fill. Anyway, I set up their tree in the main lobby. I can't tell you the number of people, residents, staff, even visitors who would stop and look at the tree. Talk about six degrees of separation, Daniel. People would comment on what a fabulously interesting history the tree represented. A few even claimed to recognize certain names they remembered from old movies, as some of Ira's relatives came from the entertainment field. Even Harriet Gobble startled everyone when she saw the tree and gleefully shouted out that she remembered a comedian from the forties and fifties whose name was Jack Durant. It really is amazing, Daniel, the occasional expression on their faces when I take someone through their own family tree, and they react with glee at some long-forgotten name. At least in the moment, they remember."

"Seems like a pretty daunting task for one person to do," Daniel offered graciously, now more appreciative of her efforts.

"Between time-consuming online research and corresponding with family members, it's a slow process at best, and in fairness a task I really don't have the time to do justice. Thank God for Samantha and her amazing network of volunteers," responded Jane, in an even more spirited tone. "After talking with her about the Gardens' Family Tree as she called it, Sam took it upon herself to contact US GenWeb.org. It's a nationwide organization of volunteers who help people trace their family lineage. They have a local chapter right here in Charleston. They've agreed to send some volunteers to work with assigned residents in constructing their family trees. They'll do all the online research necessary and then work with each resident and their family members to obtain as much information as they can to fill in the branches."

With the ding of the timer, the crown rack of lamb was done.

"Time to eat," she said, as she took Daniel by the hand, a clear sign there was no resentment over his rather caustic tone earlier.

Jane grabbed her oven mitten and took the cast iron skillet out of the oven and set it on the stove top to rest.

"That looks perfect, if I do say so myself," offered up a contented chef Jane.

She started to boil a pan of water for the baby red potatoes she had rinsed. Alongside them was a small cutting board with freshly minced rosemary. Daniel, on cue, drizzled some extra virgin olive oil over the salad and gingerly sprinkled on some fifty-year-old Balsamic vinegar. A recovering Catholic, as he liked to refer to himself, Daniel started the blessing. "Bless us O Lord for these thy gifts which we are about to receive through thy bounty, through Christ Our Lord, Amen." This seemed much quicker and equally as devotional as the itemized blessings Jane, a born-again Christian, would make for anyone they knew to be in need, could be in need or might even be in need, as Daniel saw it.

"That was divine," groaned Daniel, as he settled back in his chair. "Another bite and I'll explode."

Feeling equally sated, Jane set her glasses on the table and finished her wine, another cue for Daniel to attend to her empty glass.

"Have you ever thought about constructing your own family tree?" she asked.

"Not really. The Kilgore line ends with me," he said, mournfully thinking about what might have been had his son, Greg, lived. "My sister might be interested in that sort of thing."

"How about you?"

She smiled. There was precious little she had not accomplished in her lifetime. However, the fulfillment of that maternal instinct to bear children was something Jane had never achieved.

"I'm the last of the Lincolns. At times I wish that wasn't the case."

Jane was careful to properly couch the words that came next. She had thought about it from the moment she realized she was in love with Daniel, but hadn't dared bring it up for fear it might drive him away. She sipped the last of her wine.

"Ever thought about extending your own line?" she asked.

Realizing the implication of her question, Kilgore replied, "At sixty-five I hardly think that's practical, do you?"

Even more guarded in her response, she stealthy replied, "I think that depends on your definition of practical."

3

THE PROGNOSIS

Orsini had asked Kristin Andrews, a long-time colleague of hers from The Havens, an assisted living facility across town, to join her for breakfast at her cottage. They had been running partners for many years, partaking in every fun-run the city had to offer. It had been Andrew's idea to train for the Boston Marathon which had resulted in Madeline's broken ankle. Both were health addicts, so vegetarian omelets accompanied by slices of fresh grapefruit and avocados were well in keeping with their dietary regime. It was Kristin who insisted on a small bit of decadence, mimosas. Madeline used a small Cuisinart knife from a set she had received as a retirement gift from the staff, to adroitly slice a few mushrooms, mince a clove of garlic, and dice two scallions. Wanting a quick sauté, she slid them off the cutting board into a hot omelet pan in which Madeline had drizzled a bit of extra virgin olive oil. In the time it took to whisk four eggs, the vegetables were ready, Madeline poured the egg mix and flipped over the end of the omelet pan.

"Real butter or I Can't Believe It's Not Butter?" laughed Kristin, knowing Orsini abhorred any products using animal fats.

"Really?" groaned Madeline.

They ate on the patio which bordered the back of the grounds and away from most foot traffic, making it an ideal place for wildlife to gather. To Madeline's eternal delight, a mother and two small fawns were nibbling on the sweet grass. Any number of birds used their beaks to separate the grass wet with dew to retrieve that juicy earthworm just below the surface.

"To retirement and recovery!" said Kristin, as she raised her glass to Madeline.

Madeline reciprocated. They tapped glasses, then sipped the chilled combination of the bubbly and orange juice.

"Tell me about the kids," Madeline asked, as she slid her fork under a bite of her omelet.

Talking about her children was not a chore for Kristin. As a single mother who had virtually raised them on her own, she was immensely proud of each one.

"Kayla works for a financial management firm in Massachusetts. Courtney works for a software company in California. She's in charge of arranging trade show exhibitions. Ashley is in grad school majoring in biological research, and Riley works for the US Fire Service. They're all carving out their own niche in this world."

"And you?" Madeline continued.

"I travel. There's a world out there I want to see, cultures I want to experience, and now I've got the time and money to do it."

"Good for you," smiled Madeline, genuinely happy for her friend.

After a sip of her mimosa, Kristin queried her friend, "How about you? What's retirement hold for you?"

"For the moment, getting my ankle to heal is my top priority. The pins came out a week ago. Three times a week in the morning, I go to physical therapy and then an hour of aquatic therapy in the afternoon. On my off days, I usually roam around the Gardens trying to help where I can. But quite honestly, Kris, I'm already beginning to feel like a fifth wheel."

"What's the prognosis about your ankle?" asked Kristin, hoping to change to a more optimistic topic.

"Structurally, everything is okay. Strengthening the muscles and tendons might take a little time."

Madeline extended her right leg working the ankle up and down, left and right.

"See. Try doing that with a two-pound weight strapped to your foot ten times," she dared.

The flashing movement of a squirrel racing across the ground with a mouth full of nuts distracted Andrews.

"Could those creatures possibly stuff anymore into their mouths?" she mocked, as she puffed out her cheeks.

The rays of the mid-morning sun now breaking through the trees gave the two friends pause to reflect on the beauty of the wildlife parading before them; two baby fawns satisfying themselves on the milk from their mother's teats. Squirrels scurried across the lawn and up the trees to their nest after harvesting their next fare. A covey of quails was feasting on nearly invisible bugs and insects.

"Truth or dare?" Kristin asked Madeline.

"Yuk, not that game. Didn't you get enough of that when your kids were young?" groaned Orsini.

"Yes, that game," chided Kristin. "So, why haven't you ever married?"

Knowing her friend had her best interest at heart was no consolation to Orsini. She hated the question, and she hated more the answer she would give.

"I never found the right guy," Madeline answered, her focus drifting away to the mother deer and her two fawns still enjoying the sweetness of the grass, so she wouldn't have to look at the doubting eyes of her friend.

She lied, just as she had for years, every time someone had asked her the same question. Oh, she had found the right guy, and she had loved him with all her heart and soul. There hadn't been a day over the last thirty years she hadn't questioned her decision, but what choice did she have? How could she tell him they could never have what they both had dreamed of, a family, much less the reason why?

Every Sunday for years she was reminded of her loss when she saw young families with children seating themselves in pews at church. The torturous pain of remembering got to be too much to bear, so she stopped going to church at all. Not that she blamed God, life had its own way of dealing out unfairness and tragedy. For Madeline Orsini, there was no greater pain in life than to have loved and lost, and that pain never went away.

"But didn't you ever want children of your own? I know how much you love my kids."

"I had a career" was her terse response.

Again, Madeline lied. Her fork idly moved the remaining bit of her omelet on her plate. Her eyes seemed to dart in every direction at once, hoping to find some escape from her friend's prying question. At that moment, an image flickered before her eyes. She blinked several times to adjust her focus before she saw one of the baby fawns start to nurse from its mother's utter. Instantly, the wound was reopened. Her stomach muscles knotted tightly, triggered by the memory. She winced at the pain. As if she needed to remember the doctor's words, "I'm so sorry to have to tell you, but you will never be able to bear children." Every time she saw a mother with an infant or saw a mother's cooing an irritable toddler, she was reminded of what could never be. It was a living hell for Madeline. The distant look in her eyes, the pensive expression on her face belied her best efforts to keep the torment riling inside her a secret. Kristin sensed her friend's uneasiness and immediately felt guilty for asking the question in the first place.

"Look, Maddy, I'm sorry for prying. You sit. I'll do the dishes."

Kristin was the only person who knew of Madeline's nickname, Maddy. Well, that wasn't exactly true. One other person used to call her Maddy, and that memory had never left him.

SHE SAT IN THE PRIVACY OF HER SMALL PATIO LOOKING OUT TO THE expansive gardens which had started to enter into radiant bloom. Her casual attire was an indicator she wanted to avoid public contact. The rays of the rising sun began to illuminate the colorful species of asters, daisies, tulips, and daffodils planted in clusters among irregularly shaped plots lined with white granite river rocks. Madeline focused her attention on one plot, then another. She would close her eyes, then open them, close and open. Each time it was the same. Where once she saw the brightness of a variety of colors and defined shapes of floral life in the gardens, she now saw a dullness of color and fractured images. A sickening feeling came over her. She was positive she knew what the problem was, after all, she had seen it occur in countless residents over the years. She would leave confirmation of her self-diagnosis to Doctor Stuart, a well-known ophthalmologist in Charleston, who had treated many of the residents at the Gardens.

She had intended to drive herself to Doctor Stuart's office, one last defiant show of independence on her part. The first sign of trouble was her difficulty in walking to her car. Repeatedly, she stepped on the edge of the flagstone walkway, nearly tripping each time. Backing out of her parking slot was even more difficult. She had to turn her head slowly to see the whole reflection in her rear-view mirror. Shifting into drive should have been automatic, but it wasn't. In a state of self-doubt, Madeline glanced at the driving options of the steering column. They were a blur. Her small fists pounded on the dashboard, as the emotional realization of her condition overwhelmed her. With her windows rolled up, her cries of despair and frustration were muffled from anyone walking by. But for speed dial, she would have been unable to use her cell phone. She pressed one and waited for her friend to answer.

∼

KRISTIN ANDREWS FOUND MADELINE IN THE PARKING LOT STILL SEATING in her Audi.

"Move over, Maddy, I'm driving," she commanded.

Kristin quickly entered the vehicle on the driver's side and placed herself in the crème white leather driver's seat. Madeline had done her best to freshen her make-up, but she needed assurance from Andrews.

"You look fine, Maddy," said Kristin in response to Madeline's query about her make-up. She was clearly patronizing in her delivery but hoped Madeline wouldn't notice.

Madeline had no choice but to accept Kristin's assessment. She wore dark sunglasses to hide the fact that her eyes were constantly moving to see clearly.

"You know the way, right?" asked Madeline.

"I entered it into my GPS after you called. Relax and let Siri do the work," joked Kristin, as she backed out of the parking lot.

For twenty minutes, they rode without talking, the silence only interrupted with the occasional audio cues from the ever so obnoxious Siri to turn left or right in so many feet. Doctor Stuart's office occupied the first floor of an old Victorian in the historic part of Charleston. The expansive corner lot was surrounded by a wrought iron fence. Next to the gate was a sign that read, "Offices of Doctor Wallace Stuart, MD." Doctor Stuart had wisely designed a flat walkway to the doors of his offices for those with vision problems. Kristin opened the door while Madeline took off her sunglasses. No need to draw more attention to herself than necessary, she thought. Though her vision was impaired, Madeline could easily identify the receptionist station. She walked up to the sliding glass window.

"I'm Madeline Orsini. I have a ten o'clock appointment with Doctor Stuart."

Thank God, she was a returning patient or Madeline would have been forced to fill out several pages of patient information, a task that would have proven to be immensely difficult. The young receptionist, whose name tag read, "Mary," wore a sparkly pair of designer glasses, most likely a perk from one of the optometrists working with Doctor

Stuart. Taking a file off her desk, the receptionist said, "Please follow me, Ms. Orsini," as she came around the counter.

"I'll be here when you're done," Kristin said, as Madeline followed Mary down a short hallway to an examination room.

"Doctor Stuart will be right with you, Ms. Orsini," said Mary, leaving Madeline to nervously leaf through several old issues of National Geographic from a rack hanging on the wall. This was but another attempt to hide her failing eyesight.

This was not without its difficulties. Madeline realized if she could make out images and print peripherally, and if she rotated her head accordingly, she could make out details in the center of the page. Soon there was a knock on the door. It opened.

Slowly leafing through her file, Dr. Stuart commented, "Madeline, you're not due for another examination for six months. Have you experienced a change in your vision?"

Dr. Stuart wore a traditional white smock and spoke in a soft, monotone voice. His gray hair and gentle demeanor were a source of comfort for his older patients who preferred a doctor more in keeping with Marcus Welby than the avant-garde generation whose dress was more casual than professional. The accuracy of his equipment required he keep the overhead lighting very dim, more like a table in a romantic restaurant than a doctor's office. The beige walls of his office were sparsely decorated with only his medical certificates. The tiled floor enabled Stuart to use his rolling stool with ease. Her vision difficulties became apparent when she needed Stuart's hand to guide her into the examination chair. Madeline brought the doctor up to speed with her retirement plans and the unsettling vision issues she was experiencing.

"Well, let's see what we can do now," Stuart said. "Why don't you have a seat in this chair."

Stuart eased forward a black circular device with a chin support.

"Place your chin in the slot, Madeline."

When she was ready, Stuart opened and closed the center eye slot, allowing him to assess certain ocular qualities in each eye. When he was finished, he slid the device away and asked Madeline to look straight at him. He took out a small flashlight with a narrow beam.

"Try not to blink," he said, as he quickly focused the beam on the center of the eye, then moved it to the edge of the eye. He repeated this process several times.

"Okay, Madeline, I want you to move over here."

He directed Madeline to another examination station.

"I'm going to do a test to assess your visual acuity. I want you to cover one eye and then tell me what line of letters you can read."

Covering her left eye, she focused on a small card Stuart held in front of her. The first line of the card started with the largest letters with each succeeding line getting smaller and smaller. Madeline saw the first line clearly and read each letter correctly. With the next line down, she found she had to move her head slightly to identify some of the letters.

"Madeline, if you can, try to hold your head still," cautioned the soft-spoken Stuart.

Madeline was unable to get past the second line with either eye. Stuart slid his rolling stool to a cabinet on the wall. He opened it and took out a small card with horizontal and vertical lines. He rolled back in front of Madeline.

"Now, Madeline, I'm going to hold up a card that has horizontal and vertical lines on it. Covering one eye and then the other, tell me how the lines look to you."

With one eye covered, Madeline strained at the card Stuart held before her.

"Can I move my head?" she asked.

"I'd prefer you didn't," he replied.

"Then the lines look a little wavy and distorted."

Stuart placed the card in the side pocket of his smock.

"Let's sit over here," he said, as he stood and turned up the lights.

There was a small table in the corner of his examination room. A mirror rested on the table slightly tilted backward. Several diagrams of the eye with detailed imagery of blood vessels and muscles were posted on the wall behind the table. There was something about Dr. Stuart's bedside manner that automatically put Orsini at ease. However, the confirmation of her own diagnosis was shocking.

"Madeline, what you have is what we call dry eye macular degeneration. There are clear indications of blurred and reduced central vision."

The confirmation of her own self-diagnosis did little to ease the range of emotions sweeping over her. Would she ever be able to drive? Would she be able to walk without assistance? How would she even operate her microwave oven or respond to caller ID on her phone or even read? Only once before had she experienced such depths of despair, yet somehow, she survived that, but this was entirely different.

She braced herself before asking him. Her emotions were normally composed, however a wave of panic now engulfed her. "What causes it, and am I going to be blind?" The fear in her voice alerted the normally subdued Stuart. The tone of his voice never altered. Softly, he provided an explanation:

"The macula is the part of the retina responsible for clear vision in your direct line of sight. When the center of the macula becomes dislodged from the retina, you must rely on the edges of your vision circle to see, which is why you had to continually move your head to see things during the tests I conducted. But you are not going blind, Madeline. You would benefit from a magnifying light to place over materials you want to look at or read. Enlarged letters on appliances in your home would also help. Most stores carry or can order such things. Though you will not be able to drive anymore, certainly everyday walking will not be a problem."

Compassionately, Stuart pulled a tissue from a box on the table and handed it to Madeline.

"It's not fair, Dr. Stuart. I just retired. I was looking forward to some traveling, even teaching part-time at the College of Charleston. Now this!"

She no longer tried to contain her emotions.

"God, it's so unfair!" she sobbed.

Stuart sat back in his chair. He knew no theological platitude would help. Life was never intended to be fair; after all, tribulation was what was promised.

4

THE FAMILY TREE BEGINS

"Do you think this room will work?" Jane asked.

The young woman from US Gen stood next to Sam.

"It will be just fine," replied Marie Gordon, the volunteer from US Gen, who had come to assist Jane with her genealogical research.

A smiling Samantha Callahan nodded. Jane had expanded an old storage room off the library. She had three computer stations installed along with large easy-wipe boards of the end walls. Each computer station was arranged on a u-shaped table which allowed for both the researcher and the resident, if they so choose, to sit side by side while working on the resident's genealogical history.

Marie was of slender build. She looked the part of someone who spent much of her time in front of a computer or looking through large tomes in forgotten recesses of some library. Her complexion had an unusual ecru hue. Nondescript eyes rested behind a pair of black horn-rimmed glasses. The slightest trace of lip gloss and a rather neutral shade of fingernail polish were signs that enhancing her physical appearance was not a high priority for the woman.

She pulled out a chair from one of the computer tables and said in a rather matter of fact manner, "There's a few things you should know about genealogical research."

Jane sensed she was about to be given a warning about pursuing her research. Her reluctance at hearing such news was obvious as she slowly pulled out a chair electing to sit back from Marie.

"Sam has told me you've already worked a couple of family trees, but I want to warn you that there are a number of difficulties we are sure to encounter."

"Such as?" asked Jane, who had only touched the tip of the iceberg with the family trees she had constructed and was a bit naïve to the complexities of the task at hand.

"For starters, much of the information we are seeking comes from the government's ten-year census taking. Some families escaped those censuses. For another, multiple generations sometimes had family members with the same name. Also, consider the complexity of tracing an adoptive relative where it's difficult to pick up the trail of the birth mother. You need to be aware that some states, particularly in the South, kept very poor records. Lastly, with the gold rush of the 1840s, many men abandoned their families, making obtaining any information prior to the Civil War nearly impossible."

"You've certainly painted a rather bleak picture, Marie," responded an obviously disappointed Kilgore.

"These are obstacles I thought you needed to know, Jane. The good news is we can usually go back three generations without much difficulty, relying on something as simple as a family bible, recollections of any surviving siblings and their off-springs, and the always tedious library research."

"Now that's most optimistic, Marie," smiled Jane. "When would you like to start?"

"Why don't you schedule me for an hour with each resident starting next Monday. Ask them to bring a family Bible if they have one. If not, have them write down the names of parents and grandparents on both the husband and wife's side of the family. If they can remember where their parents and grandparents came from and when they were born, that would be icing on the cake."

Jane was elated at the simplicity of what she had to gather.

"Do you have time to stay for lunch? It seems the least I can do," responded a gleeful Kilgore.

Marie took out her day planner from her valise.

"Nothing on my schedule for the rest of the day, so sure. I'm famished."

She took them to the dining room and seated them at a table near the window. Molly McGuire, who oversaw the kitchen staff, asked if there was anything she could get them.

"Coffee or tea, Marie?" Jane asked.

"Coffee would be just fine," replied Marie.

"Coffee it is, and Molly, could you bring some French Vanilla creamer for me?"

"Not a problem, Mrs. Kilgore. Give me a few minutes to brew a fresh pot for you."

Molly McGuire was not what Marie Gordon had expected in someone who worked in the kitchen of an assisted living facility.

Rather than a short, plump woman wearing an institutional style white dress with ankle-high soft black leather shoes and a hairnet to cover her graying hair, Molly McGuire wore modestly high, open-toed heels. Her tan business pants complimented a breezy looking cotton blouse with streaks of blue and green hues. Her brown hair was neatly trimmed to below the ears. She wore enough makeup to look professional yet not look like someone who craved attention.

"She seems very attentive to her job," said Marie, as she unfolded her napkin and laid it across her leg.

Jane nodded.

"Molly has been a tremendous addition to our team at the Gardens. She spent years running a five-star restaurant in Charleston. Her father was a resident here. When he passed away, he left Molly with a sizable estate. Molly decided to return to the other residents some of the attention and care her father had received. She asked me if she could look over our kitchen operation to see where it could be improved. Providing fine food had been her career, and I think she felt our residents deserved the same. By the time she was done, she had proposed using students from the Charleston Culinary Institute as interns in the kitchen. She arranged for a local community garden to provide all our fruits and vegetables for free. We offered her the job to run our kitchen operations and the rest, as they say, is history."

"You know Marie, I wish my husband, Daniel, was here to hear you talk. He started here at the Gardens as a volunteer hoping to help the residents build a bridge to their past and forgotten memories. In a way, that's exactly what a family tree does. It connects you with your past."

"There's another aspect of a family tree that most people don't realize," said Marie, who was stirring her cup of coffee that Molly had placed on the table.

"I'm not sure I follow you," said Jane, puzzled by the woman's observation.

"In every sense of the word, a family tree reflects the dreams and aspirations others would hold for future generations. Think about it this way, Jane, every addition to a family tree perpetuates the history and the future of that family and whatever astounding and magical contributions some family member may make."

What an astute observation, Jane thought, and the notion to subtly introduce to her husband to that concept entered her mind.

∾

MARIE GORDON HAD INTENDED ON ARRIVING AT THE GARDENS EARLY that morning. She was anxious to get started on the family trees for the two residents Jane had selected, Willard Castleberry and Sally Gunderson. A dense morning fog hugged the ground, making the drive from Marie's home longer and a bit stressful as she slowly maneuvered along streets where she was guided only by the sound of hitting the white road discs glued to the divided white line on the streets. Upon exiting her car, Marie tightened the belt on her camel's hair coat that reached her knees and triple wrapped a long tan knitted scarf around her neck.

"That fog is bitter cold," said Marie, as she patted her hands together, hoping to return some circulation to her frigid fingers. Her thin black leather gloves, which she thought attractive, did little to insulate her hands from the chilling fog. Jane had greeted Marie at the entrance, as she too was concerned about the driving conditions. Marie's physical expression of her chill made Jane immediately desirous of a warm beverage.

"Let's get you a cup of coffee," she said.

Marie nodded in grateful anticipation of the French Roast Starbucks she knew Jane had the kitchen staff brew for guests. As they seated themselves at the table in the dining room, a young kitchen aide dressed in black slacks and a freshly pressed chef's jacket approached them.

"Mrs. McGuire said to expect you and a guest, Mrs. Kilgore. Coffee with French Vanilla creamer - correct?" she asked, as she set two freshly poured cups of coffee on the table along with a small crystal bowl of the creamer.

"It's most appreciated, Carol," replied Jane.

Marie smiled, as she used both hands to raise the coffee cup to her lips. The warmth from the coffee cup gave her cold hands an additional thawing. Jane waited for Marie to savor a few sips of the rich flavor of the Starbucks blend before talking.

"You got the list I emailed you?" she asked.

Dabbing her lips with her napkin, Marie replied, "Yes. What can you tell me about them?"

"Willard Castleberry is a widower who just turned seventy. He carries himself as if he were descended from the aristocratic old South. He claims his grandfather, Harrison Castleberry, was a Civil War General. After the war, Harrison Castleberry had the foresight to realize the Agrarian South was gone. According to Willard, his grandfather sold five hundred acres of prime cotton land to diehards who thought the South would rise again and started an iron and steel plant in Mobile, Alabama. Harrison Castleberry was one of the first southern millionaires after the war; that much happens to be true according to the Charleston Historical Society," smirked Jane, as if one truth validates every claim of the pretentious Castleberry. She made no attempt to shield her amused contempt. "Willard's father, Beauregard Castleberry, was the Cadet Commander at VMI and served with General Pershing in World War I."

Kilgore continued. "Willard keeps his silver-gray hair in a dated pompadour akin to Elvis Presley and dresses impeccably, always in a suit and tie: his favorite being white cotton slacks and coat, with a thin black bola tie. The staff refers to him the Colonel, after Colonel Sanders of KFC fame, only not to his face."

"I'll bet not," chuckled Marie, taking another sip of her splendid brew.

"He takes to ordering the staff to do things instead of asking them. One of his many annoying peculiarities is that he shows a certain disdain whenever he has to deal with one of our African-American staff."

"Odd for this day and age, don't you think?" remarked Marie.

"For sure," responded Jane, a frown forming on her face.

Gordon had not failed to notice her reaction.

"Why the face?" she asked.

"Willard has a perpetual George Hamilton tan complexion causing some of us to speculate on the purity of his bloodline, if you get my drift?"

Quite familiar with discovering mixed bloodlines in her work, Marie laughed, "Be careful who you disdain because you just might be a part of their very group."

In turn, Jane joined her in the enjoyment of such irony. Marie glanced at the list of names she had placed on the table. After the moments of humor paused, she returned to business.

"What about Sally Gunderson?"

"That poor dear deserved to have Willard's upbringing," replied

Jane. "Thanks to an estate left her by her sister, Millie Haggarty, who passed away recently, Sally is able to live here. I suspect she'll be moving into our dementia wing soon, but in the meantime, she can be quite conversant."

"What was her background?" asked an inquisitive Marie.

"Sally's a widow. When her husband, George, passed away a year ago, Sally's sister, Millie Haggarty, brought Sally to the Gardens. You couldn't ask for a sweeter, kinder person than Sally Gunderson. All the staff love her. She even goes so far as to write Get Well cards to residents who are feeling under the weather. For family information, I'd suggest you talk with her sister."

"Did George and Sally list any children?"

"No," Jane replied. "Her sister used to come and see her, though it's been some time since she last visited. I think she lives out of state somewhere. Up North, I believe. I can get you her contact information when you need it."

Marie pursued the tracing of someone's family tree the way some reporters doggedly go after a story. There would be no stone unturned in the pursuit of an elusive relative, no question too sensitive to ask, or even avoiding the revelation of some hidden secret discovered in a long-lost document. She would have her start with Willard Castleberry and then Sally Gunderson.

5

A VISIT TO THE FUTURE

Jane peered nervously out the kitchen window expecting to see Daniel arrive any minute. She was excited to tell him the news. The aroma of chicken soup simmering on the stove, and fresh sourdough biscuits baking in the oven, brought back memories of her childhood in Norfolk, Virginia. Jane was a military brat, the only child born to John and Betty Lincoln. Her father was a Chief Petty Officer in the navy. Betty was a stay-at-home mom who catered to her only daughter's every whim. They lived in base housing in a modest two-bedroom red brick home built during the buildup to WWII when the Norfolk Naval Base was one the busiest ports on the east coast. Though not large, the kitchen had sufficient room for a small dining table. A white enamel four-burner gas stove afforded Jane's mother ample cooking space and a source of heat during those cold winter mornings. A mudroom off the kitchen served a dual purpose. It contained an old-fashioned agitating washing machine with a set of rollers on top to run freshly done clothes through and a large built-in pantry with a vegetable cooler that had a wire mesh covering over the hole in the floor. Jane often wondered how critters didn't make their way into the vegetables and fruit stored there.

34

Jane's fondest memory growing up was helping her mother in the kitchen. Sometimes baking together when Jane would take swipes of cookie dough from a large mustard yellow mixing bowl when her mother wasn't looking. In later years, Betty would let Jane help prepare the salad, peel potatoes; or if she was lucky, dredge pieces of chicken in seasoned flour and shake them inside a brown paper bag. The inevitable white cloud of dust would eventually settle on them, evoking giddy laughter from mother and daughter. These were only some of the memories Jane had hoped to recreate with her own children. Fate would take Jane in a different direction.

The sound of the Dodge pickup coming up the driveway alerted Jane to Daniel's arrival. The distinctive rumble of the Hemi-powered pickup was unmistakable. Daniel had convinced Jane of the need for the used truck as he had become something of an urban farmer. Kilgore had installed several raised vegetable beds and added on a small workshop to the back of the garage. With well-worn boots, faded blue jeans, and a work shirt frayed around each cuff, Daniel Kilgore was a far cry from the nicely dressed Director of Volunteers at Magnolia Gardens. It tickled Jane to watch Daniel get into his truck on weekends and put on an old weathered tan cowboy hat spotted with sweat stains and any other number of mystery substances Daniel had a need to use. *Good*, she thought, as she watched him get out of his truck with shopping bags in both arms, *he hadn't forgotten after all.*

"Home at last," she called out from the front porch, holding the side entrance door, stained glass on the upper half and solid oak on the bottom, to the kitchen for him.

With over-loaded grocery bags in each arm, Kilgore took the small flight of stairs two at a time. The annoyance of the note fueled his energy.

"Did you really think I needed the shopping list you taped to the steering wheel?" he chuckled. There was a slightly sarcastic tone in his voice as if to say, *I can remember without a written reminder.*

"You're right," grimaced Jane, as she wiped her hands on her blue apron and feeling apologetic for her actions. "But we are having company tomorrow and I couldn't do without the things on that list."

It was so like her hyper-organized, slightly controlling personality.

Danial stomped his feet on the doormat to ensure he didn't track dirt into the house before making his way into the kitchen. He set the bags on the white pine kitchen table they had purchased from a wood-maker at the local flea market. Looking slightly confused, he asked, "What company?"

Feeling the need to ease his spirits since he didn't take well to surprises, Jane put her arms around him, "First, a kiss, Mr. Kilgore."

After a kiss that was longer and a bit more passionate than he expected, Daniel tilted his head backward and even more curious than before said; "Like I asked, what company?", his arms still around Jane's waist.

"Your niece, Michelle, and her husband, Peter, are coming for a visit and they're bringing little Danny with them."

As a great uncle, Daniel enjoyed his namesake, but at one year old and starting to walk, the boy was like one of those round battery-oper-ated floor cleaners they advertise on TV. They ran randomly about the room, bumping into one object, switching directions, then bumping into another object, and so on. Their previous visits had left Daniel tired and a bit frustrated over the young parents treating the Kilgore home as a *No Rules* zone for their child. Deeper in his heart were the bitter-sweet memories of his son, Greg, who had been killed in Afghanistan over thirty years ago. Being around the toddler exacer-bated the sense of loss his heart could never forget.

"Think we need to kid-proof the house before they get here?" he asked, half-joking but half-serious.

Jane was clearly annoyed by her husband's line of inquiry.

"I think we need to make them feel welcome and not like their child is entering a 'look but don't touch zone' in a store."

Daniel smiled, partially because he knew his wife was right, but mostly because he knew any other reaction would be futile. He took a seat at the kitchen table anticipating Jane was not done with him. He was right. Feeling Daniel needed a bit more assurance about the impending visit, Jane opened the refrigerator and took out a chilled bottle of Bogle Chardonnay. She slipped two glasses off the hanging rack over the kitchen island and set them on the table. As she poured, she began.

"Ever since her father's death, Michelle has looked to you for advice," Jane said. "Have you forgotten who she turned to when she found out she was pregnant, or who she wanted to walk her down the aisle when she and Peter got married?"

The pause to sip their wine served Daniel well. He set his glass down, slowly turning it by the stem. He thought of his son... *if only the past had a future.*

"He is cute, isn't he?" he said, still staring at the wine slowly swirling in the glass. For a moment, Daniel felt envious, even cheated, as his mind drifted back to the days of his son's first steps and the time the training wheels came off Greg's two-wheeler. No father was prouder. *God, to have those days back again.*

～

AT JANE'S REQUEST, KILGORE WOVE HIS WAY BETWEEN THE VEGETABLE garden beds harvesting a colorful array of lettuce, tomatoes, scallions, and bell peppers, the makings of one of Jane's delightful salads. His fingers gently lifted the greenery of snow pea vines which he expected should be bearing fruit. They were his favorite. As he admired the product of his gardening efforts, his thoughts turned to his niece's visit. His original reaction to the surprise visit of his niece, Michelle, and her family had quickly dissipated. Michelle had inherited her mother's good looks; stunning hazel eyes, auburn hair in a shag cut, orthodontically perfect teeth, and the complexion of a college homecoming queen which she had been. He was particularly fond of her husband, Peter, who, like Kilgore, was a teacher, though not in elementary school. Peter was an English teacher at the high school level. At six foot two, ebony hair fashionably in need of a trim, and a swarthy complexion, Daniel was sure Peter caused many a female student's heart to swoon when he came into the classroom. He and Kilgore rooted for the same college team, Clemson, Kilgore's alma mater. They also shared the same politics, liberal Democrats, which made any discussion of politics with others in the red state of South Carolina sometimes uncomfortable, if not infuriating.

He had just shut the wire gate to the garden when he saw the blue Subaru Cross Trek coming up the driveway. Daniel pointed for them to pull in the breezeway between the garage and the house. With a colander full of garden pickings in hand, Daniel made his way up the driveway to greet them.

When they married, Daniel and Jane had both wanted a fresh canvass to paint their lives together on and quickly agreed to sell Daniel's old home and Jane's and start anew. Their mutual desire for a rural setting helped the real estate agent locate a tranquil four acres that had once been part of breeding farm for Arabian quarter horses. Looking out at pastures of green clover grass and bordered with high white painted fences, they told their contractor this was where the house was to be built. A large country style farmhouse with a wrap-around porch. White, trimmed in gray, with a green metal roof, the home looked like an authentic vintage structure from a Norman Rockwell painting. They elected a road base driveway over asphalt and a maze of pathways to the front door and around the house to the garage and from the garage to the house consisting of pea gravel and flagstone stepping stones. The detached garage had ample space for three cars and a work area for Daniel in the back. Blooming Bougainvillea vines wove themselves through trellises edging the front of the house

"Uncle Dan, you look great!" beamed Michelle, as she exited the car with a bouncing toddler in her arms.

She adjusted the small towel on her shoulder, then placed the baby's head on it. With her one free arm she hugged her uncle. Daniel did the same.

"And you too, sweetheart," smiled Daniel. "Let's trade loads?"

Eager for a break from holding onto an infant in constant wiggle mode, Michelle passed her son to Daniel. Michelle was certainly not a clothes horse, and it was a good thing considering her husband's salary did not lend itself to designer clothes. A pair of sunglasses rested atop her auburn hair, less of a distraction to the ever-searching hands of her son. A loose-fitting Wilson High t-shirt, jean shorts, and sandals completed her attire.

Kilgore lifted the one-year-old into the air and chimed, "How's my All-American tiger?" His acclamation was met with a burp and an ungodly amount of regurgitated baby food which landed on Kilgore's shirt.

"I'm so sorry, Uncle Dan, I had to feed him on the way over," apologized Michelle, obviously embarrassed.

She quickly took the towel off her shoulder. Kilgore lowered the infant to a safer level while Michelle wiped off the mess left by her baby on her uncle's shirt.

"Hazards of having a baby, Dan," grinned Peter, who had opened the hatchback and began removing an incredible amount of infant care devices—stroller, extra car carrier, expandable swing, and a collapsible crib. He was comically relieved that it had happened to someone besides himself.

Michelle's husband took the term casual wear to a new level, which was fine with Daniel, who loathed the ads on TV pushing the latest trendy clothing line. Irregular lengths of brown hair extended below a Carolina Jaguar cap. Sunglasses rested on the bill of his cap. He sported a Clemson Tiger t-shirt with matching orange polyester pants and a very worn pair of brown leather sandals.

Jane had seen them from the kitchen window pull into the breezeway and went out to greet them. She had formed a friendship with Michelle and her mother, Kristin, during the time Jane had cared for Daniel's wife, Vivian. Michelle's words when Jane and Daniel married only endeared her more to Jane. *He deserves someone like you!* Michelle had insisted Jane not fuss over their visit, which pleased Jane. She had to maintain a professional demeanor and appearance at work, and weekends were a time to ratchet things down a bit. Bobby pins held her shoulder-length auburn hair in place. A small dish towel was draped over her right shoulder. She wore her paisley yoga pants around the house. Occasionally they inspired her to twist and contort her body into any number of yoga poses. She wore one of what she called multi-purpose blouses, a solid color slipover casual enough to wear around the house, yet sufficiently stylish to wear to the store, if necessary.

Her enthusiasm for the two was genuine "It's so good to see you kids," Jane happily exclaimed, as she hugged Peter, then Michelle, and then quickly relieved Daniel of his charge. She smothered the infant with hugs and kisses, eliciting a beaming smile from the child.

"I'll take Danny, Daniel. You help the kids get settled in the spare bedroom," ordered Jane, who then proceeded to leave everyone behind as she headed in the house, cooing and cuddling the infant to the exclusion of all others.

"I'm going with Jane," said Michelle, leaving the men to bring in multiple pieces of luggage.

The two women proceeded down the pea gravel pathway to the back deck. The rhythmic crunching sound was occasionally interrupted as Michelle stopped to kick out bits of gravel that had worked their way into her sandals. Looking at the contents of the unloaded car, Daniel couldn't help but ask, "And you're staying how long?"

"You tell me," sighed the young father. "She insisted on being prepared for any emergency. Maybe in the future, I'd better get a trailer."

The two laughed as they gathered up an endless number of suitcases, tote bags, baby equipment, and headed into the house. Once in the bedroom, Peter deftly assembled the crib and filled one corner of the bedroom with the remaining luggage. Daniel carried the expandable swing into the living room.

"Where do you want this?" asked Daniel, referring to the swing he had in his hands.

"Anywhere I can keep an eye on him," called out Michelle, who was in the kitchen rinsing off the vegetables, while Jane's attention was completely devoted to young Timmy.

"Thank God, you didn't get this from IKEA," said Daniel, who still had nightmares from trying to assemble a desk from the Swedish furniture company with directions listing parts that weren't there and connection points that didn't exist. Daniel easily managed to erect the plastic swing set and even figure out how to connect the overhead collage of objects for the baby to focus on.

Jane emerged from the kitchen with Danny clinging to her blouse. "Honey, would you mind pouring everyone some wine? My hands are full."

Leaving young Danny in the living room rocking gently in the swing seat, his eyelids fighting a losing battle to stay open, the four adults settled around the back-porch table. The double French doors to the living room allowed the young mother to keep an eye on her infant and still allow for a suitable conversation to proceed.

"To our family!" toasted Jane, raising her glass toward the others.

After the clink of glasses, the chilled libation was met with smiles from all. Daniel clearly had some sort of agenda in mind, turning directly toward the young teacher, he stated, "How are your classes this year, Peter?" asked Daniel. His opening inquiry was an obvious ruse for Daniel's true interest.

"Besides four classes of English, my principal asked me to take on a Creative Writing class. The regular teacher is out on maternity leave," replied Peter, while reaching for a handful of mixed nuts Jane had placed on the table. His hand caused the crystal container to wobble slightly before returning to its stable position.

"That must be a challenge?" smiled Daniel, remembering the strain of grading essays from his middle school students.

"The beauty of descriptive language, coupled with an enriched vocabulary, can be difficult concepts for anyone who enjoys writing to grasp, much less high school juniors and seniors. It just does not come naturally to the majority of us."

Sensing an opportunity to take advantage of his nephew-in-law's talents, Daniel offered up the bait. He was surprised that the opportunity so readily presented itself.

"Peter, I've been working on writing another book, and I would really appreciate it if you would look at what I've done so far. You know, the same kind of thing your students are struggling to grasp."

Daniel was as aware of his own limitations as he was of Peter's abilities.

Sensing Peter was caught in a potentially awkward situation, Jane tried to come to his aid but in a manner that he would accept.

"Honestly, Daniel, I'm sure Peter is much too busy considering his teaching load."

Jane was sincere in this gesture but had not taken the time to consider whether Peter might find Daniel's project a challenge.

"Just the opposite," replied an excited Peter. "It would be refreshing compared to what my young Hemmingways and Steinbecks hand me." His comment was intended more for amusement than sarcasm.

Eager to put his draft in Peter's hand, Daniel slid his chair back.

"I'll get it for you. It's in the office."

A brief sensation of panic engulfed Jane as she realized her own secret was lying on her desktop and about to be exposed. Jane nervously said, "You stay here, honey. I'll get it."

She hurried off to the office where she picked up Daniel's manuscript from the small table Daniel used, and then surreptitiously slid the trifold pamphlet on her desk under her computer. Jane was relieved the pamphlet was temporarily out of sight. She wouldn't make that mistake again. She had once broached the subject with Daniel and his less than receptive response was a sign to her the idea needed time to germinate in him. She did not want Daniel to think she was going behind his back, but then that's exactly what she was doing.

"You'll be sorry," she said mockingly, handing the partially completed manuscript to Peter.

Peter thumbed through the nearly one hundred-page unfinished work, then asked, "You're not in any hurry, I hope." This obviously was not going to be a Sunday afternoon project.

"I so appreciate that you'd even consider looking at it that time is not an issue," answered Daniel.

"Interesting title," said Peter, as he reached for his wine glass. "Forgotten Flowers. Where did you come up with that?"

"It flows out of the story," smiled Daniel, at what he thought was a compliment.

The awakening child started to fuss in the swing set.

"I better see to him," said Michelle. "He has a bit of a stubborn streak when he first wakes up."

"And I'll get more snacks," replied Jane, feeling vaguely guilty about not having a greater variety to offer. "Don't forget you're barbecuing, sweetheart."

Daniel had recently purchased a barrel smoker which he found infinitely simpler to operate than Jane's old propane unit. The smoker rested on a bed of gravel Daniel had encased with cobblestones. All he had to do was to fill the firebox with briquettes and light them with starter fluid. Thirty minutes later, he would hang the seasoned tri-tip from a rod extending across the grate and put the top on the barrel. Forty-five minutes later, the roast was done, no turning, no basting.

"I've never seen how a barrel smoker is used, mind if I tagged along," asked Peter.

"Follow me and learn from a master," clowned Daniel.

At her request, Michelle had surrendered the wiggly one-year-old to Jane, who now rocked slowly back and forth in the solitude of the living room, hoping to soothe the agitated child into a peaceful sleep.

In the kitchen, Daniel placed the roast on a cookie sheet and brushed on a coat of olive oil. Then he liberally sprinkled on his favorite dry rub. Using both hands, he massaged the rub into the roast.

"This is the trick. Make sure you work the rub in really good," Daniel said. Looking at the clock, Daniel made a mental note when to put the roast in the barrel.

"So, what does the future hold for you, Peter? Grad school, administration, what?" Having lost his own son, Daniel had developed a growing interest in this young man's life.

"My future is there," he said, as he motioned to his son in the living room, now serenely nestled in Jane's arms.

Feeling Peter had missed his point, Daniel pressed the issue.

"No, I mean your career. Do you see your future in the classroom or some other level of education?"

"My Master's adviser told me administrators develop policy, teachers develop minds. Despite the daily struggle with adolescent angst, I think the classroom is my future, at least for the time being."

Noble sentiments, Daniel thought, whose own idealism of the future had been shattered when two young Marines came knocking at his door to inform him of the death of his son, Greg, in Afghanistan. *Making the world a better place may come at a steep cost.*

"What about your future, Dan, you and Jane, I mean. What's on the horizon for you two?"

"Jane is acting Director at Magnolia Gardens, and there's a good chance it will become permanent. I still volunteer there and keep busy with writing and odd jobs around here. Four acres takes more time than some people realize."

From the way Jane attended to his son, Peter knew instinctively that was not the future Jane had in mind. *She sees more than work and her husband's hobbies in her future.*

"There could be more, you know," answered the young father.

Michelle smiled at Jane, who now blushed at what she felt was a not so subtle suggestion for family expansion.

Catching the time on the kitchen wall clock, Daniel said hurriedly, "Whoa, time for the meat to go on."

Peter immediately felt uneasy when Daniel moved quickly to take the meat to the smoker.

"Did I speak out of turn?" he asked the two women.

"Not at all," answered Jane, hoping to ease the young man's fear that he had spoken out of turn. "He has his view of the future, and I have mine."

∿

"FIVE MORE MINUTES ON THE MEAT," DANIEL CALLED OUT, AS HE LIFTED the lid to the smoker to check on the meat.

"He really means ten minutes. He'll insist on letting the meat rest for five minutes," laughed Jane. "We've got time for one more glass of wine."

Jane and Michelle sat in the living room dutifully watching young Danny work his way around the coffee table on wobbling legs. Every few steps he would raise his hand in the air as if to proclaim, "I don't need to hang on anymore," and then with a buckling of one knee and a look of fear on his face, he quickly returned his hand to the table to secure his balance. At that moment, Daniel and Peter came parading in, Daniel balancing a wooden carving board holding the tri-tip roast wrapped in aluminum foil.

"That's our cue," winked Jane, as she and Michelle marched in step to the kitchen.

The farmhouse style kitchen was something both Daniel and Jane had insisted be included in the plans drawn up by their contractor. A modern stainless steel six-burner stove had a built-in grill and an oven capable of radiant or convection cooking. A large black wrought iron pot and pan rack hung over the stove. The prep island had a deep country sink and came with foot-operated hot and cold water pedals, an indulgence Daniel had insisted on having. Jane got her white cabinets and black granite countertops. A large, stainless steel side-by-side freezer/refrigerator unit was another of Jane's wishes come true. Dark hardwood flooring ran from the kitchen throughout the house.

Jane took the crystal salad bowl from the refrigerator and set it on the table. The farmhouse style table was made from an eight-foot slab of white oak. Jane had insisted the builder keep the rough-hewn edges. Complimenting the table was a set of eight matching oak chairs made from carefully selected limbs from the same tree that produced the table. At Jane's direction, Michelle took a fork from the silverware drawer. Opening the oven, she gently poked at the foil-wrapped baked potatoes in the oven. The ease with which the fork went in and withdrew told Michelle the potatoes were done.

"Voila! Done to perfection," said Michelle, who then went to the refrigerator to get the sour cream, chopped chives, and butter.

Jane filled the pot she had taken off the rack with water and started to heat it for the steamed the broccoli.

Noticing they had done quite a bit of damage to the bottle of Chardonnay, Jane asked Daniel to open another bottle.

"I'll get that," replied Peter. "You do the carving."

Noticing the water for the broccoli was at a full boil, Jane said, "Go ahead, honey."

She deftly hooked the streamer basket full of broccoli bits to the edge of the pan of boiling water, then placed a glass lid on the pot. With three of them attending to the last-minute details of dinner, Michelle took the opportunity to set up Danny's highchair between her and Peter. She placed him in the chair, adjusted the seat belt, then slid on the tray. Danny's hands began a not-so-rhythmic beat on the tray. Michelle fed him a little applesauce to take the edge off the toddler's appetite. Jane set a steaming bowl of broccoli on the table. The sumptuous vegetable dish nearly spilled out of the antique white bowl with a chip in it.

"Daniel, would you give the blessing?" Jane asked.

Both Daniel and Peter were holding hands with heads bowed, not so subtly indicating someone else would have to take the responsibility of expressing thankfulness. Jane mockingly looked upward and said, "Forgive them, Lord."

As plates of food were passed around the table, Michelle asked Jane if she liked being the interim director at the Gardens.

"It's not without its challenges. There's a myriad of state and federal regulations to know. A violation of any one could potentially put the Gardens' license at risk. There's more paperwork than I would have ever imagined, and juggling the egos of five department heads, each of whom can at times think Magnolia Gardens would fail without them is an invitation to a catfight. All that being said, the job is beginning to grow on me."

"Do you think you'll take it full time if they offer it to you?" quizzed Michelle.

Jane's circumspect answer caught Daniel off guard.

"Unless something else comes up to occupy my time, probably yes."

Michelle, hoping to get Jane to broach the subject of family expansion, continued to press Jane.

"Have you and Daniel thought about children?"

This was a subject she did not want brought up until she had a chance to discuss it with her husband.

"That is a complicated question, Michelle, that needs a lot of discussion."

Discussion that hadn't taken place as of yet, Michelle thought. She decided to change topics.

"How's that family tree thing you mentioned earlier coming along at work?"

"I tried my hand at a couple of really easy ones for two of the residents. Surprisingly, they created quite a bit of interest not only for themselves, but also their family members who saw the names of relatives they never knew existed. It also stirred up a bit of jealousy among some other residents who wanted to know how their family trees could be put on display in the hallway, so I hired a volunteer from a local genealogical society to work with some selected residents to build their tree. We'll see how that works out."

"You know, Jane," responded Michelle, "conceptually, a family tree is like the juxtaposition of two different images."

"That sounds rather profound," smiled Daniel, as the flavor of the last bit of Chardonnay flowed across his palate.

"Think about it, Uncle Dan. If you look at a family tree in reverse, it traces your family history backward in time. Look at it in the opposite direction, and you see the future of succeeding generations; sons and daughters, nephews and nieces, aunts and uncles, cousins by blood and by marriage. It's a document that relives the past and points to the future at the same time. How many times in history books have we read where it's written that when this or that technology or invention came along and changed the future of the world. A family tree is historical and futuristic at the same time."

The adults were so absorbed in Michelle's oration, they didn't notice young Danny lift the bowl containing diced strawberries and cottage cheese form the table and empty the contents on his head. A screech of joy was soon replaced by cries as the juice from the contents of the bowl reached the boy's eyes. The boy's antics required a bath and complete change of clothing. Michelle did not need any help, but she knew it would hurt Jane's feeling to deny her request for assistance. Daniel and Peter were left to handle the dishes.

6

TIME TO DECIDE?

Daniel rose early the next morning, not having slept well that night. He found himself in recurrent dreams where he was being cross-examined by some district attorney. Just as the final question was about to be asked, trapping him into a corner, he woke up. There had been too much conversation recently about lineage for him not to suspect Jane's vision of the future was more than a duality. Still in his flannel pajamas and fur-lined slippers, Daniel savored his morning coffee. The rays of the morning sun reflected through a large lead glass kitchen window, casting momentary shadows across the kitchen table, set with a plate of sliced cantaloupe and glasses of fresh-squeezed orange juice. A bowl of sourdough pancake mix and a package of breakfast sausage awaited the arrival of the still sleeping bodies. Jane soon arrived carrying young Danny.

"I thought I'd let them sleep in a little bit," said Jane, as she cooed and tickled the baby's chin.

"Shall I make him his first pancake?" asked Daniel, as he poured a cup of coffee for Jane. He shuffled around in the kitchen junk drawer and was surprised to find a pattern mold that he could employ for cartoon figure pancakes. He had thought it had been discarded years ago, yet here it was. And then the pain came like a knife plunged deep into his heart. He had used the mold to make pancakes for his son, Greg, when he was a child.

Jane nodded as she sipped her coffee, *"Thank you for remembering my French Vanilla flavoring."* Never a huge fan of coffee flavor, she found the brew much more tolerable this way.

Daniel had the griddle plugged in on the island. He set the temperature to 350° and began whisking the water and batter combination. The bubbling of a small gob of batter dropped on the griddle told him it was ready. He poured enough batter for two small pancakes. Jane slid the highchair up to the table, set the boy in it, and attached the tray. Daniel placed the plate on the table, spreading a little butter on the pancakes and applying a liberal dose of Mrs. Butterworth's Maple Syrup. Anticipating the boy's first taste of pancakes would bring, he stated, "Eat up, young man," placing the plate on the tray.

"Daniel, let me cut them up first," chided Jane.

"Why," laughed Daniel, as the baby had grabbed one pancake, putting it up to his mouth. "He's doing fine on his own."

Daniel's pleasure at the boy's antics was bittersweet as the memory of his son at this age emerged from the past.

What butter and syrup that didn't end up in his mouth ran down his cheeks and onto his pajamas. Jane smiled in resignation that utensils were completely useless. By the time Peter and Michelle strolled into the kitchen, half of the second pancake was gone.

She quickly blurted, "Shall I clean him up before we eat?"

Michelle was instantly reassuring. "Not necessary, Jane. Cleaning up after him is a continuous process in his waking hours. Let's take a break when we can."

Daniel turned his attention to preparing more pancakes and getting the sausage links on the griddle. When he had completed his happy task, they enjoyed a leisurely meal with casual conversation intended to avoid the emotionally charged issues of future or family.

Once they were finished with breakfast, Michelle took Danny to the bathroom for a bath and change of clothes while Daniel helped Peter load up their Subaru.

"Next time we expect a longer visit. Our home is your home, understood!" said Jane, as if to scold the young couple. She smiled at them, but her eyes were unmistakably fixed on the infant.

Her bond with Michelle provided Jane with an enjoyable mother-daughter type relationship, but the infant, Danny, had temporarily filled the void that had plagued Jane since her marriage to Daniel.

"Are you sure you can handle it" queried Peter, "Turning Danny lose for more than a day or two can be quite a handful."

Peter had detected several brief moments when Daniel, while pandering to Danny's needs, suddenly paused, staring at the child as if he were some long lost-treasure now rediscovered.

"Not to worry, Peter. We can handle it," assured Jane.

Daniel was not so assured. Too often, lingering memories had short-circuited the pleasures of the moment with the infant. He said nothing to alert the others of his feelings.

Tapping his bag, Peter said, "I'll get started on your manuscript as soon as I can."

"Like I said, I appreciate whatever you can do, whenever you can do it," smiled Daniel. He was confident Peter would enjoy the experience of "Book Editor," and the manuscript would only benefit from his efforts.

They watched until the Subaru disappeared down the long driveway and into the greenery of the South Carolina countryside.

"Nice kids," sighed Jane, "and that Danny is adorable."

It was evident she was bearing her heart to him. Daniel was never one to seek out confrontation, but in this instance, he preferred confrontation to the alternative, ignoring the undercurrents of the cauldron of emotions brewing within Jane's heart.

"I want to show you something," Daniel said, taking Jane by the hand.

"What?" she asked as she intertwined her fingers with his.

"Something in the garden."

They walked down the asphalt driveway which Daniel had installed last fall to prevent the winter rains from creating ruts across the road base surface. Once inside the fenced garden, Daniel pointed to the far corner.

"I could squeeze one or two more beds if you want them?" he said.

"I don't know, honey, don't you think we have enough already?" Jane replied, musing over what additions they could possibly need to their already expansive garden. She knew her husband was using the garden in some manner to express what he truly wanted to say.

Daniel took her hands in his, pausing to stare affectionately into her deep blue, hazel eyes.

"I think we've got enough in this garden and in our lives, but if you don't, if you do want more, I want you to have your heart's desire. What husband wouldn't want this for his wife? You to tell me what's in your heart?"

Unprepared for this poignant probe into her heart, Jane turned her head aside. His arms pulled her close to him. He could feel the tension in the rigidness of her body. Whatever secret she was keeping would eventually create a wedge between them that neither would be able to overcome if she didn't tell him. Never would she have imagined telling him would be so difficult, so emotionally gut-wrenching. She had fallen in love with his tenderness and compassion. Why couldn't she let herself trust in those emotions now?

"Can we sit down for this?" she asked.

Her words were more a plea than a question. Without answering, Daniel walked her to a cast iron bench to the right of the garden gate. Its flecking white paint and faded green cushions provided a comfortable resting spot when viewing the fruits of their labor. He turned to face her. He was at once, open and receptive to her entreaties.

"My darling, tell me what you think I should know. As your husband, I am prepared for anything you want to discuss."

Jane felt somewhat relieved at the sincerity of her husband's words.

A mother never forgets the scent of her freshly bathed infant, the stare of wonderment in its roving eyes, or the child's smiles or giggles as the mother plays peek-a-boo. There seems to be a mysterious maternal joy when a woman holds a sleeping infant or soothes and coos an upset infant into a state of blissful sleep. With the passing of time, those memories become more treasured, and as if through some Darwinian continuation of the species, at some point mothers seem to want to relive them once more. For Jane Kilgore, she had no such memories, but she wanted them. For years, the tragic death of her first husband, and the demands of her career made Jane think that having children was an impossible dream. After her marriage to Daniel, Jane allowed herself to speculate if the impossible could become a reality. Her experience with Peter, Michelle, and little Danny only fueled that speculation. After their visitors left, she realized that elation from being around Danny was all too fleeting. Despite all the logical reasons against it, Jane Kilgore wanted more than anything to be a mother. She was careful and measured in her response. She did not fear rejection, but somehow, words were still difficult.

"With only the two of us, our future is finite. It ends when we die. I want more of our future than that. I want a future where we've inspired others to dream, a future where something we've molded might change the world, a future that will live beyond some inscription on a granite tombstone. I want a future filled with more than hobbies and work."

Daniel was surprised he felt such frustration with Jane's ambiguousness. Why couldn't she just come out and say exactly what was on her mind? It was clear what Jane wanted, and there was no need for him to hear vague innuendos. Just say, "I want a baby." In truth, Daniel was disturbed with his own feelings. He had lived what Jane wanted to experience, walking the floor with a colicky baby, guiding those first attempts at walking, hovering over a teetering bicycle. And yes, there were those tumultuous teenage years filled with angst and rebelliousness. He was not sure he wanted to relive them, especially not when they end with a funeral. He stood up and took a few steps. His heart was conflicted. Perhaps it was he who needed to say what was in his heart. He turned back to face her. His words came out haltingly. He was having difficulty. Perhaps he would not be so hesitant if his previous foray into parenting had not ended so tragically.

Love is not sustained by the giving of flowers, an evening out for one's anniversary, or an exotic vacation to the Caribbean. The state of being in love, or more correctly put, staying in love, requires work. It requires attention to the slightest of details; the nuance of a missing phrase or addition of an unsuspected word, the half-smile in a situation when a full smile is expected. Love continues when one is willing to live with an uneven playing field, a playing field that will endlessly tip in one direction and then another.

"Sweetheart, do you really want...?"

Jane rose. She had somehow found the strength to cross that emotional threshold that needed to be breached.

"Yes, Daniel. What I'm trying to say is that I want to experience motherhood. I want a baby, but more importantly, I want to live the experience with you. I want us to take that journey into parenthood."

Daniel was not surprised by what his wife had revealed to him. Jane saw parenthood as her fulfillment as a woman. After the visit by Daniel's niece and husband, Jane was more convinced of the bonding a child brings to an already healthy marriage. He had suspected the surprise visit by his niece was not an accident, but more of a test to see how he would react around a young toddler. Daniel now realized the depths of Jane's yearning. *Surely, she was not naïve to the responsibilities of raising a child,* he thought. What she wanted was nothing like the occasional visit from Daniel's niece where playing with their child, feeding him, bathing him were temporary diversions in her life. There would be no day and no night where the presence of a child would not determine what they did or where they would go. The physical and emotional needs of a child would become the primary factor in every aspect of their lives. Jane was perfectly willing to change their lives forever to assume this responsibility, but Daniel was not. He had lived that phase of his life. He had lived through the joys and burdens of parenthood. It took strength, patience, love, and discipline to be a parent, all virtues in endless supply in the young. Not young anymore, Daniel questioned if he had the requisite qualities needed to be a parent at his age. He chose his words carefully, holding on to her all the while. His voice was raspy, choked with emotion. His grip tightened slightly, unconsciously thinking she might slip through his arms when he spoke.

"What you're asking of me, Jane, is to change every dream we've ever had for each other. And not just change, in some cases, dreams that will never become reality. In another time, a younger time, yes, unequivocally yes, but I can't give you an answer, not right here, not right now!"

Jane knew this was an emotionally charged decision she was asking Daniel to make, not unlike when a couple considered Magnolia Gardens for a loved one. These were uncharted and potentially dangerous waters for their marriage. There at least she knew what to do. Show the family the facility and all its amenities. Assure them their loved one would be well-loved and cared for by compassionate staff trained in dealing with an aged population. Jane would give them time to make their decision, which was usually pragmatic at the core, though not without its share of guilt. If they could continue to care for their loved one at home, they would. If they could not, then Magnolia Gardens was the answer. Aware she needed to give Daniel what he was asking for, Jane resisted the urge to tell him time was not an option, that she needed an answer now.

"I know what I'm asking you, Daniel, and the sacrifices I'm asking you to make, especially at this stage of your life. You've lived through the death of your son, and I can't imagine that doesn't prey on your mind. I'm so sorry I didn't tell you when these feelings first occurred. Please do not say yes just because I'm asking. This must be a mutual decision and not an acquiescence to my wishes."

Daniel hated the thought of disappointing her. The finding of a second love brought Daniel a sense of happiness he never thought he would experience again. He did not want to lose that, nor did he want a "no" decision to become a wedge between the two of them. In the moments that they sat next to each other, neither holding the other one's hand, neither offering arms for support, each found themselves in a confluence of emotional conflict. Was there enough love in him to say yes? Was there enough love in her to accept no?

7

THE SEARCH FOR LINAGE

Madeline Orsini was maneuvering quite well with her cane after the surgery to remove four metal pins from her ankle. She had taken her doctor's advice to heart. Forcing herself to endure daily sessions with a physical therapist, she inherently knew that this displeasure would likely lead to a quicker and fuller recovery. After her session, she found salvation in the heated waters of a spa in the aquatic room. Madeline would return to her suite where she would apply an ice pack to the injured ankle. With her foot elevated atop an ottoman, she would enjoy a cup of her new favorite Macha tea. One morning after a morning jaunt around the immediate area around her suite, she noted a carefully folded piece of paper deftly inserted in the door jamb of her front door. Opening it, it was apparent as much by the tell-tale handwriting as by the careful signature, that it was written by Jane Kilgore. Jane was requesting a meeting. The brevity of the note did not express alarm, but somehow Madeline sensed it anyway. Rather than call, Madeline passed on her usual habit of wearing professional-looking slacks and complimentary blouse, a throwback to her working days, and hurriedly put on her favorite maroon nylon leisure pants and a sleeveless rose print blouse. As she made her way through the main hallway, now slowly filling with staff helping residents in wheelchairs and walkers make their way to the dining room for the lunch meal, Madeline was greeted warmly with, "Causal Tuesday, Madeline?" by the staff. She smiled back. Madeline had instituted a policy of "Casual Friday" attire for the staff the last year she served as Director. It was her way of hoping to lessen the effect of the "TGIF" syndrome which frequently left some of the staff less than attentive to the residents. "You could only hope," she replied. Just before the entrance to the dining room, Madeline turned left down the hallway where the administrative offices were located. Her unsteady gait quickened as her apprehension grew. Belaying her mounting anxiety, she paused at the office door, took a deep breath, and then gave three quick raps with the handle of her cane.

"Come in," replied the voice inside.

As she opened the door, Orsini felt a twinge of remorse. Glancing around the office, the noticeable change in office décor, the replacement of her personal items with those of Jane Kilgore was unavoidable. It gave her pause to mourn briefly for the days when she was in charge.

"Hello there, Jane. I'm answering your message," said Madeline, as she pulled out a chair from the oak conference table, another somewhat painful reminder of her past as Director.

The anxiety on her face and sense of urgency in her voice caused Jane to wish she had chosen less ambiguous language in her message.

"Gosh, Madeline, I didn't mean to alarm you. What with our annual family day celebration a few months away, I had an idea I wanted to discuss with you," replied Jane. Hoping to ease Madeline's perceptible nervousness, Jane offered her a beverage. "Can I get you something to drink?"

"A cold water would be fine. That aqua therapy can create quite a thirst," replied Madeline, who raised her surgically repaired ankle to rest on a chair.

Unconcerned with the informality of the gesture, Jane went to the small refrigerator in the corner of the office, one of the few holdovers from Madeline's tenure, and took out two chilled bottles of Perrier; this was yet another sign of change as Madeline had stocked the refrigerator with bottles of Crystal Geyser. Jane set two glasses on the table. She twisted off the cap of her bottle and slowly poured the contents into one of the glasses. Madeline did the same while subtly studying Kilgore's face to detect some indication of what was to come.

"You know I've tried my hand at constructing a family tree for two of our residents," she began. "I thought they might serve staff in drawing out old memories from the residents."

"No, actually, I hadn't," responded Orsini, who had purposely stayed out of the main facility as she wanted Jane to have a seamless transition as Director without Madeline's presence inhibiting the process. Even with the surgery, this was not an easy step for her.

Feeling not at all humble, Jane gloated, "It's been a wonderful success for Lettie Lamberson and the Levinson's. The staff working with Lettie and the Levinson's have reported how much talking about names off their trees has sparked the recollection of other names and incidents from their pasts. Not only that, other residents had stopped to look at the posters of the trees positioned outside the dining room and that has generating conversations between the residents, some even asking if we could do their family tree."

"I'm happy for them, Jane, but what exactly has that to do with me?"

Any effort that added to the lives of the residents was a plus for her. Eager to share her idea, Jane leaned forward, a sheen of excitement spread over her face.

"With Samantha's help, I've got a volunteer, Marie Gordon, a volunteer from US Gen, an organization specializing in tracing family trees, who's working with two of our residents. If we're lucky, Gordon will have the trees finished by the family day celebration and we can display them along the main hallway."

Sensing the direction of the conversion, Madeline's resistance was reflected in the sharpness of her response, if not in the flushed redness forming on her unsmiling face.

"You're not suggesting what I think you are, are you?"

It was more a statement than a question.

Jane's own excitement blinded her to the tone of Madeline's words.

"Madeline, you are an icon here at Magnolia Gardens. The Board of Directors has recognized twenty-five years of your work by arranging for your living quarters. Generations of families owe whatever happiness their loved ones received to your conscientious efforts to make the Gardens a home, not an institution; and I can't count the number of volunteers you've influenced to pursue careers in the field of aging programs. Who better to have their family tree exhibited alongside our residents than you!"

Jane's laudatory remarks did little to ease the pain at the possibility of having her tortured past revealed. There could never be a family tree for Madeline Orsini because there was no Mr. Orsini. Even more agonizing, there never would be any heirs added onto the Orsini family tree. The thought of endless expressions of sympathy from well-meaning people, or testimonials to her strength of character to have carried on in spite the tragedies heaped upon her, made her back arch as if she had been pressed against shards of glass. Madeline desperately needed the privacy of her suite lest her tormented screams alert staff to some nonexistent emergency. Years of questioning and self-doubt opened a floodgate of emotions she could not control. She grabbed for her cane, awkwardly knocking it to the floor. She bent over, her left hand randomly moving across the floor until she found it. She picked it up and without turning around, headed for the door. Madeline's uncontrollable sobbing prevented her from saying anything more than, "Please, Jane, no." Her voice was no longer angry but pitiful in tone.

Completely taken aback by this shocking display of emotions, Kilgore was left with her mouth agape.

~

OF THE TWO NAMES OF RESIDENTS WHO HAD AGREED TO HAVE MARIE
Gordon research their family trees, Marie had elected to start with
Willard Castleberry, partially because she was a bit of an aficionado of
South Carolina history, and Castleberry's claim to a lineage of the aristocratic antebellum South intrigued her. A more personal reason lay in
Marie's own background. She was the child of a bi-racial marriage.
Her father was African American, and her mother was white. The
mixture of those bloodlines resulted in Marie's stunningly beautiful
light caramel complexion. As a result, Marie Gordon was not shy
about addressing the undercurrent of racism wherever she saw it. Jane
had described Willard Castleberry as somewhat arrogant, particularly
around the African American staff at the Gardens. *She circled the date of
their first interview in her day planner. Let's see what falls out of your tree,
Willard,* she mused. Her anticipation caused a gleeful chuckle to
escape from her sensual lips.

~

WILLARD CASTLEBERRY SAT IN THE LIBRARY AWAITING THE ARRIVAL OF
Marie Gordon. Castleberry had been unusually accommodating when
he was approached by Jane Kilgore to see if he was interested in
having his family tree researched and placed on display at the
Gardens. "Of course, my dear. You do know my bloodlines pre-dated
the Civil War?" he had asked her. The hubris of his remark could not
be overemphasized. Willard saw this as an opportunity to enlighten
the other residents as to his historical importance. He dressed north of
casual for the meeting, wearing white oxford shoes and gray polyester
pants. His white dress shirt was freshly pressed and opened at the
collar to display an elegantly tied teal silk ascot. An emerald green
blazer crowned his attire. Out of vanity, he kept his glasses in a case in
the inside pocket of his blazer. Though desperately needed for proper
vision, they seldom made an appearance.

"Mr. Castleberry, my name is Marie Gordon. I'm here about your family tree. I believe Mrs. Kilgore told you I'd be coming," said a very cordial Gordon.

Castleberry rose to meet her and did his best to exude his finest refined southern gentleman persona.

"Yes, my dear, she certainly did, and may I add you look quite lovely," he said, while politely taking her hand in his and bringing it to his lips.

It was all quite feigned and nauseating to Gordon. She found nothing attractive in Castleberry's archaic display of politeness. To the contrary, she saw it as condescending and sexist. The old fellow was completely aware of the perceptual abilities of this young woman. Marie acted quickly to disarm the old gentleman.

"Then perhaps we should get started," replied Gordon, who casually brushed the back of her hand against her dress.

Willard followed her into the room off the library which Kilgore had arranged to be Gordon's work area. For their initial meeting, Gordon would only require that Castleberry give her the names of parents and grandparents on both sides of the family. Then she would use any one of several genealogical search engines to expand the family tree.

"May I call you Willard, Mr. Castleberry? I find being on a first name basis much less officious," she asked, smilingly sweetly, belying her growing distaste for this man.

Smitten with Gordon's presence, Castleberry quickly succumbed to her charm. It had been some time since he had the undivided attention of a lovely young woman, and he was going to make the most of it.

"Please call me Willard and may I be allowed to call you Marie?"

Marie nodded as she took out her notebook from her valise. She was already more interested in the task than him.

"Let's start with your parents, shall we?" she asked with pen in hand.

The braggadocios Castleberry wasted little time in enlightening Gordon. He could barely contain his pride when he smoothly replied,

"You may not know that I was the youngest state senator ever to serve the great state of South Carolina. I represented Calhoun County for over thirty years. My father, Beauregard Castleberry, was the Cadet Commander at VMI, having graduated in 1897. He served alongside General John J. Pershing in Mexico and later in France during World War I. Some say it was my father and not Pershing who brought victory to the Allies."

Castleberry delivered this outrageous falsehood without one twinge of regret. Once she wrote down Beauregard Castleberry, Gordon's pen rested on her notebook. Castleberry never noticed due to his deep state of self-absorption.

"After the war, my father married my mother, Sarah Lattimore Broadbent. The Broadbent family fortune was made in the railroad business. She, unfortunately, died when I was only a year old. I believe it was consumption."

Barely pausing to take a breath, Castleberry went on.

"My grandfather was Colonel Harrison Castleberry. He commanded the 17th Carolina Volunteers during the Civil War."

For the first time, Castleberry's enthusiasm waned. The disappointment in his voice became obvious. The man appeared capable of some genuine human emotion.

"After the war, grandfather lost all his plantation to northern carpetbaggers. All he was able to salvage was a sawmill operation. Fortunately, there was a good market for pine tar, and grandfather did quite well."

Any energy Castleberry had lost painting up his exaggerated lineage, was quickly regained. Castleberry straightened his posture as he proudly announced, "Grandfather went on to become the first Grand Wizard of the Knights of the Klu Klux Klan of South Carolina," using the Greek name as some sort of legitimacy. "The Klan is a terribly misunderstood organization, Ms. Gordon. I myself served as the Grand Giant for Calhoun County, and I can tell you we were a service to many Carolinians."

Internally, Marie was nauseated at the notion that Castleberry

Marie's mother. Her rectangular kitchen had an old fashion three burner stove with an oven suitable only for storing pots and pans. She had an equally old-fashioned refrigerator which needed defrosting more often than Marie liked. Her father had converted one end of the kitchen into a large enclosed pantry. The other end was the dining area that overlooked the front yard. Vintage might sound cute, but it had its disadvantages. The doors were narrower than normal, thus making moving in a queen size bed difficult. The crystal knobs were continually loose, and often came off when pulled too hard. Though Marie loved the claw foot bathtub, she did not appreciate the lack of electrical outlets in the bathroom needed for a water pic, hair blower, curling iron, and a makeup mirror.

Upon entering her home, she screamed, "That son-of-bitch!" throwing her bag on the couch. No need for propriety here. She went immediately to the bathroom. Turning on the cold-water handle on her antique porcelain pedestal style sink, she wet her hands and then dabbed her face. The cool water brought her some measure of relief, but she wanted more. She turned to the claw foot bathtub and turned on the hot water. Retreating to her bedroom, she took off her clothes and then scampered quickly down the short hallway to the bathroom. Then sprinkling in a liberal dose of bath salts, she stepped into bubbling warm water. For an hour or so, she leaned her head against the back of the tub and soaked in the sublime waters. When her anger had sufficiently subsided, Marie rose to her feet. She grabbed a large terry-cloth towel hanging on the wall and dried herself off. Then, putting on her favorite yellow bathrobe, she returned to her combination living room and office. At least she would be comfortable. The US Gen Society had graciously provided Marie with two large-screen computers allowing her to search multiple genealogical websites at the same time. She rolled her chair from one screen to another until she had a search engine on each screen: Family Genealogy Bank and Ancestery.com.

"Now Mr. Willard Castleberry, let's see what we can find."

Her scathing sarcasm could not have been any more intense if Castleberry were there.

Starting with Family Genealogy Bank, she entered the names of Castleberry's father and mother focusing on South Carolina. Marie soon discovered Castleberry was a somewhat common name at the time. To eliminating duplicate names, she had to search many possibilities until she was sure they could be excluded. After several hours, she was able to confirm his lineage, at least back to his grandfather. She had made note of the birth dates Castleberry had given her. They matched the dates listed in the records. It was senseless to attempt to go further as birth records prior to the Civil War were often inaccurate if they even existed. Census information which began in 1790 was even more unreliable as census takers often avoided canvasing the more rural areas of the country. In an exercise in futility, she tried both other search sites only to confirm what she already knew. On the surface, Willard Castleberry's lineage was exactly as he had stated. Marie Gordon did not consider herself a vengeful person, but she was genuinely disappointed she had been unable to bring the pompous Castleberry down a notch or two. Then she remembered something she had scribbled in her notebook. The bag lay on the couch, its contents half spilled out from an anger-filled toss when she first came home. Finding the notebook half under an end pillow, she hastily flipped through several pages. There it was. Castleberry's grandfather had served with the 17th Carolina Volunteers. The answer to her hidden agenda just might lie in some long-forgotten receptacle of South Carolina Civil War records.

8

THE HIDDEN HORRORS OF WILLARD CASTLEBERRY

The next morning after a breakfast of scrambled eggs, wheat toast, and coffee, Marie Gordon took off on the two-hour drive to the South Carolina State Library in Columbia, South Carolina. The four-story State Library building was typical of southern architecture through much of the mid-nineteenth century. Large white marble columns adorned the front and side entrances. She passed a couple of yards along the way where Confederate flags hung from multiple masts around the structure as some morbid reminder of a war where brothers killed brothers. There were any number of statues of famous military leaders on horseback from the Civil War. Male and female docents were dressed in period customs. The men were in Confederate uniforms and the women in brightly colored hoop skirts, broad brim hats, and parasols. *No wonder there's still a racial divide in this country,* she thought. As she exited the revolving door on the first floor, Gordon was greeted by a docent whose name tag read, "Sergeant Matthews." He asked if he might be of some help.

"Yes, Sergeant Matthews, can you direct me to the archives, especially those dedicated to military units active during the Civil War?"

The elderly man with silver hair straightened his stooped shoulders at being referred to by his rank. Grabbing the handle of the saber that hung from his belt, he removed his hat, and sweeping it across his body, bowed slightly at the waist. It played more to a time when the display of genteel manners was expected from southern gentlemen.

"Yes, Ma'am. Take the elevator to your left to the fourth floor. The archive section you are looking for is in the very back."

Now to play her own part, Gordon offered a slight curtsy in appreciation for his help. She made her way across the black and white marble tiled floor to the elevator. Once out of the elevator, she saw a pair of large dark Mahogany doors with a brass plate above them that read, "Archives." Once inside, Gordon stood in awe of the history that now surrounded her. Along every wall were bookcases that extended twenty feet high. The shelves were deep enough to accommodate thousands of volumes of leather-bound ledgers, each containing a trove of historical information. Each wall had several rolling ladders for staff to use. There were three long rows of research tables. The rows were twenty tables deep with lamps and electrical outlets a researcher might need. Gordon approached the receptionist desk. A nameplate on the countertop read, "Mrs. Estelle Blair." A rather matronly woman sat behind a computer screen. Her dark hair was neatly combed, but certainly not stylish. A bit on the heavy side, with reading glasses that rested near the end of her nose, she looked up at Gordon.

"What is it you need, young lady?" She seemed to evaluate Marie for a moment, as if trying to determine why someone so young would be interested in musty history.

"I hope so, Mrs. Blair. If it's not too much trouble, I was wondering if you could direct me to the archives pertaining to South Carolina military units serving in the Civil War, specifically the 17th Carolina Volunteers."

The pleasantness in Gordon's voice and the beam on her face caused Mrs. Blair to smile. She was accustomed to the more direct and curt requests from rude researchers who treated the library staff as servants whose only perceived purpose was to answer their every beck and call.

She considered the request before answering, "I think I have just the answer for you, Miss..."

"Oh, I'm so sorry. My name is Marie Gordon, and I'm doing some genealogical research for a resident at Magnolia Gardens."

"My goodness, young lady," Mrs. Blair said with great surprise. "My mother lived there until her death two years past. I'll take special care of you. Come with me."

This small admission had created an instant bond between the two women. Gordon followed her to the back of the archives room. The back end of the room was separated by a wooden rail. An elderly looking black man sat at a large desk, peering over several opened volumes. The bill on his visor had a clear plastic section which allowed light to come through, an advantage for one with poor eyesight.

"Calvin Nations, I'd like you to meet Ms. Marie Gordon. She needs your expertise. Calvin here knows more about South Carolina's participation in the Civil War than any man alive."

When he stood up, Gordon realized Calvin was no taller than she, at barely five feet tall. He took off thick rimless glasses, squinting his eyes to focus on the woman standing before him. His smile revealed two gold-capped front teeth. A snowy white mustache matched the hair that grew barely above his ears exposing a shiny bald head. He wore a black vest over a white long-sleeved shirt in need of ironing.

"I'm sorry, Missy, at seventy-two my hearing isn't what it once was. What was your name again?" He was slightly embarrassed but eager to please this lovely young woman.

"Gordon, Marie Gordon."

"Well, Ms. Gordon, why don't you have a seat and tell me how I can help you?"

The long fingers of his hand pulled a chair out next to his desk for her. Gordon couldn't help but notice the yellowish tone to his fingernails. *No doubt from years of smoking unfiltered cigarettes,* she thought.

Seeing that her charge was in good hands, Blair stated, "I'll leave you two alone. Thank you, Calvin," said Blair, as she headed back to her desk.

Gordon leaned slightly forward as she spoke in deference to his hearing difficulty.

"I'm constructing a family tree for a resident at Magnolia Garden Assisted Living Facility, and I need to verify some of the gentleman's information, specifically his grandfather's involvement with the 17th Charleston Volunteers, Mr. Nations."

"Y'all call me Calvin," he smiled. "I heard about these family trees. Sorta confounding that people is really interested in that kinda stuff. What makes his military service so important?"

Gordon was not prepared to reveal her true motivation. How could she, after all? Her quest was motivated by racial prejudice as much as historical accuracy. She hoped her ruse would work. Somewhat conflicted by this less than positive motivation, she was undeterred in her quest for the truth.

"The gentleman's father was a VMI graduate and a decorated veteran of World War I, serving with General John J. Pershing. I'm hoping to provide the gentleman with more accurate details about his grandfather's service with the 17th Carolina Volunteers."

Calvin took a white handkerchief from his back pocket and gently rubbed the lenses of his glasses. Accepting her at face value, Calvin put his glasses on and announced, "Let's see what I can find for you, Missy." He walked back to his desk and after closing the opened ledgers on his desktop revealed a laptop computer. He flipped up the top and pressed the "on" button.

"Never have liked these kinda machines," he said, as his eyes search for the start button. "It can make one lazy, but the older I get I can tolerate a bit of laziness," chuckling at his own sense of humor.

Clicking on his search bar, he typed in 17th Carolina Volunteers. In less than a second, the screen displayed the following information, *17th Charleston Volunteers activated April 11, 1861—surrendered April 9, 1865 at Appomattox. June 23, February 15, 1865. Row 3, Volume 13.*

"Come with me, Missy," Calvin said, as he stood up.

His left hand hung at his side. *A slight though persistent shake was surely a sign of Parkinson's Disease,* she thought. He walked stooped shouldered with knees that bent awkwardly with each step. Marie followed him to the back wall to a seemingly endless row of similarity bound volumes. Calvin went to the beginning of the third row. Bending at the waist, he muttered in exasperation as he squinted, "Damn small numbers!"

Embarrassed at his use of a minor profanity, he quickly responded, "Sorry, Missy."

Marie was immediately taken back to a time when such an utterance would have brought the overseer's whip across Calvin's shoulders. He moved slowly down the row, his hand dusting off the brass numbered plates with his handkerchief. Finally, he stopped.

"Yes," he said, sounding pleased with his discovery. He carefully and with genuine deference pulled out a large leather-bound ledger trimmed in red. He took Marie over to one of two long tables and set the ledger on it.

"The 17th Carolina Volunteers right here."

In a moment of sincere reflection, Calvin stared at the ledger, his fingers slowly tracing the embossed lettering on the ledger. Without looking up, he sighed, "Ain't no peace at Appomattox, Missy, not for peoples like me."

Marie set her valise on the table and took out her notebook. Putting on her square prescription reading glasses, she meticulously turned page after page, intently following the flowing handwriting on brownish paper held between protective sheets of polyester Melinex. For over an hour, Gordon's eyes strained to find that one hidden bit of information she was sure was there. *Thomas Jefferson had his Sally Hemings, and she was sure Harrison Castleberry did too.* Vexed by her fatigue, Marie closed the ledger with a thud that caught Calvin's attention. He walked over to the table and sat beside her. The kindness of his words soothed the ire building inside her. She had to remind herself that historical research is like peeling back the layers of an onion. It's slow, methodical work.

Sensing her frustration and having been drawn to the kindness in her voice, Calvin wanted to help even more.

"Missy, tell me more 'bout what you're lookin' for."

If Calvin were to help her, Marie realized she would have to be more honest with the object of her quest.

"The man whose tree I'm working on is Willard Castleberry. There is, in fact, a lineage that I can trace back to the Civil War and the 17th Carolina Volunteers. This is the clincher, Willard Castleberry is an avowed racist, past Wizard of the Klan during the fifties in South Carolina, and grandson of Harrison Castleberry, who Willard says was the first Grand Wizard of the Klan in South Carolina. Willard's skin tone, a perpetual light tan complexion, suggests to me his bloodline may be less than pure southern white. Calvin, I'm the child of a black father and a white mother, and I'm proud of my heritage. It's not something to be hidden but embraced. If there were evidence of mixed blood in his background, perhaps Willard Castleberry would realize the futility of hating what is in his own lineage. I'm sorry, Calvin, I probably should have told you this in the beginning."

The moment he heard the name Castleberry, an eerie feeling came over Calvin Nations. He took off his glasses and set them on the table. He crossed his arms and laid his head on the table. His shoulders shuddered; an audible moan emanated from his mouth. Without lifting his head, he asked, "You did say, Harrison Castleberry, didn't you?"

"Yes," replied Gordon. "Do you think you can help me?"

As Nations raised his head, Marie could see tears coming down his face. He straightened himself, taking in a deep breath.

"Yes, Missy, I can help."

His arthritic fingers attempted to pull a pocket watch from the pocket of his black vest. Embarrassed by his efforts, he finally retrieved the watch. "Fingers ain't what they use to be," he said. He pressed the watch open, looked at the time, snapped it shut, and returned it to his pocket.

"Bout closing time," he said.

He could not make eye contact with Marie. What he was about to ask was unheard of in his younger days and would undoubtedly bring unwanted attention even today. He would understand if she said no.

"I got something at home you need to see."

Calvin's emotional reaction and his rather cryptic answer that he could help her, but not for the reasons she might think, made it impossible for her not to respond in the affirmative.

"Of course, I can."

∾

MARIE WAITED IN THE PARKING LOT FOR CALVIN. AFTER A FEW MINUTES, he appeared. His right hand held a brass cane used to steady an uneven gait. He walked over to her car. Unable to shake the racial separatism of his time when a white woman riding with a black man would result in violence, he said, "I think you should follow me, Missy."

Marie nodded. Nations lived in the predominately black part of Charleston known as "The Swamp." It bordered the rail yards to the south and the Santee River to the west. Homes in the area ranged from single dwelling homes in the Craftsman style of the early forties and fifties on the fringe of "The Swamps" to blocks of public housing apartment buildings for low-income families. Calvin pulled into the driveway of his corner house and indicated to Marie to park along the curb. It pleased Marie to see that houses on Calvin's street were not the stereotypical rundown structures so common in photographs of areas targeted for urban renewal. Some needed yard work or perhaps a new coat of paint, but in general they did not deserve the unflattering nickname of "The Swamp."

Having made his way up the four wooden steps of his porch, he leaned his cane against the railing and offered up an apology.

"Please excuse the mess, Missy. My wife passed some time back n' I ain't much of a housekeeper."

"No apologies needed, Calvin," replied Marie, as she noted the well-worn swing cushion and the rusted three-legged wrought iron flower stand with an ashtray full of snuffed out hand-rolled cigarettes.

Calvin noted her gaze.

"She never wanted me to smoke inside. Still don't," he said in a rather melancholy tone.

Calvin held the door open as Marie entered his home. The living room was small and somewhat cluttered. Days of old newspapers were stacked on the end table next to a badly faded and saggy couch which was covered with a brown knitted afghan. A chair was posed against the door wall. It served as a resting place for Calvin's jacket. Its matched pair was against the opposite wall in the corner. Free of clutter, it must be used by any company Calvin may have. The TV tray at one end of the couch where Calvin took his meals still had his coffee cup on it. A large area rug covered a wood floor scared with scratches and grooves from moving furniture over the years. An array of family photos was arranged on the mantle of a fireplace no longer used. It was clear Calvin Nation's entire life was on display. Marie scanned each of them. She had long ago learned that such photos often contained clues

"I can see you are proud of your family," Marie asked.

The floor creaked as Calvin walked over to the mantel. He took down the first photo, a black and white of a young black man in a dark suit and a very young black woman in a white cotton dress, wearing a broad brim white straw hat. "My wife, Betty. Just a girl when we married up in Bowman. Sharecropped 'bout fifty acres. Had a roof over our heads and food on the table. Knew where to go, and who to talk to. By the time the boys were ready for high school, Betty wanted more for them. We moved to Charleston, and I took a job as a floor sweep in a steel mill." Thinking of their years together brought an immediate flow of tears to Calvin's eyes. Unashamed, he offered up a poignant observation. "You can't hold a memory, Missy." He took out a handkerchief from his back pocket and gently dusted the oak frame.

The remaining photos showed two children at various stages of growth, from infancy to school years, family activities, and graduation photos.

Calvin picked up the graduation photo of two boys in their cap and gowns.

"My twin boys, John and Wilbert." Tears continued a slow ebb down his face. "John died from tuberculosis, at least that's what the VA said. He served in Desert Storm. That boy was never sick a day in his life until he went over there. Wilbert here, he became a preacher. First in the family." A momentary smile formed on his face, then he set the photo back on the mantle.

"He died in 1995 up in Columbia leading a march to have Martin Luther King Day declared a state holiday. Some Klan members didn't take a likin' to that. The police found his body the next day a mile or two outside of town. He'd been shot."

Marie had grown up in a different era. Campus marches in support of affirmative action or sit-ins protesting lack of care for the homeless were hardly life-threatening endeavors for social justice. She said all she could. "Calvin, I'm so sorry."

The old man began to tremble slightly at the remembrance of his loss.

"Now this isn't why I asked you over here," he said, as he moved away from Marie. "I got a terrible thirst and need a smoke. Missy, mind waiting on the porch swing for a moment?"

Marie sat down on the aged porch swing missing much of its original paint. Her anticipation was building. Several minutes passed before Calvin came out to the porch. He had a glass tumbler in one hand with ice cubes and filled half-way with a rich brown liquid. He set his drink on the glass top of the flower stand and rested a Bible in his lap as he sat next to her. Fingers twisted by arthritis took out a small pouch of tobacco and rolling papers from his vest pocket. Deftly cradling the curved paper between two fingers, he used his teeth to pull open the pouch of tobacco. The slight tremor in his hand caused as much of the rough-cut brown leaves to fall on his leg as in the curved paper. Once the paper held the appropriate amount of tobacco, he carefully ran his tongue along one edge of the paper. Once the paper was properly sealed, he lightly twisted both ends. He lifted his drink and smiled at Marie. He closed his eyes for a moment as his palette savored the flavor of Crown Royal on the rocks. He brought the cigarette to his mouth and slid open a small box of matches next to the ashtray. Taking out a match, he lit it with his thumbnail and held it to the end of his smoke. He inhaled deeply and then slowly exhaled a stream of smoke.

"Nothing like a good smoke and a glass of Crown," he said with a smile.

Calvin set his cigarette in the ashtray. The smoke lazily left the tray and drifted off away from Marie, saving her from the bulk of the noxious odor. As he picked up his Bible, his smile was gone, replaced by a look of dreadful trepidation as he opened the cover of his Bible.

"This is what I wanted you to see, Missy," he said. Holding the Bible in his hand, he turned it toward her. "This here Bible was passed down through three generations of my mother's family. Look at the note my grandmother wrote next to her husband's name. As the head maid overseeing the operations of the plantation owner's house, grandmother had been taught to write by his wife."

Marie took the Bible from Calvin. Between the paper, crinkled and brown with age, and the faded letters, Marie needed her glasses to read the note. Hanging from a sterling silver chain around her neck, she placed them on her small nose and strained to make out the note. When she did, she gasped, "No, it's not possible!" looking at Calvin.

"Go ahead, read it out aloud," Calvin said, as he exhaled the smoke from another drag off his cigarette.

Marie turned her attention back to the opened page. There, next to the name John Withers was printed, *Harrison Castleberry did murder*

with his favorite revolver John Withers for being with Mrs. Castleberry.
Calvin took a final drag off his cigarette then crushed it out in the
ashtray. He raised his glass, tipping it politely at Marie and slowly
drained its contents. Normally a lightweight drinker at best, Marie
Gordon could see its value in these circumstances.

"May I have one of those?" she asked.

Obliging as always, Calvin rose and went into the house. He
returned with a glass tumbler filled with ice cubes and a lady's
amount of Crown Royal. He handed it to her. Unaccustomed to
drinking straight alcohol, Marie coughed a bit. A blush appeared on
her cheeks. She waved her hand in front of her face to create a breeze.

"So, I was right after all," she said, closing the bible.

"Yes'm," replied Calvin. "You know and I know Harrison Castleberry kilt my grandpa and probably has a little of my blood in him.
But what'a ya do just cuz you're right. Tellin' him gonna change him,
make him feel different about people like me? Think about this, Missy,
being right and doin' right, two different things."

What had once been so clear to Marie Gordon now was clouded
with uncertainty. Calvin's words rang true, but Marie had been
blinded by her own anger. She loathed William Castleberry for never
having to endure the bi-racial prejudices that she did growing up. She
wanted Willard Castleberry to experience what her life had been like.
Rather than elation at confronting Willard with her findings, Marie
began to feel pity for him; more importantly, anger at herself. How
would what she wanted to do honor her father and mother and the
values they instilled in her?

"Calvin, thank you so much for your time and sharing with me
this information. I've got some thinking to do."

"It's been my pleasure, Missy Gordon," he replied.

As she got in her car, Marie looked at Calvin, who had lit another
rolled smoke and emptied the last of his cherished Crown. He looked
smaller and even more wrinkled than before.

9

INSIGHT AND HOPE

After several restless nights, Marie Gordon decided to seek the counsel of her father and mother. Franklin Gordon was a professor of African Studies at South Carolina State University. Her mother, Alice, was a social worker for the city of Charleston. Marie had been raised in the upper-class area of Mount Pleasant thanks to a bit of chicanery on her mother's part. As a biracial couple, Franklin and Alice knew there were certain areas a realtor would not take them. When they decided to buy in Mount Pleasant, Franklin and Alice spent weeks driving the area looking for just the right home. When they narrowed their choices down to their dream home, it was Alice who went to the listing agent's office. Under the pretense that her husband was out of town for an extended period, the agent would be dealing solely with Alice. For years the family laughed about the day the agent brought over a housewarming gift only to be greeted by Franklin Gordon, a six-foot-four two-hundred-pound black man.

"You're staying for dinner? Your father would be so disappointed if he missed a chance to visit with you," said Alice, as she and Marie settled down on the living room sofa.

"Absolutely," replied Marie. "There's something I want to talk over with you and Daddy."

"Fabulous," responded Alice. Though her daughter, Alice treated Marie more as an equal. "Let me get us something to drink."

With her mother in the kitchen, Marie kicked off her shoes and rested her feet on the glass top of the coffee table, a no-no if her father had been home. She hadn't lived at home for nearly three years and nothing had changed. The same brick fireplace her father had converted to gas, so he didn't have to bother with the burden of maintaining a constant supply of wood in the winter. The eight-foot-long beige cloth sofa bought specifically to accommodate her father's lanky frame was as comfortable as ever. Her father's fifty-two inch HDTV occupied the front corner of the living room. The rich dark mahogany wood floor, a concession to Alice in exchange for the gas fireplace, held wonderful memories of her father sliding her across the floor in her pajamas as a young child. Her mother soon appeared carrying a tray with a pitcher of lemonade, glasses, and a small plate of homemade oatmeal cookies. As the two women feasted on the cookies, Marie told her mother of the project she had taken on at Magnolia Gardens.

"You couldn't have found a project closer to your heart than that," smiled Alice.

Placing her head on the back of the sofa, Marie groaned, "That's the problem, Mom. It's what my heart was telling me."

"I think this is where we wait for your father, don't you?"

Marie nodded. Alice took the tray back to the kitchen, leaving her daughter deep in thought. Hearing the garage door roll up, Alice knew her husband was home. Opening the door from the garage to the kitchen, Franklin lay his faux leather valise on a small secretariat in the hallway. Though not fond of stereotypes, Franklin dearly loved his professorial looking tweed jacket with patches on the elbows. He wore a gray stubble of a beard due to razor bumps and kept his curly hair neatly trimmed.

"Is that my baby's car in the driveway?" he called out, after giving his wife a hug and kiss.

"Daddy!" yelped Marie, who ran to her father's open arms.

Franklin had unabashedly spoiled Marie when she was growing up. Although he and Alice insisted Marie help around the house, earn good grades, and in high school earn her own spending money, she was rewarded generously. He had no problem hefting his diminutive daughter in the air for a kiss and hug. Franklin had played college football at Clemson and still maintained a rigorous exercise regime.

After setting his daughter down, he called out to his wife, "Do you need any help with dinner?"

"When it's time, the kabobs are marinating in the frig. But Marie has something she wants to talk to you about."

Detailed by nature, Franklin set the timer on his wristwatch for thirty minutes after lighting the coals in his Smokey Joe barbecue on the back porch.

"Then let's sit at the bar and I'll make you a libation," Franklin smiled broadly.

Alice had purchased a small wet bar with three bar stools for her husband's last birthday. The dark oak of the bar complemented the room's hard wood flooring. The bar had a brass foot bar and black granite top. On either end of the bar, Franklin kept a small bowl of mixed nuts.

"Now my dear, what can I prepare for you?" Franklin asked.

Franklin was not much of a drinker, but when he did imbibe, he preferred the more expensive brands of liquor. He dismissed less costly liquor as not worth spending his hard-earned money on. It also enhanced his reputation as a barista with his friends.

"Daddy, could you make me a Crown Royal on the rocks, with maybe a splash of water?"

Looking quite surprised at his daughter's choice, he hesitated momentarily to comply. "When did you develop a taste for Crown?"

Marie appeared embarrassed at her father's query. She was never good at hiding much of anything from him.

"I can explain. It's part of the story I wanted to talk to you about."

Obliging his daughter, Franklin took a crystal tumbler off the glass rack behind the table. A small refrigerator behind the bar provided the ice cubes. He slowly poured from the bottle of Crown until it reached the half-way point on the glass. Then he held it under the water filter and gave it a gentle application of H_2O. Franklin reached for a Martini glass and made himself his favorite, a vodka Martini with Kettle One, no olive, no twist.

As the two clinked glasses, Franklin asked, "What's on your mind?"

Marie took a small sip of her drink. The addition of water took just enough of the edge on the Crown so that she didn't choke as she did with Calvin's offering. She proceeded to tell her father about her project at Magnolia Gardens, her interview with Willard Castleberry and her resulting visit with Calvin Nations.

"The past marks all of us, sweetheart" sighed her father, as he took a healthy sip of his Martini."

"Daddy, you have no idea how much pleasure I experienced at the thought of telling Willard Castleberry he had mixed blood in his background."

"An assumption not a fact," responded her father.

"A fairly good assumption considering the times and Castleberry's complexion, don't you think? After all, look at me."

Franklin smiled. The most pronounced feature of his daughter's mixed blood came from her black hair which she elected to wear in short maroon tresses. Her caramel complexion was the result of Franklin's own biracial background. His father was a noted jazz musician who had one fan, a white woman from Chicago, who cared more about his music than the color of his skin. When Marie was growing up, Franklin and Alice encouraged her to address the leers or rejections that Marie felt was the result of her skin color, but to do so respectfully. Marie grew to enjoy asking when necessary, "Is there something about my skin color that bothers you? or "Considering I have equal if not better qualifications than the other selectees, did my skin color factor into your decision to exclude me? It gave her a surprising sense of empowerment.

Franklin considered his daughter's remarks. He wrinkled his large forehead, which was always a giveaway that he had some doubts about what was said. He wondered if his daughter had truly learned the lessons he had inculcated into her from a young age.

"Are you angry that Mr. Castleberry never endured some of the childhood taunts and adult prejudices that you did?"

Confronted with a rather blunt but perceptive question from her father, Marie felt flushed with embarrassment. She took another sip of her Crown and replied, "Yes, I'm ashamed to say; yes, I am."

Her lovely face assumed a contoured look. It was apparent she was displeased with herself. Franklin slowly turned the stem of his Martini glass with his well-formed and manicured hands. He formed his thoughts carefully, his words even more so.

"I want you to think about this, you can't make Mr. Castleberry live what you lived. At his age, what useful purpose would that serve? The belief systems of men like Willard Castleberry are entrenched in the belief that you must denigrate others to elevate yourself. No genealogical fact or assumption will ever change them. If you are determined to introduce your findings or suppositions, you should consider implicit inference as opposed to explicit confrontation. The former is more likely to be successful than the later. The operative word being likely."

The resonance of his melodic baritone voice gave emphasis to his words and caused a momentary reflection on Marie's part. The aroma of barbecue coals wafting in from the back porch barbecue grill alerted Franklin's olfactory sensors at the same moment his wristwatch started to chime.

"Time for the kabobs to go on," Alice announced, breaking up the seriousness of the conversation.

∼

MARIE GORDON'S TIME WITH WILLARD CASTLEBERRY HAD TAXED HER emotions and resolve to continue, but she had given her word to Jane Kilgore. She hoped Sally Gunderson's case would be different. Gordon would never have imagined how different it would be.

"I'm here to see Sally Gunderson. I have an appointment with her," Marie told the new receptionist whom Marie did not recognize. "I'm sorry, but are you new here?"

"Yes, I only started last week," said Kelly Rae, a retired schoolteacher who took the job to supplement her meager retirement income. "Let me check the schedule," she said apologetically.

Marie was patient as Rae reached for one binder after another until she found the right one. Her fumbling efforts reinforced her image as a new hire.

"Here it is," she said triumphantly. "All this is so new to me, but I'll get faster with time." This was spoken with much more confidence.

Marie appreciated the enthusiasm the woman displayed. She exuded a sense of enthusiasm missing from the other receptionists who approached their job with the emotions of an android. From her complexion and sun-bleached hair, Marie judged Rae to be someone to like to spend time at the shore. Curiosity got the best of Gordon.

"Do you spend much time at the shore? I mean what with your complexion and hair. Kind of a natural assumption," she said.

Daily use of a moisturizing cream had not only kept her skin smooth but helped her deeply bronzed complexion. Her naturally curly hair, bleached by years in the sun and saltwater, hung in fashionable ringlets exuding her laissez-faire approach to life. Rae grinned. Having gone to college in California, it amused her that people on the east coast referred to the beach as the coast.

"Thirty years as a surf bum, yeah you could say I've spent time at the shore and teaching PE all that time didn't hurt. Come with me."

The two walked over to the double French doors leading to the veranda.

Pointing to the far end of the veranda, Rae said, "She's over there with a small reading group. Virginia is the staff member."

"Thanks for your help," replied Marie with a smile.

Marie walked through the double French doors leading to the veranda. Once outside, she paused for a moment to scan the area. There in the far corner was the small group of four Rae had referenced. Virginia, the staff member conducting the group, had two books on the table in front of her. She petitioned the group, "Shall I read from *Under the Tuscan Sun* or *Where the Heart Grows*." The lack of a response from anyone pleased her, as she could now read from her favorite love story.

"Okay, *Under the Tuscan Sun* it is."

To call it a reading group was a humorous misnomer. One of the four sat in a wheelchair. Her name tag, carelessly pinned at an angle on the front of her blue cotton blouse, read Margaret. Her head hung at an awkward angle. Marie could tell she was sleeping, unbothered by the staff member's recitation or the rhythmic tones from a wind chime hanging from an overhead beam. The Cater sisters sat next to each other. Ethel, the older of the two, repeatedly adjusted her silver-framed glasses as she seemed transfixed by several hummingbirds feasting on the nectar from a hanging basket of Zinnias. Enamored by their beauty and whirling movements, she would interrupt the reading by saying, "They're such beautiful creatures." Ethel's young sister, Sarah, giving a maximum effort to listen to the story, would respond with a gentle rebuke, "Shush, I'm can't hear when you talk." She then adjusted the crimson shawl lying across her lap and leaned forward, more intent than ever not to miss anything. Ethel pursed her lips at the recrimination from her young sister. The fourth member of the group was Sally Gunderson, Marie's interviewee. Sally seemed amused by the banter of the Carter sisters and offered her own peace offering. "Girls, you are sisters and sisters should get along." Ethel lost her focus on the hummingbirds. A bit of wonderment spread across her face. "What did she say?" referring to Sally's caution. By now Sarah, sufficiently annoyed at the stream of interruptions, forcefully tapped the table with her cane like a queen demanding order in her court.

Marie approached slowly, lest Sarah Carter be bothered by yet another interruption. Seeing Marie standing there, Virginia closed the book in her hands and asked, "May I help you?"

"I'm sorry to interrupt, Virginia, but my name is Marie Gordon, and I'm scheduled to spend some time with Sally Gunderson today. Would this be a good time?"

Sally had momentarily closed her eyes, yet another victim of the hypnotic wind chime. Virginia responded, smiling, "I think this would be a perfect time."

Virginia rose and walked over to Sally. Kneeling in front of her, Virginia gently placed her hand on Sally's arm.

"Sally, dear, there's someone here to see you."

Upon opening her eyes, Sally saw Virginia kneeling in front of her. Always concerned about others, she was embarrassed that she had done something to disrupt the session.

"I'm sorry, Virginia. I only closed my eyes for a second. Please continue reading."

"On no, Sally. You've done nothing wrong. There's someone here to see you, her name is Marie Gordon."

Aware that a stranger was looking at her, Sally gently cupped her thinning brown hair to maintain the new coiffure she had received yesterday. An acceptable form of vanity for a woman of any age. Sally was never one to be impressed with stylish clothing, but her hair was a different matter. It was going to be the way she wanted it. Unaccustomed to visitors and certainly from an attractive young woman, Sally straightened herself in her wheelchair, adjusting the knitted shawl that laid across her lap. Anxious to meet her guest, she extended her hand and inquired, "I don't think I know you, young lady. I'm Sally Gunderson."

Marie was impressed by the woman's state of awareness and hoped to capitalize on it. She was also taken by Sally's stunning hazel eyes and radiant smile. There was an aura about the older woman that immediately put Marie as ease, much like Marie's own grandmother. Sally turned to Virginia.

"Would that be alright, Virginia? You are right in the middle of our reading, and I wouldn't want to disappoint you by leaving."

"Not at all, Sally, we'll be fine. You go with Ms. Gordon."

Virginia pointed to an area at the opposite end of the veranda now totally shaded from the afternoon sun. There was an attractive white wicker chair and table ensemble in the area. The staff had recently changed the seasonal blooms in the vase on the table. The area literally beamed a welcome to the new acquaintances.

"That will be a quiet spot over there."

Marie stepped behind the wheelchair.

"Would you mind holding my bag while I push?"

Sally looked back at the group. Her eyes beamed with delight.

"They're such a lovely group of friends when they care to be," she said.

Marie mused at Sally's perceptive remark.

"And how exactly does that happen, Sally?"

"Oh, I always tell them how important they are to me. It makes them feel wanted and appreciated. Just like children, don't you know."

Marie would come to learn that philosophy had been the cornerstone of Sally Gunderson's life, and reveal a treasure trove of recipients. Marie was smitten with Sally's humility, a stark contrast to Willard Castleberry's smug arrogance. When they reached the location Virginia had directed them to, Marie locked the wheels of the chair and pulled up a wicker chair in front of Sally. Marie watched as Sally gently adjusted her cotton dress of forget-me-not flowers. She noticed the simple but elegant turquoise ring on Sally's right hand and her perfectly maintained nails. Her smile was infectious. The tone of her voice was melodic, if not angelic.

"You must be a very special person to spend time with an old lady like me?"

I must be talking to my grandmother, Gordon thought. Melba Franklin, Marie's paternal grandmother, always greeted Marie with a similar expression whenever Marie stopped by to see her.

"You've blessed my day by coming here, Marie." The mere recollection brought a small tear to her eye.

"Jane Kilgore told me you might be interested in having me construct your family tree. So I thought we could talk about it."

Sally tilted her head a bit. A quizzical look formed on her face. Her eyes slightly squinting, she said, "She did?"

"You don't remember?" asked Gordon.

"I'm afraid I don't."

It wasn't that she didn't believe this young woman, she did. It's just the fact that she couldn't remember again. Her eyes brightened. An accommodating grin began to form.

"But if it will help you, please let's do it."

Gordon opened her beige leather shoulder bag and took out her notebook.

"I have your birth date as October 15, 1938. Is that correct?"

"Goodness, that was such a long time ago," she said with a devilish gleam in her eyes. "I guess so."

Of course she had not forgotten, Marie thought, *this was but a bit of comedic vanity on Sally's part.* Gordon chuckled at the woman's sense of humor, or was it a failed attempt to disguise her memory loss? Of course it was!

"And your husband, George, was born May 19, 1939?"

The aura of awareness in the moment quickly faded, only to be replaced by eyes that stared out into the distance, as if the answer to Gordon's question would mysteriously appear in some cloud formation.

"Husband, you say?"

Her voice was subdued and lacked focus. Marie feared Sally's questioning response was an indication that any further questioning would be futile. Gordon decided to be more open-ended with her next question. Hoping Sally's blithe spirit would return, she asked, "Well then, how about your sister, Betty. What can you tell me about her?"

Unfortunately, the fog of early dementia reappeared. Sally no longer struggled to remember. She reached out and gently patted Gordon on the hand.

"I hope I been of some help to you."

Marie closed her tattered notebook. She hoped Sally's vision was as poor as her memory, so she would not see the tears beginning to flow down Gordon's lovely face. Initially, the interview had seemed so promising. Sally was genuinely accommodating and displayed a subtle sense of humor. In but a few minutes, it was all gone. Marie could not hide her despair. The golden ring had slipped through her fingers and Marie agonized over how many more opportunities would be lost.

"Yes you have, Sally, and I'll be back again to see you. I promise."

Gordon slung her leather bag over her shoulder and then wheeled Sally back to her reading group where she said goodbye to Virginia and the group. On her way out to the parking lot, Marie promised herself to recreate Sally Gunderson's past before it would be too late for any measure of recollection. She headed home to begin her quest.

10

SALLY GUNDERSON: AN UNDISCOVERED PAST

arie turned on her computer, logged onto Family Search, and began. Armed with Sally's date of birth and that of her husband, George, she quickly discovered George Gunderson, born May 19, 1938, in Trenton, New Jersey. On the admissions paperwork at the Gardens, Sally had listed her name as Sally London Gunderson. *London could be a middle name or her maiden name,* Gordon thought. *Bingo,* she muttered after typing in Sally London. A Sally London was born on October 15, 1939, to Arthur and Louise London in Eatontown, New Jersey. With George passed on and Sally's mind being what it was, Marie could only hope she'd get more information from Sally's sister, Millie Haggarty. Marie dialed the contact number she had been given by Kilgore and waited. After several rings, a young female voice finally answered, "Haggarty residence. This is Ashley."

Marie introduced herself and explained the nature of her call. She hoped the stranger would be receptive to her request.

"A family tree about my great aunt Sally, that's exciting. I barely remember her. How can I help?" Ashley said, enthusiastically.

She went on to explain that her great aunt had passed away about six months ago, and Ashley and her new husband, Lee Edwards, were living there until all her great aunt's personal property could be disposed of.

"Do you recall the names of any of your grandmother's relatives such as their mothers and fathers, any brothers and sisters they may have had; and don't leave out your own mother and father? You are part of this tree as well," Marie said, almost apologetically.

The newlywed felt a need for maternal permission before answering Marie's request.

"I'll have to check with my mom. She's kind of the keeper of the family history. I'm sure she has all that information."

Though thankful for the sense of co-operation she got from the young woman, Marie was sensitive to the young woman hesitancy.

"I think it would be easier for you if I talk directly with your mother. Would you mind giving me her number, so I can contact her?"

Ashley eagerly surrendered the information as she could devote more time to the tasks at hand, the disposal of her great aunt's property and a new husband.

After hanging up, Marie immediately placed a call to Ashley's mother, Harriet Nelson, in Tacoma, Washington. The sense of urgency for Marie after visiting with Sally would not permit any delays. A pleasant-sounding woman answered, "Hello."

"Is this Harriet Nelson, mother of Ashley Edwards?"

"Why, yes. Is there some sort of problem?" asked the anxious woman alarmed by the formality of Gordon's question.

"I'm so sorry, Mrs. Nelson. I didn't mean to shock you. My name is Marie Gordon. I live in Charleston, South Carolina. I'm doing some work at Magnolia Gardens, an assisted living facility here where your aunt lives. I'm developing a family tree for your aunt, and I was wondering if you might provide me with some information about her family?"

Relieved at the nature of the call, Harriet Nelson let out a sigh of relief.

"Of course. The last time I saw her was when my husband and I got married right after high school. The military sent him to out west to Seattle, Washington, and we've been here ever since."

"Ashley told me you're considered the keeper of the family history, so I thought you might be able to help."

The woman chuckled at the reference.

"I've always been interested in family history though I can assure you there are no famous or infamous relatives in my family. That aside, how can I help you?"

Marie explained that she needed the names of any relatives on Harriet's mother's side of the family and any children of those relatives. Dates of birth would be particularly helpful.

"My mother, who passed away shortly before Ashley was born, I don't recall her ever saying that her sister and her husband had any children. I think there may have been a rift between the two, about what I'm not sure. But mom hoarded, as my children would say, all sorts of family pictures and old letters. I'll go through them and see what I can find. Give me your contact information. and I'll get back to you."

"I can't tell you how much I appreciate that, Mrs. Nelson. I'll look forward to hearing from you."

Several weeks later, after returning home from dinner with her parents, she found a small manila envelope at her doorstep. The return address was Harriet Nelson, 1324 Willow Ave, Tacoma, Washington. Marie hurried inside, anxious to see what trove of information Harriet had provided her. One thing Marie did not inherit from her mother was a sense of neatness in the home. The back of a chair served fine as a coat hanger. The small oval-shaped glass coffee table edged in dark mahogany wood was a landing area for mail, old and new, the latest issue of the Charleston Herald, and the occasional box or two of take-out Chinese food from the Orient Express. Marie shuffled the papers into somewhat of a stack and tossed the day-old boxes of pork fried rice and Hunan Beef in the kitchen trash can. Sitting on the couch, she gently opened the manila envelope and slid the contents onto the newly cleared area on the coffee table. A hand-written note was paper clipped to a sheet of paper folded around some photographs. Marie took off the clip and read the note.

> Dear Ms. Gordon,
> Attached you will find a list of names and dates of birth for as many relatives on my side of the family as I could find or remember. I've included some old photographs which I thought might interest you. Please return them when you are finished with your project.
> Sincerely,
> Harriet Nelson

Marie scanned the list of names provided her. Harriet had done well. Sally's tree would grow exponentially with the names of grand-parents, aunts, uncles, and cousins. But it was the small groups of photographs that would provide the greatest mystery. Among the dozen or so old black and white photos, one perplexed Marie. The small scalloped-edged faded black and white photograph showed a woman sitting on porch steps, surrounded by four young children ranging in age from probably two to maybe eight, Marie guessed. The woman was cradling a toddler in her arms. On the back of the picture was written *the newest member of our family, Andrew Collins.* Confused and bewildered, Marie slumped back against the couch. She stared again at the photo. And why the name Collins and not Gunderson? She doubted genealogy would provide much help. The answer would lie much closer to home than Marie could have imagined.

~

MARIE'S MOTHER HAD WORKED FOR YEARS IN SOCIAL WORK. PERHAPS those years of experience would benefit Marie in her quest. She imme-diately dialed her work number.

"Mom, can I stop by your work today? There's something I need help with," asked Marie over the phone.

It was unlike Marie to sound anything but confident, and the request for help caused immediate concern in Alice

"Absolutely," Alice responded. "Folks here will be glad to see you."

"Who will we be glad to see?" asked Florence Abby, a fellow social worker who had a desk opposite Alice Franklin for years.

"Marie. She's coming by today to see me."

"It seems like forever since I've seen that child," smiled Florence, who had served as a second mother to Marie over the years.

Alice and Florence were something of a legend within the Social Services Department in Charleston, South Carolina. Social Services often sent them on difficult and complex cases together. Alice Gordon was a diminutive white woman in her fifties. She was an outspoken advocate for the rights of children, and Lord forbid the case involving child abuse or neglect that landed on her desk. That child became her child, and Alice protected them like a mother lion protects her young. Alice had received many certificates of achievement over the years, and she had an equal number of written reprimands for procedural violations or ignoring jurisdictional lines of authority. Florence Abby, several years younger than Alice, still proudly wore her hair in an Afro akin to Diana Ross. She had a degree in social welfare from Rutgers University and had graduated at the top of her law school class from Duke. After passing the South Carolina Bar examination, she was hired by a firm doing product liability research. There was nothing intellectually stimulating or socially redeeming about product liability research, and Florence soon found herself working for the Charleston Department of Social Services. Her ability to quote paragraph, section, and subsection of criminal law and departmental regulations, some real, some not, intimidated more than one hostile parent or pettifogger, as she liked to refer to unscrupulous lawyers, to crumble to her demands.

"What is my baby doing these days?" asked Florence as she

checked her day planner, hoping there was nothing that would prevent a long lunch with Alice and Marie.

"She works for a company called US Gen. They specialize in doing genealogical research. Right now, she's working with some clients at Magnolia Gardens."

"God that sounds mind-numbing," groaned Florence, thinking back to her days do product liability research.

With the tell-tale shrug of her shoulders indicating you can lead a horse to water, but you can't make it drink, Alice responded, "She's on the right path, however, her destination is still unknown."

Florence, who had grown up on the East coast and was a huge New York Yankee's fan, quoted her favorite Yogism.

"Remember what the Yogi used to say, 'when you come to a fork in the road, take it.' She'll find hers."

As the two women enjoyed a laugh, Alice's cell phone rang. She answered it.

"Send her in," replied Alice. "It's Marie. She's here."

Alice and Florence grabbed their bags and headed to the lobby to the awaiting Marie.

"Auntie Flo, gee I'm glad you're here," said the gleeful Marie.

The two embraced in a long hug. It pleased Alice immensely that Florence had formed such a close relationship with her daughter. She had often been that second set of ears Marie could vent to during the onset of womanhood, a time when Marie felt her mother had no understanding of what she was going through

Alice smiled and said, "It's lunchtime. Where do you want to go?"

"How about the Dawg Doctor in the park? The weather's great outside," Marie asked, as her appetite had returned after her scant breakfast toast and coffee.

"The Dawg Doctor is it," answered Florence. "Let's go."

The three walked two short blocks to the downtown park. Lined with blooming magnolias and a bubbling marble fountain in the center, the park was a beacon for those seeking a get-a-way from crowded cafes and bistros. Fluffy white cumulus clouds drifted across the blue sky occasionally blocking the noonday sun much to the relief of those standing in line at the "Dawg Doctor."

He called his truck, "The Dawg Doctor." John Collins had owned an auto body and fender paint shop for years before following his true vocation of cooking. He had taken a twenty-five-foot long 1990 Winnebago Chieftain and completely refurbished the inside with a grill, triple fryers, with refrigeration boxes. The designs on the sides of his truck reflected his artistic ability with a paint gun. Brightly painted caricatures of everything hot dog he sold greeted a customer's eyes. A rotund black man, Big John Collins, sold every imaginable type of hot dog known to mankind: Cajun, Kielbasa, Italian, Polish, Hot Link, even Nathan's Kosher Ball Park Franks. For those with true South Carolina backgrounds, he also had a variety of alligator products, fried, grilled, and steamed. Throw in French fries and onion rings, he had it all. John's wife made him a batch of fresh Cole slaw daily with just the right amount of diced okra and jalapeños for heat. He had finished checking his propane tanks on the back of the truck when he saw Alice, Florence, and Marie crossing the street. His deep baritone voice called out, "Lordy, is that my Miss Marie?

In addition to his regular clientele from the businesses around the park, Big John had a cult-like following among the students at Clinton High school, three blocks west of the park. Thanks to an open campus policy at lunchtime, for years throngs of high schoolers would regularly make the three-block walk to savor their favorite dog at the "Dawg Doctor."

Big John held his arms open, and Marie unashamedly gave him a long hug. His bald head glistened with sweat, and his white t-shirt and apron were stained with perspiration due to the heat inside the truck. As he hugged Marie, he smiled at Alice and Florence and nodded for them to head to the truck.

"Are you heading up City Hall yet?" he asked Marie.

Though not a man of formal education, John Collins had street cred, as they say, and an excellent judge of human nature. He had followed her career at Clinton High where she was student body president as a senior and had organized the first-ever monthly student-run food bank. Later at the College of Charleston, Marie organized student groups to advocate for mobile medical services for the homeless, and student tutors for underachieving students in the poorer schools. John had recognized Marie's ability to work with people, to build consensus, and he thought public service was a perfect fit for her.

"I don't think politics are for me, John," replied Marie, as she walked arm in arm with him to the back of the truck.

"My girl, don't confuse politics with public service. One is merely the means to the greater good."

John stepped up into his truck and headed to the order window.

"Same as always?" he called out.

"No way he remembers," said Marie.

"Same as always, John," Alice replied, confident John's memory was as good as his food. She wasn't disappointed.

Several minutes later, John called out through the small window, "One Cajun dog with onion rings and coleslaw, one Kosher with mustard and fries, and one Italian smothered with grilled onions and bell peppers."

"I don't believe it!" laughed Marie.

Alice walked up to the window to pay. She handed John two twenties and told him to keep the change. John smiled. The three women headed to one of the park tables. John followed them and said, "You forgot your change." He placed an assortment of paper bills and an assortment of coins on the table.

Florence asked Alice, "Are you thinking what I am?"

"Yep."

Alice counted out the bills and coins John had left. It totaled forty dollars. The silence over the next ten minutes was a tribute to the quality of Big John's food.

Wiping her face with a napkin, Alice asked, "So what exactly do you need help with?"

Marie opened her bag and took out the picture of Sally Gunderson and the children sitting on the steps of a porch.

"I'm doing a family tree on this woman," pointing to the picture of Sally. "Her husband passed away about a year ago. Her memory is fading, and I'm anxious to figure this thing out. According to her niece, Sally and her husband never had any child, but the niece sent me this picture along with other letters and pictures. Look at what's written on the back."

Alice flipped the photo over then handed it to Florence.

"I don't get it, Mom. If Sally and her husband never had any children, who are the kids on the porch and how do you explain what's written on the back, the latest addition to our family?"

"I'm not sure, sweetheart," answered Alice, befuddled by her daughter's dilemma.

"May I look at it again?" asked Florence.

Marie handed the photo to her. She gazed intently at the images. Noticing the wide range of ages, and the lack of any apparent facial similarities, Florence had an idea, but she was in no hurry to disappoint Marie if she was wrong. It was only speculation on Florence's part, but she wanted something concrete before revealing her thoughts to Marie.

"Where was this picture taken?"

"Trenton, New Jersey. Why?" answered Marie, her interest piqued at Florence's question.

Florence had grown up in Secaucus, New Jersey, and had done her undergraduate work at Rutgers. She knew exactly who to call to confirm her suspicions.

"Listen, sweetie, I'll need to make a few calls first and then if we're lucky I'll have to run the information through a number of public agencies on the computer at work. Use of the computers at work for private interest is frowned on, to say the least, so I'll have to go in on the weekend."

Marie grimaced at the thought her auntie might get in trouble.

"Auntie, I've got two computers at home for work. Us Gen gave me access to any number of public agencies for my research for them. Why not do the work at my house? Your work would never know."

Florence Abby had a bit of riverboat gambler in her blood, but losing her job over inappropriate use of state resources was enough to readily accept Marie's offer.

"Okay, but this stays between you, me, and your mom, got it?"

"Auntie Flo, that would mean so much to me. Thank you," smiled an ever so appreciative Marie, not realize she could be considered as an accomplice if her auntie's scheme went awry.

"How about your issue with the other resident, Willard? What have you decided to do?"" asked Alice, devouring the last of her seasoned fries.

"Ooh, I like issues. Tell me more," chimed Florence, squeezing the last bit of ketchup from the plastic bottle.

Marie recounted her experience at the state library with Calvin Nations and the resulting meeting at his home. Florence, who had had her share of struggles with civil rights issues and been on the receiving end of nightsticks, slowly shook her head.

"Part of me wants to lay it out in front of him what I think happened and that he's more like me than he would ever suspect. You know, take him down a notch or two," said Marie.

"But you're not sure what to do, are you?" asked Florence.

Marie nodded.

"Want some advice from your second mom?"

"Sure."

"Nothing productive will come from revealing your findings to him of an incident in his family's past that he had absolutely no control over. He owns his past just like my father owns his. To this day, dad will still step to the side when a white woman walks toward him on the sidewalk. Mr. Castleberry's reactions to blacks, like my dad's to white women, are reflexive, not intuitive. His treatment of others, not his mixed blood, should be your focus."

Marie felt ashamed. She realized she was treating Willard Castleberry exactly like he treated people of color. She wanted to demean him over something he had no control over.

"I thought I was a better person, Auntie Flo. I'm not so sure now."

"Honey, you are a better person, just not a perfect person," smiled Florence, sensing nothing more needed to be said on the matter.

11

MADELINE'S PRIVATE HELL

The gentle but persistent knocking at the door awoke Madeline from a blissful nap, causing a sense of irritation to be her first conscious thought. A sense of melancholy had plagued her ever since her appointment with Doctor Wallace. Like the downward slide of the residents at Magnolia Gardens, Madeline was helpless to prevent the progressive eye deterioration of Macular Degeneration. Adding to that sense of melancholy was her self-destructive need to read again those letters that had come back stamped Return to Sender, a dozen in all with the same request: *There's something I must tell you, Eddie, and not in writing, but face to face.* She had wondered for years if he had found someone else, or worse, did something happen to him while on a mission? While a member of Seal Team 4, he had been allowed to leave her an innocuous message like, *Business calls,* code for another mission. But when he was accepted to Seal Team 6, all that changed. No more forewarning, nothing, only meals he didn't show up for or stealthy departures in the middle of the night. The letters were scattered about on her bed when she rose to answer the knock on her door.

"Yes?" she asked, more than a little annoyed while straightening her rumpled blouse.

"Yes, that's all you've got to say. I've got a piping hot pepperoni and sausage pizza from Luigi's that I'll eat myself if you don't open this door right now."

The sound of her friend's voice lifted her spirits. She opened the door to see Kristin Andrews standing there with a most impatient expression on her face. She held the large gaily decorated pizza box firmly in front of her, which somehow lent emphasis to her apparently petulant state of mind.

"Really, yes? You're the one who asked me to pick up a pizza from Luigi's or had you forgotten?" chided Andrews, who quickly brushed by Madeline and headed to the kitchen to offload the steaming hot pizza from its box.

Embarrassed at her memory lapse, Madeline hugged her friend saying, "Sorry. Guess I haven't been myself lately."

Ever since their return from Doctor Stuart's office, it had amazed Kristin how often Madeline wove a sense of fatal inevitability into her life. She was sure Madeline saw herself as one step away from living an existence dependent on a white cane or a seeing-eye dog. Psychologically predisposed for that outcome, Madeline had taken to wearing dark sunglasses even when inside her suite.

"Inside or out?" asked Kristin, holding up two paper plates with pizza slices on them, and napkins.

"Outside," replied Orsini, whose appetite was now stimulated by the aroma of the hot pizza. "I love the sound of the birds this time of day."

Madeline took a couple of bottles of water from the refrigerator and followed Kristin out to the patio table. Kristin pulled out a white wicker chair for Madeline and one for herself. The pizza rested in the middle of the glass tabletop. Kristin was not a patient person went it came to eating one of Luigi's masterpieces. She had already taken a healthy bite before Madeline even sat down.

Seeing Kristin had already taken a bit of pizza, Madeline asked, "Hungry?"

Pointing to her mouth and rolling her eyes skyward as her taste buds exploded, Kristin could only reply, "Mmmmm!"

"I hope it's as good as it sounds," said Madeline, her sarcasm the result of lingering resentment at being woken from her nap.

An ardent admirer of the plentiful wildlife surrounding Magnolia Gardens, Madeline found herself even more attuned to the sounds of nature since her diagnosis.

"Listen," she said, as she stared off in the direction of a large Magnolia tree. Her head swaying to the competitive chirping of the Blue-winged Warblers and Carolina Wrens. Her face exuded a peaceful contentment which was soon to be interrupted.

"It's so beautiful," sighed Madeline, whose hunger had been momentarily abated by the warbling symphony. She leaned forward in the direction of the medley in the trees, her tense posture reflecting her resolve to locate the source of the sounds.

"So is this," mumbled Kristin, trying to speak clearly while chewing a mouthful of pizza. She laid a brochure on the table.

"What's that?" Madeline asked, taking her first bite of pizza.

"It's a brochure from Viking Cruise Lines. I'm taking their Rhine River Cruise in six months. It includes seven cities and four countries, The Netherlands, Germany, France, and Switzerland. Maddy, I've dreamed of a European vacation for years and now I'm taking one," beamed her exuberant friend.

Wanting to share in her friend's happiness, Madeline started to rise.

"Where are you going?" asked Kristin.

"Well, I'd like to see these places you're going. I need my magnifying glass, which is on the stand next to my bed."

"I'll get it. You stay," responded her friend.

Madeline rested her head against the back of her chair, holding the brochure in one hand, and listened to the sounds of the orchestral gathering of birds in the trees. When she entered Madeline's bedroom, Kristin immediately spotted the silver-handled magnifying glass on the bed stand. She also noticed several letters scattered about the bedspread. From the faded color of the envelopes and outdated cursive handwriting, Kristin supposed these letters had been written long ago. *Why keep them?* she thought. *Obviously, they must be special to Madeline, but why?* Like finding someone's diary left out in the open, she was overcome by a morbid sense of curiosity. She reached down and picked up one of the letters. It was addressed to a Lieutenant Edward T. Orsini, Seal Team Six, Naval Air Station, Oceana, Virginia. If the addressee wasn't confusing enough, the return address brought a tsunami of confusion and doubt. It read Madeline O'Connor, 27 Ivy Lane, Brockton, Mass. The Madeline Orsini Kristin had known for over twenty-five years was really Madeline O'Connor? The Madeline Orsini who had never been married had the last name of a Naval Lieutenant? *What the hell was going on?*

Kristin put the letter back on the bedspread. She picked up the magnifying glass and returned to the patio. Thoughts were racing through her head so fast her emotions could barely keep up. *Was this her husband? Why hadn't Maddy ever told me about him? Wasn't I her best friend? I deserved to know about him.*

Handing Madeline the brochure, she said, "Take a look."

Madeline took the brochure in one hand and held the magnifying glass over it with her other hand. She moved the glass slowly as she absorbed every bit of detail and beauty. The regal century-old castles, cities with churches, and buildings dating back to the sixteenth and seventeenth centuries took her breath away.

"My God, Kristin. These pictures are unbelievable. I'm so envious."

Madeline's enthusiastic response was lost on Kristin who was trying to determine how to approach her friend about the letters, a subtle or frontal approach. Her faced grimaced with concern. She sat on her hands in an attempt to further hide her anxiety. The noise her chair made on the patio tile from constantly shifting her position began to annoy Madeline, who felt compelled to confront her friend.

"What are you so antsy about?"

Sure that her face would betray the guilt she felt for examining the letters on the bed, Kristin stood up and walked to the wrought iron fence at the edge of the patio. Her grip on the top rail was like a vice as she sought to control her emotions. Without turning around, she said, "We've been friends forever haven't we, Maddy?"

Still enamored at the pictures in the brochure, Madeline answered, "Sure," not yet sensing the foreboding tone in her friend's voice.

"You know I love you like you're my own sister," Kristin continued.

Still oblivious to her line of questioning, Maddy casually replied, "Me too, Kris."

When Kristin turned around to her friend, tears were freely flowing down her face. Her voice choked from the combination of guilt and anger she was feeling.

"I'm sorry, Maddy, but I saw the letters on your bed."

There, it was out. No more evasiveness, no more misleading answers. Kristin thought she knew Madeline better than anyone. Their twenty-plus year friendship was filled with shared secrets and dreams. What Kristin was about to hear was a nightmare and not a dream. The brochure dropped from Madeline's hand. Her pulse rate went out of control. Her lungs struggled as if they couldn't get enough air to breathe. Madeline slammed her hands on the tabletop, causing pieces of pizza to bounce in the air. There was no need to see the rage burning in Madeline's eyes. The crumbled brochure fell to the ground. Madeline's jaw clinched like a vise. Her cheeks tightened. Her lips quivered in anger. Madeline jerked her hands back and lurched to her feet. She threw off her glasses and stared at her betrayer, her best friend.

"You read my letters!" she screamed. "What gave you the right to pry into my past?" Madeline's rage frightened Kristin when Madeline threw her chair to the ground and stormed back into her apartment.

Kristin remained calm, at least on the outside. On the inside, her heart was breaking. She had no intention of betraying their friendship, but she realized now that's exactly how Maddy saw things. Madeline was sitting at one end of the couch. Kristin took a seat at the other end. With a tranquil tone, she answered the accusation. "I did not pry, Maddy. They were lying out in the open. I have always respected your privacy."

It has been said that time heals all wounds. In Madeline's case, the adage did not apply. Time did not heal her wounds. Time allowed for scars to cover them, scars that were an ever-present sign of what she had endured. And now her best friend had literally torn off those scars, exposing Madeline to having to live the past all over again. It was too much for Madeline. Never one to use alcohol as a crutch, Madeline walked to the kitchen. She took a bottle of Chardonnay from the refrigerator and lifted two glasses from the glass rack hanging over the kitchen counter. For several minutes, they sat in silence. Kristin fidgeted in her seat. Her fingers nervously twisting the edges of her blouse. Madeline sat erect, staring straight ahead.

There was no warmth in Madeline's voice, more like royalty directing a servant. Kristin had never heard such a distant and aloof tone from Madeline. After Madeline's reaction on the patio, Kristin sat paralyzed at what might come next, another screaming rebuke, what? She felt chilled at the icy tone of Maddy's command.

"Pour, please."

No celebratory clinking of the glasses, no "Here's to us" toast, just a piercing foreboding quietness. Kristin lifted her glass and took a small sip. Madeline leaned forward, her elbows resting on her knees. She reached out as if to pick up her glass of wine, but instead picked up the handful of letters, clutching them in her hand. She never once looked at Kristin. Instead, she stared straight ahead.

Seizing the moment, Kristin asked what only a sister of the heart could,

"Who is he?"

Her face was expressionless. Her eyes were fixed in a death-like stare. She spoke in a monotone voice as if she were in an out-of-body state removed from all emotions.

"His name was Edward T. Orsini. He was a Navy Seal assigned to Seal Team Six. We lived in a small apartment in Little Creek, Virginia, home base for his team. We were to be married when he was suddenly deployed on a mission. No warning, no nothing. One day I came home from work, and he was gone. It wasn't like it hadn't happened before. They used to refer to us as Seal Widows. You came to accept it. It was no use asking questions. Rumor was, some of their missions were so secret only the President knew about them. Anyway, one night after work, a couple of girlfriends and I went out for drinks."

Madeline paused. It had been decades since she had talked about what had happened that night. Her words were as apologetic now as they were when she had been questioned by the police.

"With his team deployed for God knows how long, I joined some Seal widows as we called ourselves, for drinks. Eddie and his friends liked to unwind at a local spot called the Landing Zone. Us wives and girlfriends gathered there as well when the team was gone. It was kind of like having them home when they weren't," she said.

"Anyway, some Romeo decided to try his luck. First, he asked if he could buy us a round of drinks. My friend, Sheila, told him no thanks. He made some reference to Seal Widows needing company, and he was the person to provide it. That infuriated Shelia, who proceeded to tell him where to put his company. When he walked away, we thought it was over. After our second round of drinks, he came back to our table and asked if anyone wanted to dance. Before anyone could say anything, he grabbed my hand, demanding I dance with him. Eddie had taught me a few self-defense moves. I drove the heel of my shoe onto the arch of his foot. He let out a yell, then cursed me as he hobbled back to his bar stool. That got the caught the attention of the bartender, Red. He was a retired Chief Boatswain's Mate who looked after women in his place like they were his own daughters, and he didn't take kindly to anyone disrespecting them in his place. He was around the bar in a flash. He grabbed Romeo's arm with his hand and bent it back until it practically reached the base of his neck. The yelp of pain brought a smile to Red's face. Anyway, Red literally threw him out the door."

Kristin was mesmerized by Madeline's story. It was like reading a mystery novel, afraid to turn the page fearful of the terror that was about to befall the heroine. She reached for another sip of wine. Madeline's monotone voice continued.

"Around ten that night, we left the bar and headed to our own cars. I waved good-bye to Sheila and Colleen. I had parked around the corner from the bar. The street wasn't very well lit. As I got to my car door, a hand suddenly covered my mouth. I was dragged into an alley. The first slap stung, but it was the fists that hurt the most, that is until I passed out. When I woke up, I was in the hospital. I had been in a coma for several days."

She stopped, like a driver coming upon a fork in the road, uncertain as to which one to take. Madeline began wringing her hands as if to summon up some last bit of courage before continuing. Taking off her dark glasses, she turned to Kristin, her eyes pleading for understanding and not condemnation for the nightmare that had changed her life forever.

"I had no idea of the extent of the rape or the beating I had received."

It was as if Kristin had been kicked in the stomach. Air rushed from her lungs. Her mind rejected the words she had heard. *Not to my friend, nothing that horrible could have happened to her.* She seized Madeline's hands literally shouting, "My God! Maddy. That son-of-a-bitch!"

The sudden profanity seemed to give Madeline the strength to continue. The monotone voice disappeared, replaced by anger and rage. Her face became furrowed with rage. Oddly, there were no tears as her recollection of the past continued.

"I had a broken jaw, broken orbital bones in my face, and I had been raped. The rape was so savage the doctor told me I could never bear children. That bastard took my dreams away! I knew I'd have to tell Eddie, but not in a letter. It had to be face to face, which is what I wrote to him for months. Eventually, my letters came back stamped Return to Sender. I didn't know what Eddie thought, maybe I had found someone else, and the letters were a Dear John warning when he got home. I don't know. Months passed. The Navy won't tell me anything. I wrote letters to anyone and everyone who might know something. Eventually, the Secretary of the Navy wrote me. He went around and round. The Seals are this, the Seals are that. Missions are highly secret. The honor with which the Seals serve their country. But nothing about Eddie, was he dead, was he alive, had he been captured, what?"

The eruption of such volatile memories left Madeline emotionally exhausted. She slumped back against the couch and closed her eyes. Kristin nervously waited for her to speak. After several excruciating minutes, Madeline opened her eyes and sat upright.

"I had lost everything, the man I loved, the children I thought we would have, all gone. But there was one thing of his I could keep, that no one would ever be able to take away. It would bind us like marriage vows. After I got out of the hospital, I legally changed my last name to Orsini. In my mind, it kept us together."

Her emotions spent, Madeline laid her head against the back of the couch. Not a drop of adrenaline remained in her body. She might have been dead if not for the shallowest of breathing. In a strange way, Madeline felt relieved. The weight of her secret and the toll of repressed pain and anger that had tortured her for years had at the moment been lifted from her. However, such was not the case for her friend, Kristin. She felt as if she had been at Ground Zero of an atomic bomb explosion. The weight of her friend's years of secrecy squeezed the breath out of her. Her vision was blurred by the fountain of tears pouring down her face. She couldn't hear her own thoughts. Kristin could not imagine the agony her friend had endured over the years, coming to every one of Kristin's kid's birthdays, graduations, and weddings. No words could possibly ease her pain. Consumed by guilt for opening this door to Madeline's past, Kristin reached out with an apologizing request.

"Please forgive me. I should have never asked."

Her previous anger had not completely dissipated, though their years of friendship was beginning to tip the scales.

"Maybe so," Madeline replied, searching for the words to soothe her friends' angst. "But then good friends do ask."

"I'm not sure I follow," responded Kristin, hoping there was some sort of pardon in the midst.

"Good friends ask when they care."

Relieved that she had not be exiled to some island, never to see her friend again, Kristin reached out to hug Maddy.

"I'll always care."

Sensing there was more to her answer, Madeline asked, "You're going to look into this, aren't you?"

Her stomach knotted with anxiety as she awaited Kristin's answer. *Would she be successful; much more, did Madeline want her to be successful?*

"Yes, that's what friends do when they care."

In the security of her friend's arms, part of Madeline Orsini had been reborn. She was no longer a secret keeper. Emotional strength long spent stifling the past could now be spent embracing the future. Even if Madeline seemed at peace accepting the unknown about Edward, Kristin was not. There remained just this one last piece of the puzzle to be found.

12

CONFLICTIONS OF THE HEART

Their conversation in the garden about children had plagued both Daniel and Jane. His nights were interrupted with dreams of raising his son. It was always the same, in that magical moment of hearing the boy's laughter, or the smile on his face after having accomplished some boyhood task, suddenly the boy disappeared. Daniel would scream, but there was no sound. Jane's dreams were equally painful. Every scene had the same ending. She could be bathing her child or trying to coax a spoonful of baby food into a closed mouth, or urging the child to take its first steps with the words, "Come to Mommy" when suddenly she heard Daniel's voice yelling, "No."

Every conversation was affected by the growing tension between the two. Their normal chatty conversations in the morning before Jane jetted off to work had become business-like, void of the usual humorous repartee the two had enjoyed. Evenings were worse. They had taken to eating in front of the television, lest they have to make eye contact if sitting at the dining room table. If either one asked, "How was your day?" the other answered, "Fine" or "Just another day, no big deal." The intimacy they had enjoyed listening to the events that had occupied each other's day, the encouragement given to each other, had devolved into an awkwardness akin to two strangers riding in an elevator.

For Jane, there could be no greater fulfillment in life, no greater statement to the purpose of life than parenthood. Daniel had experienced that fulfillment and a parent's worst nightmare as well—the death of a child. Jane was asking Daniel to gamble that fate would be different this time. It would not take this child. He or she would grow to be a happy, successful person, and that Daniel would live to witness it. It was a huge gamble for a man just passed sixty. Daniel Kilgore did not see himself as a gambler or a risk-taker, particularly at this stage of life.

～

JANE HAD CALLED TO SAY SHE WOULD BE A LITTLE LATE GETTING HOME, something about a staff meeting. She was uncomfortable with deception at all times and in particular with her loving husband. The obvious truth neither of them was willing to address only added to her angst.

"I'm sorry, but there's been a medical emergency with one of the residents, and the ambulance crew has just arrived. I'll be home when I can."

Of course, the emergency meeting was a complete fabrication. After hanging up the phone, she leaned back in her chair, her eyes fixated on the golden chandelier hanging from the ceiling. Freed from the thought of another silent meal, Jane allowed herself to be hypnotized by the dancing reflections of light radiating through the crystal prisms of the chandelier onto the ceiling. Her relief was fleeting. Dinner could only be postponed, then what? What about breakfast the next morning or dinner the following night? She roiled on the inside. Her anger reflected by her clinched jaw and pursed lips. She repeatedly poked her pencil onto her desk pad until it snapped in her hand. *Damn him,* she thought, as she threw the pieces of broken pencil into the trash can near her desk. Her anger toward her husband was genuine. When you love someone, you'll do anything to make them happy. Was that such a difficult concept for him to understand?

Daniel held the receiver to his ear muttering, "Uh-huh" at the news of Jane's unexpected emergency. In the past, such news would have been greeted with disappointment as he and Jane both enjoyed a pre-meal glass of wine and a hug to said, "I missed you." The discussion on having a child had changed all that. Plagued by the thoughts of parenthood, Daniel had become more distant, finding any excuse to be outside and away from Jane when she was home. He cared less about his personal appearance, now sporting a perpetual five o'clock shadow much to the chagrin of Jane, who preferred his clean jawline to the stubble that now covered his face. His face was haggard from the growing tension between him and Jane that had given him far too many sleepless nights. After hanging up, he slumped into a kitchen chair, engulfed by an overwhelming sense of defeatism that swept over him. *Where had he gone wrong? How had he so misread Jane?* The palms of his hands massaged each temple, failing to ease the constant mental fatigue that was his daily companion. Grimacing at the gurgling in his stomach, he stood up and went to a counter drawer that held a hodgepodge of health aids such as aspirin, Aleve, and antacid tablets. After taking two Roll-Aide tablets, he let the water run for a moment, splashing a couple of handfuls of water to his face. He placed his hands on the kitchen sink and straightened up, not bothering to wipe his face or the back of his neck, preferring to let gravity control where the water went. Staring out the kitchen window at the garden, he saw several blackbirds attempting to get through the netting he had placed over the peach tree to protect the nearly ripe corp. Shifting his focus to the tomato plants, he saw another group of birds feasting on ripened cherry tomatoes. Transferring his anger to the scavenging feathered thieves, he raised the window and screamed, "Get out of there!" Without so much as a glance in the direction of the alarming sound, the birds continued their orgy.

He was on his way to the porch swing with a photo album where

Jane had called. He picked up the album and headed to the porch swing. He found the view over the expansive pastures to be meditative. Though normally not a person given to solitude, Daniel found a peculiar sense of peace in those periods of time without Jane at his side. Once taken with her hazel eyes, Daniel now found them to be reflections of condemnation for his hesitancy to fulfill Jane's desire to have children. Even the sound of her sweet southern voice had begun to sound like an interrogator probing the basis for every decision he made. There seemed to be no middle ground for his dilemma.

How ironic that Daniel now found himself drawn to the very thing he did not want to relive, the past. He rested the photo album in his lap and slowly opened the cover. *God, was he ever really that small?* Daniel thought, gazing down on a photo of his son's Baptism. Vivian had filled the album with photographs of every event she deemed important in her son's life. With a broad brush, she applied that definition to such mundane moments as changing his diapers, his first spoon of Gerber's baby food, and bathing in the kitchen sink. Later, there would be more embarrassing moments like his first venture standing on a footstool in front of the toilet, his bare bottom exposed for future viewers to see. It was the array of photos of family vacations that brought back a smile to Daniel's face; teaching Greg to fish on a vacation at Herring Creek, campouts on the shore roasting marshmallows and hot dogs, and the smile on Greg's face the first time he stood up while learning to water ski. The high back Adirondack swing provided a resting place for Daniel's head as he closed his eyes, gently pushing the swing with his feet. Could time have made those memories sweeter than the actual event? Had time dimmed the frustrations of chores left undone, homework put off to the last minute, and the volcanic eruptions stemming from a teenager hyperloaded with testosterone. More times than he would want to admit, Daniel's patience meter was calibrated from six to ten during those years. Yet somehow everyone survived.

Suddenly, his mental alarm clock went off. He had promised Jane he would have dinner ready when she got home. What with the tension between the two, Daniel did not want there to be any reason for more discord. Leaving the album on the swing, Daniel hurried to the kitchen, letting the screen door slam behind him. The bowl of mixed vegetables from the garden on the dining room table could provide a quick salad. *That will be last,* he thought, as he opened the refrigerator scanning the contents for something quick and easy to prepare. Two boneless chicken breasts wrapped in cellophane gave him his inspiration. *Find something she won't complain about,* he thought, scanning the contents in the refrigerator. He grabbed the chicken breasts and a half-empty box of mushrooms then slammed the door shut so hard he could hear the rattling of bottoms in the rack of the refrigerator door. Putting them on a cutting broad, Daniel retrieved a shallot and several cloves of garlic from their resting place on a shelf above the stove. Using the flat side of a carving knife, he smashed the garlic cloves and quickly discarded the peels. More careful with the shallot, Daniel carefully peeled off the skin and then finely diced both the garlic cloves and the shallot. Sliding them off to one corner of the cutting board, Daniel unwrapped the chicken breasts. Gently holding the top of each breast, he carefully sliced it longways, giving him several long thin strips. He glanced up at the clock on the wall. *Damn, 6:15pm, if only she had given him an estimate of when she'd be getting home,* he thought. He only needed a small bowl of seasoned flour to be ready the minute she walked in. The adage haste makes waste proved costly for Daniel. First, the top of the flour canister popped off as he took it off the shelf in the pantry, spilling some on the pantry floor. Standing at the prep island, he tried shaking out some flour into the bowl. More than a bit came out, causing a fine cloud of white powder to rise and then slowly settle on the kitchen's dark wood floor, leaving a distinct outline around the edge of the island. Scooping up the excess with his hands only exacerbated the mess. As he was slicing a large Meyer Lemon in half, he heard Jane's car coming up the driveway. *Almost there,* he thought, hastily reaching for a cast iron skillet from the rack above the stove. He had enough time to set two wine glasses on the table next to a chilled bottle of

Chardonnay from the wine cooler when he heard the door from the back door close.

It had been a frustrating ending to the day for Jane. She had hoped to use the time of the fictitious medical emergency to examine the conflict between her and Daniel. Instead, Marie Gordon appeared at her door, insisting on talking with her about Jane's project of creating family trees for some residents. Her temples began to throb. She still had to face Daniel and somehow tip-toe through meaningless conversation without amping up the tension between the two.

"I'm home," she called out from the hallway. She dropped her bag at the foot the coat tree in her office and listlessly hung her coat on the tree, not bothering to pull out of the sleeves now inside out from its hasty removal. An unusual oversight for one considered conspicuously ordered by friends.

"In the kitchen," answered a monotone Daniel, as he wiped up the last of the spilled flour.

Once in the doorway to the kitchen, she asked, "What's for dinner?" Completely ignoring Daniel, Jane walked to the kitchen sink to wash her hands and dab her face with a damp towel.

Without looking at her, almost automatically, he uttered, "Chicken Piccata. Would you care for a glass of wine?"

He hoped Jane would not notice the residue of flour swirls on the floor, and another argument would be avoided.

"Sure," responded an agreeable Jane, hoping the wine would ease what had become their normal stale, antiseptic conversations. Inspired by thoughts of their former intimacy, she gently cooed, "Darling, do you think you could massage my neck? I'm really tense."

This type of physicality seemed a small price to pay to avoid the paramount issue in their lives. He said, "Stand still."

There was a time when Daniel would have viewed such an invitation as a precursor to greater intimacy. Now he approached it like a factory worker on an assembly line. Unemotional and dispassionately, he walked behind her and using the palms of his hands, he worked the trapezius muscles at the base of her neck and along the top of her back to the shoulder joints, all the while staring mindlessly at the second hand of the wall clock slowly making its circular orbit. The effects were instantaneous as Jane let out a barely audible sigh of relief. Unphased by this audible cue, Daniel continued using his thumbs to work her shoulder blade muscles. When he felt a knotted muscle, he would pause, moving his thumbs back and forth until the knot disappeared.

After several minutes, with the tenseness gone and the symptoms of her headache waning, Jane sighed, "Thanks."

Daniel's response to Jane's appreciative remark was an empty, "Sure."

Daniel missed the times when, after such a massage, there was a playful kiss. Maybe even more. He was tempted to caress her neck but withheld the urge. Daniel got a bottle of Chardonnay from the refrigerator and two glasses from the cupboard. He followed Jane out to the deck. Jane settled down on the thick green cushion tied to the swing. She wanted to initiate a conversation with him, but the complete lack of eye contact made that impossible. Daniel set the wine and glasses on a small table he had made out of a bough of a Southern Magnolia tree. He used an irregularly shaped slab of Magnolia wood for the top which he had been sanded and then applied numerous coats of clear Varathane stain. Jane noticed the picture album lying on the table. She recognized it immediately, Daniel's family photo album. *Was he still so tortured by the past?* she wondered. She decided to let Daniel answer that question if he so chose, not wanting to appear too inquisitive.

After pouring the wine, Daniel and Jane sat in silence, the photo album between them. Jane rubbed the chilled wine glass across her forehead. The iciness providing an element of relief to the tension between them. From the corner of his eye, Daniel caught Jane's movement. Not being completely insensitive to her condition, he asked, "What was the medical emergency about?"

Jane took a rather healthy sip of wine. Time to tell the truth or continue the deception. She chose the latter as it was the least threatening to the controlled calmness between the two.

"Enda Thompson had some sort of allergic reaction to her new heart medicine. It put her husband, William, in a panic attack. The paramedics attended to Enda while I worked to keep William clam."

Jane began to slowly rotate her neck to prevent the returning of tightening muscle brought on by her continued deception.

"How are they now?" Daniel asked, finding himself genuinely interested in their welfare.

"The paramedics got Edna's breathing under control and were able to lower her soaring blood pressure. When William saw she was going to be okay, his anxiety eased immediately. Once that situation was taken care of, Marie Gordon had to talk with me. She's having second thoughts about the need to research our client's family trees, something about letting the past be. It's not like I was asking her to dig up anyone's family skeletons."

"There are times when the past should not be revisited," responded Daniel as he moved the album to make room for their glasses.

Jane thought of herself as an insightful person, but this time, she completely missed the cryptic message in Daniel's words. This was more of a conversation than they had had in weeks, and it felt good. A bit of awkwardness lingered in the air. He wished he had put the album away before she had gotten home. Daniel saw Jane's eyes darting back and forth at the album. He knew he had to address why it was out. He reached out, his hands tracing the hardbound cover. His throat tightened. His words became raspy as he spoke.

"I wanted to see him again, to remember the sound of his laughter. Vivian was a bit of a photo maniac. She took pictures of him everywhere. The last one she ever took was Greg and me the day Greg graduated from Marine Corps boot camp at Camp Lejeune."

Unashamed by his tears, his voice barely above a whisper, he said, "Raising him gave us the happiest moments of our lives. His death was agony beyond belief. I don't think I could survive it again." His words trailed off into silence.

There was no need to say anything. Jane let the motion of the swing help anesthetize Daniel's pain. She reached out, placing her hand on his leg, hoping to comfort him. Involuntarily, his body tightened at her touch. Was his reaction a rejection or merely a physiological response.? Jane hoped the latter. Had Jane understood the implication in his words? Had she grasped the abject fear gripping his heart?

Jane kicked off her shoes, got off the swing, and walked to the deck railing. The setting sun, shown through puffy white clouds, created a strange formation of shadows over the fenced pasture lands. A gentle southerly breeze drove off the normally pesty infestation of gnats, bugs, and other mysterious flying creatures that gathered at that time of day. She slowly turned her glass as it rested on the rail. Her mind struggled with the realization forming in her mind. Without turning back to face him, she spoke.

"Daniel, there's something I have to say to you."

As if to prepare himself for some apocalyptic pronouncement, Daniel emptied his half-full glass of wine. Jane turned around. Fraught with anxiety, she cleared her throat before speaking.

"The loss of a child at any age is agony beyond description. Time is supposed to heal all wounds, but it doesn't always work out that way for some. I'm so sorry to have put you through this. I think maybe my mom was wrong. Maybe it's better to live with old memories than pay Russian Roulette making new ones."

Her attempt to appease Daniel's fears had little effect on him. He lowered his head. His knuckles turned white from gripping the edge of the seat. Suddenly, his hands formed into fists and he beat the swing seat and screamed, "Why God? Why my son?" He never wanted to feel such agony again. His chest heaved as his lungs sucked in needed air. He brought the album up to his chest, squeezing it tightly as if to draw from mysterious strength from its pages. His eyes were shut, but that did not prevent the flow of tears rolling down his face.

"A parent isn't supposed to bury his own child," he wept. "When it happens, it makes you question why even ..."

He caught himself before uttering the unthinkable. But he had thought it back then. Ten years ago, in that horrible, tragic moment, he had questioned why had God allowed such joy and happiness into his and Vivian's life only to tear it from them later? Life and death are not like the ends of a scale where the joy of life balances out the agony of death.

Daniel's unfinished sentence was a jolt to Jane's sensibilities. Had she really been that insensitive to Daniel's past? Her eyes welled up with tears. Her professional comments had not accounted for the limits of the human heart. When the subject had first been broached, he had spoken of the never-ending pain at the loss of his son, and she had selfishly decided to pursue the subject. She had naively thought time would be the answer to resolving Daniel's problem. It agonized her soul to realize the pain she had so thoughtlessly been willing to have him endure so she could have her dream. She thought back to that awkward moment the morning after their first night together, when the conflicted emotions of Vivian's memories and the joy he had experienced in Jane's arms collided. It was Jane's wisdom to assure him, in time, he could have both. Where was that wisdom now? She went to the swing and sat by his side. With the last of the setting sun, shadows covered the porch. Jane reached out with her hand for Daniel's head, which hung over the edge of the photo album he still clutched in his arms. She guided his head until it rested on her shoulder.

Discreetly wiping the dampness from the side of her face, she said, "Darling, I want your love. I want to share in your happiness. I do not want to be the cause of your pain anymore."

Jane had hoped by releasing him from the implied deadline of *time* it would bring some measure of relief for Daniel. In fact, her reprieve had just the opposite effect. In that seminal moment, though relieved of one burden, Daniel now felt a more paralyzing realization. He felt a need to do something in return, to reciprocate with a sacrifice of equal emotional impact. Perhaps he was being too analytical also. A marriage can not survive a quid pro quo relationship. Daniel now wondered if their union was meant to continue. That in and of itself was a profound shock.

13

THE FAMILY TREE OF SALLY GUNDERSON

The results of delving into Willard Castleberry's history had Marie Gordon questioning the purpose of her efforts in constructing family trees. Accidental or not, what is to be gained from discovering the family skeleton lurking in someone's past? How does it benefit a person to learn some distant relative was involved in a horrible scandal or some morally repugnant behavior? When historic curiosity results in painful revelations, what responsibility does the discoverer have? Reveal it, regardless of the pain it will cause; or make the decision all that's needed in a family tree are names and not the sins or human foibles of one's ancestors?

With her conscience clear as to how she would handle Willard Castleberry, Marie Gordon approached Sally Gunderson's case with a renewed enthusiasm, bolstered by her Auntie Flo's offer to help. Offering her home as a place to work would serve a dual purpose. One, it forced Marie to do some much-needed house cleaning; and two, it would allow Marie to use her multiple computers at her Aunt Flo's direction. US Gen had given Marie access to numerous agencies connected to public information. It would prove invaluable for cross-referencing any information her aunt might uncover.

Of all the genetic traits that could have been passed down to her from her parents, domestic neatness was not one of them. Her twist on the old adage, "A place for everything and everything in its place," was "Everything has a place and where I drop it is it's place." After hastily picking up a number of pieces of clothing strewn throughout the living room, Marie made a quick pass over her wooden floors with an economy-sized Oreck vacuum cleaner. The empty boxes of takeout from Fong's Authentic Chinese Food Restaurant and an old pizza box from Papa John's, both signs of Marie's lack of culinary skills, left a strangely odd combination of odors lingering in the front room. After taking the food containers to the trash can on her back porch, she lit several scented Yankee candles strategically placed throughout the living room hoping to mask the offensive aromas. After straightening up the files cluttering her worktable, Marie made a pitcher of lemonade and placed it in the refrigerator to chill. Her time in the noon heat with her mother and aunt at the Dawg Doctor, coupled with her hurried efforts to clean her home, left Marie with an uncomfortable sensation of drops of perspiration running down her back. After a quick shower and a change of clothes into her favorite tank top and shorts, she poured herself a glass of cold lemonade and headed to the front porch for a meditative moment on the swing.

There was a refreshing breeze that tempered the heat of the later afternoon. Holding the glass of lemonade to her forehead, Marie felt the coolness slow the sense of anticipation she had over her aunt's efforts to help. She was glad she had placed several sprigs of mint in the lemonade pitcher. It was a southern tradition which added an additional layer of taste and fragrance to the drink. Marie had not bothered to plan for a meal as her Aunt Flo was known to never arrive anywhere without bringing something to eat. Marie would not be disappointed. Two quick honks of a car horn told Marie her aunt had arrived. As her maroon Fiat Spider rolled slowly down the drive, Florence hollered, "I'm here." With the car stopped, she quickly primped her Afro which had been disheveled a bit from the drive over. Exiting her treasured vehicle, Florence held up two bags, gleefully announcing, "Ribs from Ribs and Things!" For genuine soul food, Ribs and Things was the best in all of Charleston.

"Come on in," Marie said, holding open the screen door.

With both hands full, her aunt carefully traversed the gravel walkway. Her low heel shoes were no match for the gravel base causing her aunt to wobble with the agility of a two-year-old taking its first steps. Upon reaching the front door, she kissed Marie on the cheek and asked, "Where do these go?"

"The kitchen counter."

Walking from the living room to the kitchen, Florence noticed the burning candles, and the telltale dust line left along the floor molding that the vacuum cleaner missed. Tongue in cheek, she commented, "I see you've got your mother's gift for housecleaning."

Appreciating the left-handed compliment, Marie laughed, "Yeah, right! Mom's gift, as you call it, is really a curse and one I am proud to say I did not inherit. Care for something cold to drink?"

Marie's question seemed rhetorical. Flo's cotton blouse stuck to her body, a consequence of southern humidity. Reflecting off her ebony complexion was a glistening of minute beads of perspiration.

"Need I say yes?" Flo responded, as she dabbed her face with a damp paper towel from a roll on the kitchen.

Marie poured her aunt a glass of lemonade. Leaning against the kitchen counter, the two women allowed the chilled lemonade to quench their thirst and relieve an uncomfortable level of body heat. There was no sense in counting calories as Marie opened the two to-go boxes from Ribs and Things. Food from Ribs and Things was intended to warm your stomach, not balanced one's caloric intake. With plastic silverware in hand, the two settled on the couch with plates of food in their laps.

"So, what's your plan, Auntie," Marie asked, as she bit into her first rib. Her curiosity had been piqued by her aunt's need to avoid using her workplace computers to access records. Flo ignored her question, preferring to savor the rich barbecue sauce layered across the baby-back rib in her hand. Patience was not one of Marie's strong points, as she continued, "Well?"

Demonstrating the best of southern table manners, Flo held up one finger indicating she would answer only after the last remnants of pork had been swallowed.

"Child, lets at least enjoy this food before we start work, okay?"

Marie dropped her head slightly, furrowed her eyebrows, and gave her auntie a childlike, pouty stare. Chuckling at the adolescent reaction so inappropriate for a twenty-five-year-old, Flo responded, "Now where did that look come from?"

Recognizing her act would not produce the desired effect, Marie grinned and responded, "It works with dad, sometimes."

"Well, I ain't your daddy," chided Flo, choosing an expression associated with her ethnic background for emphasis.

Little else was said, as the two finished the ribs followed by the greens and slaw. Neither cared for the mac and cheese which had become gooey form the rib sauce seeping into it. Thank God, Ribs and Things provided ample napkins. Between the condensation on their glasses from the ice-cold lemonade and the rib sauce coating their fingers, holding onto their glasses was like trying to control a freshly caught fish. After licking each finger that was covered with sauce, the two used every napkin they had to remove any evidence of their ravenous eating. Flo turned to face Marie —her arm draped over the back of the couch.

"Here's my idea, Marie. You've got no records that Sally Gunderson ever had any children, but you've got that mysterious photo of her sitting with several children, and written on the back of the photo a note about the family's latest addition, right?"

Marie nodded, as she nervously twirled the pen she was holding, anxiously waiting for more of her aunt's thoughts.

"In my world, baby, either your Mrs. Gunderson ran a daycare program, or she took in..."

The light bulb in her head didn't just go off, it virtually exploded.

"How could I have missed it! What with you and mom working

for Social Services," screeched Marie," I should have known. Sally took in foster children."

Pleased at her niece's belated use of her deductive powers, Florence set herself upright, eager to get started.

"Yes, indeed," beamed her aunt. "Now let's see if your auntie still got game. You say Sally Gunderson lived in Trenton, New Jersey, right?"

"According to the family I contacted," responded Marie.

"So, I'll contact Social Services in Trenton, and see what shakes from the tree?"

Marie hurried to her worktable. Flo sat next to her, laying her iPhone 10 on the table next to her.

"What do you need?" asked Marie, clearly excited that they had, at last, started on their journey.

"Google Social Services, Trenton, New Jersey, and get a contact number."

Marie's large, twenty-two-inch screen was illuminated with images that Marie rapidly clicked on until she got what she wanted.

"609-457-3340," announced Marie.

Florence had her iPhone in hand. As fast as Marie called out the number, Florence's thumbs tapped the appropriate square. She touched "speaker," then put the phone on the table. After several rings, a voice answered.

"Social Services, how may I direct your call?"

Flo lost any trace of an ethnic accent. Speaking in the King's English, she asked, "May I speak with someone in the Foster Care Program."

"Are you currently a foster care parent, or are you interested in becoming a foster parent?" replied the rather business-like voice on the other end.

"Actually, neither," answered Florence. "I'm trying to track down a former foster parent..."

With typical bureaucratic indifference, the voice interrupted Florence. "I'm afraid that information is confidential."

Flo' s face grimaced. Marie could tell from her aunt's furrowed brow and pursed lips that she was not going to play nice anymore. Marie nervously clicked the top of her pen trying to anticipate her auntie's response.

"I'm an attorney with the South Carolina State's Attorney General's office. I want to speak with someone who can make it not confidential."

Florence looked at her niece, and anticipated her disapproval mouthed the words, "A white lie."

"One moment, please," answered the voice, now sufficiently alerted this was not an ordinary inquiry.

The obnoxious organ music in the background played for several minutes, indicating to Florence that her inquiry was being passed up several layers of command. Marie stared at the cell phone, as if, magically, a face would appear.

"This is Dr. Guillory. I'm sorry, but the receptionist did not get your name. Whom am I speaking with?"

Florence quickly turned her phone over.

"Did we ever hit a gold mine or what!" announced the excited aunt.

Turning the phone back over, Flo asked, "Joann, Joann Guillory, past president of Delta Sigma Theta at Rutgers, that Joann Guillory?"

"My God! Is this who I think it is? My forever friend Florence Abby who only calls once a year? Ahola, Kaikaina!"

Marie's heartbeat elevated as the friendship between her auntie and Joann Guillory became more apparent though she was confused at the terms of endearment the women used for each other. Marie mouthed the word, "What" to her aunt. Flo scribbled sister in Hawaiian on her notepad in order to keep continuity with her friend.

Flo was elated at Guillory's reaction. Reconnecting with an old friend, or *ohana* (family in Hawaiian) as Joann called her, had a way of bridging the time of disconnection.

"*Aloha* to you, *Haikuahine*, and yes, I'm delinquent in keeping in touch. How is John, still working?"

At the mention of her husband's name, Joann glanced at a photo-graph of her husband, John, she kept on her desk in his number twenty-five football jersey when he played defensive halfback at Stan-ford University. *He's as handsome as he ever was,* she thought.

"Flo, you know John, the quest for that one final development project was too much to pass up, especially when it's on Maui. It's a big one, over 800 acres, but when it's complete, we're both retiring back to the island."

Flo was genuinely sorry for not having maintained closer contact with her friend. Different life choices and the resulting circuitous paths they took made contacting each other something akin to a New Year's Resolution that faded after a few weeks into the New Year. At the sound of each other's voices, the old friends were as close as ever. The gleeful mirth in the women's voices erased any feeling of anxiety in Marie, but she was anxious to move forward. She tapped her auntie on the shoulder, pointing to herself and then her auntie. Flo nodded.

"Joann, I've got a bit of a problem here, and I was wondering if you could help me out?"

"If I can, you know I will," answered Joann, whose momentary annoyance with her friend for not keeping in regular contact had faded.

"I'll let my niece explain," said Flor. "Her name is Marie Gordon, and she's working with a resident at a local assisted living facility on a project that could use your help. Would you mind if I put the phone on record, Marie is hyper-detailed and being able to refer to the tape will really help her?"

"I appreciate her desire for accuracy. Absolutely, use the recorder."

Marie leaned in the direction of her aunt's phone, elated at the chance to talk with her auntie's friend.

"Hello, Dr. Guillory. I'm Marie Gordon."

"Please call me Joann, Marie. I use the title "Doctor" to open doors, not when speaking with friends. Tell me about your project."

"I'm afraid there's no Reader's Digest version to this. It may take some time to explain."

Marie and her aunt heard Joann call out to her secretary, "Edith, hold my calls."

With that, Marie began her story. She started with the invitation from Jane Kilgore to do family trees for some residents, to her encounter with Willard Castleberry, and lastly Sally Gunderson.

"Goodness, you did say Sally Gunderson?" asked the excited friend of her aunt's.

Joann's reaction only served to heighten the expectation of good news.

"Yes. Why?"

"Marie, Sally Gunderson is a legend in the foster care program. She has had articles about her written in all the major east coast papers. She even appeared on Sixty Minutes with Mike Wallace. Let me tell you about Sally Gunderson."

Marie quickly took pen to hand. She wanted to write down every detail Joann Guillory would tell her. After only a few minutes, Marie put her pen down. The awe and wonderment of what she heard left her spellbound. Sally Gunderson and her husband took in their first foster child when Sally was twenty-five. She and her husband, George, had learned Sally could never bear children of her own. George knew how much his wife yearned to have children, and he was willing to take in foster children if it made her happy. Over the years, Sally and George had taken in over forty foster children, some as infants, others from toddler to teenagers, some with physical and mental disabilities. When Sally broke her leg at age 66, caring for their last foster child became impossible. Florence listened intently to her friend's account of the Gunderson's, wishing she had had such parents on her caseload.

"Marie, Sally Gunderson was the Mother Teresa of foster parents," said Joann. "Whenever the program had to remove a child from her care, she always told them, 'Someone else is going to take care of you from now on, but remember, I will always be your mother, no matter what.' "

Joann's eyes began to tear as she heard the sound of the two women on the other end of the phone using tissues.

"Joann, is there any way I can get the names of any of the Gunderson's foster kids?" pleaded Marie.

"The state of New Jersey only keeps foster parent records active for seven years after they leave the program. After that, the records are sent to archives and then scheduled for incineration. Let me check something quickly," Joann said.

She placed her phone on the desk and spun her chair to the large computer screen. After entering the requisite information, she clicked search. In a nanosecond, the names Sally and George Gunderson appeared. Joann's hope for good news was soon dashed when she saw the year of termination, July 7, 2005. Their records had been in archives for nearly eight years. Not anxious to give Marie the bad news, Joann hesitated before picking up her phone.

"Marie, I'm afraid I've got bad news. The records of Sally and George Gunderson were sent to archives nearly eight years ago. In all likelihood, they've already been destroyed."

It was crushing news for Marie to hear, who slumped back in her chair. So much hope, so much expectation, now lost. Her complexion mirrored the abject dejection that overwhelmed her. She looked pale. Her eyes stared aimlessly toward the ceiling. Her imagination ran wild. Deep in the basement of some archaic building were countless shelves, filled with cardboard boxes, stamped with a "Destroy by date." Faceless figures pushed carts loaded with boxes down dimly lit aisles to industrial shredders. The chances were a million to one that Sally Gunderson's records hadn't already been destroyed. What if they were gone? How could she ever trace Sally's children? Would all her efforts be for naught? Suddenly she sprung forward in her chair. Her face was alive with the anticipation of what might be if she had heard Joann correctly. Her sudden movement startled Flo.

"What is it?" she asked.

Ignoring her aunt's question, Marie picked up her aunt's phone. Her excitement caused her to practically shout her question.

"Joann, you did say in all likelihood, right?"

"That's right, why?"

Bolstered by a sudden surge of optimism, Marie responded, "In all likelihood is not a certainty, so it's possible, just maybe, that Sally's records might not have been destroyed?"

Joann had seen more than her share of disappointments in her career with the Foster Care Program: uncaring bureaucrats deciding by the letter of the law instead of the spirit of the law, abusive and greedy foster parents, and children scared by a system with not enough people who care to serve those who need care. She was not going to disappoint another with false hope.

"Marie, searching for those records would be like looking for the world's smallest needle in the world's largest haystack. I'm certain it would be a waste of your time and efforts."

Determined to the point of being pigheaded, Marie asserted herself in a most challenging manner.

"Joann, I assure you my time and efforts will not be wasted. Let me try, at least before I'm predestined to failure," she pleaded.

Realizing she was not going to dissuade the young woman, Joann capitulated.

"Okay, I hope this doesn't turn out to be an I-told-you-so situation. There are several shredding centers the State of New Jersey uses. We send our archives to the Board of Children's Guardians Shredding Center in the Piper Building, 338 North Broad St. If you must, the contact person is Daniel Hahn. His number is 609-289-4455. I will notify him you will be calling, but do not expect a warm welcome. Mr. Hahn views human contact as an unwanted and unnecessary interruption with his love affair with the hi-tech industrial shredders he maintains."

Having written the name and number down, Marie left Joann and Flo to reminisce about the old days. She had packing to do and precious little time to accomplish her goal. Family Day was but a few weeks away.

14

NEVER FORGOTTEN

With information Madeline had revealed during their conversation, Kristin Andrews prepared for her journey. She was determined to succeed where Madeline had failed - finding Edward Orsini. She was convinced someone, the Navy, Eddy's family, had to know what had happened to him. The need for secrecy can't mean that his past was obliterated forever. Kristin was offered help from someone she least expected, her daughter, Kayla Andrews.

"Are you sure you want to tackle this, Mom? After all, it's been nearly twenty-five years, and Maddy seems to have made her peace with it," Kayla said, as she settled into the large overstuffed sofa in her mother's living room. She adjusted her bathrobe after curling her feet underneath her, a large coffee mug balanced precariously on the arm of the sofa. With a flip of her hand, she moved her long brownish blonde hair to the side, wanting to keep it from dipping into her coffee mug. She closed her enormously blue eyes, savoring the aroma of her favorite fresh brew she had brought with her from Massachusetts. She had earned a well-deserved vacation from her job as a financial manager for East Coast Asset Management, LLC in Essex, Mass-achusetts. The long hours required by her work left little time for any kind of a relationship. Kayla was not necessarily disappointed by this absence in her life. Her observations of the follies of romance, in particular her parent's divorce during her impressionable teenage years, left her jaded on the subject. Kayla found little value in giving her heart to another.

"You really think she's made peace, honey?" asked her mother, as she nestled into the other end of the sofa. She cupped her mug with both hands, as she raised it to her face and inhaled deeply.

"This is the best," she sighed, taking her first sip as if to skirt the issue.

"Well, hasn't she?" mused Kayla, "after all, she's never mentioned his name or anything about him in all the years we've known her."

Kristin grappled with the thought, then quickly realized introspection would give Kayla her answer. There were parallels in both of their lives.

"Honey, it' been seventeen years since your father and I got divorced. Have you made peace with the turmoil that created in your life?"

This was a subject Kristin had never broached with Kayla or any of her children. The children were given the stereotypical and blameless explanation that Kristin and the kid's father had grown apart. Each assured the children they loved them dearly and would never do anything to hurt them. Kayla fidgeted in her seat, clearly bothered by her mother's question. The emotionally charged issue put Kayla at a loss for words. She turned to her mother. She wrapped her arms around her legs, resting her chin on her knees. Her mind struggled with the reality that she had so efficiently compartmentalized over the years.

"None of us kids ever understood why," she said. "It was just the way things were." This inconvenient truth caused her to clear her throat. Kayla and her siblings were young at the time of her parent's divorce and may not have been mature enough to understand the emotional complexities of a divorce, but they were certainly old enough to understand what was not told to them. People don't just drift apart for no reason. There had been many late-night conversations with her siblings as to what those reasons might be.

"I guess the answer to your question is no. We accepted it without ever really knowing why."

Kristin enjoyed another sip of the exquisite brew before continuing. "I think it's the same with Maddy. After a while, she accepted that fact that she would never know what had happened to him, but no, she was never at peace with it. One way or the other, I want Maddy to have her peace."

Shifting her focus from her own unanswered past, Kayla replied, "Where do we start?"

Equally anxious to move past a subject that even she had not made peace with, Kristin responded, "The US Navy."

THE DECISION WAS MADE TO DO AS MUCH GROUNDWORK AS POSSIBLE OUT of Kristin's spacious two-bedroom townhouse before considering the need to travel. Located in a development called Charleston Shores, her townhouse offered her privacy and a view. Kristin's unit was at the far end of Charleston Shores, away from the community pool, tennis courts and other gathering places for residents and guests. She had a pristine view of the white sandy beach from her back patio, unencumbered by trees or shrubbery.

The noise of running water told Kristin her daughter was already up. Kristin took this opportunity to make a batch of almond-flavored scones. They had been one of Kayla's favorite breakfast snacks when she was young. Kristin no longer made them from scratch, as there were no longer young ones at home who needed to participate in cracking eggs, stirring, and tasting the sweet batter with their fingers. A box of Sara Lee's scone mix would be much less mess. The results were not nearly as satisfying to the palette, but less mess justified the change.

As if on cue in some Hollywood movie, the oven timer went off just as Kayla emerged from the downstairs bathroom. Her finders swished through her shoulder-length hair as she moved her head side to side. The warm temperature afforded her the opportunity to wear a tank-top stenciled with the image of a porpoise leaping out of the water. Her chic jeans were studded with bling along with stylish tears at the knees, something that flabbergasted Kristin. She had wondered why her daughter didn't buy her pants at a thrift store instead of paying eighty dollars at Chico's for the same pants. The slightest application of facial powder and lip gloss accentuated her natural beauty.

"They smell scrumptious, Mom," responded Kayla, now captivated by the aroma of the scones cooling on the kitchen counter. As if not believing the law of nature about the temperature of something just taken out of a hot oven, Kayla touched one of the scones with her finger.

"And still hot!" as she put blew on her sensitive fingertip.

Not surprised by her daughter's foolish mistake, Kristin stated, "There's fresh coffee, and I've left a list of places to contact on the patio table. Look them over while I shower."

Walking out the sliding glass door, Kayla entered the patio. Not only had Kristin left the contact list on the small glass patio table, but she also left a small jar of orange marmalade, a crystal butter tray and a small silver butter knife. Kayla poured herself a cup of fresh brew then placed a couple of scones on a small plate her mother had set next to the tray. Skillfully using her elbow to open the sliding door to the patio without spilling a drop of coffee, Kayla set her morning snack on the tabletop. She gently dusted off the seafoam green cushion on the white wicker chair before sitting down.

"First things first," she said, as she took the butter knife and cut a scone in half. She then applied a liberal covering of butter and a layer of orange marmalade to each half. As the heat of the scone reduced the butter and marmalade into a wonderful yellow and orange goo, Kayla glanced at the list of contacts. There were five in all: The Department of the Navy website, The Navy Seal Foundation,

The National Military Personnel Records, the National Archives, and lastly a site to file a Freedom of Information Act request. Odd she thought, *why a website for the Freedom of Information Act?* With that thought, she picked up half of her scone. The combination of almond flavor with the butter and marmalade sent her palette into culinary heaven. She closed her eyes at the first swallow and took great delight in its passage to her awaiting stomach. Kayla wasted no time in devouring the rest of the scones. Much to the delight of several Carolina wrens roaming the lawn near the patio, Kayla wiped the crumbs on her lap onto the tiled stone patio. They feasted on the wipings off Kayla's lap. Casting aside any fear of the nearby human, the bravest of the feathered creatures perched itself on the edge of the patio table, obviously too dignified to eat on the ground. However defiant to their hunger they might have been, the wrens quickly took flight when Kristin opened the slider and entered the patio.

"What do you think of the list?" asked Kristin, as she took her seat at the patio table. Wearing a colorful blue sarong imprinted with the image of the bird of paradise sitting amongst blossoms of Plumeria, she carefully poured a bit of French Vanilla flavoring into her hot coffee cup. "I had Samantha's husband, Mike, help me with it. He's a sergeant on the Charleston Police Department and a veteran."

Kayla stared at the list momentarily before exclaiming, "I get most of them, but why the site about the Freedom of Information Act?"

"Mike suggested it, a kind of last resort in case the Navy won't give us any information."

"Image that," replied a comically sarcastic Kayla, "a cover-up by the military."

Kristin chuckled at her daughter's remark. Growing up, Kayla was never one to get interested in political or governmental scandals. Her remark told Kristin an evolution had taken place in her daughter's assessment of such things. She was not displeased by this change.

"No scones, Mom?" asked Kayla, noting the bowl of sliced cantaloupe and berries topped with yogurt in front of her mother.

"All I have to do is look at scones, and I feel my butt getting bigger! No, fruit and yogurt is just fine for me."

Kayla smiled at her mother's on-going battle with what in reality was an imperceptible weight gain as far as Kayla was concerned. She adjusted her chair to get a wider view of the inlet from the ocean that flowed by her mother's condo. White egrets floated among the clumps of cattails near the shoreline. A mother duck waddled near the water's edge, her brood of young ones following dutifully in line. An occasional sea erne would swoop down eager to snag any number of small fish swimming near the surface. Interrupting the serene scene was Kayla's rising curiosity about a possible military cover-up."

"Mom, I think we ought to get started on finding Aunt Maddy's boyfriend."

Finishing the last of her fruit bowl, Kristin wiped her mouth with a napkin and responded. Well aware of her daughter's propensity to dive headfirst into a challenge, she reluctantly stated, "Okay, let's do it. I'll just finish the dishes."

Preferring the couch to a desk or tabletop as a workplace, Kayla assumed a cross-legged position, her computer rested on her lap, a notepad at her side.

She called out to her mother, "I'm going to try a couple of the websites you have."

Kayla smiled to herself. Once again, she had found a way to get out of the most minimal of household chores. Kristin wondered about the domestic organization or lack thereof in her single daughter's one-bedroom apartment.

"Mom, I've hit a bit of a snag," Kayla called out. Her face grimaced, her lips pursed with frustration

Having finished cleaning up, Kristin wiped her hands with a kitchen towel slung over her shoulder, and went to sit down next to her daughter. Kayla was rubbing her aching temples, the result of maneuvering through endless boxes lined with red reading *this information is required.*

"I tried these two sites," Kayla said, pointing to the top two websites on her list. "At first, I thought it would be a snap. Both sites lead you to believe by entering in certain information, you can view records online. So, I started with the National Military Personnel Center. Entered all the information they asked for. You know, like first name, middle initial, last name, branch of service, date of enlistment, social security number. All the stuff Aunt Maddy gave you. The screen indicated no records for an Edward T. Orsini being a member of the US Navy. Then I tried the National Archives Center. Same thing, I entered all the information they asked for and again, no record of any Edward T. Orsini. It was really starting to piss me off, so I tried the service telephone numbers they provided and that only made me madder," groaned Kayla.

Puzzled that her genius daughter had hit a snag so soon, Kristin inquired, "First things first. Have you entered incorrect data, a misspelling, a middle initial, DOB? Did any boxes require case sensitive replies?"

"No, I doubled checked everything, Mom."

There is something inherently frustrating about dealing with online technology. There's no human voice to vent to, to hear your pleas for help.

"How about a customer service number?" Kristin asked.

"The android-like human voices all sounded alike," Kayla groaned.

Her nostrils flared as she could no longer control her anger at the not so user-friendly websites.

Venting to her mother, "This is the help I got!" Folding three fingers, she put her thumb and little finger to her ear as if she was speaking into a telephone. "I would like to speak to someone about accessing the records of a Lieutenant Edward T. Orsini, US Navy." Then switch hands, Kayla mocked the person on the other end. "Yes, Maam, let me connect you with the appropriate division."

Grimacing, she slapped her hands on the couch. "After ten minutes of elevator music, a recorded voice said, "Thank you for calling the National Military Personnel Center, and the line went dead."

Kayla clinched her fists and shook her head in frustration. Sympathetic to her daughter's thwarted efforts, Kristin said, "Perhaps a more personal approach would help. Let me try the next one."

Kristin called the contact number for the Navy Seal Foundation. It rang several times. A recorded voice took Kristin through several menu options before she settled on number six for records. A voice answered, "Navy Seals Foundation, Seaman Styles speaking, how may I help you?"

From the tone of his voice, Kristin surmised she was speaking to a very young sailor. Kristin cleared her throat and put forth her best mother pleading voice.

"Seaman Styles, thank you for taking the time to speak with me. My name is Kristin Andrews, and I'm coordinating the thirtieth reunion for Brockton High School, Class of 1973. I'm trying to locate an address for one of our classmates, an Edward T. Orsini. He joined the Navy out of high school and became a Navy Seal. I was wondering if you could help me?"

Creating a fabrication requires a fast mind, and Kristin's mind now raced to find convincing terms to employ. To her advantage, the young man was particularly susceptible to Kristin's motherly voice.

"I will certainly try, Maam," came the response. "Can you give me your friend's full name, date of enlistment, and social security number if available."

After giving him the requested information, Kristin heard, "Give me a minute, Ms. Andrews."

The young man's sincerity was evident by the tone of his voice. The tell-tale sound of fingers working a keyboard resonated through Kristin's cell phone. After several minutes in which Kristin's apprehension about getting information rose, Seaman Styles said, "I'm sorry, Ms. Lewis, but at my level, I'm not able to find any record of an Edward T. Orsini."

The seaman sounded just as disappointed with the results as she had been. His phrasing reflected a certain lack of sophistication. At my level, both Kayla and Kristin turned toward each other. Kayla mouth the words, *what level do we need to go to?*

Wanting at all cost to avoid sounding condescending, Kristin asked, "Perhaps, you can direct me to someone who might be able to assist me?"

The pause was telling, as if someone was standing next to the seaman, ready to give him directions as to what to say.

"One moment, Ms. Andrews."

Immediately, a voice came on the line.

"Lieutenant Corrigan. I'm the supervisor of this division. I'm prepared to answer your questions."

Both Kristin and Kayla were sure this Lieutenant had overheard the prior conversation, which lowered their expectations for a positive outcome. The Lieutenant's reply was quite evasive.

"Ms. Lewis, the records of any Seal operation, past and present are considered confidential. I'm sure you understand, national security and all that goes with it."

Kristin's frustration now matched her daughter's.

Making no attempt to hide her sarcasm, Kristin stated firmly, "Lieutenant, I am not asking about Seal operations, past or present. I'm asking about one particular Navy Seal, Edward T. Orsini."

The pause was an indication the Lieutenant was carefully choosing his words.

"Ms. Lewis, I must reiterate the confidentiality of Seal operations is of the highest nature."

"And the confidentiality of Seal Team Six would certainly meet that highest of standards, wouldn't it, Lieutenant?"

Another pause.

"Yes, it would and I'm afraid I have no further information to give you," came the reply.

Kayla nearly jumped off the couch in surprise. She placed her hand over her mother's phone and said excitedly, "Well, didn't he just let the cat out of the bag?"

"I know," responded an equally aroused Kristin. Kristin had dealt with more than her share of sanctimonious, self-indulged doctors in her career. It was not uncommon for an underappreciated nurse to refer to the letter M.D. before a name tag as Mentally Deficient. No longer willing to play nice, Kristin firmed her voice and offered a command, not a request.

"And I'm sure you understand the power of a Freedom of Information Request, Lieutenant. But in case you don't, may I speak with your superior officer?"

There was a moment's hesitation before the Lieutenant uttered, "One moment, Ms. Andrews." It was a statement made reluctantly.

One moment led to several moments, which led to several minutes before another voice came over the phone.

"Ms. Lewis, I am Commander Jenkins. Lieutenant Corrigan has explained your request to me. I'm sorry the Seals Foundation will not be able to help you. Certain operations have not been declassified and therefore do not fall within the preview of the Freedom of Information Act. Again, I'm sorry we are unable to help you."

"So, Lieutenant Orsini, a member of Seal Team Six, was involved in a still-classified Seal Operation and you're unable to give me any information about him? Do I understand you correctly, Commander?"

The line went dead. Both Kristin and Kayla stared at the phone in disbelief.

"I don't believe it," shouted Kayla, who now was pacing back and forth in front of the couch. "That was nothing but coverup BS!"

Kristin placed her hands behind her head and looked up to the ceiling.

"You're right, Honey, so how do we uncover the coverup?"

Kayla continued her pacing, her mind racing through each and every possibility, discarding them one by one after thoughtful consideration. Suddenly she stopped, pivoting back to her mother.

"Orsini is Italian, right?"

"Yes, but why?" asked Kristin.

"Ever know an Italian family without relatives somewhere. I need to do a search of his last name. Let's see if there are Navy records of anyone named Orsini."

At last, some luck for Kayla, on one Navy website the first name was not a required field to be filled out. The screen showed several Orsini's, but only one with the same enlistment date as Edward Orsini.

"Gotcha!" yelled Kayla, as she set her computer on the couch. Like a boxer who had just won a championship, she stood up and pranced around the living room, her arms raised triumphantly over her head.

"You found him?" asked Kristin, anxious to partake in her daughter's discovery.

Kayla bounced onto the couch next to her mother with the enthusiasm of a child about to share a special secret with her mother.

"If by him, you mean Edward Orsini, no. But I did find an Andrew Orsini who enlisted on the same day as Edward Orsini, that can't be a coincidence."

"Maybe not, but how do we find this Andrew Orsini?"

"Where do you find anybody these days, Mom, social media."

Quickly opening her laptop, she logged into her Instagram account and typed in the search box, Andrew Orsini. Several names appeared. Focusing only on those who were listed as living on the East Coast, she asked each if they were related to Edward Orsini.

"This will take no time at all if this guy lives in the world of social media like Facebook, Instagram or Twitter the way some of my friends do," Kayla said, as she stretched her legs now cramping from sitting too long in a yoga position.

Those addicted to social media through Facebook, Instagram, Twitter, or any of the others need to be connected with everything in an instant and cannot resist the possibility of a new contact. Andrew Orsini was one of those.

"Yes!" announced an excited Kayla, as her screen lit up.

Kristin leaned over Kayla's shoulder as her fingers moved with lighting speed asking questions and responding to the answers. She could feel the energy exuding from her daughter's body in the process. The last question she asked was, "Can we talk?" Immediately a number appeared on the screen followed by a Yes.

"He's Edward Orsini's second cousin," shouted an exuberant Kayla.

Kristin grabbed for her cell phone and dialed the number. After several rings, a voice answered, "Hello."

"Andrew Orsini?" Kristin asked, hoping the voice would be as responsive on the phone as he was on Instagram. She would not be disappointed.

"Yes. You must be Kayla?"

"Actually, I'm her mother. She's the one with the computer skills. She's sitting here with me now. May I put you on speaker?"

"Certainly," replied a confident-sounding voice.

Kristin spent the next several minutes explaining her relationship with Madeline Orsini, the letters Madeline had sent Edward Orsini, and their failed effort to get any cooperation from the Navy in locating Edward Orsini.

"My God! Kristin. I haven't heard her name in years. Eddy never talked about her once he got out of the hospital."

"Andrew, it's really important we meet. There are things about Maddy and the Navy we have to clear up."

His voice rose in intensity, making no attempt to disguise his anger. "The Navy screwed Eddy, yes I'll talk with you. But what about Maddy?"

"Let's share together, shall we?" responded Kristin. "How can we meet?"

Anger turned to excitement as Andrew Orsini was finally going to get a chance to tell his cousin' story.

"I live in Beaufort, about ninety miles from Charleston. 20034 Walnut Lane."

"Not to be too pushy, but would you be available to see us today?"

The voice shared the same sense of urgency.

"Absolutely."

Looking at her wristwatch, Kristin responded, "See you about eleven."

"Eleven it is," Orsini replied. The call ended.

Kristin struggled to contain her enthusiasm. Twenty-five years of lies and deception were about to be uncovered. There was a fierce determination in her voice as she announced, "We are taking a road trip."

15

THE QUEST FOR RECORDS

The generosity of Joann Guillory to pick her up at the airport in Trenton was much appreciated by Marie Gordon. It not only saved Marie the expense of a rental car, but Joann also agreed to take Marie to the Document Shredding Center and thus avoid a dconfrontation on her own with Daniel Hahn, the supervisor of the shredding center, who Joann had described as reclusive and anti-social in his dealings with others. Marie stood atop the escalator holding her two pieces of carry-on luggage. The scene reminded her of an ant farm she had as a young child. People rising on the one escalator, others descending on another. On the main floor there was a steady flow of people going and coming. Some appeared lost as they stopped occasionally to look at an endless array of arrival and departure boards. Others towed multiple pieces of luggage while holding a cell phone, oblivious to the flow of humanity around them. Halfway down the escalator, Marie noticed a sign waving back and forth in the air above the crowded concourse. It read, "Marie Gordon." Marie raised her hand and waved back and forth to signal Joann Guillory she had seen the sign.

Stepping off the escalator, Marie was greeted with a lei and a smiling "Aloha" from Joann Guillory.

"Some traditions are hard to break," said Joann, after placing a lei of scented Palmeria over Marie's head.

"Thank you. Aunt Flo said you were Hawaiian and to expect to be treated like family.

"Ohana, or family in Hawaiian, is woven into every fabric of Hawaiian culture. Your Aunt Flo was like a sister to me in school, helping to adjust to living on the east coast after living on Maui all my life. I'm only returning the favor."

"I don't have the words to express my appreciation for all you're doing," smiled Marie.

"Ohana, remember," smiled Joann. "Now follow me."

Guillory walked quickly down the sidewalk outside the terminal, skillfully avoiding the clusters of arrivals bunching up at various shuttle pickup point. She was equally adept at skirting the countless travelers who constantly seemed to stop and focus on the overhead signs indicating specific airlines. With a wave from a traffic guard, they crossed the street to the parking building where Guillory's husband's company maintained several reserved parking slots.

This is us, "said Joann as she pressed the button on her fob which lit up the interior lights of a late model Mercedes Bentz AMG C63. With another press of a button on the fob, the trunk lid was unlocked.

Marie stopped in her tracks. "Oh My God, a Mercedes Benz AMG! My dad would croak if he knew I was riding in one. He's wanted one of these all his life, but mom kept his choices of cars to a more frugal standard."

"I'm of a similar mindset," replied Joann. "It was my husband's decision. Let's say he had a rather frugal upbringing and occasionally likes to indulge himself in something expensive."

Marie's two pieces of luggage could have easily fit in the backseat of the Mercedes, but Joann placed them in the spacious truck. Once inside the car, Marie understood why. The interior was upholstered with an expensive black Italian leather. Even the floor mats were a custom-made black carpet weave by Lloyd's.

"Shall we get a bite to eat?"" asked Joann. "I can't imagine you got any food on that commuter flight."

"Only a cup of weak coffee and a stale Bear Claw by Sara Lee."

"We're stopping!" laughed Joann, who now hastily drove toward the exit sign.

Twenty minutes down Interstate 35 now void of the early morning commuters so famous for bringing traffic to a crawl, Joann took exit B to an upscale downtown development of office buildings, shops, bodegas, and a number of taverns selling local craft beers. Joann cut in front of a taxi loading its fare at the curb and shot into a parking spot in front of "Ohana's Grill." Marie let out a subtle sigh of relief that did not go unnoticed by Joann.

"Not used to east coast driving?"

"Things are a little slower in Charleston," replied Marie, hoping she had not offended Joann.

"I know," answered an apologetic Joann. "Whenever we go back to Maui, I really have to scale back my need for speed!"

The Ohana Grill had half a dozen tables down the middle of the eating area. Another dozen wooden booths lined both walls. The back of the restaurant had a large open view kitchen with its signature open fire pit with a rotating grill. Hot coals were neatly arranged in several piles separated by open space so the cook could rotate food from hot to cool places. Marie had half expected to see walls covered with bamboo with strategically places starfish and seashells, maybe even table lamps in the shape of palm trees. She was quite surprised at the décor. The center tables had white table cloths with silverware carefully rolled in cloth napkins with the name "Ohana" showing face up. In the center of each table was a crystal bowl filled with water. A tea candle rested in the middle. White ginger leaves were carefully placed around the candle, infusing the air with a mild ginger scent. The booths were similarly decorated along with matching ruby red seat cushions. The only thing stereotypical about the Ohana Grill was the beautifully colored Hawaiian shirts worn by the male staff. The waitresses wore sarongs printed with Hawaiian beaches and landmarks.

A stunningly beautiful young woman approached Joann and Marie.

"Table for two?"

"Please," replied Joann. "And let Alani know Joann Guillory is here."

The waitress led them to a table near the back, leaving them with menus to peruse.

"How did you pick this place," asked Marie, as she focused on the menu items described in bold italic font.

"Aside from the name, it's only three blocks from the Shredding Center. Once fortified with good Hawaiian food, you'll be in better shape to deal with Mr. Hahn."

Their conversation was interrupted by a shout of "Aloha, Sista." Standing next to the table was a woman who verged on being obese. Her hair was pulled tightly back into a pigtail. She wore a flowered muumuu with a necklace of white shinny seashells around her neck. Joann got to her feet and hugged the woman.

"Auntie Alani, so good to see you."

The woman's large fleshy arms engulfed the slender Guillory who was now standing on her tiptoes.

"Little one, you betta come see me more often," replied Alani, as she released Joann from her grasp. "Who your friend, anotha sista?"

Joann took a needed breath and introduced Marie as she stood up.

"She's the niece of my friend Flo from college. The one you always referred to as 'Big Hair.'" Remembering the friend with the exaggerated Afro, Alani exploded in laughter. The term Ohana was liberally applied to family, friends of family and friends of friends of family. With the introduction made, Alani hugged Marie with the same enthusiasm as she did Joann and announced, "Well, you Ohana, now." Marie found the woman's broken English charming. Seeing several more couples enter the restaurant, Alani said, "I got more people to greet. You two enjoy. It's on me. Ohana, you know!"

Joann ordered a cob salad while Marie was overcome by the description of the Hawaiian short ribs with poi cakes. Every bite of her ribs elicited a "Yummm," from Marie which delighted Joann. With nary a crumb left on Marie's plate, Joann said, "You were hungry, weren't you?" With the last bit still in her mouth, Marie could only nod. Joann glanced at her wristwatch.

"Well, I either need to feed the meter, or we have to go."

"No, we need to go, Joann. I scheduled a return flight for 3pm, which gives us about two hours with Mr. Hahn."

"Then let's go meet Mr. Friendly," chuckled Joann.

$\sim$

IN THREE CITY BLOCKS, MARIE HAD GONE FROM TOWERING OFFICE buildings with tinted glass windows, trendy shops, and eateries to an area of urban blight. There were old warehouses, with countless broken out windows. Small manufacturing businesses provided most of the employment in the area. Every street seemed to have one neon sign flashing "Bar" or "Tavern." There were numerous small ethnic restaurants. Each restaurant had its own sign describing its cuisine as authentic this or that type of food. Joann pulled up at the corner of North Broad and Washington.

"Here we are."

Marie looked out the window at the four-story brick building with faded silver letters reading, "The Piper Building." Not surprising, the letter P was missing.

"The state spares no expense in maintaining renting buildings," mocked Joann, as she stepped out of her car.

A security guard approached them. Hired by the state to make random rounds in front of the building, he provided little more than window dressing for protection. The old black gentleman walked with a noticeable limp. A long flashlight bounced awkwardly against his leg with each step.

"Are you two ladies going into the Piper Building?" he asked.

"Yes, we are, Lester," replied Joann, after looking at the name's plastic name tag.

"I think I'll just stay here," he said, glancing at the expensive Mercedes which would undoubtedly attract attention from the unsavory element that frequent such areas.

"Hopefully we won't be long. Thank you, Lester," responded Joann.

Lester used his right-hand pointer finger to touch the bill of his black cap, embossed with Security Guard in golden thread. Marie followed Joann up a short flight of stone steps to the entrance. The double glass door with trimmed in gilded gold now chipped and faded.

"The top two floors are vacant. The state rents out the first and second floors to some several mail-out businesses, and we get the basement," moaned Joann.

The black and white diamond-shaped tile floor must have been stunning in its day. Now, it was marred with scuff marks, stains of spilt coffee or other unknown liquids. The elevator was no longer serviceable, so Joann and Marie headed down the stairs to the basement. Neither bothered to use the handrail. Even before entering the area marked "Shredding Area," the drone of machinery could be heard through the heavy metal doors. The sign on the door read, "State Shredding Center #2." As improbable of it seemed, the heavy metal door opened quite easily.

Marie had to blink her eyes several times to adjust to the glare from row upon row of fluorescent lights hanging from the false ceiling. The illumination made looking up painful on one's eyes. The air was stale thanks to a lack of adequate ventilation. The heat emitted by a dozen industrial size shredder made breathing labored. What laid before her was not what Marie had expected. In an area the size of a high school gymnasium, there were rows of metal pushcarts the type used at Home Deport for people to load heavy materials on. Each was loaded to handle height with cardboard boxes. Each box had a termination date stamped with large red numbers. Marie estimated thirty rows in all. It was the state of organization that caught her eye. The carts were in perfect alignment. The boxes were stacked on one another symmetrically, not a one seemed to extend over the edge of the box it rested on. Unlike the tiled floor in the foyer, the gray painted cement floor was spotless, not a shred of torn paper or debris anywhere. A smallish man with a clipboard in hand paused in front of each cart in the front of every row, carefully making notes on the clipboard he carried. His jet-black hair was meticulously combed off to one side. He wore a short-sleeve white shirt already stained with perspiration with a leather pouch in one pocket for his black horn-rimmed glasses. On the other pocket was a black plastic name tag with white letters reading "Daniel Hahn." He walked with quick short steps. Above the droning of the shredders, Joann had to shout to get his attention as the man was so focused on what appeared to be a rather mundane task.

"Dan," she called out.

The man continued his note taking.

Again, Joann called out, "Dan!"

Still no response. Joann went to the nearby wall and flipped the light switch back and forth several times. Startled by the blinking of the florescent lights, he immediately looked upward and then toward the two women standing at the entrance. Without saying a word, he approached them.

"Mrs. Guillory, I don't often see you down here," he said, as he carefully removed his glasses and placed them in their leather pouch.

"Dan, I'd like to introduce you to a friend of mine, Marie Gordon. She's here to search some records on a former foster family."

"I'm on a strict schedule. Even with my part-time helper, Robert, I can barely keep up with the work. Will this take much time?"

"I hope not," interjected Marie, hoping to establish some sort of rapport with the reported recluse. "I'm looking for the records of George and Sally Gunderson."

"Let me check my database. Please follow me."

Hahn led them to a small glass-walled cubical near the first shredder. Joann felt sorry for the man. There was not a single photo on his desk, a standard state gray desk with a well-worn desk pad. A small round cylinder contained several very sharp pencils and pens, along with a green plastic ruler.

"I made this database myself," Hahn said proudly, as he turned on the computer screen resting on the side of his desk. "It tells me the date a box arrived, the names on the files in it, and the shredding date. It's important that I keep to a precise schedule, you know."

"Oh, yes. I completely understand," replied Joann, barely able to maintain her composure in the face of the self-anointed importance Hahn gave his creation, a creation that any tech-savvy thirteen-year-old could do.

After typing in the name Gunderson, he ran his finger across the spreadsheet that appeared on his screen. Then Hahn picked up his clipboard.

"I'm afraid that box is on the shredding line as we speak."

Both Joann and Marie looked through the glass window to the line of shredders. There was a large feeding box on the top of each machine. Hahn's part-time helper could be seen emptying one box at a time into each loader.

"Please Mr. Hahn. This is so important. Can't you stop the shredders for just a moment until we locate the box with the Gunderson's file? Surely that won't delay you too much," Marie pleaded.

Untouched by the woman's emotional request, Hahn clicked off his computer.

"Unfortunately, I can't. Procedure precludes me from shutting the system down except in emergencies."

Marie's affected state at the disappointing news may have blinded her to the pathetic nature of Hahn's statement, but it did not escape the astute Joann Guillory.

"Well, Daniel. since procedure states no one is to operate a shredder with a long sleeve shirt, you may want to check the long sleeve shirt your helper is wearing. And you do follow all procedures, don't you, Daniel?"

Hahn jumped to his feet. His eyes darted left and right until he spotted his helper. He moved quickly to the wall of the cubical and threw a large black switch labeled "Power" to the off position. He literally ran out of the office. Marie believing the ploy used by Joann, quickly followed. The thought that the information she needed was gone, much less that someone had been hurt, caused Marie to gasp. Joann picked up the clipboard off Hahn's desk, and calmly followed, enjoying the false sense of anxiety she had caused Hahn to endure.

"Robert, are you okay?" Hahn asked, still under the illusion there had been a potential emergency.

Robert Allen, a student at Rider University, majoring in accounting, seemed startled by the question. A lacrosse player at Rider, Allen stood a six-foot-three and a solid two hundred pounds. *Please give me a problem, this brainless work is killing me,* he thought.

"There's no problem here, why?"

Before Hahn could answer, Joann spoke.

"Robert, I'm Dr. Joann Guillory, Director of Social Services for the city of Trenton." Glancing down at the clipboard she took off Hahn's desk she said, "I'm looking for a box number 8-32. Can you find it for me?"

"I can, in part," replied the accounting major with an eye for numbers. "I'd just started putting the contents into the hopper when the power went off. What's left is right over here."

The threesome followed Allen down to the fourth shredder. He lifted off the box in front of the hopper.

"8-32. Here it is," he said.

The rush of apprehension from Marie's body led her to grab the edge of the conveyor belt for balance. Allen placed the box on the short conveyor line holding the next boxes for destruction. Joann preferred to keep the ruse official, so she quickly rifled through the remaining files in box 8-32. It was as Allen as said. The files were placed in the box in alphabetical order. A through F were gone. It took Joann but a minute to locate the file of George and Sally Gunderson or what was left of it. It seems, in an effort to increase efficiency, Hahn had instructed his helper to feed the shredder with parts of files instead of whole files. It was faster and caused less clogging, or so Hahn thought.

With the file in hand, Joann thanked Robert for his help then turned to Hahn.

"Well, Daniel, I think you can restart your system now. It appears from Mr. Allen's shirt that proper procedure is being followed."

Knowing Hahn would not make eye contact, Joann smirked as he took out his glass case, and using the small cloth inside, started to clean his glasses. "Schedules and procedures are important," he said without looking up.

Working their way back up the stairs to the lobby, Guillory cautioned Marie to avoid a syringe and needle she spotted on the landing.

Shaking her head, Joann commented, "A shame to waste a life on that crap."

Lester, the protective security guard, was standing by Guillory's car.

"No one came near it," he beamed with the satisfaction of someone who been protected the King's jewels.

"Thank you, Lester," replied Guillory, as she accepted the courtesy of Lester holding open the driver's door.

Seeing Marie hug the file they had retrieved from the basement, Joann said, "Promise me you'll let me know how things work out."

"I promise."

16

THE UNRAVELING OF THE PAST

"He sounded really angry about the Navy, didn't he," asked Kayla, as they headed up I-14 to Beaufort.

Kristin had allowed herself to become absorbed with the marshy coastal waterways they had crossed. Flocks of Sandpipers would suddenly swoop into the air as if escaping from some predatory foe. Unconcerned by the flight of the Sandpipers, hundreds of light gray Willets moved slowly between large clumps of reeds looking for that ideal nesting place. The air conditioning in Kayla's well-used Volkswagen Jetta hadn't worked in months, forcing the women to rely on the coolness of the mid-morning breeze coming through opened windows to refresh them. Thanks to Kayla's heavy foot on the gas pedal, they had covered the ninety miles to Beaufort in a little over an hour. As they passed a mileage sign indicating Beaufort was ten miles away, Kayla pressed the home button on her phone.

"Directions to 20034 Walnut Lane."

"Don't want me to use a map?"

"Mom, you're so last-gen," said Kayla, laughing at her mother's antiquated method of finding directions.

"In three miles, take Exit 2B," stated the GPS.

"Sit and let Siri do the work," laughed Kayla, as an obvious sense of smugness spread over her face.

The overhead sign reading Exit 2B prompted Siri to speak.

"Take Exit 2B and turn left onto Beaumont Blvd. Proceed two miles to Walnut Lane and then turn right. Your destination will be on your left."

The morning commute traffic had disappeared, allowing easy maneuvering across the four-lane Beaumont Blvd. After turn right onto Walnut Lane, Kayla drove slowly as her mother tracked the numbers on the houses.

They drove several blocks before Kristin announced, "There," pointing to a single-story red-brick Tudor style house. The windows and eaves were trimmed in brown rough-hewn wooden beams. Wooden window coverings exposed three tall, thin windows with thin wooden grids on each. There was an absence of any shrubby in a narrow earthen path along the front of the house probably a sign a green thumb didn't reside there. The vibrancy of the verdant lawn sparkled as the approaching noon sun broke through a partially clouded sky. A line of tilted red bricks separated the lawn and the sideway and extended along the driveway. Kayla pulled into the driveway and parked behind a late model Ford pickup truck with a license frame reading "All gave some, some gave all."

Kristin and Kayla followed a cobbled stone walkway to the front door. Several raps with a large wrought iron knocker hanging on a wooden plank door announced their presence.

"Kristin and Kayla, I presume," said Andrew Orsini, a smallish man who might have stood five feet eight if stretched on a medieval torture device. A pair of reading glasses sat atop a bald head that glistened from a recent application of Palmer's Coconut Cream. "Please come in."

Brushing their feet on a coarse hair doormat, Kristin and Kayla entered a residence clearly intended to resemble an English countryside home. In the living room, white walls were roughly textured with swirl marks, the result of a rough-edged trowel. A large hall tree on the right afforded a place to hang coats and umbrellas. A leaded mirror in the hall tree gave arrivals and departures a last chance to check their appearance. The seat hinged to expose a storage area for footwear. The exposed beamed ceiling lent further charm to the home. Several area rugs were neatly displayed over a dark wooden floor. A large dark leather couch faced a fireplace with a wood stove insert. A number of period pieces of furniture provided further ambiance of medieval England. Completely out of place with the medieval motif was a large HD television on the wall next to the fireplace. A high back sitting chair matching the leather of the couch sat in front of the TV. A small end table next to the chair was the home of the remote control and a bowl of pistachio nuts. Pistachio shells littered the table-top, indicative of a one not prone to housecleaning.

"Please, have a sit," said Andrew, as he turned his TV chair to face them. "Can I get either of you something to drink, water, water, or water?"

His sense of humor was amusing, causing both women to chuckle. Equally adept at comedic repartee, Kayla responded, "No, water will be fine."

Sensing he had met his match, Orsini laughed back, "Touche."

Curious over the lack of any personal pictures, but uncomfortable with a direct approach with a near stranger, Kristin asked," Your wife must love this home?"

At the mention of a wife, Orsini looked away. His hand began to rub his forehead as if reacting to a tension headache.

"She died a few years ago, cancer."

Orsini stood up and stared toward the windows.

"The last months were difficult, and I don't need a picture to remind me or prompt questions."

Guilt swept over Kristin for her unnecessary inquiry into Orsini's family. Changing subjects, she said, "I can't tell you how much we appreciate your meeting with us. We only know the tip of the iceberg. Maddy deserves more than to live with an unknown."

Orsini returned to his chair. He split open several pistachios and tossed them into his mouth as he began to speak. This was an annoyance to Kristin who had been raised by a mother who insisted on every bit of food being swallowed before one spoke. With a wipe of the back of his hand across his mouth, Orsini began.

"Eddy and I joined the Navy together on the buddy system. We were planning on becoming Navy Seals. Eddy was something of a family legend, high school All-American, drafted by the Yankees in the first round. Anyway, at our first orientation to the Seals training program, we were told that becoming a Seal would require toughness, determination, and excellent physical conditioning. I knew then I had better pick another enlistment option."

Kristin found Orsini's self-deprecating sense of humor appealing.

"Eddy made it through the program. I went into electronics. I don't know the details of what actually happened. Eddy never told me, but this much I do know. He was the lone survivor of a mission that went bad. He was horribly burned, losing an arm and a leg. He was determined to be able to walk and have his burns heal as best they could before telling Maddy. It was almost two years of skin grafts and other operations. During that time her letters starting coming about having to tell him something face to face, Eddy suspected what had happened. With no news from him or the Navy, Maddy had moved on and found someone else. Shortly before he was discharged, he told me the Navy had insisted on a name change, new social security number, something about mission security. Anyway, he's gone by Allen Pinafore for nearly twenty-five years."

The mere mention that Maddy would have left Eddy for someone else blurred her thinking as to Edward's wounds. Kristin stood up. The sternness on her face, her clenched jaw and pursed lips should have alerted Andrew to Kristin's emotional state. Speaking in defense of her friend, her words were emphatic.

"You and your cousin were so wrong. There was no other guy. Maddy had experienced a horrible tragedy, and she wanted to tell Eddy in person, not in a letter."

Andrew found himself pushing against the back of his chair as if to avoid more of Kristin's visible rage. His face blushed with embarrassment. He started to stand up to defend himself.

"No, you sit and listen," commanded Kristin."

For the next hour, Kristin paced back and forth in front of Andrew, like a district attorney addressing the jury. She told him about every ugly and sorted detail of Maddy's sexual assault and the effects of that assault on her ability to have children. Telling him of the progressive case of macular degeneration only added more urgency to her request.

Feeling she may have been too rough on him, Kristin placed her hand on Andrew's shoulder. In a voice much softer and more tender, she said, "Your cousin needs to know about Maddy's scars and trauma, and she needs to know about his."

For a man who normally channeled his emotions under a layer of machismo, Andrew turned to Kristin. His eyes pleaded for understanding.

"Eddy was everything I ever wanted to be. He's a hero in my eyes, and I would never want him to feel I betrayed his confidence by talking with you. When you talk with him, please don't mention you've talked to me. He works at the Naval Hospital on the other side of Beaufort."

There were heartfelt hugs and assurances that they would respect his privacy.

Heading back to Beaumont Blvd, Kayla pushed a button on her phone, sitting in a cradle on her dashboard.

"Directions to the Naval Hospital in Beaufort."

Smiling at her mother, she said, "Siri will do the work."

As an afterthought, Kayla said, "If we're going to keep our talk with Albert a secret, we'd better come up a reason for our visit."

"Did Albert say the Navy gave Edward a new social security number?" asked Kristin.

"Yeah, but I don't see how that helps?" replied Kayla, whose eyes were focused on the cross-traffic as they headed up the ramp onto the cross-town freeway.

"History, think history, Honey," prompted Kristin.

Suddenly, Kayla swerved into the righthand lane. She barely made it to the exit lane. After rolling through the stop sign at the bottom, she turned into a small rest area.

White knuckled after her daughter's driving maneuvers, and red-faced from holding her breath, Kristin blurted out, "What was that all about!"

"That's it, mom, history. I can tell you one thing, even if the Navy gave Edward a new social security number, his old credit records would follow the new number. We could say we are looking into a question of identity theft. You know new social number linked to old credit records with the social security number of Edward Orsini."

"Well, aren't you the Sherlock Holmes," beamed Kristin at her daughter's ingenuity.

"Elementary, Mom, elementary."

They shared a moment of laughter before getting back onto the freeway.

Within moments, the directions started. "In approximately ten miles take Exit 13."

As they neared Exit 13, Siri spoke again.

"Take Exit 13 and turn right onto Calhoun Boulevard. Your destination will be two miles on your left."

The absence of commuter traffic made the transition off Exit 13 onto the four-lane Calhoun Boulevard smooth. Slowly moving to the extreme left-hand lane, Kayla anticipated Siri's next command. Before it came, she saw the hospital on her left.

"Your destination is on your left."

"Got it, Siri, thanks."

Kristin chuckled at her daughter's conversation with the android voice of Siri. A large sign extending over the Boulevard read "Visitor Parking" and an arrow curving to the right. It took some time to find an empty space. Between visitors for the two hundred patients at Beaufort, and those staff under the rank of Petty Officer Third Class whom the Navy determined to be unworthy of their own parking space, Kayla finally found a slot in the very back corner of Visitor Parking. The noon breeze coming off Albergottie Creek provided minimal relief to the now oppressive humidity. Feeling the need to look more professional than casual, Kayla wore a blue pants suit with matching blazer which she now regretted. Once inside, she dared not take off her blazer lest she reveal a perspiration stained light blue cotton blouse. Kristin was a bit manipulative in her choice of appeal. She wore her nurse's whites, complete with cap and her name tag hanging from a lanyard around her neck. After all, this was a hospital and looking official couldn't hurt.

Standing at the crosswalk across from the hospital, the two women marveled at the size of the medical complex. The Administration building was four stories tall. A long concourse behind it led to three wings, each four stories high. Kristin and Kayla hurried down the marble stone walkway to a series of multiple automatic front doors. As the door opened to them, a rush of air-conditioned air met them. They paused for a moment to enjoy the coolness before proceeding further. The white marble floor was spotless. A janitorial staff in green pants and shirt meandered back and forth brushing up almost imperceptible pieces of dust orbs into a handheld scoop. The older black man walked with a shuffle. His shoulders stooped from years of bending over the castaways of the careless who gave no thought to who would pick up their discards. Along the left wall were pictures of the hospital's staff in gilded gold frames, starting with the female commanding officer, which pleased Kristin. Despite the growing number of women doctors and nurses in the medical field, Kristin still found it to be, in many ways, a good ole boy system. Beneath the director were several rows of division heads, ranging from medical to administrative services types. Many in dress uniforms, some in suits. An array of personnel, some in Naval uniforms, some in Marine uniforms strolled through the lobby. The monotonous ping of the elevator indicated that one of four doors was about to open. Kayla was focusing on the staff directory on the wall to the right.

"Here he is, Mom. Allen Pinafore, Director of Veteran Placement, first floor, suite 104."

Kayla looked up to an overhead sign with arrows indicating suites 100 to 120 to the left, and suites 121 to 140 to the right. As Kayla turned to her mother, she took notice of the staff portraits on the opposite wall.

"Hmmm, I wonder why Mr. Pinafore's picture isn't up there with the other directors?"

Soon she would have her answer. They proceeded down the left hallway but a short distance before they stood before a large maple wood door with Allen Pinafore's name above it.

"Why the wide doorways?" asked Kayla.

"Have you forgotten, handicapped accessibility," responded her mother.

"Oops!" muttered Kayla at her momentary lack of sensibility.

Expecting more pictures of military personnel on the wall, Kristin was pleasantly surprised to see several paintings of seascapes, mountain streams, and lakes. They were certainly intended to create a calm and serene mood for those wounded servicemen and women seeking help. Four personnel were waiting to be seen, not a one with a complete body. Three were in wheelchairs, each missing an arm or a leg. In one case, a double amputee sat mindlessly thumbing through a travel magazine, letting the colored pictures take him to a better place than he had been. One soldier with dark sunglasses sat quietly stroking the head of his service dog. Kristin and Kayla approached the receptionist who sat behind a sliding glass window. An electric sensor alerted her to the new arrivals.

"Director's Pinafore's office, how can I help you?"

It was probably protocol, but with his brass name plate on the door, was it really necessary to tell someone this was Allen Pinafore's office, Kristin thought.

"We'd like to see Mr. Pinafore, please," Kristin said.

"May I ask what about?" asked the receptionist who had a clipboard in hand and seemed ready to hand it to them.

Kristin leaned forward. Keeping her voice low, she said, "I'm Kristin Andrews, and this is my daughter, Kayla Andrews. We're here to see Mr. Pinafore about a confidential matter."

Recognizing Kristin's medical attire, the receptionist smiled and responded, "A medical confidentiality."

Sensing Kristin and the receptionist were about to play twenty questions, Kayla leaned forward and whispered. "I'm afraid it's a matter of identity theft."

The receptionist with two diagonal stripes on her sleeve indicating she was an E-2 in the Medical Corps hastily responded, "Please take the door to your left. Mr. Pinafore's office is at the end of the hallway."

As they turned to their left, Kristin saw the receptionist pick up an inter-office phone and push a button—obviously letting her boss know they were coming. Once again, Kristin was pleased with the decorative prints on the hallway walls. More of the same soothing pictures, this time of ocean beaches, most appearing to have been taken in the Pacific. Small signs to the side of each door indicating the service provided: housing, education benefits, out-patient therapy, to name a few. After knocking gently on Pinafore's door, a deep voice from within called out with an unexpected familiarity, "No need to knock, come on it."

For someone with the title of Director of Veterans Placement, Allen Pinafore's office was uncommonly common. No rich carpeting or expensive tile, only the aesthetically pleasing tight woven seafoam carpeting intended to put Pinafore's visitors in a better place mentally. Prints on the walls were intended to produce the same effect. One showed the sun dipping below the horizon at sea with broken reddish clouds overhead. Another, a herd of sheep lazily grazing on a grassy hillside. There was a sunrise over an expansive white sand beach contrasted with a mountain pasture with a creek whose waters rolled over half-exposed stones. An inspirational quote was painted in the center of one wall. It read, "I may not be able to do what I used to so I will learn to do new things." A not so new steel desk with a patina sheen sat angled in one corner of the room. A large, five-drawer metal cabinet was directly behind Pinafore's desk pushed into the corner. Along the two walls were wooden oak cabinets about three feet tall. A medium-size rectangular, metal gray table occupied an area in front of one wall adjacent to Pinafore's desk. Three heavily cushioned metal chairs were arranged around the table.

A rather tall man with his back to them was placing a file back in the top drawer of the gray metal cabinet. The left sleeve of his long sleeve white cotton shirt was neatly folded and pinned underneath what was left of his upper arm. When he turned around, Kayla had her answer as to why his portrait was not hanging in the foyer. The right side of his face had been horribly burned. The scar extended from his collar line to above his ear or what was left of his ear. It covered nearly half his face. The scar tissue appeared to be stretched over this area. Any skin pigment in the burnt area was pale and stood out noticeably against the man's unaffected facial area. Kristin had spent some time in a burn unit during nursing school. She could only imagine the horrible pain this man must have endured only to be left with half a face. Walking to a small table, his uneven gait was probably an indication Pinafore was a double amputee.

Smiling, he held his hand out and said, "Let's sit at the table. It's less formal. My receptionist tells me there's an issue of possible identity theft. Now, who's Kristin and who's Kayla?"

"I'm Kristin Andrews, and this is my daughter, Kayla Andrews."

"And I'm Allen. Can we do first name basis?"

His charming style elicited nods from both Kristin and Kaya. Kristin, in particular, was taken with his pleasant manner.

"A nurse I see," said Pinafore, again with that magical smile.

"Yes, I ran an assisted living facility in Charleston for a number of years."

"And you, young lady," turning his attention to Kayla.

Blushing, she answered, "I'm a financial manager for a large investment firm in Massachusetts."

As he pulled out two chairs for the women, he noticed Kayla was not making eye contact. Pinafore experienced this type of reaction on a daily basis. Strangers at the store, a bank teller, a sale clerk, all avoided eye contact as if not looking at it would make the grotesque scarring go away. Pinafore had a strange sense of compassion for such people. He could not make his appearance change, but he could effect a change in those who saw him.

"It quit hurting years ago," he said, as he gently moved the fingers of his right hand on the scarring. "I think of it as my beauty mark. You know like Kirk Douglas' dimples or Ben Affleck's chin. What do you think?" he said, as he turned his head to the right giving Kristin and Kayla a semi profile pose while glancing back at them.

Now forced to look, Kayla felt her stomach gurgle. Pinafore's smile was electric. His ebony hair had but a trace of gray through the temples. Blue eyes radiating out over a sharply defined cheek line only accented his attractiveness. She smiled nervously.

"See what I mean," Pinafore said, a smile forming on his face. "Excuse my manners, but can I get either of you something to drink, a water, or soda?"

"Nothing for me," responded Kayla, still suffering from some strange sense of infatuation.

"None for me either," echoed Kristin.

"Well then, tell me about this identity theft issue."

Kayla slid her chair forward, closer to the table. It had been decided she would take the lead in their ruse. Kristin tried to put herself at ease, but the narrative of his past as revealed by his cousin, Andrew, had her conflicted. This man had suffered so much, and it was inevitable that when he would hear of Maddy's tragedy, his anguish would only increase. She watched his mannerism for any sign of an emotional breakthrough.

"In researching a client's account, I discovered that two men had been assigned the same social security number. One of those men is you, Mr. Pinafore. Your social security number had also been assigned to an Edward T. Orsini. It's a rather perplexing problem and one my contact at the IRS is intent on solving."

Pinafore's pleasant and charming manner changed suddenly. His fingers rolled nervously on the tabletop. His eyes blinked rapidly, avoiding eye contact with either woman. He had been taught during the multiple skin graph operations that the best way to deal with the pain was to mentally put himself in another place. To focus so intently on the imagery of waves gently rolling up a beach or the wind blowing on his face or the laughter of those at a party, that the physical pain could not penetrate those thoughts. The idea of explaining the past was both emotionally and physically devastating. He tried to control his fear, but his shallow breaths now on the increase belayed the anxiety that was overtaking him. He tried to steady his nerves, but the possibility of the unraveling of his past caused his dry throat to cough several times.

"Excuse me, the IRS you say. They know of this mix-up?"

"Yes, they do," responded Kayla, struggling to maintain the facade of a financial investigator working in collaboration with the IRS.

Struggling to present himself as cooperative, Pinafore asked, "Perhaps you could give me your IRS friend's contact number? I could call and clear up this situation."

He removed a pen from his shirt pocket and gave it to Kayla along with a piece of paper torn from a small notepad lying on the table. His evasiveness began to bother Kristin.

"I apologize, Mr. Pinafore. I don't mean to be forward but..."

"Please, Allen, remember, and there's no need to apologize. Go on."

That invitation would take Allen Pinafore down a road he had long ago blocked from his mind. He struggled to control his breathing. His pupils dilated due to the anxiety taking control of him. He steadied himself for more questions.

"In our research, we found that this Edward Orsini had been in the Navy at one time, a Navy Seal, actually. But every overture to the Navy for information led us to one bureaucratic stone wall after another. The issue of the social security number led us to you."

Pinafore sat silent. For the first time in years, he felt unable to avoid or evade what was coming. He would make one more attempt to misdirect the inquisitive pair.

"This theft issue sounds like something that should be referred to the NCIS, our Naval Criminal Investigative Services Unit. They're good at this type of thing, you know."

Getting Pinafore to recognize his culpability was like trying to nail Jell-O to a wall.

"You'll have to forgive me if I don't have the same degree of faith you have in the Navy," sighed a dejected Kayla.

Kristin could no longer tolerate watching the man's emotional torture. She realized every attempt by Pinafore to redirect the inquiry was his way of avoiding the past. Kristin knew his past was his salvation, not his downfall.

"If you insist, but I doubt another investigation will be beneficial to either of you or do you any good."

Had he let the issue lie, Allen Pinafore would be able to live his life secure within the web of governmental sight of hand magic. But the reference to "either of you" was too enticing.

"You said either of us, what exactly do you mean?"

The name Pinafore was about to hear would put him near the edge of an emotional collapse.

"You and my friend, Madeline, Madeline Orsini. She told me that her fiancée, Edward Orsini, went on some sort of deployment and never turned. She had written him numerous letters, but Orsini never responded. The Navy gave her no assistance. Their story was Seal operations are highly confidential, Blah, Blah, Blah. Their love for each other was so eternal, Maddy legally changed her last name to Orsini. I don't think she can survive another rejection by the military."

The sound of her name broke every fiber of resistance Pinafore had been able to maintain. He sat in silence, unable to control the floor of memories pouring from his past. His eyes welled up. His right hand began to tremble. The photographs on the wall meant to ease the nightmares that lived within his clients now failed him. His voice choked with emotion; his words, barely audible.

"Maddy?"

Kristin and Kayla both knew now was the time to tell him.

"Allen, or Edward, whatever name you want to go by, Maddy never stopped loving you," Kristin said. "Never stopped dreaming of a life together. But when her letters came back stamped Return to Sender, what was she to think?"

Allen Pinafore couldn't take any more, no more deceptions, no more lies. He pushed his chair away from the table. With the use of his right hand, he rose awkwardly from his chair and walked over to his desk. The mechanics of his prosthetic leg suddenly locked. He grabbed the edge of his desk when he started to trip. Another sign he was not the man he used to be. Pulling open the middle drawer of his desk, he took out a small envelope and returned to the table. He placed it in from the Kristin and Kayla.

"I never stopped loving her, either." Words he had only spoken in his dreams.

He had not been called that name in nearly twenty-five years, nor had he wanted to. The name Allen Pinafore had given him a way to move beyond what had left him a double amputee with horrible scars. His heart had told him Maddy had done the same, but had she? He had lived a lie for too many years, pretending he was doing the right thing. Pinafore saw understanding and compassion in the eyes of the women sitting across the table from him. He decided these would be the first people with whom he would share his secret. He reached for the small envelope he had placed before them. The fingers of one hand worked awkwardly to open it. Using one finger, he slowly pulled out a small photograph, a beautiful young woman in a stylish dinner grown and a very handsome Naval officer in his dress whites. His eyes fixated on the snapshot for a moment before passing it to Kristin.

"Maddy and I on our engagement day," he said. "Our wedding date was set for early June. She always said she wanted a June wedding."

He paused as the recollection of those failed plans brought back the pain of memories he had compartmentalized for decades.

"Do either of you remember the Iran-Contra scandal of the '80s?" he asked.

Kayla shook her head, being four years old at that time.

"Sorry," replied Kristin. "I was pretty well occupied with raising four children."

The mere mention of the scandal released the suppressed anger that had festered in him for years. Pinafore sat erect. His right hand rested on the table. His words were emphatic, almost angry as he recounted the events at the time.

"Our government was secretly selling arms to Iran, in direct violation of legislation passed by Congress. The money was then funneled to Nicaragua to fund the Contra rebels fighting the military regime. Complicating the situation was the fact that negotiations with Iran to release seven hostages were not going well. The decision was made to send a Seal team in to extract the hostages and thereby gain an edge in the negotiations."

"That would be your team?" asked Kristin, now enthralled by the mystery being unveiled before her.

Pinafore nodded.

"What we didn't know was that the person handling the money between Iran and the Contras felt if the hostages were freed, Iran's leverage to demand more money would disappear, and he was making a lot of money brokering those transactions."

With every bit of information Pinafore gave the women, his determination to make them understand what had happened grew.

"We launched our helicopter off a small destroyer near the coast of Iran around midnight. The first sign there was trouble was when we cleared a small range of coastal mountains. We were about three hundred feet when we started taking anti-aircraft fire. You could hear the ping of rounds hitting the chopper. Then a SAM rocket hit us midship. The explosion killed seven of my team immediately. I was in the back of the chopper. You couldn't see anything through the fire and smoke: fire was everywhere. I could feel the flames hit my face. I tried to help those that were alive, but my left arm was useless. It hung by my side, covered in blood. I couldn't even feel my right leg. I had to crawl to those I tried to help. The rocket also damaged the steering mechanism. The pilot tried to head to our safe zone near the Saudi border. We were about a mile away when we crashed. I was told later a Saudi army unit picked up those who survived."

Kristin and Kayla sat frozen in their chair, paralyzed by the horrific details they had just heard. Whatever anger or frustration they had felt toward Pinafore was now replaced by an overwhelming sense of sorrow for what he had endured.

"I woke up in a burn unit in the military hospital in Kaiserslautern, Germany. My left arm was gone along with my right leg, half my face covered with bandages. The doctors told me I was facing multiple skin graft operations as well as operations on my left shoulder and right leg to see if prosthetic devices were an option. I was the lone survivor. Someone up the chain of command determined that the loss of a complete Seal team might put more pressure on Iran to release the hostages. Turns out he was right. Hence the new name, and everything else that went with it."

"Edward, why didn't you tell Maddy what happened?" asked Kristin, who unashamedly wiped tears from her eyes.

"I didn't want her to see me like I was. I wanted to see how the skin grafts went, and I wanted to be able to walk before I saw her. It was over a year before the doctors told me about my future. During that time, I started getting letters from her about needing to tell me something, face to face, not in a letter. I'd see this happen before: girl waits at home without any news, days turn into weeks, weeks into months; and before long, the girl finds someone who can be there. Maddy had found someone else, but I'll give her credit. She never put it in a letter. She had the guts to want to tell me to my face."

"Oh, my God! Edward. If you only knew," sighed Kristin, as she started to weep.

"Knew what?" he asked.

Edward was about to hear of an equally tragic and devastating story. One that would challenge his sense of commitment. Kristin began with the night of the rape. With every detail she could remember his rage grew. Then the news from the doctor about never being able to bear children.

"She knew what having children meant to you. The shame she felt over the rape and never being able to bear your children wasn't something she wanted you to read in a letter. She wanted to tell you directly. I think there was a part of her that doubted you would still want her after knowing what had happened."

"No!" he screamed, slamming his right hand on the tabletop. "How could she even think that would matter. Nothing could have ever changed my love for her, Nothing!"

His eruption caused Kayla to nearly fall out of her chair. Kristin stayed focused on Edward.

"Don't you see, Edward, both of you questioned the strength of the other's commitment. You with a body she might not be able to deal with, and Maddy with the stigma of a being a rape victim and all that went with it.

He struggled with the logic of her words. He rose slowly from his chair and walked to the window overlooking the expansive lawn outside. Edward Orsini had never run away from a fight in his life. There was never a challenge he didn't embrace, never a struggle that he didn't think he would prevail against, that is until the aftermath of a failed covert operation. He had failed his own core value, worse yet, he had failed Maddy. He turned to Kristin and Kayla. It seemed he stood a little more erect, more in command of his body. His eyes conveyed a sense of determination.

"I need to see her. I need to explain everything."

Kristin took Kayla's hand in hers and squeezed. They had accomplished what they set out to do, to somehow bring Maddy and her Eddy together one more time. There was one more thing to tell him.

As Kristin wrote down the location of Magnolia Gardens and the phone number she said, "One last thing, Edward. Maddy has developed a vision problem. It's called Macular Degeneration. Her vision is severely impaired."

With a newfound sense of understanding and commitment to making things right between he and Maddy, Orsini looked at Kristin and replied, "It's what I want her to hear, not to see, that matters."

17
FOREVER LOVED

As Marie slowly made her way down the aisle of the forty-seat commuter plane, patiently waiting as people hurriedly tried to cram their carry-on luggage into the overhead storage bins, she thought maybe her luck had changed. There were two seats on either side of the aisle. Marie had seat 14B, an aisle seat. With most of the plane loaded, there was no one in 14A, the window seat. Hoping it would remain empty, Marie took a chance and sat in it, after quickly flashing her ticket to the attendant who was checking to see that everyone sat in their assigned seat.

After placing her shoulder bag under the seat in front of her, she settled back for what she had hoped would be a tranquil flight back to Charleston, affording her the opportunity to develop a plan for contacting the names of Sally Gunderson's foster children. That expectation was soon shattered by a loud voice, pleading repeatedly, "Sorry. Excuse me." Marie leaned outward to see the source of the commotion. To her horror, she was greeted by the sight of a very overweight man sweating profusely while juggling a brown paper tray with a tall cup of coffee and a large raspberry Danish in one hand and two carry-on pieces in his other hand. Walking sideways, his luggage managed to hit everyone sitting in an aisle seat. He stopped next to Marie, then glanced at the crumpled boarding pass on his paper tray.

"Sorry," he said solemnly, "but you're in my seat."

Perspiration stains dotted his white shirt along with a trail of raspberry drippings. The thought of being trapped between him and the window for an hour and a half brought a wave of nausea over Marie.

Hoping to salvage some sort of peace from this dilemma, she implored with her best puppy dog eyes, "Would you mind if we traded seats?"

The late arrival had no patience for Marie's request.

"Look," he demanded. "I took a redeye from Chicago at two in the morning. All I want to do is sleep."

Realizing the futility of any further pleading on her part, Marie stood up and stepped into the aisle.

"Hold this, would ya?" he said, handing Marie his paper tray.

Marie obliged if only to end any further conversation with him. As he stretched to cramp his luggage pieces into what little space was left in the overhead bin, the stench of his body order reached her nostrils. She turned her head to keep from gagging. With his luggage finally secured, her new seat companion awkwardly bent forward as he squeezed into his seat.

"Thanks," he said, as he extended his hand to take the tray Marie was holding.

She smirked a very insincere smile and said, "Sure."

Marie slid as far as she could to her left, hoping to avoid any contact with the man's very hairy and tattooed left arm which covered the armrest and then some. For the next hour and a half, Marie was serenaded by slurps of coffee, belches, and the sounds of an opened mouth rapidly devouring several raspberry Danishes in a manner as unbecoming to watch as it was to hear.

～

As the jet came to a stop next to the jet bridge connecting the plane with the terminal, Marie Gordon leaped to her feet, determined to exit the plane as fast as possible. The past hour and a half having to breathe in the odorous smells emanating from her travel companion had left her on the verge of vomiting. Moving quickly down the aisle, she thanked the flight attendant and proceeded to the terminal. Ignoring the escalator, Marie hurried through the concourse to the parking lot across the street. Her key fob quickly located her car, now parked between two large vans and out of her immediate sight. She tossed her luggage into the back seat of a Silver 2009 sporty looking Nissan 370Z. Marie followed the exit arrows as if she were driving at La Mans. She was anxious to get home with her treasure trove of information on some twenty-five foster children cared for by George and Sally Gunderson.

～

After multiple applications of scented bath soap, Marie stood under the pulsating showerhead, hoping the steaming flow of hot water would help rid herself of the pernicious odors which seemed to have attached themselves permanently to her body, no matter how hard she scrubbed away at them.

Her initial euphoria over the information Joann Guillory had provided her had ebbed somewhat when she thought of the abbreviated time frame she had to work with and the sensitivity of her inquiry. It was not as easy as merely saying, "Hi, I'm Marie Gordon, and I want to talk to you about your time as a foster child with George and Sally Gunderson." Maybe being a foster child was better kept a secret for some. For others, any delving into their foster care history might dredge up horrible memories of how they came into the foster care system in the first place; abusive parents, drug or alcohol problems, even abandonment. As the child of a social worker, Marie Gordon was all too familiar with the heartbreaking circumstances endured by children who had to be placed in alternative home placement, a euphemism for foster care. Other logistical considerations were name changes for girls who might have married, and what about those who had moved to God knows where, or even died. What at first glance had appeared to be a fairly simple process now seemed fraught with potential failures and disappointments. The chirp of the Keurig coffee maker signaled to Marie that her brew was ready as if the aroma of freshly ground coffee beans wafting through the house hadn't already done that. Donning a yellow bathrobe and wrapping her wet hair in turban fashion with a terry cloth towel, Marie shuffled her way to the kitchen in her oversized Bugs Bunny slippers, a childhood favorite she had never been able to discard. Pouring her mega-sized coffee cup three-quarters full, she added a healthy dose of agave. Marie preferred the natural sweetener to commercial sweeteners that were laced with chemicals. She headed to the living room seeking the comfort of her couch where she could enjoy her ritual of that first cup of coffee while listening to the morning news. Once curled into the soft cushions of the couch, she reached for the remote control. At the sound of "Here's Pete Williams from the White House lawn," Marie pressed the mute button. The thought of having to listen to the voice of the "The most Superlative President ever" as she called him, was enough to cause her stomach to turn.

Marie used the silence to plan her search strategy. She would rely on various social media sources. She savored each sip of her coffee while enjoying the sight of a charm of yellow finches fight for space around the circular feeder hanging from the porch eave. With her coffee done, Marie went to the bedroom to change into her favorite work-at-home clothes, a Clemson University t-shirt, crimson nylon pants, and an Atlanta Braves baseball cap. On her way back to the front room, Marie detoured to the kitchen for a second cup of coffee and then headed to her worktable in the living room.

With one hand holding her coffee cup, Marie used her other hand to open the file she and Joann Guillory had retrieved from the shredding center and the possessive hands of Dan Hahn. *How thoughtful,* she thought, *the names of the children cared for by George and Sally*

Gunderson were listed in chronological order by date of placement. Though the most recent date was well over seven years ago, Marie decided to start there with a boy named James Austin. This was the most laborious part, dutifully entering the same question twenty-five times into five different social networks with a different name. "My name is Marie Gordon and I'm looking for...who might know George and Sally Gunderson. If you know them, please respond by such and such a date". First, there was Google, then Facebook, Who's Talking, YoName, and Bing Social. Marie had consciously decided to omit any reference to foster care in the event anyone may have felt a stigma from such a placement. The process was much like chumming when you go fishing - throw a lot of bait into the water and hope you get a bite.

With the last name entered into the last search engine, Marie pushed her chair away from the table. Her back ached from the not so ergonomically correct chair she had spent the last two hours in while hunched over her computer. Her neck muscles were taut, and her eyes were irritated from staring at the computer screen. Seeking relief, she closed her eyes and began to slowly rotate her head, first clockwise then counterclockwise. The temporary relief was interrupted by the ring tone of a text message from her cell phone. Rubbing her eyes, Marie glanced at the text, "I'm in the driveway, Aunt Flo." Clearly, there was no time for picking up the assortment of sweaters, shawls, and hats, strewn over the back of the couch, and a stack of old newspapers by the door which never made it to the trash can. Oh well, at least her aunt could be greeted with a fresh cup of coffee. Marie hurried to the kitchen. In the dish rack on the counter, there were several plates, cups and some silverware left to dry from the day before. Anything Marie washed and left in the rack to dry rarely made it back to the leaded glass door cabinet above the sink. Marie believed in the principle of quintessential laziness: why put it away if I have to use it again. She grabbed a cup from the rack and opened the refrigerator door, hoping the can of evaporated milk had not spoiled. Her aunt was old school when it came to coffee sweeteners, preferring Eagle Evaporated Milk to any of the modern sweeteners. The opened can passed the smell test as Marie held it to her nose and inhaled deeply.

"No need to open the door, I'll just let myself in," responded her aunt, obviously irritated that her niece had not been responsive to her text by greeting her at the door. Flo held a bag in one arm from the Queen's Bakery, full of freshly baked croissants filled with cream cheese and fruit, and her computer bag in the other. The aroma alone from the oven-fresh pastries was enough to push one's blood sugar to severely diabetic levels.

"Sorry, Auntie Flo," called out Marie from the kitchen. "I'm getting your coffee ready." After a dash of evaporated milk and a quick swirl with a spoon, Marie headed to the living room.

"For you," Marie said, handing her aunt her coffee.

Flo had long ago convinced Marie to use a combination of chicory and French Roast beans, giving her coffee a pronounced woody and peppery taste. Marie found it had the same effect as a double espresso. She needed the jolt after completing the mind-numbing entry of data she had just completed.

"Any for you, my dear?" answered Flo, handing Marie the bag of pastries.

"From the Queen's?" Marie asked, as she savored the aroma from the contents in the bag.

"None other," smiled Flo, as she sipped her weird combination of coffee brew.

Marie eagerly reached in the bag of sweet delights and pulled out a croissant. Her first bite was anything but ladylike, as she practically devoured half the croissant. Crumbs fell haphazardly from her mouth onto her lap, causing her aunt to retreat into the kitchen for napkins.

"Here," she said, returning to the couch and handing Marie a napkin. "Forget how to use one?"

The twinkle in her aunt's eyes softened the terseness of her rebuke. With her cheeks pooched out with a gargantuan mouthful of croissant, Marie raised her finger into the air, signaling she was going to enjoy every morsel before answering. With the last bit of croissant gone and her palate cleansed with a generous sip of coffee, Marie sighed, "That was made in heaven!"

Using more daintiness than displayed by her niece, Flo sampled her own croissant with a genteel bite, gently dabbing her lips with her napkin. After a sip of her coffee, Flo asked, "So how was your trip to Trenton?"

Marie set her coffee cup on the end table next to her and delicately placed the last bit of her croissant in her mouth. Not wanting to repeat her previous display of bad manners, Marie made sure she swallowed the last crumb before answering.

"It was great, Auntie," she said, with rising enthusiasm in her voice.

"We were only able to retrieve about half the names of the Gunderson's foster children from the shredding center, but that still amounted to twenty-five names, and I'm sure I'll get some contacts from the social media sites I used."

Marie went on to explain how she had saturated several social media sites with requests to hear from this name or that name and if they had ever lived with George and Sally Gunderson in Trenton, New Jersey.

"I just finished when you arrived," Marie said.

"People today are addicted to their favorite social media site like addicts to heroin. They crave the instant communication ability to respond to whatever inane posting appears. Your request certainly has more credibility than responding to a posting of a sunset picture taken by someone's ten-year-old boy."

"I hope so, Auntie," sighed Marie, with a twinge of despair in her voice. "The Family Day celebration Jane has planned at the Gardens is a month away and that doesn't leave much time for anyone who contacts me to arrange to come."

"I'm a bit more optimistic, sweetie," smiled Flo. "If the Gunderson's were everything Joann said they were as foster parents, any of their care would move heaven and earth to get to Family Day and see Sally."

Marie hoped her aunt was right. She needed time away from her computer. The gratuitous calories from the croissant caused Marie to think a mid-morning jog was just what she needed.

"Auntie, could we meet for breakfast tomorrow? If I gaze at a computer screen again today, I'll go blind, and thanks to your thoughtful gift of croissants from the Queen, I need to work off those calories before they solidify to my waist."

Flo chuckled at her niece who in the past had abhorred exercise of any kind, but shopping for a dress for your best friend's wedding and finding out you've gone from a size ten to a size fourteen can be a strong motivator to lose weight.

"Sure. Let's meet at Le Petite, say eight?"

The suggestion of Le Petite was no accident. A treasured part of Florence Abby's past, as well as a secret part of her current life, was there. She never suspected her niece's prying nature would force its revelation.

"Sounds great, Auntie. Maybe I'll have had some contacts by then."

Marie had no idea how fate would grant her wish.

18

SIX DEGREES OF SEPARATION

I n the gentrified section of old Charleston, on the corner of a long block of quaint boutiques featuring locally made leather goods, kitchen pottery, and custom jewelry, sat Le Petite. It was as if the eatery had been transported from the West Bank of the Seine in Paris and placed in Charleston. A large pink canopy covered two rows of small round oak stained wooden tables with cane chairs. In the middle of a white tablecloth with the letters "LP" embroidered along the edges, a vase held a freshly placed white rose. Resting next to the vase was the menu. Henri Broussard, the original owner, would have never tolerated a printed sheet inside a plastic protector to describe his food. Besides, smudges of whatever was on the hands of the previous patrons was not what Broussard wanted his next patrons to see. His menus were a folded piece of scallop-edged cream paper, no bigger than a Christmas card, embossed on the outside by the river Seine. On the inside, each item was handwritten in beautiful sweeping penmanship. After each seating, along with a new tablecloth, and silverware, a new menu was placed on the table. By design, Henri Broussard had aligned the tables so that pedestrian traffic had to walk between the rows to get to the corner, exposing them to the aromas and sight of Henri's fabulously prepared European foods. Soft accordion music piped through several speakers added to the Parisian atmosphere.

Broussard's arrangement of the inside was equally as clever as his sidewalk design. Henri felt meals were a time for intimacy and good conversation among friends. Accordingly, throughout the cafe, large oak barrels with floral arrays of northern maidenhair ferns were strategically placed, giving the illusion of privacy and acting as sound barriers. Brightness of color was important to the artistic side of Broussard. Cream stucco walls had numerous built-in arched grottos filled with Dwarf Iris, Eastern Bluestar, and Carolina Lupine.

Le Petite had a decades-long reputation for serving the finest breakfast in town. Unlike the mantra of many cafes in Charleston that bragged about serving authentic Southern Comfort foods, Le Petite used the slogan, *Local Ingredients with European inspiration.* Using his connections at the local farmers' market, Broussard bought only locally grown grains, potatoes, free-range chicken eggs, and herbs. Even his pancetta and prosciutto were prepared at a local Italian deli. From these ingredients, his inspiration created an array of muffins, puffs, pastries, several types of quiches, crispy potato balls, and pancakes. Not to be forgotten were Broussard's famous crepes.

～

"I KNEW IT WAS GOING TO BE CROWDED, SATURDAYS ALWAYS ARE," groaned Marie, as she and her aunt approached Le Petite. Marie had dressed casually hoping to find seating outside and avoid the disapproving eyes of those offended by Marie's stylish jeans with several frayed areas exposing her bare legs or her Polynesian colored polyester off the shoulder blouse that could have been a little less revealing as far as Flo was concerned. Though in her mid-fifties, Flo would have passed for much younger. She enjoyed high heels because they added precious inches to her five-foot three height, which Flo always detested. Unlike her niece, Flo preferred blouses, usually short sleeved. The only trace of a femme fatale were the top two buttons left unbuttoned. The Afro from her days of political activism had been replaced by a stylish tapered scarlet pixie with a layered top. Belonging to a running club kept unwanted pounds off, but it was her eyes that were the focal point of her appearance. High cheekbones and long eyelashes made her brown eyes a magnet for the attention of others. Every outside table was occupied, and Marie had no doubt that the inside was equally full. Broussard's rather unsophisticated way to avoid taking reservations was to use a large blackboard on the outside wall next to the door. Customers would write their names on the blackboard and the number in their group, and as tables became available, a waiter or waitress would check the board to see who was next to be seated. Her appetite grew exponentially as she followed her aunt down the aisle between tables to the chalkboard.

After writing her name on the board, Flo turned to Marie and said, "It shouldn't be long. The inside doesn't look too crowded."

Suddenly, a voice from behind her called out, "Florence, mon ami. It has been too, too, long."

Flo turned around. Marie did not recognize the man, though it was eminently clear from the smile of her aunt's face she did.

"Yes, it has, Henri. I apologize for that," replied Flo, whose awkwardness at the sudden appearance of an old acquaintance had caught her off guard.

"Please, no, my dear. No apologies necessary," the man replied, who took one of her aunt's hands and brought it to his lips. Then he gently drew her to him and placed a soft kiss on each cheek.

"And who is this beautiful young lady?" he asked, turning his attention to Marie.

There was little Henri Broussard knew about Florence Abby's personal life and she about his, a decision mutually made by both. But this revelation would have to be made.

"Henri, this is my niece, Marie Gordon. Marie, this is my old friend, Henri Broussard."

"Not so old, I hope," smiled Broussard, who took Marie's hand in his.

Marie was mesmerized by Henri Broussard. She guessed him to be about her father's height, six foot four inches, though with a more slender build. His white chef coat was sparkling white, a sign Henri had delegated much of the cooking responsibilities to other kitchen staff. The top button of the collar was left unbuttoned as if to add an air of casualness to his appearance. A pair of reading glasses sat atop his closely cropped black hair. Traces of silver hair were sprinkled about his temples. With piercing blue eyes, dimples, and a chiseled jawline, Henri Broussard could have easily passed for an aged movie star who still had that "It" factor.

"There is no need to place your name on the board," he grinned. "Follow me."

Broussard led them to a table nestled in a triangle of floral oak barrels.

"Bon Appetit," he said, again taking Flo's hand and placing a gentle kiss on the back.

Marie's eyes followed him as he walked away, and Flo took notice of her niece's interest. Hopefully, there would be no questions. Such would not be the case.

"Care to look at the menu?" Flo asked her niece. "I highly recommend the egg and spinach crepes."

Marie was much more interested in the apparent chemistry between Broussard and her aunt.

"Let's start with a little conversation about your friend Henri Broussard, Auntie?" queried Marie. "There was more than politeness to his attention." It was obvious that Marie was enjoying this line of questioning with her aunt.

"Don't be silly, girl! He's just an old friend," replied Flo, hoping to avoid any more questioning by her niece. Despite her bold front, Flo was clearly unnerved by Marie's questions.

"Then what was it like when you were just young friends? You know I'm not going to give up until you tell me," smirked Marie, as she placed her elbows on the table and rested her chin on folded hands.

Flo knew her niece had the persistence of a CIA interrogator, and she would have to tell her something or Flo would have no rest from the questioning. Just then, the waitress brought them two cups of coffee and a St. Honore pastry.

"Compliments of Monsieur Broussard."

Marie leaned back in her chair, the broad smile on her face was a reflection of the smugness she felt on the inside. *Just old friends, right!*

Flo poured a dash of cream into her coffee and slowly swirled her spoon through the mixture. Did her niece really need to know the history between her and Broussard? More importantly, was she experienced enough to understand? If revelation was really necessary, Flo would have preferred a more private place, but then this was Henri's place, a place of his inspiration, so why not here.

"Other than your mother, no one knows about this, and I prefer it that way. Am I clear?"

There was an unfamiliar edginess to her aunt's words. A determined demand of the conditions she had set forth; Marie did not sense anger in Flor's voice, only a stern demand for compliance with the conditions she had set forth. Flo steadied herself as her past, and present relationship with Henri Broussard was something she held close to her heart. The words expressed did not come easily.

"I was not much older than you when I finished law school. Four years of undergraduate work and three years of law school took a toll on me. I needed a break. I had taken French as a foreign language, so an extended vacation to France seemed ideal. The Culinary Institute of Paris offered discounted meals prepared by its students, and being on a limited budget, I took full advantage of the special pricing. In time, something more than the price of the meals kept me coming back. He was gorgeous beyond belief. Tall, black hair, ivory white teeth, and blue eyes that could melt ice. I think the attraction was mutual because whenever I came in, he always seemed to find a way to be my waiter."

Marie turned toward the door where Henri Broussard was greeting customers.

"Let me guess," she said, nodding in his direction. "That Henri Broussard?"

No longer feeling a need to be circumspect, the surging of memories brought a smile of joy to Flo's face. "Yes, that Henri Broussard, my Henri Broussard."

The rapturous nature of her aunt's past had Marie spellbound. The most romantic story of all times was playing itself out right in front of her.

"We soon were spending every free moment of time we could together. He showed me places in Paris and the French countryside the average tourist never sees. We hosteled our way across Europe to save money. He took me to the most beautiful spots on earth: Lake Como in Italy, Lucerne in Switzerland, the banks of the Loire. We toured the great cathedrals and famous museums. He filled my soul with his dreams, and I returned the favor. He wanted to change the world through cooking, and I wanted to make change as a social worker."

Flo's voice began to fade slightly.

"And then what?" Marie asked anxiously, as if to fast forward to the romantic ending of a Hollywood love story.

"Henri's father died suddenly of a heart attack. There were no brothers and sisters to look after his mother, who was grief-stricken by the death of her husband of nearly forty-five years. After graduation, Henri took a job at a resort hotel outside Paris so he could care for his mother. I had an internship awaiting me back in the states. We both knew any future together would have to be in the far-off future, if at all."

Her energy spent recalling this most heartbreaking part of her past, Flo took a final sip of her coffee, then lean back in her chair, perhaps to savor one more time what might have been.

Let there be no doubt, Marie Gordon was a romantic, but not a naive romantic. She had spent time in Italy after college, a graduation gift from her parents. In Venice, a young tour guide led her group through Saint Mark's Basilica and the most romantic little cafes along the canal. Marie's favorite had been the boat tours to the island of Murano with their exquisite works of blown glass. When her group headed off to Florence, Marie had her own private tour guide for her remaining time in Italy. Their connection had been magical, passionate, and intense. She had lived in the moment, but when the time came to an end, she realized it that been just that, a moment in time, but one she would cherish privately for the rest of her life. She would try one more time, leaving subtlety aside.

"So, you and this young man had an affair?"

Flo sat more erect, surprised at her lack of embarrassment at her niece's bold declaration. She smiled at the inner emotion of romance that filled her heart. Yes, it had been an affair, but also much more than an affair. An affair ends, but a romance continues.

"No, Marie, what we shared was not an affair. Ours was a love story, a love story cruelly interrupted by circumstances neither one of us could control. Nearly twenty-five years later, Henri came to the United States to open his own restaurant in New York City. He was wildly successful, opening two more restaurants over the next ten years. We reconnected whenever we could. Eventually, he sold his restaurants and moved to Charleston and opened Le Petite. Running a restaurant consumed much of his time, but at least we were closer, and our love continues to this day."

Feeling like she was in a Hallmark movie, tears began to flow down Marie's cheeks. "Auntie, that's so beautiful."

Marie could never be anything but sincere, and heartfelt feeling expressed in this simple statement was profound.

Mercifully, the waiter appeared to take their order, breaking the emotionally charged atmosphere. Almost absentmindedly, Flo uttered: "Two spinach crepes, please."

Hoping to avoid her own floodgate of emotions, Flo made a quick segue to the original purpose of their breakfast meeting.

"Let's get to how the search for the Gunderson's foster children is going?"

Sitting over to the side of a trio of oak wine barrels, barely visible through a cluster of decorative ferns on the barrel tops, sat a young man making notes from some sort of manual. He stopped abruptly when he heard the word, Gunderson. He leaned his head towards the ferns, curious how he had heard a name from his past.

"Not good, if you count the number of responses I got as of this morning: three," replied an obviously dejected Marie.

"Give yourself a few more days, then consider a more direct approach. Sally and George Gunderson were like saints according to Joann Guillory, and I doubt any of their foster care children looked on placement with them as something not to be remembered. My guess is anyone of them who heard you were looking for Sally or George Gunderson's foster children would knock down doors to get to you."

The young man abruptly closed his notebook and stood up, making sure he could see who was seated on the other side of the oaken barrels. He made his way down the short aisle and turned up the next aisle.

"If only the world was that small, Auntie," Marie sighed, trying without success to be optimistic.

Suddenly, a man approached them dressed in the uniform of a Charleston Police Officer.

"I beg your pardon, but I couldn't help but overhear your conversation."

"I tend to talk loudly. I only hope we haven't annoyed you?" said Flo.

"No, not at all," replied the young officer, his uniform hat tucked under one arm. He seemed painfully embarrassed by Flo's remarks.

"My name is Joe Collier. I was wondering if I might ask you a few questions?"

"Joe, not Joseph?" asked Flo after looking at the young man's name tag.

The young officer glanced at his name tag and smiled.

"Officially, it's Joseph for the Department, Joe for my friends, and Joey, for really close friends."

Marie found the young officer's selective use of his name charming. She also found his smile, his eyes, his voice, and practically every-thing else about him charming. This attraction did not go unnoticed by her aunt.

"Please, have a seat, Joe," Flo responded.

As he settled into his chair, Flo asked, "What was it you heard that intrigued you?" She was not at all offended by his uninvited intrusion.

"Did you say you were looking for children of Sally and George Gunderson?"

"I'm not, but my niece is," Flo said, pointing to Marie.

"Marie Gordon," Marie said, extending her hand to the officer.

Marie was surprised at the tender grip with which his large hand held hers. He paused just long enough to take in her alluring smile before releasing it. Then he stammered, "Joe, Joe Collier."

Now it was Flo's turn to muse. "So, it's "Joe" friend, not "Joseph" official.

"Would that be Sally and George Gunderson from Trenton, New Jersey?" the young officer asked.

"As a matter of fact, yes," responded Marie with sufficient enthu-siasm she almost knocked over her coffee cup. "I'm doing some research for a project I'm working on for some residents at an assisted living facility here in Charleston. Magnolia Gardens, you may have heard of it."

The young officer sat silent, trying to compose his thoughts. As he did, his eyes moistened. Flo and Marie looked on in amazement.

"I'm sorry I don't, but I do know Sally and George Gunderson, they were my foster parents. They were the only real parents I ever had. I mean, my father was killed in an automobile accident when I was four. My mom found comfort in drugs and alcohol. I wasn't an easy kid to handle back then, so when I was seven, she had me placed in foster care. Sally and George raised me until I was eighteen and aged out of foster care. Without their love and support, I probably would have wound up in prison. They were the most loving, caring people I've ever known."

There was a tenderness to this young man that caused her heart to palpitate. Instinctively, she started to reach out to touch his hand but stopped. Too soon, her brain told her, but it was too late, her heart had been smitten.

There was a pause as he picked up a napkin from the table and not so discreetly dabbed at his eyes. There was only so much emotion he could hold back when speaking of Sally and George Gunderson. "Allergies," he said. "Probably someone near us has a cat. Anyway, I wasn't sure where I was headed after aging out of foster care. It was George who told me to think about the Marine Corps. He said they would become my new family. He was right. They finished molding what Sally and George started. Four years later, I discharged at the Marine Base in Beaufort. I wrote to them often when I was in the Corps, but after a while I stopped getting letters. I never knew what happened to them. Anyway, long story short, I liked it here, so I joined the Charleston PD, and here we are."

Marie was moved by his failed attempt to hide his emotions, but she had not lost track of how she hoped he could help.

"Do you know of any of the other foster children they had?"

"Lots," replied Collier, as he placed the napkin on the table. "You'd be surprised how many of them would come back to see Mom and Dad over the years. They would talk about how their lives were going, and the influence Mom and Dad had on them. Several got in the habit of writing to those of us in the home, to kind of offer support and encouragement. I'm not afraid to admit this, but aging out of foster care was frightening, at least for me. I guess the others as well. We all used to get letters from kids who had aged out, letting us know how things were going with them."

A sudden somberness came over him. He stared downward. "Sometimes they were happy letters, sometimes not." This was the treasure trove of information Marie had hoped to find. She explained to Collier what had happened to Sally and George and of the Family Day Celebration that was being organized at Magnolia Gardens.

"I want to get ahold of as many of their foster children as I can and invite them to the Family Day Celebration. Would you be willing to help me, Joe?"

"Absolutely!" he practically screamed. "It would be like a family reunion."

There was a sense of elation in Marie's eyes that Flo felt went beyond finding Joe's help. After exchanging phone numbers, he asked, "When would you like to start?"

Unwilling to play coy with the attractive officer, Marie blurted out, "How about tomorrow? I've already mailed out invitations to the residents' families so the sooner we get started on Sally's children, the better."

"Tomorrow would be fine," Collier responded, secretly wishing they could start right now, but he still had four hours left on his shift, and his lunch break was nearly over.

"I've got a little time left before I'm back on the clock, where exactly do you live?"

Taking her cue, Flo said, "Look, if it's not too inconvenient, I've got to get back to the office. Joe, would you mind taking Marie home. That way, you'll know exactly where to go tomorrow."

Stumbling like some sort of country bumpkin, Collier said, "Sure, that is if it's okay with you," looking at Marie. *If only looks could talk...*

19

A MEETING OF FATES

Beaufort, South Carolina was only ninety miles from Charleston, an hour and a half maybe at normal speed. Allen Pinafore had that much time to formulate his thoughts, to choose the words he would use when he would meet the love of his life. The confidence he felt after his meeting with Kristin and her daughter, Kayla, had given way to doubt and fear. The small box in his pocket containing the wedding ring he had never given her gave him little inspiration. Could he avoid suggesting that Madeline had decided not to wait for him, and instead moved on with her life with someone else, or would he sound like he had doubted her ability to love him despite his horrific injuries? This was a man who had faced incredible dangers, accepted death as a possible consequence for being a Navy Seal, and yet Allen Pinafore was terrified. Could any words make a difference? Nothing could have prepared him for what he was about to encounter.

∽

"How do you think she's going to react when she meets him?" Kayla asked her mother as she snuggled into an oversized blanket on the couch.

Kristin had been pacing about the living room anxiously awaiting a call from Pinafore that he was near. She had been so focused on confronting Pinafore, so determined to get at the truth, she had completely forgotten about how this encounter would affect Madeline. She was as much part of the story as he was, and yet Kristin had failed to consider her feelings. She stood in front of the window, one hand holding back the curtain to expose her view of the street.

"I don't know, honey, I suppose there will an eruption of all sorts of emotions; disbelief, an immense sense of euphoria and then probably anger."

A quizzical look came over Kayla's face.

"I would have never guessed anger," she mused.

Turning around to face her daughter, Kristin said, "That's because you've never thought you had lost someone you loved only to find out they were okay."

Though well into her twenties, this was a complex bundle of human emotions Kayla had not yet encountered. In order to bring understanding to her daughter, Kristin harkened back to an event that would illustrate what she was attempting to convey.

"You were just about eight and wanted to play in the front yard. I was leery because we hadn't yet put in a fence, but you had an annoying persistence even at that age, so I said okay, but I told you to stay on the lawn. To this day I can still remember the screeching sound of a car hitting its brakes. When I ran to the window, a man was getting out of his car, and you were nowhere in sight. I screamed your name as I ran into the street expecting to see your body on the ground. Instead, you were in the neighbor's yard playing with the new puppy they had just brought home. There was unimaginable relief when I picked you up and squeezed you to my breast. By the time I got you back home, that feeling had changed to anger because you had not listened to me, and then I hugged you again."

"But not before a few not so gentle whacks to my butt!" laughed Kayla.

"Yes," as Kristin joined her daughter in laughter.

Just then Kristin got a text alert on her phone. She glanced at the screen.

"GPS has me three blocks away. Allen."

"He's almost here," Kristin announced, as she headed to the front door. Her mind was awash with conflicting emotions, still uncertain if this was right for Madeline.

She was standing on the brick porch when a late model Subaru Outback pulled up to the curb. When the driver got out, Kristin's grip on the wrought iron handrail tightened. *My God, he's handsome*, she thought. Pinafore adjusted his white dress hat. He preferred a snug fit set squarely on his head. He tugged at the hem of his tropical worsted wool coat, smoothing out any lines from the drive. Kristin marveled at the rows of medals and ribbons on his uniform and the three gold stripes on the end of one sleeve only added to the luster of his Commander's uniform. She hadn't even noticed the folded up left sleeve nor the discolored scar tissue on his left cheek. Pinafore had become so adept with his prosthetic leg, his limp was barely perceptible. As he made his way up the drive, he smiled. *God, what a smile*, Kristin thought. *Those eyes. That chin!*

"You made good time," Kristin said, extending her to hand him. "And so dressed up!" referring to his dress uniform.

"Try to equate twenty-five years with ninety minutes. It goes faster than you think," Pinafore replied. "As for the uniform, it's the Navy's way of compensation, I guess. I was retired at the rank of a commander."

There was a long pause before he continued.

"The last time Maddy and I were together was the Navy Birthday Ball. I was in my dress blues. So I thought, you know, that wearing it might help somehow. I don't know. What do you think?"

Touched by his thoughtfulness, Kristin answered, "I don't think it will matter what you wear. What with her vision problem, she'll be more focused on your voice, not the uniform."

"Hi, Allen," Kayla called out from the porch. She had decided to stay home and let her mother orchestrate the reunion.

"Hello to you," Pinafore replied, cheerfully waving to Kayla.

Turning to Kristin, he asked, "Have you arranged the meeting?"

The anxiety in his words caused him to cough slightly. The uncertainty of the meeting coupled with his horrendous injuries only added to his anxiety.

"It's all arranged," Kristin said. "I already called her to say there's a representative from the Navy who wants to see her, and I'm bringing him over this afternoon. She knows we're were looking into this whole Navy thing so that shouldn't surprise her. She has an appointment with her ophthalmologist this morning, so I'll take you directly to her place rather than use a room in the facility. The rest is up to you."

The emotional enormity of the encounter caused Pinafore to pause. His mind was awash with unfamiliar emotion. His decades-long deceptions had helped no one and likely harmed the one he loved most.

"I know. I hope I don't fail her again."

With her purse in hand, Kristin commanded, "Okay, then, follow me," as she headed to her car.

As HE EXITED HIS CAR, PINAFORE MARVELED AT THE BEAUTY AND SERENITY of Magnolia Gardens. The afternoon sun filtered through the branches of massive Magnolia trees like bolts of lightning, casting irregular shadows on the ground. The air was filled with the chirping of several species of birds, each trying to outperform the other. There was a distinct sweetness in the air caused by the blossoming jasmine hedges bordering the main building.

"This way," Kristin said, as she headed down a stamped concrete pathway around the front of the building to Madeline's private side entrance. Pinafore followed, rehearsing in his mind what his first words would be.

Knocking on the door, Kristin announced, "Maddy, it's me. I've got that Navy representative I told you about."

Madeline called out, "Give me a minute, just got back from the ophthalmologist. He dilated my pupils as if I need something else to blur my vision!" She exclaimed facetiously.

There was little to cause apprehension in Madeline who had long ago given up hope of ever finding out what happened to her Eddy. This was probably another meaningless though polite way for the Navy to put an end to the issue. There was the stereotypical sound of her cane tapping on the tiled floor as she approached the door. Madeline had chosen a stylish dress not only because she had been to the doctor's, but also because of this unknown visitor. After all, what woman doesn't want to look her best in such a situation? Her auburn hair was pulled back into a bun accentuating her high cheekbones and hazel eyes. Despite her vision limitation, Madeline was still able to expertly apply her makeup, giving her another facet of attractiveness. With a last-minute adjustment of her dress and the dark sunglasses she wore as the result of the dilation, she opened the door.

"Hi stranger, come on in."

"Maddy, this is the navy representative I told you about, Commander Allan Pinafore."

There was no hiding the sarcasm in her voice at the words "Navy Representative."

"Huh, I've never heard anything good from the Navy, but if Kristin brought you, come on it, I guess."

Despite the less than warm greeting, the mere sound of her voice sent shock waves through his body. Pinafore looked at Kristin. His eyes pleading, *What am I supposed to say to her? How do I explain what happened?* Ever since that meeting with Kristin and her daughter in his office, he had been tortured with how to explain the unexplainable, yet make it believable and sincere. At that moment, he realized the futility of trying to mend twenty-five years of deception and self-pity. He turned to walk away when Kristin grabbed him by the arm and whispered in his ear, "Trust your heart and trust hers."

Pinafore followed Kristin inside.

"Shall we sit at the dining room table?" Madeline said.

It was less comfortable than the couch, and that feature alone might hasten the end of what Madeline was positive would be an uneasy conversation. She purposely avoided offering coffee, tea, water, or any gesture of civility. She wanted to get this over with as quickly as possible. Pinafore pulled out a chair for Kristin and then one for himself. In those precious few seconds, Madeline's mind moved at warp speed recalling every unsuccessful attempt to get information from the Navy, years of frustration and finally the resignation that she would never know what had happened to her Eddie.

"So, what has the Navy got for me, Commander?" The caustic tone in her words was intentional and well deserved as far as Madeline was concerned.

Realizing Madeline's words had done nothing to establish an open line of communication between Pinafore and Madeline, Kristin interjected.

"Look, Maddy, this isn't like an unanswered letter or another evasive phone call to the Navy. The Commander came here to personally speak to you. What have you got to lose by listening to him?" Her words were a mix between a scolding and a plea.

Madeline stood up and turned her back to the two at the table. Barely able to contain any semblance of civility, she snapped, "Fine!" With that, Madeline turned and sat down. The rigidity of her posture, her arms folded across her chest, and a clenched jaw were signs she had lost little of her disdain for the Navy and their representative. Kristin nodded to Pinafore as a precursor of what was to come.

"Maddy, what you need now is some privacy, so I'll let myself out," Kristin responded. As she stood up, she looked at Pinafore and added, "Don't mess up this opportunity, Commander. There might never be another."

Madeline was so entrenched in past memories she failed to grasp the cryptic warning to Pinafore, but not the Commander.

"I won't," he responded.

Madeline sat silent. The awkwardness of being there alone with a stranger was compounded by the anger and rage that now boiled inside her. The United States Navy had taken the love of her life without any explanation as to what had happened. Using any justification they could muster, the Navy refused every effort Madeline had made over the years to find out what had happened to her Eddie, and now they had the audacity to send a representative to see her. For what reason, another lie, another coverup? Every muscle in her body was taunt, every nerve primed to react. Pinafore waited for Kristin to shut the door. He wanted to reach out and hold her hand before saying anything, but he held back. Then he spoke softly as he began to reveal the truth.

"Ms. Orsini, my name is Commander Allen Pinafore, and I am here to tell you about Lt. Edward Orsini."

He watched her for some kind of reaction, a facial twitch, a jerk of her body, anything to indicate she had heard his words. Suddenly, Madeline slammed her fist on the table.

"So, you're going to tell me about Edward Orsini, are you! " She shouted, "And just what do you think you can tell me that I don't already know. Where he went to high school, where he proposed to me, our first house together, our wedding plans?"

This time she slammed both fists on the tabletop and leaned forward screaming with the rage of a madwoman, "What do you know about Edward Orsini or me!"

Pinafore flinched at the volcanic intensity of her words. He steadied himself as he looked at the woman he had never stopped loving, the woman who's heart he now wanted desperately to salvage. The tone in his voice was timid, even shy for a man of his military experience.

"I know everything about you and Edward Orsini."

The furor that consumed her left her deaf to Pinafore's words or the memory of his voice. With one last emotional eruption she shrieked, "The hell you do!"

This last rebuke caused tears to flow freely down Pinafore's face. She was slipping away from him, and there seemed nothing he could do to stop her. Fear and desperation brought him to the emotional precipice of his life. The lifeline to any happiness he could ever have was sitting there in front of him. He was not about to let go now. He had hardly an ounce of adrenaline left. Barely above a whisper he said, "Maddy, I do know you."

In that fractured moment of reality, something reconnected in Madeline's brain. She rubbed her temples as the pain of an emerging realization intensified.

"What did you just say?"

"I said, Maddy, I do know you," he added with emphasis.

There is was; that oft-made fun of New England accent. The softness and tenderness of a voice not heard in decades. She felt his memory like it was yesterday. Her heart surged with emotion. *It couldn't be,* she thought. *There's no way.* She threw off her dark sunglasses and rapidly jerked her head, first to one side and then the other, then up and down, trying desperately to find one of those random spots of clear vision. It was as if a ghost had spoken to her. She bolted to her feet, knocking over her chair. She pressed herself against the wall desperately trying to escape from the voice she knew could not be real. Her hand clutched the drapes covering the window. She could barely get the words out, "Eddy?"

Pinafore stood up and walked over to face her.

"Yes, Maddy, it's me," he said quietly and soothingly.

That voice, his voice, sent her mind reeling out of control. She was seized with the most horrible sense of panic. She pressed herself even harder against the wall crying out, "I don't understand! What's happening!"

He wanted to blurt out everything, but a sense of reason had come over him. *Start slowly, the mission, the crash, the recovery, but first tell her you love her.* His words were soft and gentle as he tried to reassure her of the most important thing.

"Maddy, all this time, all these years, I never stopped loving you. I never stopped wanting you."

His words had the desired effect. Her rigid body began to relax. The lingering effects of the dilation blurred any details of the face that had just spoken. Her hands reached out tentatively. First, she felt his shoulders. Slowly, she moved up to his face. When her hand came into contact with his scarred cheek, she stopped. There was a distinct gasp for air. He understood and said nothing. She wanted to believe it was really him. She wanted to believe it with all her heart that he was really standing in front of her; then he spoke.

"Remember whenever you told me, I love you? I would tell you I love you more."

Those words unleashed a flood gate of emotions. It was him. She threw her arms around his neck. It was the same tender voice that had pledged his everlasting love. Still, a nagging iota of doubt remained. If this was real, she was holding on forever. If it was an illusion, she would hang on until reality exposed the truth. Her breathing seemed nonexistent. Her lungs burned as she tried to find air to breathe. Her heartbeat was out of control. Her grip tightened as she buried her head against his chest.

As air found its way into her lungs, hysterical sobs of joy erupted. Neither knew how long they held each other, five minutes, ten minutes. It didn't really matter. Once more, Eddy Orsini held the love of his life. Every memory of her touch, her scent, the sound of her laughter, spewed out of the past like a volcanic eruption. Through his own tears, Eddy continually mumbled, "I love you. I love you." Madeline responded by nodding her head and somehow managed to utter, "Me too."

The first barrier, meeting again after twenty-five years, had been breached. The second barrier, why had it happened in the first place, would test the resolve of both Madeline and Eddy.

He could feel her legs begin to wobble. Navy Commander or not, this was a lot to process, let alone endure.

"Maybe we should sit down," he said.

"If we don't, I'm about to collapse," replied Maddy, a smile returning to her face as he took her hand and walked her to the couch.

It was then, as she curled up next to him and extended her arm around his chest that she noticed she could not feel his other arm. Her rationality, previously clouded by the explosive emotions she had just experienced, now returned. The mere thought that her intuition might be true sent Maddy to the edge of another emotional whirlpool. Her question was more of an urgent demand than a gentle inquiry. She sat upright facing him. She blinked her eyes repeatedly as the effects of the dilation were fading.

"My God! Eddy, what happened to your arm?" she snapped, not so much out of anger, but out of a sense of urgency. Then remembering that strange feeling when her hand had touched his face, she added, "and your face."

He should have felt relief that at last, he would be able to tell her what had happened, but the ninety-mile drive from Beaufort had given him pause to reflect on his real motives for allowing their estrangement to even begin. He was deeply ashamed.

"I got the page to report to base just after midnight. You were sound asleep and even if I woke you, there was nothing I could tell you, so I left you knowing you'd figure out that I had probably been sent on a mission."

"You got that much right," replied Maddy, as she now held his right hand to her breast.

"Anyway," he continued. "Halfway to our objective, our copter was hit by a SAM, a surface to air missile along with heavy ground fire. The explosion killed everyone but me. When I woke up in the hospital in Germany, I realized I had lost my left arm, the fire had burnt my face badly, and I had lost my right leg."

Maddy's hand dropped to his right leg. She could feel the prosthetic leg where it was attached mid-thigh. Maddy was not the squeamish type, but the thought of all he had endured nearly caused her to wretch right there on the couch. She placed both her hands on his face. She implored him.

"Eddy, why didn't you tell me? I would have been there for you."

"I didn't want you to see me like that, I guess."

He turned his head fearing she would see the humiliation on his face.

"Well, for God's sake, why didn't you answer any of my letters?"

"You wrote there was something you wanted to tell me. Maddy, if you had found someone else, what could I have done about it?"

Suddenly, Maddy realized what Eddy had said. It infuriated her. *How dare he,* she thought, *did he really have such little faith in her?* She rose to her feet afraid that in her fury she might strike out at him. Ignoring her cane, she used her hand to guide her to the other side of the coffee table where she turned to face him.

"So, you thought so little of my love for you that you thought I had found someone else? You actually thought I would throw away the life we had planned together, the dreams we had made for someone else?"

"Maddy, please, it wasn't like that," he pleaded.

"Oh yes, it was like that," she yelled back. "And don't give me that lame excuse you didn't want me to see you with those injures. What you were really afraid of was that I would be so repulsed at what had happened to you that I would turn away from you, isn't that right Eddy!"

Having his real motives exposed, Edward Orsini sat silent. What could he say that would make any difference? His silence gave rise to one more tirade from Maddy.

In an explosive rant, she screamed, "I hate you, Eddy Orsini. I hate you!"

For twenty-five years, Edward Orsini had dealt with the loss of the love of his life. Now, he had lost her again, and this time there would be no turning back. He hated himself. He got to his feet and walked to the table to retrieve his hat. He was not prone to accept failure but felt he had no choice.

"I guess that's my cue to leave," he said.

As he made his way to the door, Maddy stepped in front of him.

"Where the hell do you think you're going!"

"Maddy, you pretty much told me what you think of me."

She put both hands on her hips and, with more defiance than he had ever seen from her, she shouted, "And you don't think that I've got the right to be angry? You don't think that you had an ass-chewing coming?"

"No, of course. You're right on both accounts," he answered meekly.

Humble pie was never a favorite of Edward Orsini, but this time he knew what he had to eat. He stood there silently for several minutes before saying, "Good-bye, Maddy."

He was halted by the strangest response.

"Not so fast, Commander Edward Orsini. Hell yes, I'm mad, and yes, I hate you, but only in the moment. Do you really think I'm going to let you walk out of my life over a moment of anger and whatever else I said? This moment will pass, but what will not pass is that I love you. I've always loved you, and we will have that life we dreamed of, but there's one more thing you need to hear."

He struggled to comprehend what he heard. She was angry. She was mad. She hated him, yet she loved him still, and their life together would become a reality and not remain some lost dream. How could any human being still love someone who had failed them the way Orsini had failed Madeline? Speechless and dumbfounded, she led him back to the couch. Maddy thought very carefully before she spoke. She was about to tell him there was one dream of theirs that been shattered years ago, a dream that had meant the world to both of them. The mere thought of recounting that experience to him would force her to relive it all over again. Knowing was the only way she could explain to him that her letters were not meant to reveal a perfidious act on her part, but to prepare him for a lost dream. She gripped his hand tightly, hoping to control her rising heartbeat. Her throat became parched, her voice raspy.

"You had been gone for several weeks when some of the girls wanted to go to the Landing Zone for drinks. It seemed harmless, besides what danger was there in having a few drinks in a bar frequented by Navy Seals and their friends."

"I haven't thought about that place in forever," Eddy said.

"I wish I could say the same," Madeline grimaced, reflecting on the memories that had plagued her for years. "Anyway, when the group decided to leave, I headed around the corner where I had parked. That's when it happened."

"That's when what happened, Maddy?" Her introductory remarks had done nothing to ease his level of anxiety.

She squeezed his hand a little tighter.

"Someone grabbed me from behind and attacked me, Eddy. When I woke up, I was in the hospital."

His anxiety turned to anger, or more accurately rage. Instinctively he knew he should have been there. If not to protect her from the attack, then at least to be with her in the hospital. He had failed her again. Quickly, his thoughts turned back to her. He moved to release her grip, then put his arm around her and pulled her to him. Something in her words told him there was more to her story. You don't awake in a hospital unless something serious had occurred.

"Maddy, waking up in a hospital means more than just waking up. What had happened?"

She placed her arms around him, her face pressed to his chest.

"I had a broken jaw, broken orbital bones to my right eye and..." She stopped. "Eddy, I wasn't just attacked." She paused again. "I was raped!"

He had cursed the loss of his arm in the past, but never more than now. He wanted both arms to hold her, to assure her of his love. He also wanted both arms as he fantasized beating the person responsible for this to within an inch of his life.

"Did they catch the guy?"

"No, he vanished into the dark. No one heard or saw anything."

Mustering up a final bit of courage, she said, "Eddy, the doctor told me I would never be able to have children. We would never have the family we dreamed of. I could never bear you a son or daughter."

With her story out, there was no need to continue to restrain her emotions. At first, there were only a few gentle sobs separated by shallow gasps for air. Then the sobs became deep, loud, hysterical outbursts. He felt the spasmatic jerking of her body as the wailing escalated to a frightening level. Eddy was afraid she might have a heart attack. The volcanic eruption of pent up emotions continued for several minutes until she became exhausted and lay limp in his arms.

Now he understood. Who would want to read of this in a letter, especially when you're thousands of miles away and couldn't do anything about it? Had he only trusted in her love, how much of this agony could have been avoided? With his one hand, he tilted her head backward and lowered his head to kiss her. At first, she was unresponsive to the touch of his lips. As he maneuvered his lips over hers, an awakening of feelings long only dreamed about came to the surface. She put her arms around his neck. She returned his caress with increasing passion and intensity and he reciprocated. Eventually their mouths parted, partially to catch their breaths.

"There's so much more I want to say to you," Eddy whispered in her ear.

"Can it wait until morning, my love?"

20

LOVE HASTENED

He was tempted to light up his patrol car as morning traffic was seriously impeding his arrival time at her house. *Perhaps a phone call to alert her he was going to be late. He could at least hear her voice again.* He had gotten her number when he dropped her off after their chance meeting at Le Petite, entered it into his cell phone and placed it on speed dial. His fingers drummed on the steering wheel as the dial tone droned until it went to voice mail. *Dammit,* he thought. Just then a hurried voice answered, "This is Marie."

"Marie, Joe Collier. Listen, traffic is really bad. I'm still about twenty minutes from your place. Sorry for the delay."

"Don't be silly. Get here when you can."

"Copy that," came the response.

Must be some sort of police code talk, Marie thought, as she set her cell phone back on the desk. The delay was fortuitous as it gave Marie an opportunity to finish her makeup and hair. She had been smitten by the officer and had found herself in the uncharacteristic mode of wanting to look her best, even a bit seductive if she were to admit it. With her dryer in hand, she lightly feathered her layered hair until it was perfect. She stared into the makeup mirror, carefully applying the final touches of mascara to her long eyelashes, and with a final application of bronze lipstick, she put on her chic Calvin Klein jeans, turned to the mirror to see that the fit was right and by right, she meant tight, but not crammed. With a smile of self-assurance, she slipped into a long-sleeved black polyester blouse with slits from the elbows to the shoulders. She tugged lightly at the bottom of the blouse to ensure her scoop neck exposed just the proper amount of cleavage. This was to be his second visit and Marie wanted to test the temperature of the water, so to speak. He had been so, so proper at Le Petite, and even at their first meeting he remained at bit gentlemanly shy. Not that Marie saw herself as a temptress, but she certainly felt an attraction to him, and she hoped to sense the same from him.

Their first visit was a bit formal. Marie had shared with him the information she had retrieved from foster care records of Sally and George Gunderson. They sat on the couch, he on one end, she on the other, as he scanned the list of names. At one point, he started to laugh, "Man, do I remember him. Secretly tried my first and last cigarette with Billy. George abhorred the thought that any of his kids would take up the habit."

When he came to the name Melissa Banks, the sweetest of smiles spread across his face.

"What?" asked Marie, who had been focusing on his face, delighting in the sparkle in his eyes whenever a name evoked a memory from his past.

"Melissa Banks," he said. "She was three years younger than me and had a hard time fitting in at school. Most of us foster kids had the same problem. We didn't want or need pity. Some kids looked at us like we had leprosy. Anyway, I had been in the Marines for a couple of years when I got a letter from Sally that Melissa was really depressed. She had asked a guy from school to take her to the Sadie Hawkins dance, and he turned her down. To add insult to injury, the jerk told his friends. Melissa got a lot of taunting from them."

Joe set the letter down on the couch and looked at Marie. There was the tenderest of smiles spreading across his face.

"You should have seen her face when I showed up in my dress blues to take her to that dance. Man, she was on cloud nine when we walked into the gym at school. She got payback in spades," he laughed, remembering the jealous stares from the petty onlookers.

Marie's heart warmed at the act of kindness to a young girl who undoubtedly would remember it for the rest of her life. She tempered her desire to move closer to him.

"If it's okay with you, I'll take this list home and match it with any addresses I have, then I'll get back to you."

"Sounds great," Marie responded.

Hoping to extend the visit, she had offered to make coffee for them.

"I wish I could, but I just got off a ten-hour shift and coffee is the last thing I need," he joked. "But I'll take a rain check."

She smiled at him. "A rain check it is," she answered.

"I really should be going," Joe said, as he stood up with Marie's folder in his hand.

"I understand," Marie said, dejected that her ploy had failed.

The formality of another handshake would not express the gratitude she felt for his assistance nor would it appease the surging desire to hold more than his hand. Unashamedly, she found herself hugging him.

"Joe, I can't tell you how much I appreciate what you're doing."

He was caught off guard by her sudden display of affection; however, it offered an opportunity for him to reciprocate. As he hugged her back, he said, "No need to thank me, Marie."

Intoxicated by her perfume, Tabu if he were to guess, and aroused by the feel of her body next to his, he allowed the hug to continue until a sense of awkwardness caused him to release her.

"See you next week," Marie said, a little embarrassed herself at the duration of the hug, though not regretting it one bit.

"Unless you call you first," he replied, with his own bit of flirtatious behavior.

~

TWO DAYS HAD PASSED WHEN COLLIER, FINISHING THE END OF HIS TEN-hour shift, decided he could not wait another two days to see Marie or at least hear her voice. The scent of her perfume, the image of her smile, and the thought of more than just a hug at their next meeting had made sleeping at night difficult for the smitten officer. As his '86 Dodge pickup came to a stop in his garage, Collier picked up his cell phone and dialed Marie's number. It was six at night, and he desperately hoped she had not made plans for the evening.

"Joe?" Marie asked.

Embarrassed at the adolescent reaction the sound of her voice caused, Collier fumbled his first few words. "Uh, yeah. I mean yes, it's me, Joe."

Had he been able to see her, his teenage-like angst would have disappeared as Marie felt exactly the same. He had left her feeling intoxicated at the thought of their next meeting, and a four-day delay was not acceptable to a young woman who had not experienced such an emotion in a long time. Marie threw on a quilted afghan over her and snuggled into the softness of her couch.

"To what do I owe the pleasure of your call?" she said, using all her feminine wiles to sound exotic.

"I thought maybe I could bring over some pizza and we could make a few calls tonight rather than wait until my RDO's. We might be more likely to find folks at home in the evening."

Marie mused as she traced her lips with her tongue. "Greek artisan with anchovies from Luigi's. I'll supply the wine."

"A lady after my own heart," beamed Joe. "I'll call it in now. See you in forty-five minutes or thereabouts."

Taking the steps two at a time, Joe hurried through the back door into his house. The normally neat Collier, who had been trained to keep his quarters squared away at all times in the Marine Corps, reverted back to those days when the expression "everything in its place and a place for everything" meant wherever he dropped it. His duty belt fell onto one of the kitchen chairs. His bulletproof vest landed on another kitchen chair. Uniform shirt and pants that normally hung neatly on a hanger and were placed on a hook behind his bedroom door were tossed on his bed. Grabbing his cell phone before jumping into the shower, he called in the pizza order. He didn't wait for the shower water to get hot. Cold water would clean just as well and be a bit more refreshing. Collier gave new meaning to a Navy shower and within minutes left a damp towel hanging on the shower door while he hurried to dress. After a quick spray of Jovan Musk, he slipped on his Levi's, Nike shoes, a t-shirt which showed off a very toned physique and was out the door.

Marie was also preparing for their unplanned evening together. Foregoing her normal long hot soaking bath, she opted for a much quicker shower, being careful not to get her hair wet. She dried quickly, then headed to her bedroom. She took the stopper from her Tabu perfume bottle on her vanity and slowly ran two lines from both ears down her neck to her throat. A bit of an overkill maybe, but Marie was taking no chances of getting another hug at the end of the evening. She held up two pair of jeans, trying to remember which one she had worn to Le Petite when they first met. She settled on the Calvin Klein's. Her cream color chiffon blouse added another layer of enticement. When she got to the living room, she took a quick visual. Thanks to a few extra visits from her aunt Flo, any extra picking up around her cottage was at a minimum. *Okay,* she thought. *Get the wine ready.* She was in the kitchen, opening a bottle of Pinot when the motion sensor lights her father had installed for her safety lit up. She went out to the porch to see an unfamiliar older pickup come to a stop. When she realized this might not be Joe, she stepped back behind the corner of the porch.

"It's me, Joe," he called out.

With the fear that it might be a stranger now gone, Marie stepped out to greet him.

"You're earlier than I expected," she said, greeting him with a smile.

"That's a good thing, isn't it?" he joked.

"Absolutely," she replied.

As he approached with the pizza in hand, Marie wet her lips.

"My gosh, that smells heavenly."

"Nobody makes them like Luigi," responded Joe, who tried not to stare at the alluring figure standing under the porch light.

Marie held the door open for Joe. As he passed, she could not help but notice the scent of Jovan Musk cologne.

"Set it on the coffee table. We'll keep this informal," smiled Marie.

Joe had his orders. He set the pizza box on the coffee table which had been cleared of all her magazines and unopened mail. He opened the lid and took out several packets of cheese and crushed hot peppers. Marie had never thought of herself as a wine snob, normally deferring to whatever wine was on sale, but her mother had convinced Marie to join a wine club, and as an introductory gift, the club gave Marie a crystal aerator. With two glasses in one hand and the wine and small box containing the aerator in the other, Marie made her way from the kitchen to the living room. She found Joe standing dutifully until her arrival. *Nice touch of courtesy,* she thought.

"Ever use one of these things? It's called an aerator." Marie asked, as she set the glasses on the end of the oval-shaped coffee table.

"Sure," Joe replied. "One year at the Marine Corps Birthday Ball, every table had one. Our commanding officer's family own a vineyard in North Carolina, and he supplied all the wine."

Joe opened the box and took out the aerator.

"Crystal, no less. Very impressive."

Taking the aerator in hand, Joe said, "It's intended to soften the taste of the tannins in red wines. It's normally used for Merlots and heavier reds, but it can be used for any wines, really."

"My, my, one judging you to be some beer-guzzling ex-Marine would be sorely mistaken," joked Marie.

"That would be former Marine," he quipped, "And I'm not really much of a beer drinker. In fact, thanks to my mother's battle with alcohol, a glass of wine or two is pretty much my limit," Joe responded.

From the somberness in his voice, Marie felt badly at her choice of jokes. He held it over each glass and slowly poured from the bottle. The wine gurgled through the wire screen at the bottom of the aerator and into the glass. When he was finished, he set the aerator back in its red velvet box and took a seat next to Marie. Handing her a glass, he said, "To your work." *Not so fast, Mister, this is a joint project,* Marie thought. "To our work."

They savored their first sip, then started in on Luigi's creation. There was little conversation as they lost themselves in the delight of the Kalamata olives, anchovies, feta cheese, and tender chunks of roasted lamb.

"Would you think me a hog if I had another piece?" Joe asked. "I only had time for half a sandwich today."

Marie smiled. "Go right ahead. I'll put the rest in a baggie for you to take home."

She felt strangely comfortable in tending to the welfare of the young man sitting on her couch. Deep within her stirred a desire to tend to more of his needs. When she returned from the kitchen after splitting the remaining pizza into two baggies, she found Joe had carefully laid out two lines of letters, a piece of paper with several phone numbers on it, and a small leather address book. She took a seat next to him, no longer willing to maintain some Victorian standard of an appropriate distance between a young man and a young woman sitting on a couch unescorted.

"What's this?" Marie asked, leaning forward to look at the letters on the coffee table. Inadvertently, their knees touched. Neither made a move to end the contact.

"These are letters I got from other foster kids that George and Sally raised. I've kept in touch with some. I guess it's kind of odd that a guy would save stuff like this, but they were the only real brothers and sisters I ever had. They're reminders of a better time in my life. The paper had some phone numbers of others I've kept in contact with. I could call them if you'd like."

"That's so much more current that the information in the records I have," smiled Marie. Turning to Joe, she placed her hand on his knee and softly said, "Thank you for caring so much."

21

CONNECTIONS WITH THE PAST

J oe had carefully controlled his desire for Marie. She was different than most of the women he had dated. Some wanted only a live-in relationship, but with no commitment. Some wanted an open relationship so they could see others. None had the wit, charm, and depth of compassion that Marie possessed. If Sally and George Gunderson had taught him anything, it was the importance of being committed to those you love. Joe wanted a committed relationship, and luring Marie into bed after a couple of dates would send the wrong message. However, the scent of her perfume, the softness of her hand on his knee, and the way she now looked at him broke down his defenses. He slid his arm around her waist. That was all the prompting Marie needed. She placed her hand around Joe's neck and tilted her head back. A rousing sensuality seemed to radiate from her body as Joe gently pulled her closer and lowered his lips to hers. If not for an immediate need to pursue the information Joe had brought, Marie would have had their kiss last much longer. As their lips parted, Marie whispered, "We've got some work to do, don't we?"

"Unfortunately, we do," replied Joe, who had the same desire to continue, as did Marie. "If you want to look at the letters and write down their return addresses, I'll start making some phone calls."

The few steps it took to walk to her desk and retrieve a pad of paper and pen gave Marie a brief respite from the romantic rush that had engulfed her after their kiss. However, given the right opportunity, the evening would not end with another hug. She returned to the couch and began making careful note of the names and addresses of the senders on the letter, and then began to silently read the contents. Joe took out his cell phone and began calling.

"Hi, Melissa, this is Joe, Joe Collier. Have you got a minute to talk?"

From the gleeful shout coming from Joe's cell, Marie judged the answer was yes.

"Listen, Melissa, I'm here with a friend who is working on a project involving Mom, and she'd like to talk with you." He paused then said, "Uh-huh, sure." Looking at Marie, he said, "She wants me to put the phone on speaker." After tapping the speaker icon, he said, "Go ahead, Melissa."

"So, you're Joey's friend," giggled a woman's voice. "I hope you're a she."

Marie chuckled both at the reference to Joey and the gender speculation.

"As a matter of fact, I am. My name is Marie. Why?"

"Because I think the world of Joey, Marie. I named my son after him, and he deserves the best. I hope you're it."

Embarrassed by the implication of a future union, Marie cleared her throat and said, "Well, time will tell." Looking at Joe, she gave him a slight shrug of her shoulders and a whimsical smile suggesting, *who knows!*

Joe had a look of confidence on his face, causing Marie to wonder if it were some strange sign of affirmation.

"Marie, what's this project Joey says you're working on for Mom?" Melissa asked.

Joe handed his cell to Marie. She went on to explain to Melissa about the Family Day Celebration at Magnolia Gardens in Charleston, and her plans to get as many of Sally and George's former foster kids to come, along with their family members.

"My gosh, I lost track of Mom and Dad some years back. I can't believe they're still alive."

Marie detested being the bearer of bad news, but it was unavoidable.

"Melissa, I'm sorry, but George passed away about three years ago. Sally is still alive, though she's not as sharp mentally as she used to be, which is why there's a sense of urgency about contacting her children about the Family Day Celebration. It's only a month away."

Melissa exploded with excitement. "Marie, count me in, and my husband and three kids. We're only an hour and a half away in Wilmington, North Carolina."

Melissa then gave Marie another trove of information.

"Marie, I've kept in touch with several others who lived with Sally and George. If you'd like, I'd be glad to call them and tell them about the Family Day Celebration and maybe even ask them to contact any other kids with whom they may have remained close."

Marie was positive a contact from a former foster child of Sally and George's would reap huge rewards. "Gosh, I'd really appreciate that, Melissa."

"Consider it done. Give me your contact information, and I'll get back to you as soon as I can. Also, the date of the celebration."

Marie gave Melissa her cell number and home address while Joe drew a line through her name.

"And Joey, you'll be surprised I married a Marine, Matt Fogerty. He's a captain stationed at the Marine Corps Weather Station in Wilmington."

Again that glorious laughter bellowed from the phone.

"Not a zero," groaned Joe, an uncomplimentary reference to the Marine's ranking of officers, O1 a First Lieutenant, O2 a Second Lieutenant, etc. etc.

"Yes, but he's a mustang, Joey. Surely that counts for something."

Now it was Joe's turn to laugh.

"Makes all the difference, little sister."

After trading a few "Do you remember when stories," Melissa said, "Joey, I got kids to put to bed. Keep in touch, big brother. I love you."

Smiling, Joe said, "Love you too, sis," and ended the call.

Marie curled her legs underneath her and laid her arm on the back of the couch. She had a quizzical look on her face which only acted to add an impish charm to her attractiveness. She blurted out, "What the heck is a mustang?"

"It means an officer who came up through the enlisted ranks. In the eyes of grunts in the field, he has more credibility than some Academy grad."

"And you were what, a grunt?" she asked, baffled by this strange language she was hearing.

Joe smiled at Marie's lack of knowledge about military parlance.

"O311 infantry," he explained with an unabashed sense of pride as only one who passed through the halls of the Marine Corps Infantry Training School at Camp Lejune could possess.

It was almost an afterthought. *What about Hank Connors?* Joe thought.

"Marie, there's a name in my old address book I'd like to call. It's someone I haven't talked with in years, but he played a pretty important part in my life when I was living with Mom and Dad. He might be one who had kept contact with other kids long before I came along."

"Call him. I'll straighten up these letters."

Marie made a neat stack of the letters. She took them to her desk where she bundled them up with a rubber band from a small tray used to keep paper clips and rubber bands, then snuggled up next to Joe. He began to flip through the pages of his address book.

"There he is," Joe said excitedly. "I sure hope he's still at this number."

Joe had started keeping phone numbers when he lived with the

Gunderson's, which accounted for the faded yellow pages and diffi-cult numbers to read. Joe squinted as he tapped the numbers into his phone. After several rings, a voice answered.

"Connors' residence," a young-sounding voice answered.

Joe pumped his fist. *Yeah!*

"May I speak with Hank Connors, please."

The young voice called out, "Dad, it's for you. Just a minute, sir."

"This is Hank Connors. To whom am I speaking?"

"Hank, I hope you remember me. I'm Joe Collier. I lived with Sally and George Gunderson from the time I was seven until I aged out."

There was a long pause and then a roar of laughter.

"Well I'll be dammed, Joey Collier. How the hell have you been son? It's been some time since we've last talked."

Elated that Connors remembered him, Joe proceeded to bring him up to date with his life; the Marine Corps, the police force. Then he returned to matters at hand and stated, "There's someone here I'd like you to talk with, Hank. It's about Mom."

The unmistakable sound of a throat tightening came over the phone.

"I saw Mom and Dad just after she broke her leg. Last I heard they had moved to some place in South Carolina."

"My friend can tell you all about it. Her name is Marie."

By force of habit, Joe tapped the speaker icon.

"Hello, Mr. Connors. This is Marie Gordon."

"Please, call me Hank. How can I help you?"

Marie went on to explain the Family Day Celebration and her desire to get as many of the foster children who had lived with the Gunderson's over the years to come.

"I take it you were a foster child with Sally and George?"

"Oh yeah! I was what you'd call the runt of the litter, a half black, half white child during a time when that type of blood mix was diffi-cult to adopt. With a teenage white mother who couldn't handle the circumstances and a black father not in the picture, foster care was the only option short of an orphanage."

Marie felt an immediate kinship for Connors and felt sorry he had not had the loving parents she had.

"Joe told me you were a real important part of his life when he lived with the Gunderson's."

"Do tell? That's not exactly how I remembered it," laughed Connors.

Joe grimaced as he was sure Connors was about to reveal more than Joe wanted.

"When I aged out, the Gunderson's let me live in a converted garage studio apartment while I went to community college, and later to Rutgers in return for helping with the smaller kids. I was like the play yard monitor, errand runner, homework helper, you name it. As I remember, Joey was quite the handful back then. He had lots of attitude, and that translated to lots of fights."

Joe rolled his eyes back as Marie stared at him as if it couldn't be true what she was hearing.

"It's hard to imagine him being such a bully, Mr. Connors. I mean, Hank," Marie said, while giving Joe that *so now I get the truth!* glance.

"Oh, Joey wasn't a bully. He was a protector. Let anyone at school tease him about being a foster kid or tease any of the other kids from the Gunderson's, they'd have to deal with Joey. He wasn't the biggest kid around, but he had the heart of a tiger and was tough as nails. Hey Joey, remember the time the cops had to come to the theater that Saturday afternoon after you handled business? I laughed about that for years."

Joe was mortified that Marie was hearing about his tumultuous years. He had learned from Connors that there's no benefit in striking out at others without sufficient provocation. The problem with young Joey Collier was that he had an abundance of provocation.

"Hank, do we really have to get into that?" Joe pleaded, remembering nothing comical about the incident.

Marie was of no help.

"Please, Hank, just this one story," Marie asked, while placing her finger on Joe's lips, then rested her head on his shoulders.

Resigned to the inevitable, Joe groaned, "I guess it's no use to argue."

Hank began. "I had dropped off Joey and three of kids at the theater for the Saturday afternoon matinee. I was at Rutgers at the time and needed to check some books out of the library. I was back just as the Matinee was over. There were three patrol cars and an ambulance parked out front. There were four teenagers sitting on the curb. A paramedic was tending to split lips, black eyes, and one possible broken arm. Joey was in the back of one of the patrol cars. When he saw me approaching the cops, he bowed his head, probably thought he was going to get an ass chewing. I told them I was from the foster home and asked what had happened. They said the police had received a call about a gang fight in front of the theater. Expecting to find a dozen or so thugs duking it out with clubs and knives, they found four beaten teens on the ground and Joey standing over them. His shirt was ripped in half. He had a bloody nose, a split lip and the makings of a great shiner. He was in a rage according to them. It seems they had started making fun of the kids all holding arms as they exited the theater. It was a safety thing Sally and George insisted on. When one pushed his way between the kids, Joey came to their defense. He got his lumps, but he gave better in return. To this day, he can't bend his nose to the right."

More laughter roared from the phone. Marie kissed him on his cheek and whispered, "My hero."

"Listen, Marie, I've got some old numbers. I'd be glad to contact them about the celebration. Count on my family being there along with our five kids. Joey, you take care."

With the call ended, Marie presented a much-exaggerated scowl of disapproval on her face. Joe pleaded defensively, "I told you I was a bit much to handle back then."

"And that's why you have the heart you do," Marie said. "So don't apologize to me."

She curled even closer to him, her arms around his neck. Time had passed much too fast, and Joe had another ten-hour shift in front of him. Better judgment, not desire, ruled the day.

"Marie, I've got to be going. My shift starts at six a.m."

There was a profound sense of belonging in his arms that Marie did not want to end, not this moment. She squeezed just a little tighter so his scent would last her through the night. He returned the gesture. Suddenly, Marie remembered.

"I almost forgot. Your leftover pizza for tomorrow's dinner."

Joe Collier took a gamble, though, in reality, it was a certainty.

"Any chance we could have it tomorrow night here?"

Perhaps fate had brought Marie and Joe together that fateful day at Le Petite. She didn't know, and at that moment she didn't care. Whether he knew it or not, he had embraced her heart. One of them had to take the first step. Pride would not be a barrier.

"I've got a better idea," she said. "How about we have breakfast tomorrow?"

He answered with a kiss and said, "Yes."

With her arms still around his neck, Marie titled her head back and with a sensuous smile of guile on her face asked, "Should I call you or nudge you?"

For a second, Collier was caught off guard by her boldness. In that thoughtful pause, Marie released her arms from around his neck and held out both hands, palms up.

"It's not a difficult question, Officer Collier," she jokingly said. Raising one palm, she said, "Call." Then raising the other hand, she said, "Nudge."

Putting his embarrassment aside, Collier replied with a bit of his own romantic repartee, "Yes."

Marie sealed their fate.

"Then nudge it is,"

22

CONVERGENCE

The schism between Daniel and Jane Kilgore had shrunk in recent months. He had made a conscious decision to acquiesce to many of Jane's requests. Simple agreements led to a restoration of refreshing pleasantries between him and Jane. For her part, she made sure she didn't ask Daniel to decide on anything too far in the future. When she realized Daniel was torn by the thought of what the future might hold should they decide to have children, she kept most discussions in the present tense. This change brought about the renewal of some old traditions.

The porch swing had once again become a welcome gathering spot at the end of the day for the two to enjoy a glass of chilled wine. As Jane was still working as the interim director at the Gardens, Daniel had become the principal homemaker, a task he found both enjoyable and somewhat irritating. Yard work, shopping, and cooking had become second nature to him. However, he seemed unable to grasp the intricacies of vacuuming behind furniture, dusting from the top down, and the folding of laundry. Their newest favorite wine was a reserve Windy Oaks Pinot, a small California winery club they had recently joined. Employing French oak casks for aging of their wines resulted in low tannins and a distinctly "oaky" bouquet. This made their wines a hit in the Kilgore household. Daniel had started work on a new manuscript and Jane had resumed her editorial duties as before. Jane felt he had developed an affinity for connecting unrelated situations with cleverly crafted transitions. He had also learned that with the use of descriptive language he could make the reader feel they were in the story, and not just reading the story.

"That is good," sighed Jane, as she slowly allowed the wine to move across her palate.

Daniel nodded as he twirled his glass, then held it up to allow the setting sun to accentuate the legs forming in his glass. Daniel allowed her head to rest on his shoulder, a contact he would have avoided not that long ago. He reciprocated by reaching out to hold her hand. In that moment of silence, they savored the fragile peace between the two that seemed to be growing.

"How's the manuscript coming along?" she asked. "You haven't given me any new pages in a week or so."

Daniel sipped his wine pensively.

"I know. I kind of have this writer's block. My main characters need to resolve a serious conflict that is threatening their relationship. I need to find a way for them to come together, but not like a Hallmark movie. I need a twist, something profound and unexpected to surprise the reader."

A sense of satisfaction began to swell in Jane. Reminiscent of their efforts with Daniel's first novel, they were working together again. Jane began to feel that initial attraction to Daniel all over again.

"I'm sure you'll come up with something," she said, then suddenly she remembered. "I almost forgot," Jane said, as she stood up and went into the house. Retrieving a small envelope from her purse, she returned to the porch swing.

"This is to us," she said. "It's our invitation to the Family Day Celebration at the Gardens next month."

As the former Director of Volunteer Services, Daniel knew the tremendous amount of work that went into such an event, and he was thankful that responsibility now fell on someone else's shoulders.

"I don't envy what Samantha has had to do, but knowing her, it's going to be great."

Hoping she had read his enthusiastic response as a desire to attend, Jane asked, "So you're going?"

"I won't miss it for the world, sweetheart."

Neither Daniel Kilgore nor his wife had any idea that their attendance at the Family Day Celebration would change their lives forever.

~

FROM ALL ALONG THE EAST COAST AND EXTENDING TO THE MIDWEST, A caravan of nearly thirty brothers and sisters (if not by blood, then certainly of the heart), began a pilgrimage to Charleston, South Carolina. Their destination was Magnolia Gardens. Their purpose was to see, perhaps for the last time, the woman who had loved them unconditionally, who had accepted them into her heart without reservation, the woman who each referred to as "Mom." One, the eldest of them all, would bring with him a gift, albeit an unintended one, but its recipient's heart would be moved in a direction long ago closed off.

~

FOR MARIE GORDON, THE PAST MONTH HAD BEEN AN EMOTIONAL whirlwind. Not that she hadn't thought about finding Mr. Right someday, but it never occurred to her that he would appear out of nowhere in a restaurant after overhearing a conversation between her and her aunt. That's what happens in the movies, but not in real life. However, it did happen, and Marie was now faced with the most anxiety-laden moment of her life, telling her mother and father.

Alice busied herself in the kitchen, humming the Beatle's song "And I Love Her." Her daughter's news that she wanted to talk about her work on Sally Gunderson, and "Oh, by the way, I'm bringing a friend over for dinner" sent Alice's imagination into overdrive. She hadn't even met this person, but Alice was already speculating it was a "he," a nice "he," she hoped. Alice knew her daughter. After college, Marie had dated some, but never felt the need or desire to bring anyone home. Marie referred to them as just a friend, nothing serious. Marie's words that she wanted her mother and father to meet her friend was code talk that the mysterious "he" was something special. Franklin had spent much of the day in the garage tinkering with the 1970 Ford Mustang he was restoring. The garage had become his sanctuary for the past several days to avoid Alice's constant maternal inquisitiveness and speculation about Marie's friend.

～

"THERE," MARIE SAID, POINTING TO HER PARENTS' HOME.

Joe pulled up to the curb, pausing to collect his thoughts about the impending conversation he knew he wanted to have with Marie's father. Joe seemed preoccupied with the purring of the original rebuilt Dodge motor as he let the engine idle for a moment. Marie felt his hesitation, sensing it had more to do with talking to her father than the sound of his prized engine.

"Joey, there's nothing to be nervous about," she said with a smile. "All I told Mom was I was bringing home a friend who has been helping me with the Family Day Celebration. It's no big deal," she said, hoping to soothe what she was sure was his anxiety over meeting her parents. She couldn't have been more wrong.

Collier rehearsed his words in his mind one more time, then said, "Absolutely. Let's go."

Franklin came out from under the hood of his truck to listen to the sound of the engine outside his house. *Sweet,* he thought, *somebody knows how to work on engines,* not realizing he was about to meet its driver.

Marie opened the door without knocking and announced, "Mom, Dad, we're here!"

The words "We're here" brought a weird kind of comfort to Collier. He was part of a "We." Not since his days with the Gundersons had he felt that way. An iron confidence replaced his trepidation.

"In the kitchen, sweetheart," hollered Alice, who tossed the kitchen towel hanging around her neck onto the counter. She straightened her dress as she rounded the kitchen corner to meet Marie's friend.

Marie gave her mother a hug, then turned to Joey.

"Mom, this is Joey Collier. He's the one I told you who was helping me with the Family Day Celebration."

Collier respectfully extended his hand to Alice and said, "It's very nice to meet you, Mrs. Gordon."

"Friends don't handshake, we hug," Alice replied, as she put her arms around Collier and gave him a big hug.

Looking around the living room, Marie asked, "Where's Daddy?"

"Where do you think he is when he wants to avoid me?" she laughed, pointing to the door leading into the garage.

Marie took Joe in hand and headed into the garage. Joe was impressed. A nicely painted gray concrete floor was spotless. A rolling toolbox alongside a creeper was next to an older model Ford Mustang, its front resting on two jack stands. Marie waited as her dad made the last of several adjustments to the rebuilt carburetor. What fascinated any man about working on cars and engines baffled her.

Marie hollered out, "Daddy!"

As the engine revved down to a decibel level the human ear could tolerate, Franklin Gordon looked up from underneath the Mustang's hood. His smile put Marie at ease, though Collier was certain he detected a waning of that smile when Franklin turned his attention to Collier.

"Hey, sweetheart. How about a hug for your father?"

"Daddy, please! Not with those overalls on," chided Marie comically. "Oil and grease stains just don't appeal to me."

Franklin unzipped the upper half of his mechanic's overalls, letting it fall to his waist."

"How about now?" he grinned.

"I love you, Daddy," she whispered to him as he hugged his only child.

After releasing Marie, Franklin turned his attention to the young man standing behind her.

"You must be the person helping Marie with her project?"

Trying to sound self-assured, Collier extended his right hand and responded, "Yes, Sir. I'm Joe Collier. It's nice to meet you."

Franklin liked the young man's grip. It was firm, but not overly aggressive, a trait the timid often use to compensate for their lack of confidence. Franklin was slightly taller than the young man, and he liked that. No doubt a macho thing to be able to look down on someone of lesser stature. There was something about the young man's eyes that intrigued Franklin. They exuded confidence, not intimidation, something Franklin would have expected from a young white man shaking hands with a taller, well-constructed black man. Collier had made a good first impression. Testing Collier's resolve a bit, Franklin said, "You don't mind the smell of oil and grease?" as their hands were clasped together.

An exasperated Marie groaned, "Daddy, don't!" Collier replied, "No, sir. I kinda like tinkering with engines myself. I've got a rebuilt '86 Dodge pickup."

"Is that what I heard outside?" Franklin asked, turning his head toward the open garage door.

Sensing there was a bit of curiosity in his voice, Collier asked, "Yes sir, would you like to see it?"

Feeling a bit like a fifth wheel, Marie said, "You two go. I'll help Mom with dinner."

As they approached the curb, Franklin noticed a disturbing sight. There was a noticeable bulge under the back of Collier's untucked shirt. Franklin had friends who were policemen, and it always bothered him that they felt the need to carry a concealed weapon when they were off duty. He hoped his question to Collier would be answered in the negative.

"Joe, I don't mean to pry, but are you carrying a weapon?"

Instinctively Collier reached behind him and gave the back of his shirt a tug, hoping his holster hadn't been exposed. He was wrong. Caught, he had no choice.

"Yes, sir, it is."

"Then I can assume you are a police officer?"

"Yes again, Mr. Franklin, Charleston PD."

"That will come as quite a surprise to my wife."

"I hope it's not a disappointment, Mr. Franklin, to either your wife or you. We all make different choices how to serve. This was mine."

Good answer, Franklin thought. He was taken with Collier's sense of commitment to a greater good. He then switched his focus to Collier's truck. Every bit of chrome was polished. A coat of Armor All gave the tires a special sheen. The two-tone white and red paint job had to be a custom job, Franklin thought. Collier went to the driver's door. He opened it and then popped the hood lever just under the steering wheel. Taking the rod clipped to the top of the radiator, Collier propped up the hood.

"A 318 bored out to 340, hydraulic flat tappet camshaft and lifter kite with a two-barrel carburetor."

The words flowed out of his mouth as if Collier was describing a great piece of art. Franklin rested his hands on the edge of the engine space, silently admiring the work of art before him. However, a lifetime Ford lover could not let Collier go unchallenged.

"I prefer Ford myself," said Franklin, with a hint of smugness in his voice. "Motor Trend rated them the best truck in America for the last ten years."

Forgetting his main purpose in meeting Marie's father, Collier let his own prejudice slip out.

"Hard to image their reasoning, sir. Doesn't Ford stand for fix or repair daily?"

Franklin cringed on the inside. How had he let that door open in front of a Dodge lover? But he did admire the young man's chutzpah. There seemed to be an instant kinship between two men that loved their vehicles. Franklin watched as Collier lowered the hood and then, using both hands gently pushed the hood shut.

"We do love our motors, don't we?" Franklin remarked with a smile as they walked back up the driveway and into the garage.

That smile would soon disappear with Collier's response.

"Among other things, yes, sir."

Franklin tried not to react to the possibilities racing through his mind. *What other things, a career, a home, another hobby? What was he referring to?* An intelligent man might ponder many possibilities. A father meeting his daughter's friend for the first time, the first time ever she had brought a friend home, would conclude only one thing. Normally a patient man, Franklin had no such virtue when it came to Marie's best interest, at least what Franklin considered to be in her best interest. The small refrigerator on the end of his workbench held a variety of sodas and bottled water. With his hand on the door, Franklin asked Collier, "Soda, water, or something stronger?"

"Water would be fine, sir," Collier replied.

"Water it is," said Franklin, as he handed Collier a cold H_2O. "I think I'll have something stronger," added Franklin. He took a small glass jar off the shelf above his workbench. It was labeled "Starter Fluid." From behind a large Chilton's Truck Manual, Franklin retrieved a bottle of Gray Goose Vodka. He poured two fingers of the fine vodka and then took out two ice cubes from the refrigerator's small freezer section. Raising his glass to Collier, Franklin chuckled, "What happens in the garage, stays in the garage." Leaning back against the workbench, Franklin let the Grey Goose move slowly down his throat. Collier removed the cap to his water bottle and took a healthy swig. Again, that subtle confidence that had impressed Franklin. There was no need to be subtle, Franklin thought.

"So, what other things do you love besides that '86 Dodge?"

Franklin Gordon had given Joe Collier the perfect opportunity, and he wasn't about to squander it.

"Mr. Franklin, I am in love with your daughter, and I would like your permission to marry her."

Franklin Gordon stood silent. He knew he would hear these words someday, but someday could have been years down the road, as far as he was concerned. There had been no time to get to know this young man, no time to learn about his family or anything else about him. A virtual stranger had just asked for his daughter's hand in marriage. Franklin Gordon was at a loss for words. The silence was killing Collier. Had he been too blunt? Should he have waited until Marie's mother and father got to know him? For Franklin Gordon, it was deja vu. Nearly thirty years ago, a young black man was going to meet his girlfriend's parents for the first time. They had fallen in love while in college, and she had only told her parents she was bringing a friend home. If the color of his skin hadn't been enough of a shock, blurting out at the dinner table that he was in love with this man's daughter and wanted to marry her could have started WW III. But the girl's parents were more tolerant and open-minded than the times allowed and being cognizant of the power of the human heart, they welcomed the young man into their family. Franklin took another sip of his hidden treasure and walked the two or three steps to face Collier. A smile came over his face.

"Should I call you Joseph or Joe?"

"I like to go by Joey to my friends, sir."

"Then Joey it is, and since I'm going to be more than a friend, it's Franklin, not sir."

Franklin stepped out of his overalls. He emptied the glass of his treasured Grey Goose and placed it behind the Chilton Manual.

"Follow me," he said.

Franklin led Collier up the small flight of stairs and opened the door leading into the kitchen.

"Well, have you two gotten to know each other?" asked Alice.

"As a matter of fact, we have. Joey and I have an announcement."

Hearing her father refer to him as Joey put Marie into a tailspin. She turned around to face them.

"Daddy, what are you saying?"

The smile on Franklin's face said it all.

"I'm saying, yes."

23

DANIEL'S TRANSFORMATION

The very private wedding ceremony of Madeline Orsini and Alan Pinafore had all the tapestry of a royal wedding. Pinafore had invited half a dozen of his fellow department heads, all of whom wore dress uniforms with enough gold braids on their coat cuffs to be captains or admirals. The wives were attired in smartly flowered spring dresses. A few wore hats as if they were attending the Kentucky Derby. Pinafore had decided to stay with a traditional black tuxedo. A dress uniform with the customary adornments of medals and ribbons seemed unnecessary accouterments as far as Pinafore was concerned. He had enough reminders of his service without a wedding album showing him dressed in a uniform he hadn't worn in over twenty-five years. More importantly, after all Maddy had been through in her struggles to get information from the Navy as to his status, wedding pictures with him in uniform would only contaminate what should be precious memories.

◦

"I CAN'T TELL YOU HOW MUCH I VALUE EVERYTHING YOU'VE DONE, ANDY, I could have never pulled this off on my own," said the very appreciative older brother.

Andy smiled as he jokingly scolded Eddy, "Tilt your head back, or I'll never get this bow tie clipped on."

Eddy wondered if a similar type banter was taking place in the spare bedroom where Kristin Andrews was helping Maddy dress for her special day.

"I need to check on a couple of things then I'll be right back, Eddy," said Andy, who was now suffering from pre-ceremonial sweats. With his computer expertise, Andy had pre-staged several electronic cameras to record the event. He had even prepared a playlist of love songs that spoke to the union that was about to take place.

∾

ANDY ORSINI'S BACK YARD WAS IN STARK CONTRAST TO THE SPARSELY planted front yard. He definitely had the eye of a landscape architect. Stepping out of the house through double French doors onto a stamped patio of gray cement, one was greeted with a back yard off the cover of *Better Homes and Gardens*. A seven-foot-high wall of palomino paving stones with contrasting layers of colored concrete lined the twenty by forty-foot back yard. The right edge of the patio was lined with Andy's homegrown herbs, basil, rosemary, thyme, oregano, and turmeric. The left side of the patio was Andy's barbecue. Being somewhat of a purist, he had built a barbecue out of leftover palomino paving stones. He used only wood with his favorite applewood chips for smoking. He had a neighbor, who was a welder, create a firebox of quarter-inch flat steel with a hand crank to raise and lower the grill, and a hood of similar material hinged on the back. In the far left corner of the yard was a ten-foot-high, ten-foot-wide gazebo normally used for outdoor eating, but today it would be where Alan's and Madeline's wedding vows would be exchanged. The bridal path was lined with white plastic chains looped between shepherd hook stakes that had been driven into the lawn. Kentucky bluegrass seeds had produced a rich dark green lawn. The entire back yard wall was covered with trellises of blossoming jasmine emanating an almost overwhelming aroma.

~

HURRIEDLY TAKING THE STAIRS TWO AT A TIME, ANDY HASTENED TO HIS brother's room and opened the door.

"Ok, cuz, it's time."

Edward Orsini had always been the epitome of confidence, maybe even a little arrogant at time, what with being a Seal and all that. But the Edward Orsini standing in front of a full-length mirror was anything but that. His eyes darted continuously at the image in the mirror, carefully assessing his appearance for anything out of place, or not in perfect alignment. Satisfied his appearance was as good as it could be, Eddy turned to his brother.

"You know the irony of this day, Andy?" he said.

"Irony is not the word I would use to describe your wedding day." reasoned his younger brother.

"Take a seat," said Eddy.

With Andy seated on the corner of the bed, Eddy rested on a leather-lined oak chest.

"From the moment I met Maddy, I knew I wanted to marry her. I knew I wanted a life with her. After the crash, when I realized what I would look like forever and the physical limitations I would have to live with, marriage to Maddy was the last thing I could have imagined. She deserved a full man, and I didn't think I measured up to that. I should have trusted her, Andy, I should have trusted her."

His words were followed by a steady stream of tears, tears caused by shame and exhilaration. Years of emotional denial crumbled under the weight of the enormity of this moment.

"Here. You need this more than me," replied Andy, handing his brother a handkerchief.

After stemming the flow of emotionality, Eddy gave the handkerchief back to him.

With a deep breath, he resolutely announced, "Andy, I'm the luckiest man on the face of the earth."

Andy was never prouder of his older cousin. He went to the window, looking down onto the backyard. Those in attendance were mingling about, sampling the hors d'oeuvres and wine provided by Andy's catering friend.

"I think it's time to join our friends before Maddy makes her entrance.

Eddy followed Andy down the stairs and into the back yard. After greeting his guests, Eddy assumed his position under the gazebo.

∾

LOOKING OUT THE BEDROOM WINDOW, KRISTIN COULD SEE EDDY mingling with the guests.

"Maddy, I think it's time for your grand entrance."

Maddy sat on a cushioned stool staring into the gold-lined mirror in the guest bedroom's bathroom.

"Kristin, I'm as nervous as if the past twenty-five years had never happened and I'm about to walk down the aisle of Saint Patrick's Church on my father's arm."

Sensing tears were about come, Kristin walked to Maddie's side and took a tissue from a box on the marble counter. Handing Maddie the tissue, she said, "That wannabe tear will destroy that perfect make-up. Don't you dare let that happen!" The comically delivered chide cause both women to laugh.

Maddy bowed her head, and in the silence, Kristin wondered if Maddy was having any misgivings.

"Everything's okay, isn't it?" she asked.

Maddy pivoted on her stool. Looking up to Kristin, she said, "I gave up on ever finding out what had happened to him, but I never gave up on loving him, or on having a life together. For years I heard his voice when he wasn't there. I smelled his cologne in my solitude. He touched my heart in ways I could never describe. Now, we'll be together in the present and the future."

"Okay, give me that tissue box," said Kristin, now fighting her own battle to stem a flood of tears. "You've got it all now, kiddo," she replied.

Maddy lamented, "I'm ashamed to say, I want more, Kristin. I want the rest of our dream."

No one knew better than Kristin Andrews the pain of dreams left unfulfilled, and no one could have ever imagined how the fulfillment of Maddy's dream would come at such a tragic cost.

∾

THE DRIVE HOME FROM THE PRIVATE WEDDING CEREMONY OF MADELINE Orsini and Alan Pinafore at Alan's brother's home in Beaufort gave rise to a renewal of old emotions between Daniel and Jane Kilgore. The less traveled Interstate 13 from Beaufort to Charleston took Daniel and Jane through miles of rolling Carolina countryside, where blooming red and white Dogwood trees seemed to line every road. Magenta colored wisteria clumps hung from the arched gateways of rural country homes, some hardly more than shacks. Always there was the sweetness of blossoming Magnolia trees like a floral perfume that filled their lungs with every breath. Among this floral beauty, Daniel marveled at the peach and apple orchards that seemed to appear out of nowhere among the corn and wheat fields that quilted the countryside. Just past what looked to be a homemade road sign reading, "Colton population 8." Daniel saw a roadside stand advertising "Peaches and ice-cold sweet tea."

"Care for something to drink?" asked Daniel, who had grown thirsty from the afternoon heat.

Jane, who had been lost in the idyllic imagery of Madeline in her white wedding gown, and Alan, or Eddie as Maddy called him, in his black tuxedo, straightened herself in her seat and replied, "I'd love something, and I need to stretch my legs."

Daniel slowed to a snail's pace as he turned off the county road onto the dirt turnout where the unusually constructed stand stood. Centuries of water currents from flooding rivers and ocean storms had turned the surface soil into a fine powder when dry. An unavoidable cloud of the powdered soil rose slowly into the air and descended back to earth at an equally slow rate of speed. The stand consisted of a large blue tarp stretched between two ten-foot step ladders in the front corners and nailed to two stacks of wooden pallets in the back corners. A two by eight plank resting on the rungs of the two ladders served as a table to display rows of boxes of freshly picked peaches, or so the sign on the plank said. Sitting behind the plank on a five-gallon bucket turned upside down was a young African American boy who appeared to be about twelve years old. He wore faded jean overalls embroidered with the letters "TC" on the bib over a Clemson University t-shirt along with an orange cap with the Clemson "C" above the bill. As he and Jane approached, the boy stood up and through an infectious smile politely inquired, "Care for some fresh picked peaches, Ma'am?"

"I think I'll just have one of those cold sweet teas you advertise."

Smiling, the boy reached into an ice chest beside the table. He pulled out a small Mason jar filled with that dark brew so revered in the South.

"How about you, Sir, care for a sweet tea?"

Glancing at the letters on the boy's overalls, Daniel said, "You know, TC, that is your name isn't it, how about a couple of boxes of those freshly picked peaches and throw in a sweet tea for good measure."

Beaming like he had made the sale of the day, TC jumped up. His bare feet created their own dust cloud. He handed Daniel two plastic boxes of peaches then returned to the ice chest to retrieve another Mason jar of tea. By four in the afternoon, the setting sun had created a shaded area to the right of the tarp. Daniel was beginning to admire the young boy's ingenuity. TC had created a sitting area by placing a piece of plywood atop several plastic buckets. There were two molded plastic chairs, one with broken slats on the back, next to the makeshift table.

"Can we sit over there, TC?" Jane asked, referring to the shaded area with its table and chairs.

"Oh, yes, Ma'am. Let me wipe the chairs off first, this dust covers everything," said their attentive young host. Using a bright orange towel that Daniel immediately recognized as a Clemson sports item, TC soon had the chairs clean and ready for use.

As Daniel and Jane sat down, they toasted each other with their quaint Mason jars of tea.

"To us," Daniel said.

"Yes," replied Jane.

Weddings may sometimes cause people to envy the road ahead for the newlyweds, as they reflect on their own lives together. However, Madeline and Pinafore were hardly young or naive, nor were Daniel and Jane when they married.

Jane mused aloud, "They deserve so much happiness after what has happened between them."

Daniel sipped his sweet tea before replying, "They've both had a ton of life experiences which should help them get through those petty, annoying situations that will certainly arise."

Jane reflected over the past months of very strained times between her and Daniel before responding. She dared not risk raising the subject again, but still wanted to know.

"Is that what got us through our tough times?"

There had never been an explicit solution to the tension that had existed between the two over having another child, only a renewed effort to focus more on what was good in their marriage than a seemingly impassable barrier. Perhaps this moment provided such an opportunity. He reached out to hold her hand.

"Our marriage is filled with beautiful memories, and God willing, many more to come. No one memory, however tragic, should or will ever push us apart again."

The rush of emotion caused Jane to begin to tightly squeeze Daniel's hand.

"How...," she tried to continue before Daniel interrupted her, suspecting what she was going to ask.

"I never read a book or saw a movie with a tragic ending that didn't have parts of happiness and joy, the abrupt end to which is why the ending is so tragic. To focus on the ending is to ignore all the happiness and joy that made the ending so heart-wrenchingly tragic in the first place. I did that, and I'll never do it again."

Noticing the woman was crying, TC stopped tossing his football in the air and hurried to the table.

"Is there something wrong with the tea, Ma'am?"

His worry was obvious, and Jane was touched by his concern.

"No, TC," responded Jane, as she daintily dabbed at the flowing tears with a lace handkerchief she had retrieved from her clutch bag. "My husband just told me a wonderful story, and I'm a sucker when it comes to such things."

Daniel saw an opportunity to change subjects.

"So, what do the letters TC stand for?"

Cradling the football under his arms, the boy smiled and replied, "Thomas Colton, sir."

Remembering the sign reading "Colton, population eight," Daniel chuckled aloud, "You wouldn't have anything to do with that sign back the road apiece?"

Grinning that his clever secret had been discovered, TC replied, "Yes, sir, I did. There's eight in our family counting Mamma and Daddy, and I thought I could get more customers if people thought we was a real town."

"You're quite the entrepreneur, Thomas Colton," laughed Daniel.

"Yes, sir. I guess," replied Colton, clearly not sure what exactly he had been called.

Daniel sympathized with the boy's obvious lack of vocabulary and so as to not add to any further embarrassment, asked more simplified questions.

"I'm guessing from your t-shirt and cap that you're a Clemson fan?"

Again, the politeness.

"Yes, sir," he answered with a smile that couldn't spread any wider across his face. "I'm gonna play football there someday."

"You know I went to school there, TC. Let's see what kind of hands you have, said Daniel, as he rose to his feet.

TC tossed Daniel the ball. There was a large grassy area directly behind the makeshift fruit stand that TC's family used as a crop break between rows of peach trees. It was probably fifty yards deep. TC trotted out, looking backward to Daniel, who lofted a soft pass to the boy. The boy's long arms reached up and snagged the ball that Daniel had clearly thought he had overthrown.

"Nice catch!" Daniel shouted.

TC loped back to Daniel. "Can we do that again?" he asked.

Daniel nodded, then hollered. "Go."

This time TC took off in a sprint, causing Daniel to test the strength of an arm that hadn't done so since he had played catch with his son, Greg, nearly thirty-five years ago. Some sort of athletic instinct caused TC to look over his shoulder at just the right moment, and without breaking stride, he reached up and pulled in the mightily thrown football. The boy ran a bit farther and after crossing an imaginary goal line did an obviously choreographed celebratory touchdown dance. When he got back to Daniel, he said, "I can catch 'em farther, Mister."

Gently rubbing the football as if to draw some magic power from it, Daniel said, "Let's see what this old arm has left. Run to that old wheel barrel then cut left," grinned Daniel.

TC looked to the field and saw the old wheel barrel piled full of weeds he had promised his mother to empty by days end. He nodded.

"On Red," ordered the aged wannabe quarterback.

TC took his stance while Daniel looked left, then right to assess the make-believe defensive rush. He barked out, "Green, green, Red!"

The boy's high-octane speed kicked in while Daniel dropped back, spinning to avoid the rush of a defensive end, then set his feet and lofted a high pass into the air. Barely slowing down, TC planted his right foot and cut sharply to his left when he got to the wheel barrel. He had taken about four strides when the pass floated down into his outstretched hands. The moment he threw the pass, Daniel felt a sharp twinge in his throwing shoulder, the price for overtaxing an arm whose only test of strength had been a golf club in recent years. On his return to his quarterback, TC found Daniel rubbing his right shoulder, Daniel offered an excuse most men loathe to acknowledge, "TC, I don't have any more throws like that left in this old arm. How about we stick with short passes?"

Pleased to have someone throw to him besides his older brothers, TC readily agreed. For the next half hour or so, TC ran made up pass routes, while Daniel, pretending to avoid the rush of more imaginary defensive linemen, deftly threw passes that TC easily caught. There was no hiding his delight in throwing the ball to TC, and TC reveled in the suggestions and compliments Daniel gave him. No one was happier than Jane as she watched gleeful banter between Daniel and the boy. There was a joy in Daniel's expressions that she had never seen. He was reconnecting to a time in his past of special father-son moments. Daniel's last few passes were noticeably short of their mark and a clue that perhaps it was time to quit.

"TC, you worked this old guy pretty good. How about we stop now?"

Though disappointed, TC reluctantly agreed. The boy headed over to his ice chest and withdrew two jars of sweet tea. He handed one to Daniel and the other to Jane, who had already emptied her first jar.

"Aren't you going to have one, TC?" Jane asked.

"Oh, no Ma'am. I'm savin' the money I make from selling these peaches and tea to help pay for college." There was a sound of prideful self-reliance in the boy's tone.

Jane glanced at Daniel, who had already reached the same conclusion. The gleam in Daniel's eyes indicated his agreement.

"Then Daniel and I would like to help you," replied Jane.

She got up and walked over to the boxes of peaches and counted a total of twenty-five baskets, then glanced down at the ice chest TC had absentmindedly left open. About a dozen Mason jars rested on a shallow bed of ice cubes dangerously close to being completely melted. The baskets were priced at three dollars a box while a paper sign taped to the lid of the ice chest read, "Sweet tea-fifty cents each."

She returned to the table and opened her clutch bag, containing a small makeup mirror and lipstick. Jane had minimal cash, three twenties. Taking them out, she asked Daniel, "Do you have a couple of twenties?"

Fortunately for the boy, Daniel had stopped at an ATM on the way to the wedding for just such an emergency. He took out his wallet and retrieved two crisp twenty-dollar bills. Taking the additional cash, Jane turned to TC, and handing him the money said, "We'd like to buy all the peach baskets and jars of sweet tea you've got left."

TC's eyes appeared as big as saucers. He was used to being paid with one-dollar bills, and whatever assortment of spare change could be found in car consoles or empty cup holders.

"Are you serious, Ma'am? Mamma won't believe me when I tell her!" He shouted out in surprise.

"Yes, we're serious, TC, but there's a favor we'd like to ask," responded Daniel.

"Anything sir, anything at all, you just ask TC!"

The anticipation of being able to return such a favor was overwhelming as TC jumped to his feet.

"We don't have room in our car for all those baskets and jars, so would you mind keeping them? Maybe even sell them again to some lucky customer?"

Overcome with emotion at the implication of Daniel's words, TC used the back of his hand to wipe away the tears before they flowed down his cheeks. Some parts of rural South Carolina had been resistant to the advancements in race relations, preferring to remain connected to some vestige of the Reconstruction Era where the separation of the races was maintained wherever possible. The urge to hug the boy was more than Jane's emotional state could handle. She drew TC to her and hugged him. Emotionally charged by this enormous act of goodness, he returned the gesture. Lest he see her crying, she held on to him until Daniel caught her signaling to get her clutch bag containing a small lace handkerchief.

"You are a special young man, TC," Jane replied, still struggling to control her emotions.

"You got to take at least one or two baskets, Ma'am," TC pleaded, his adolescent sense of manhood resisting a complete acquiescence to their act of charity.

"Fine," smiled Daniel, as he reached out and shook TC's hand.

Daniel and Jane sat mostly silent on the way home. His time with TC allowed Daniel to revisit his memories with his own son without rancor or resentment. Jane permitted herself to speculate on a long-held dream of her own.

24

FAMILY DAY

The staff at Magnolia Gardens was abuzz with the planning for the Family Day Celebration. Molly McGuire, Head of Culinary Operations, was working in tandem with Belle Deloume, owner of The Inferno, (Charleston's finest southern food restaurant), on planning the menu and who would prepare what dishes. With the responsibilities of daily meals, Molly quickly deferred to Belle when she offered to prepare the entrees and side dishes. That would leave Molly with only having to worry about the appetizers and desserts. Samantha Callahan, Daniel's replacement as Director of Volunteer Services, had sent out mailers to the families notifying them of nearby motels and hotels. She had secured the services of a local catering company to provide tables, chairs, and a dozen white canopy tents, as several hundred guests were expected for the two-day celebration. The catering crew had staked out and assembled half a dozen twenty by sixty canopy tents with interlocking rubber panels for flooring. Bouquets of 'Cajun Blue' Scaevola in shallow copper bowls were centered on four rows of five-foot round tables with white tablecloths. Prepared place settings of ruby red napkins and silver utensils were evenly spaced around every table. Water goblets and wine glasses were turned upside down opposite each place setting. Six comfortably padded folding chairs rimmed each table. Around the pipe frame of each canopy hung baskets of Bonita Shea Begonias.

With Jane's approval as the acting Executive Director, Samantha undertook a two-month-long major landscaping do-over. Along the edges of the pergola boarding the large patio hung baskets of cherry pink Mandevilla Vogues. The white four clover blossoms were intermixed with Princess Blush Verbenas with purple centers. Steel shepherd crooks with scarlet "Stars and Stripes" patio baskets hanging in the upward curve attracted hummingbirds in aerial combat over the nectar in the blooms. Swarms of butterflies kept a safe distance from the waring hummingbirds, waiting for a chance to rest on the hanging blossoms.

~

THE ANXIETY OF THOSE PREPARING FOR THE FESTIVE EVENT PALED IN comparison to the emotional charge Sally Gunderson's foster children felt after hearing from Joe Collier and then receiving their invitations to the Family Day Celebration. Some twenty Gunderson charges were coming. The irony was some would not even know each other as their time with George and Sally consisted of a few years' time spanning nearly forty-five years. For others, it was like a family reunion. Common to all, however, was the love and support George and Sally Gunderson had given them.

~

THE RANK OF DETECTIVE SERGEANT DID NOT IMPRESS SAMANTHA Callahan, who was busily ordering her newly promoted husband, Mike, around like an abused manservant. He was headed to the office to pick up some fliers for the arriving guests when Samantha called out, "And don't forget to check at the desk about those sparkling lights. I need them hung around the edges of the canopies."

The harried husband, without turning around, waved in acknowledgment, keeping his frustration out of sight of his momentarily annoying but still loving wife. He couldn't wait for someone he knew to show up, hoping his presence would ease the burden of being a mere lackey.

~

Marie balanced a stack of paperwork on her lap as Joe maneuvered his truck through unusually slow traffic caused by a burst water main.

"Got everything?" he asked his fiancé.

Marie placed the papers in her valise and leaned back against the headrest.

"I'm exhausted. All I have had to do was send out the invitations, confirm Sally's kids arrived, and make sure they're all seated in the same area. I can't imagine how Samantha's handled everything she had on her plate without losing her mind."

"Undoubtedly, she has an underappreciated assistant willing to subjugate himself to her every wish," Joe said, grinning to himself about a connection of which Marie had no knowledge.

Marie reached over and gently tugged on Joe's ear.

"Aren't you the profound one, and what makes you think her assistant is a guy?"

"Just call it a cop's intuition," smiled Joe.

"Oh, please!" Marie muttered in mock disdain.

Joe drove slowly up Magnolia Lane. The grounds crew had lined the entrance road to the Gardens with white containers of the South Carolina state flower, yellow jasmine. Marie had insisted they get there hours in advance of the time stated in the invitations for the start of the festivities.

"Over there," said Marie, pointing to a sign reading, "Staff Parking Only."

As Marie exited Joe's truck, she asked, "Can you get that package in the back? Samantha asked me to pick it up at Staples."

"Your wish is my command," replied Joe, as he opened the rear door to the bench seat.

Holding the package under one arm and Marie's arm under his other arm, the two headed to the entrance doors. Headed down the hallway, Marie's mind was awhirl with expectations of the reunion of the Gunderson's foster children with Sally. Joe was hoping for a special moment along with Marie, but that did not look likely given the enormity of the day's event. Mike Callahan saw Jane Kilgore standing at the front desk. Before he could say anything, a voice called out, "Semper Fi, Mike, working a little overtime?" Mike turned to see his fellow cop, and fellow Marine, Joe Collier, walking down the hallway, a package under one arm and a beautiful young woman on the other.

"Not really, just running an errand for the boss. Where would she be without this cabana boy to boss around?"

Ignoring his friend, Callahan extended his hand to Marie.

"Hi, I'm Mike Callahan. I work with Joey. You must be Marie. I've heard plenty about you."

Marie shook his hand. Then she remembered Joey's comment about a cop's intuition telling him Samantha's helper had to be a man. Scowling at him in mock anger, Marie muttered, "A cop's intuition, uh?"

Sheepishly, Joey tilted his head and shrugged his shoulders, an admission of failing to notice Marie of his relationship with Mike Callahan.

"What exactly did you tell him about me?" Marie queried.

"Everything," Joey said, with sufficient confidence that Marie would not sense another secret was being kept from her, which it was.

Satisfied she was getting the truth, Marie asked Callahan where she could find Samantha. There were some last-minute details she wanted to go over with her.

"I left her on the patio talking with the caterer," Mike answered.

"Thanks. Joey, I need you to come with me in case I need something," Marie said with enough authority in her voice to let him know this was more a command than a request.

"Look Marie, I've got to check with the desk about some sparkling lights she wants hung on the canopies. Maybe you could let Joey help me?"

"If I need him, I'll know where to find him, just don't get into any trouble," she replied with a comical admonishment.

Like two puppies eager to get outside, Mike and Joey headed to the desk. Through the open double French doors leading to the patio, Marie saw Samantha with the caterer and headed in their direction. It took the boys an hour and a half to get the sparkling lights hung around the six extra-large canopy tents.

"Now what?" asked Joey.

"Let's check in with HQ before we bug out."

Joey and Mike walked up to the patio where Samantha and Marie had papers spread out over the entire surface of a large table.

"My God, Samantha, your layout for this is unbelievably beautiful!" said an admiring Marie.

The new landscaping provided a kaleidoscope of colors the envy of works by Renoir or Van Gogh. Samantha took a break from her paperwork review with Marie and responded, "A lot of people worked very hard to make this happen." She said it modestly, but with a "Yes, I did," glow on her face.

"Wait until Jane sees how this turned out," Marie said excitedly.

Glancing at her watch, Samantha said, "She and Daniel should be arriving soon. She texted me they would be here around eight." Reminded of the pamphlets Marie had made with a diagram of the grounds of the visitors and the ones Samantha had prepared which described the activities of the day, Samantha said, "Would you and Joe take our pamphlets to the staff at the entrance door? I want them available for any early arrivals."

If his growling stomach needed another reminder, Mike Callahan seized the moment. "We'll take care of that."

Once inside the building, Joey announced, "I sure wish we could get a cup of coffee and something to munch on."

"Great minds think alike," smiled the scheming Callahan.

Unaware of Mike's plan, but with the anticipation it will lead to good things, Joey dutifully followed Mike into the dining room and then into the kitchen. The joyful sound of Belle Deloume calling out directions to the expanded kitchen staff drew Mike like a beacon.

"Belle, any chance we could get a couple of those fresh beignets and some coffee?"

The rotund legend of Southern cuisine belted out her answer.

"Darlin, for you two boys, you ask Belle for anythin'!"

Belle placed two paper towels on the stainless steel kitchen table. Using tongs, she deftly placed two beignets, fresh out of the fryer, on a rack and then sprinkled them with powdered sugar. After filling two Styrofoam cups with hot coffee, Belle used her tongs to move the hot beignets from the rack to the paper towels.

"You two enjoy and don't smear dat powda sugar on your clothes, ya hear!"

Hoping to avoid detection of the prying eyes of other staff, Mike and Joe exited the back door of the kitchen and made their way around the edge of the building to a cluster of Gold Mop Cypresses. Gently tapping their beignets to remove any excess powdered sugar, they took their first bite. It might have been the warmth of the raspberry filling, or the honey taste of the phyllo dough Belle used, either way they groaned in delight as they went from first bite to final swallow in about five seconds. The hot coffee helped fight off the chill of the high 50's mid-morning temperature. After consuming their ill-gotten snacks, Joey headed off to check the parking signs Marie had made designating where visitors for each resident should park. She had a pretty good idea based on the number of positive responses the number of parking slots to reserve for each resident. Mike checked in with the two volunteer staff at the door, making sure he gave them the pamphlets with the itinerary for the next two days. As he did, he noticed a single car slowly making its way up the winding driveway. As they got near, he recognized Daniel and Jane Kilgore.

He dutifully handed them a pamphlet remaking, "Good to see you two."

"A little cool out, isn't it?" responded Daniel, as he took the pamphlet and handed it to Jane.

"Another hour and it will warm up, Daniel. See you on the inside."

Jane leaned over toward the driver's window and thanked Mike for his help. Daniel proceeded to the Executive Director's parking slot.

When Mike redirected his attention to the driveway, he saw a long slow-moving caravan of cars headed up the driveway. He counted nearly thirty cars in all. Looking at his watch he thought, *these people are really early.* Jane headed into the building, leaving Daniel to chit-chat with Mike. He too was surprised by the large number of early arrivals. As the lead car got to the entrance, a large man, easily six-foot-four and not an ounce south of two hundred and forty pounds emerged.

Eying the man quizzically, Mike exclaimed, "Can I help you, sir?"

"Yes, my name is Hank Connors. I'm with a group to see Sally Gunderson. Can you tell me where we should park?"

"Certainly, Mr. Connors," replied Mike. "Your group is a little on the early side," he noted.

"Sally and George Gunderson weren't just any parents," replied Connors, "and their family even more so."

Connors' eyes carefully scanned the expansive property that laid before him.

Mike quickly glanced at the Marie inspired parking diagram. He stated, "Follow this road to the back of the facility. There's a gravel area normally used for the grounds crew to park their vehicles. It's been set aside specifically for your group."

Connors stared down the road, wondering logistically how the group would navigate a twisted road lined with dense shrubbery, what with any number of small children in tow, and a trove of gifts.

Sensing his apprehension, Daniel added, "Don't worry about the distance. I'll guide you."

"I'd really appreciate that," smiled Connors. His readiness to smile had the effect of offsetting his imposing physical presence.

"Then follow me, Mr. Connors," Daniel replied. He had immediately been taken with the command presence of Connors, hence the use of Mister. Yet Connors himself was not one to stand on formality.

"Please, call me Hank," came the humble reply.

"Hank it is," answered Daniel, as he headed off down the road with the Gunderson caravan inching its way behind him.

Once all the vehicles had been parked, Daniel announced to the group that they would follow Joe up the road to a gathering point in front of the main facility. To many of the youngest children, this was a new and inviting area that deserved exploration. Containing the anxious group was akin to the folly of attempting to herding cats.

"We'd better get this done quick, or I'll be making a 911 call for some missing children," joked Connors.

"Then let's load 'em up, wagon master!"

That elicited a hardy laugh from Connors reminiscent of Ward Bond in the fifties tv series "Wagon Master."

Joe Collier hollered out for everyone to follow him. Slowly, a long line began to move up the road. There was an excitement in the air as adults anticipated seeing the woman they had called Mother when they were her foster children, igniting a flood of emotions. Some of the children, now older teenagers, quizzed aloud, "I hope Gramma remembers me." Daniel and Hank Connors held back until the last of the families headed up the road. During this time, Daniel learned a bit of Hank Connors' background. He and his wife Elena had five children, two sons in high school, George Jr. a senior and Liam a junior. They were followed by three girls, Ashley age five, Courtney age three, and the youngest Sally, age two. Following college, Connors played briefly with the NFL New York Jets before a knee injury ended his career. Thanks to a degree in finance from Rutgers University, Connors did quite well in the commercial real estate market. What surprised Kilgore however, were the ages of Connor's three girls. Ashley was just five, Courtney three, and Sally, named after the matriarch of the Gunderson clan, was barely two years old.

Even with their early arrival, the group of well over a hundred individuals would present a logistical nightmare if they were not processed through quickly. Having been thoroughly briefed by Marie on the sign-in process, Joey announced, "Folks, if you'll follow me, please have your invitation in hand." At that announcement, the crowd moved slowly forward, no telling how many purses and jackets were being quickly rifled through to find invitations. This seemingly endless procession of visitors caught the attention of staff who wondered if there weren't some unknown celebrity residing at the Gardens. After checking in at the visitor counter, Marie, who was standing at the opened double French doors, said to Hank Connors who was in the lead, "Let me show you where to go, Mr. Connors."

Stepping out onto the patio, Connors was in awe at the preparations that had been made for the Family Day Celebration. The massive floral display was akin to looking at a three-dimensional version of Irises by Van Gogh. The detailed pathways leading to the canopy tents were lined with yellow plastic chains reminiscent of something out of the Wizard of Oz. The pearl canopy tents edged with sparkling lights glistened like beacons calling for Dorothy. An entire canopy had been devoted just to Sally's family. Standing at the front of their tent, Marie said, "There are water pitchers and plastic cups on each table. When the staff learned oatmeal chocolate chip cookies were Sally's favorite, they worked overtime to have plenty of them available. They're on the table to your left along with a variety of bottled waters in case plain tap water isn't to your taste. I've got to get back to the others, so please make yourself at home."

As the families seated themselves, Connors made his way to each table, his middle girl, contently resting in his arms. As the oldest child of Sally and George in attendance, Hank Connors enjoyed his own special reunion with other foster children he remembered. Working his way from table to table, Hank Connors felt more than ever that he and his wife had made the right decision in raising foster children, following in the path of his foster parents, George and Sally Gunderson. When Hank explained the reason for their decision to him, Daniel Kilgore's life would be changed forever. For well over an hour, there were conversations that started with, "Remember when..." and progressed to "Do you ever hear from..." Sometimes the answer was in the affirmative, sometimes sadly with a silent shaking of the head. The trading of memories, addresses, and introductions of family members brought a level of gaiety and laughter not often seen at the Gardens in view of the age and mental awareness of its residents. With the noise of more arrivals, Connors realized he needed to ask Marie something. Seeing her at the edge of the patio directing other families, he walked in her direction. Catching her in a rare moment alone, he asked, "Marie, is there any chance I could see Sally alone? I want to prepare her for the amount of family that are here."

Marie didn't need long to consider that possibility and quickly responded, "Good idea."

25

EMERGING EPIPHANY

T hanks to a treatment drug named Aducanumab prescribed by Sally Gunderson's doctor, symptoms of her dementia had been greatly reduced over the past few months. Periods of recollection took less prompting and seemed to last much longer, even to the point where associative memories also came to mind. Sally also seemed more inquisitive as to the goings-on around her. With the announcement of the Family Day Celebration, Sally had taken to looking through a family album. As her frail fingers lined with raised blood vessels traced over the photos, a smile spread across her aged face. Recognition was there though not completely connected with the past. Sometimes the pause was longer as Sally focused more intently, then suddenly she would blurt out a name.

~

CONNORS ATTEMPTED TO PASS OFF HIS THREE-YEAR-OLD, COURTNEY, TO his wife, but the stubborn toddler would have nothing of it. Her arms clung tightly to his neck. She was a daddy's girl for sure.

"I'm going to see Mom. Marie told me she's aware some visitors are coming today, but I think something of this nature could be over-whelming. Daniel's coming with me."

Connors' wife, Elena, shushed him away with a smile as she had her hands full with the one-year-old. He and Daniel headed up the walkway side by side. Once secured that she could stay with her father, the toddler began to maneuver herself around to sit on her father's shoulders. Hank dutifully held his hands out to help her. When she tried to begin her second attempt to climb over her father's shoulders, Hank muttered in feigned disappointment, "Not again, Courtney!" The child gave a firm response that sounded like "Uh-huh."

Daniel was amused at both the girl's actions and Hank's willing compliance. "I imagine she can be quite a handful," asked Daniel.

A broad smile formed on Hank's face.

"When we got our last child, she did not take well to the competi-tion. My wife warned me that there would be consequences for treating her like daddy's little girl. You know what, Daniel, I don't regret a day of it. Courtney seemed to transfer that feeling of protec-tiveness to her younger sister, Sally."

His choice of words—*When we got our last child*—puzzled Daniel. He put Hank Connors and his wife Cindy in their mid-fifties, and too old to be of childbearing age. Equally as intriguing were the ages of Hank Connors other children. The boys, George and Liam were in high school and the girls, Ashley five, Courtney three, and Sally, age two. Daniel had felt a strange kinship with Hank Connors but was still hesitant to pry in the strange age span of their children. Just as they approached Sally's room, Hank's eldest son, George, approached them holding Sally in his arms.

"Dad, Sally's been putting up a fuss. Mom thinks she misses Courtney. Could you take her?"

At the sight of her baby sister, Courtney held her hands out. Her fingers opened and closed rapidly as if to get ahold of her baby sister whose crying had reached the annoying point.

Somewhat irked at this sudden interruption to his plan, Connors grimaced as he pondered the logistics of presenting his two youngest children to his mother.

Daniel sensed that Connors could use some help.

"Hank, can I be of any use?"

Sally would certainly be easier to handle given Courtney's deep sense of determination, he thought.

"Daniel, it would really help if you could take little Sally."

"Not a problem, Hank. If George could just stay for a few minutes to get her familiar with me, then I'll come in."

George spent the next few minutes soothing Courtney by assuring her baby Sally would be fine. George smiled as the two children hugged. His coddling worked.

"George, I'll take your father in to see his mother, and then I'll come out to take of little Sally."

~

HANK CONNORS PREPARED HIMSELF FOR A MEETING HE HAD LONG anticipated since that phone call from Joey Collier. Daniel gently knocked on his mother's door.

"Hi Sally, it's me, Daniel. May I come in?"

The door was opened by Ellen Taggart, Sally's rec-therapist, who had helped dress Sally and positioned her in her wheelchair.

"She's all ready," Ellen announced, as she opened the door widely.

Daniel entered first, followed by Connors, holding a relaxed Courtney in his arms. Daniel announced, "Sally, there's someone here to see you."

Sally was primed for the special event. She looked up at her son, Hank Connors. The sight of his mother took Hank Connors' breath away. In that moment, Connors thought of the only mother he had ever known. Hands that had stroked his shoulders when he needed encouragement and held him in times of despair, now rested on the arms of a wheelchair, wrinkled and aged by blotches of purple skin and raised blood vessels. Legs that had chased countless children in games of tag, legs that ran to them in times of fear and panic, now rested on the metal braces of a wheelchair. After leaving the Gunderson's, the one constant for Hank Connors was the image of Sally Gunderson's face. The night he graduated from Rutgers, she appeared in a dream with a glowing expression that he had done well. Whenever he toyed with a conflict, the image of Sally appeared, reminding him to do the right thing. There were nearly thirty other people waiting to see her who felt the same. Her eyes steadied on him as he said, "Mom, it's me, Hank. Hank Connors."

At the sound of his name, Sally adjusted herself to a more erect position. She lifted her eyeglasses which hung from a gold chain around her neck and brought them to the bridge of her nose.

"Excuse me?" came the response from the frail woman, struggling to remember the name.

"Hank, Mom. Your son Hank," he added.

The first sound of recognition was a hard gasp and then a tearful weeping, "My Hank! My Hank!"

In describing her husband's personality, Elena Connors often referred to him as gentle as a lamb, despite having the size of a retired offensive lineman. Connors' reaction to his mother's response only served to reinforce that description. The huge frame of a man knelt next to her, tears unashamedly pouring down his face. He adjusted the child in his arms and leaned forward, resting his head on Sally's chest. Through the sobs, he repeated over and over, "Mom, I love you so much. We all do, and we're here to see you." The role of a caregiver never left Sally Gunderson. Her hands gently stroked Connors' head.

Sally seemed confused by his words. Her recollections of the past had improved with the new medicine her doctor had put her on, but she still had difficulty translating the collective third person "we" to the person kneeling next to her.

"We?" she questioned.

Connors raised his head. "Yes, Mellissa, Joey Collier, and plenty of others you and dad raised. We're all here to see you."

An intuitive alarm went off in Courtney's brain. *Those names aren't me. Tell Gramma I'm here too.* With a surge of determination, the three-year-old reached out and began grabbing the handle of the wheel-chair. Her efforts caught Sally's attention. Hank realized the first intro-duction was about to be made. Shifting the child to face Sally, Hank said, "Mom, this is Courtney Connors, your granddaughter." Connors' proclamation brought a renewed level of awareness in Sally. The searching hands of the precocious child immediately sought out the gold chain hanging from Sally's glasses. There was a sudden rebirth of Sally's mothering heart. She reached into the small clutch she always carried with her and withdrew a tiny charm bracelet she liked to wear when she remembered.

"Here, sweetie," dangling the bracelet in front of the child.

Without a negative word or gesture, Sally had diverted the child's attention.

"Mom, I want you to meet the rest of my kids."

"More, you say?" she beamed. "I'll keep this one," she announced, her arms now encircling Courtney who busied herself fondling the bracelet. Her stunning blue eyes radiated a sense of love that had infused the lives of so many.

～

IN THE HALLWAY, GEORGE JR. AND DANIEL HAD SPENT SEVERAL MINUTES letting little Sally adjust to Daniel. When he saw the two getting along so well, he said, "I'd better be getting back to Mom and the others." With Sally nearly asleep in his arms, Daniel pursued with George the topic he had hesitated to approach with the boy's father. He asked, "There's quite an age span between your brothers and sisters. Having children at an older age must have been hard on your mother and father?"

George Jr. radiated an immense sense of pride as he told the family story.

"Well, my brother Liam's birth was pretty difficult. The doctors told mom and dad that she shouldn't risk having any more children.

The news broke mom's heart. She wanted more children, especially girls. Several years later, what with my dad's background as a foster child, they thought, why not be foster parents and take in kids who needed love and, if fortunate, they would be able to keep them? They relished in continuing the tradition of guardianship of children who needed love and a home."

"You mean at their ages, your mom and dad decided to take in foster care children?

George proudly replied, "Yes, and luckily, I got three sisters out of it."

Kilgore seemed quite taken aback by this revelation.

"That was quite a gamble?"

Mature for his age, George Jr. emphatically exclaimed, "Not for my mom and dad. He used to tell us no child is too young to be loved, and no adult is too old to give love. I'd better get back to mom and the others."

As George headed down the hallway, Daniel found himself swaying slowly side to side, with young Sally now soundly asleep in his arms. He thought of the words Hank had told his son, George. Suddenly Sally's body jerked as if she was experiencing a disturbing dream. Daniel leaned his head down to kiss her forehead and whispered, "It's alright, little one, I'm here." He cradled her just a little closer. Not just to soothe her but to rekindle a long-lost joy hidden in himself.

～

BY THE TIME DANIEL AND HANK HAD RETURNED TO THE VERANDA, THE entire back acreage was teeming with families and their loved ones. The coolness of the late morning temperature enticed many to take their loved ones along the multiple walking paths that meandered throughout the Gardens. Some families elected to stay under their canopies as the alertness and mobility level of their loved ones, either in a wheelchair or afoot, would tax their strength to the point of needing a long rest. A steady stream of kitchen staff brought out trays of finger food and liquid refreshments. Hank steered Sally's wheelchair to their canopy. Daniel followed with a young Sally soundly asleep in his arms. Joey and Melissa were updating each other with their life status.

"She's a lucky girl, Joey," she said, after hearing of Joey's engagement to Marie.

"I think I'm the lucky one, Melissa." Glancing over at Marie, who was in a deep conversation with Elena Connors over theories of child-rearing, he added, "She's got a lot of Sally in her."

With that pronouncement, any anxiety she had of her foster brother making a hasty decision regarding a future with Marie quickly faded. Now that Jane was finally finished with processing the last of the late arrivals, she and Marie headed out to the veranda. There they were greeted with numerous congratulations for arranging the Family Day Celebration. Jane graciously deferred any credit to the staff, especially Marie Franklin, who now was blushing a bright red. Anxious to catch up with Daniel, whom she had not seen since early in the morning, she quickened her pace.

The scene inside the Gunderson canopy was akin to a high school reunion. Those who had spent time together as foster kids relished in the memories of the Gundersons. Conversations started with, "Do you remember when..." and then roars of laughter. When questions were asked about kids who were not there, the tenor of the conversations shifted. "You didn't hear," or "They just dropped off the face of the earth," were indicators where fate may not have been kind. It was Joey and Melissa who first saw Connors pushing Sally's wheelchair. Standing behind Connors and Sally were Jane Kilgore and Marie Franklin.

"My God, she looks just like the day I left," uttered Melissa.

"Hey, everyone, Mom's here," extolled Joey excitedly.

As he bent down to enter the canopy, Connors paused and whispered to Sally, "Your kids are all here, at least all that we could contact. Mom, they're here to see you." Connors gently removed

Courtney from Sally's lap. Sally stared at the line of people moving slowly to her. Her eyes strained to remember the slightest facial feature. Her heart never wanted to disappoint or hurt anyone's feelings. Joey Collier remembered that heart. He and Melissa knelt down next to her wheelchair.

"Mom, it's me, Joey Collier, and Melissa Norman. You probably remember her as Melissa Gatewood."

Sally stared into Melissa's face, her brain sifting through years of faces.

"The dance?" she said. "Did you have a good time?"

Her response evoked a flood of tears from Melissa, whose night as *the Belle of the Ball* remained one of the most cherished moments of her life.

"Oh yes I do, mom. You and Joey made it all possible." Melissa took a handkerchief from her sweater pocket and in a failed attempt to stem the flow of tears pressed it gently against her eyes.

Turning to Collier, Sally took his hand and voiced a threatening yet heartfelt caution.

"Have you been staying out of trouble or do I have to call Hank to deal with you?"

Joey looked up at Connors, who was grinning like the Cheshire cat.

"Mom, I've got someone else to keep me in tow. Her name's Marie Gordon. We're going to be married."

Joey waved to Marie to come forward. Sheepishly, Marie approached them and knelt next to Joey.

She reached out to hold Sally's hand.

"So, you'll be the one looking after my Joey?" Sally asked, with a wistful grin on her face.

Slightly embarrassed at the responsibility Sally had passed on to her, Marie answered, "I'll try to do as good a job as you did, Sally."

Sally smiled and continued her comical remembrance of history.

"Well, if he causes you any trouble, you just call Hank. He knows how to deal with that rascal."

Knowing many others wanted to speak with Sally, Joey said, "Mom, there's lots of your kids who want to see and talk to you. We'll see you later."

For the next hour or so, Sally's children knelt before her with papal reverence. Some drew remembrance in a minute or so while others took more prodding. When they were done, everyone returned to their tables to renew visiting with other foster brothers and sisters. Once his mom consumed a few petit fours and quenched her thirst with some sweet iced tea, Hank Connors dutifully guided Sally to each table for some private time with her children.

Jane had been busy answering questions from several of the visiting families when she noticed Daniel approaching holding one of the Connors' children. She was surprised yet delighted to see the unusual amount of patience he displayed with a one-year-old.

"Looks like you've been pretty busy," said Jane to Daniel, who was adjusting the drool towel Hank had given him. Young Sally was beginning to fuss.

"She takes up all of my time and attention," Daniel replied, gently dabbing the towel to the child's mouth. "But good time," he quickly added with a smile. "I don't mind it at all."

They were interrupted by Elena Connors, who approached them with a plastic bottle in hand. Long years of child-rearing had given her a wonderful sense of timing with what was necessary.

"You seem a natural with children, Daniel. Do you and Jane have any?"

He stood, twisting to and fro to settle down the child. "No, I think we're probably too old for that sort of thing."

Elena gave him a wink and said, "That's what Hank and I first thought. But it's not how old you are that matters, it's how much love you have that counts."

Reaching for the baby, she said, "She's probably ready for this. Is there a place I can warm this up?" Elena said.

Jane asked the attendant at the refreshment table to take Elena to the staff breakroom where they had a microwave. Relieved from the burden of carrying a twenty-five-pound baby, Daniel slumped down on one of the vacant chairs. Jane joined him. He was surprised how taxing it had been.

"Exhausted, huh?" she asked.

Daniel nodded and then countered with a smile, "But a good exhausted."

"You sure?" she asked, half expecting a caveat of "but not again."

Jane was taken aback by his response, a response she had prayed to hear someday, but thought it was beyond Daniel's capability to express. His eyes swept the room taking stock of the sights and sounds.

"Ever wonder if love is transgenerational? I never did until now. Through the efforts of George and Sally, countless children like these were provided a safe haven to hope when hope seemed impossible. They gave value to those that life had dealt a shorthand."

Jane was uncharacteristically silent at the depth of Daniel's words. She quietly sat in the vacant chair next to him. He took her hand in his.

"For George and Sally, there was no greater joy than loving the most vulnerable and helpless of creatures, children; unless it was being loved by them in return."

Sitting there with his arm over Jane's shoulder, Daniel and Jane soaked in the sight of smiles and the sounds of love. Jane dared not allow herself to think Daniel had experienced some sort of epiphany regarding children of their own. Daniel found himself feeling the day filled with the odor of baby powder, coos, woos, and tiny fingers grabbing at anything that sparkled or shined, had passed too soon.

26

DANIEL'S REVELATION

The following day, families dribbled in to visit Sally at staggered times depending on the length of their return trips home. One of the first was Hank Connors and his family. After finishing breakfast with her, Hank asked if they could go out onto the veranda. Ellen Taggart, who was assisting in the final day's activities, nodded. Once settled around a table, Hank put his arms around Sally's shoulders, "You know Mom, I can never thank you and dad for all you did for me and the other kids you two raised. Not a day goes by that I don't remember the love you gave us. I try to pass that love along to my kids."

Sally sat there gently patting his hand while staring off beyond those sitting at the table. His words seemed to have escaped her attention.

"He loved you, Hank."

"Who's he, Mom?" Hank asked

"What did you say?" she said, turning her head to Hank as if she hadn't heard a thing he had said.

"Who loved me, Mom?" Hank asked, fearful that his mother would soon slip into the recurring fog of dementia.

Suddenly reconnected with reality, Sally answered, "Why your father, George."

Her response seemed misdirected as Hank had not mentioned George's name. Perhaps her mental decline had confused his words, or perhaps Sally had remembered her husband's role in all they had done despite the failing struggle with dementia. Her smile at that moment told Hank it was the latter, not the former. Hank, his wife, Elena, and all five children gave Sally hugs and kisses and promised not to let so much time pass before their next visit. On seeing the Connors family make their goodbyes, Ellen went out to the veranda to check on Sally.

The previous day left Sally exhausted from the emotional reunion with her children. By days end, her mind had great difficulty recalling the faces of anyone who sat before her, though her face never failed to evoke a smile and an, "I love you too."

Bending gently down to Sally's level, Ellen quietly asked, "Is there anything I can get you, Sally?"

Sally adjusted the ends of the blue shawl around her shoulders, its ends now crossing over her lap. She hadn't responded to Taggart's request. She seemed focused on the trickle of visitors now saying their last goodbyes to loved ones. Her eyes were now bright and alert, at least for the moment.

"It was wonderful so many came," she said. A state of contentment put a smile on her face, clearly contented with the previous day's events.

Ellen was surprised Sally had so much retention of the previous day given the sheer number of families that had come to see her, and the length of time since they had left the confines of the Gunderson's home. Testing the depth of her recall, Ellen asked, "Tell me about yesterday?"

Ellen was taken aback by her response. Sally's depth of compassion for others overruled her annoyance at the inference she had not or could not remember. Somehow, she seemed to defy the presence of her dementia.

"Oh, my dear, it was wonderful," Sally said with assurance. "Hank, Joey, Melissa, so many came. They're wonderful children, don't you know."

A trace of smugness appeared as Sally steadied herself in her wheelchair. She smiled at Taggart and inquired, "My dear, could I possibly get one of those wonderful beignets and a cup of coffee?"

Another affirmation of her mental stability, albeit temporary.

Ellen answered, "Of course, I will bring them right away."

Ellen returned to the kitchen where the staff had just removed several trays of freshly baked beignets. Ellen placed one on a plate, poured a fresh cup of coffee, and returned to the veranda.

"Here you are, Sally, just as requested, a fresh beignet and a cup of coffee."

Without looking up, Sally responded, "Thank you so much, George."

~

THE FAMILY DAY CELEBRATION HAD ITS EFFECTS ON A NUMBER OF PEOPLE, a renewed sense of appreciation from the visiting families for the work the staff performed and revived promises to visit again. Perhaps none had been affected to the degree Daniel Kilgore had. The time he had spent with Hank Connors and tending to the needs of Connors' two-year old had changed him. The death of his son would never leave his memory, but Daniel could no longer allow it to dominate what could be. He needed to tell Jane.

Jane was late getting home from the Gardens after supervising the final clean-up details. Daniel had a chilled glass of their favorite red, a Windy Oaks Pinot. Daniel watched from the porch as Jane drove up the driveway and parked in front of the house. As she exited her vehicle, he thought she appeared fatigued. She took small steps; her shoulders slumped from the weight of responsibility of Family Day. Greeting her from the porch, Daniel announced like a royal page, "A glass of wine awaits my lady." His proclamation brought a quickened pace and a smile to a very tired Jane Kilgore. Daniel met her at the top of the steps.

"Let me have these, you sit," said Daniel, who relieved Jane of her valise and a grocery bag with two lamb shanks she had purchased at the local market with the expectation that Daniel would prepare them.

"What a relief," she sighed, handing over the two bags to her husband. She then proceeded to take a seat on the swing.

Daniel put away the few groceries, set Jane's valise in her office, and returned to the porch. With Daniel at her side, she lifted her glass to his and toasted, "To a wonderful day!" With a clink from the glasses, Daniel added, "and to us." There was a nuance to his words that Jane had not detected, but she soon would understand. The pinot was soft and silky, not a trace of tannic acid.

"What a wonderful day, Daniel. Marie did such a wonderful job in reuniting so many families."

"Yes, she did, and speaking of that, families I mean, there's something I'd like to talk to you about - family."

Daniel's word, "family," raised an old sense of apprehension in Jane that she had previously been able to put to rest. That apprehension surfaced again. Meeting Hank Gunderson revealed to Daniel that the trepidation about his and Jane's ages suddenly didn't seem an overwhelming barrier to child-rearing. The necessary lifestyle changes seemed less of an impossible burden and more of something to embrace considering the rewards. Even the inevitable concern of, "I'll be this old then the child is this old," was no longer an automatic rejection, but merely a fact among many to be considered. Daniel gently brushed the hair away from her face. Her eyes moistened with the expectation of a negative response. Her lips were slightly opened anticipating a gasp for air at his rejection. He placed his hands on her shoulders.

"You have fulfilled my life in ways I could have never imagined. You allowed me to feel love and hope at a time when despair nearly consumed me. That being said," he paused to take a breath.

Jane flinched at the thought that Daniel had finally decided his vision of the future did not match hers.

"At my age, I doubt I can father a child and at your age there are certainly health concerns for you. Since I doubt there's another Immaculate Conception in our future, how would you feel about trying foster care as a start?"

Jane hardly considered herself out to pasture, but Daniel was right in one respect, the health of a child. In her early fifties, there was a significant chance a baby could be born with some form of mental impairment. As for Daniel's doubts that he could father a child at his age, his renewed sense of virility over the last several months left little doubt that was a strong possibility, and if not, the effort alone was its own reward.

Her hand holding her wine glass began to tremble, causing its contents to swirl out of control. Using her other hand for control, Jane gently set her glass on the table. For a moment, Jane sat silent, staring at the pinot as its contents slowly settled to a gentle sway. His words sent shock waves through her body. Had he really changed his feelings about having children? Had he thought through the changes it would bring to their lives? Shifting her position on the swing to face him, she was stunned by the look on his face. He sat firm and resolute as if his question had been more of a statement of fact than a question of probability. Jane's throat tightened as she sought confirmation of a lifetime dream.

"Daniel, are you sure?" Her words were tentative and uncertain.

"I spent a lot of time with Hank Connors and his family over the last two days. With all its risk, I've seen the joy foster care brought to Sally Gunderson and in turn, to the Conners. Jane, I'd like us to have the chance at that same joy and happiness." He smiled as he was certain in his decision.

She grabbed his forearm and squeezed with a force of disbelief. Daniel knew she needed more conformation of his commitment. He set his glass on the table.

"Yes, Jane. I'm serious. Who is more deserving of love and

compassion than a foster child caught in a bureaucratic system which, at best, may provide mere survival? They need what every child needs and deserves, a home where love is unquestioned, and support a certainty, not a maybe."

Knowing Daniel was now in alignment with her life's dream, Jane broke into tears. Two hearts together now as never before. Her arms encircled his shoulders as a floodgate of emotions flowed down her cheeks. A sense of both contentment and anxiety filled Daniel. He was anxious to get the process started. Fortunately, Jane opened the door. She straightened herself and dabbed her eyes with the cocktail napkin from under her wine glass.

"My God, Daniel. There's so much to do, and I don't have the slightest idea where to start?"

A smile spread over Daniel's face.

"Fortunately, those long conversations with Hank Connors weren't all about football. He had a wealth of information about foster care and how to get started."

Jane took a healthy sip of wine, then faced Daniel.

"So, where do we start?"

"That's the ironic part," Daniel said with the excitement of a child about to reveal a special secret to his parents. "Right here at the Gardens. I had a chance to talk with Marie Gordon about Sally Gunderson's background, and it seems Marie Gordon's mother, Alice Gordon, works for the city of Charleston's Family Services Division, specializing in foster placement. We have an appointment with her tomorrow at ten a.m."

At that moment, Jane realized Daniel had set the appointment before he had said anything to her. *Why the secrecy about the appointment? Why hadn't he told me?*" she thought. Annoyed that he had kept this a secret from her, Jane pressed him.

"So, you made the appointment without consulting me first!" She asked, her arms now folded as if a scolding was on the horizon. Her squinting eyes and pursed lips gave further evidence of her obvious disapproval.

Her baited question had caught Daniel off guard. Frankly, he thought wanting a child would be irrelevant to the process. Realizing he was wrong, Daniel hastily tried to mend the situation.

"Jane. I know how important this is for you. Once I realized how important it had become for me, I thought I'd get things started."

His throat tightened at the thought he had misjudged her. "You're not changing your mind, are you?" The look in his eyes was like that of a child whose favorite Christmas toy was about to be taken away from him.

"This is not about starting anything, Daniel. This is about us, we, beginning the process, and I don't appreciate one bit being left out of the decision-making process."

She waited a moment to let the seriousness of her words settle in Daniel's mind. Then satisfied she had made her point, she took his hand and smiled.

"Of course, I haven't changed my mind," she replied with a chuckle. "I want that child as much as ever, and I want it with you. But in the future, let's make such decisions 'we' decisions, all right?"

Sure that Jane had been playing him, Daniel quickly responded, "Absolutely," to ensure further questioning was unnecessary.

∾

IF ALL DANIEL OR JANE THOUGHT WAS NECESSARY TO BECOME FOSTER parents was to fill out a few forms, they were sorely mistaken. They sat across from Marie's mother, Alice Franklin, the Department of Social Services Director of Out of Home Placement. On a small conference table in Alice's office was a file, three inches thick, of forms to be filled out. Alice had taken them through each one leaving Daniel and Jane thoroughly overwhelmed. Once they had provided the agency with copies of their own medical records, three years of income tax records, a list of family and friends for the agency to contact, and their own personal histories dating back to birth, the agency could begin working on their internal requirements; two days

Pre-Service training, home inspections to meet the agency's safety requirements, a psychological profile, and criminal background review.

Alice got up and walked to the window. She hated the effect of the indirect lighting generated by the neon lights hanging from the ten-foot-high ceiling. She slowly pulled on the chain to angle the shades to the level position, hoping the morning fog had cleared, and the brightness of the sun could penetrate the rather gloomy sense of depression consuming those at the table. Alice squinted as the shades opened. Thankfully, fractures in the lifting fog allowed the bright rays of the rising sun to permeate through the shades. Alice turned around and braced herself against the brass steam heater.

"Seems daunting, doesn't it?" said Alice, as she saw the "You've got to be kidding!" look on their faces. "Look," Alice continued, "each of you has worked in venues where the bureaucracy is the bandleader, ain't no music if you don't follow the bandleader."

Reminded of an old adage somewhat unflattering about bureaucracy, Daniel thought to himself, *we the unwilling who do the unnecessary to make the simple difficult.*

"Then we'd better get started," Daniel proclaimed, scooping up the initial phase of the paperwork.

Jane was uneasy with Alice's timelines of first get this done, then we'll work on the rest. "Alice, can you give me a guesstimate of how long this might take?"

Fortunately, Alice knew of their backgrounds, which freed her from the usual precautionary caveats.

"Press anyone you have to in order to get your paperwork ASAP! Flo and I will fast track the background clearance with a sergeant we work with at the Charleston PD. I'll get you on the calendar as if your paperwork has been approved for everything we need to do. We should have some potential placement candidates in ninety days. Operative word, should."

Alice's estimation eased the tension that had built up in Jane. She had expected to hear, *up to a year.* Jane took ahold of Daniel's hand.

"Shall we?" To wit, Daniel responded eagerly, "What are we waiting for?"

Alice walked them to the door of her office.

"See you soon, I hope?"

Their response was a simple wave as Daniel and Jane were consumed with the tasks ahead. Alice's experience had taught her no matter what the age of potential foster parents, there are two simultaneous thought processes taking place with each parent. Daniel and Jane both felt the apprehension of a dream that might come true. They were about to be given the responsibility of providing for a human life, materially and spiritually. That tinge of doubt peaked its ugly head, would they be up to the task. Once on the road, both kept those expectations private for the time being.

27

THE DREAM ARRIVES

The call from Daniel to meet for lunch at Belle's Inferno came as a pleasant surprise to Madeline and Jane. The two women were nearly done with the last of the touch-up painting and cleaning of Madeline's suite at the Gardens before her move to Eddy's house in Beaufort. The chance to savor one of Belle's famous shrimp Po Boy's gave the girls added motivation to wash up and change clothes. Daniel and Eddy were waiting for them when they arrived. Belle had seated the girls in the front booth. Lined with ruby red leather and an overhead crystal chandelier, the booth had been the preferred dining table for many of Charleston's finest.

"You two must be famished!" Eddy said, as he waved to the waitress to bring two more iced teas.

Jane shrugged her shoulders. She was suddenly aware of an unfamiliar ache in her shoulders and arms.

"If I have to plaster one more nail hole or roll one more wall, my arms will fall off."

Madeline knew the fault was with her and displayed an impish look while stating, "I like pictures and knickknacks. What can I say?"

Having eaten there many times, the waitress knew Jane and Madeline's favorite lunch dishes. For Jane, a bowl of jambalaya with hot sauce and for Madeline, a crawdad salad with the heads of the crawdad left on. Jane was one of the few non-creole persons Belle had ever met who took to the tradition of biting off the head of the crawdad and sucking out the juices. Nothing was said for the next several minutes as the men enjoyed their Po Boy's and the girls dove into their dishes. Only the repeated, but feigned repugnant, "Uck!," broke the silence every time Jane picked up another crawdad.

Both Daniel and Eddy had wished they hadn't ordered the full Po Boy with fries and a side. The two thought of pulling the tablecloth over their laps, in order to cover the process of loosening their respective belts. As this required more than the fabric was capable of delivering, it presented a comical scene. Their efforts at waistline deception brought a chuckle from the waitress standing nearby. With a noticeable sigh of relief at the loosening of his belt, Eddy asked, "How's that foster care process going?" Jane, who had the last mouthful of crawdad in her mouth, raised a finger to signal, "Just a minute." Daniel stepped in to answer.

"It took us about a week to get everything Alice and Flo needed. They fast-tracked everything they needed to do, to the extent of getting home inspections and expedited psychological reviews done on weekends, and with a little manipulation by Flo the agency signed off on the day's in-service training class by letting us watch a four-hour videotape. All we're waiting on now is a criminal background check, and who knows how long that will take."

The obvious frustration in Daniel's voice alerted Eddy to the fact no more questions were necessary. The waitress brought them the bill asking, "How was everything?"

"Delicious as always," replied Daniel, as he grabbed the bill, saying to Eddy, "My treat."

There was no argument from Eddy, who feigned fumbling for his wallet just long enough for Daniel to realize he had lost. The two had developed a friendly game of seeing who could stiff the other into picking up the bill whenever they went out. Slowly shaking his head,

Daniel muttered, "Next time, buddy!" Eddy enjoyed his victory with a smug acknowledgment of touching two fingers to his forehead.

At that moment, the couples were interrupted by a sergeant from the Charleston PD. "Am I glad I found you! Marie's mom has been hounding me to find you before my shift was over." Sergeant Mike Callahan scooted into the booth.

"What's the rush?" asked Daniel, as he put his wallet into his back pocket.

"I finished your background clearances. When I gave them to Alice and Flo, Alice told me to get you and Jane to their office ASAP, so get ready for a lights-but-no-siren escort," Mike said, grabbing the last of the chowder crackers from a crystal bowl on the table.

Daniel and Jane stared at each other in wonderment at the urgency of the order.

"Hey, didn't you hear the man? You do know what ASAP means?" clowned Eddy, who not so subtly started to nudge Daniel out of the booth.

Goodbyes were quick as Daniel and Jane hurried to follow Callahan outside. Stepping into his patrol car door, he warned them, "Hang on!"

～

BLACK AND WHITE FEVER, AS CALLAHAN REFERRED TO DRIVERS WHO automatically slowed down at the sight of a police car, was exacerbated by the sight of the flashing red and blue lights atop Callahan's patrol car. Taking advantage of the ruse created by his flashing lights, Callahan quickly maneuvered through the downtown traffic until he pulled up in front of the county building Children Services.

"Any idea what this is about?" asked Daniel, as he exited Callahan's patrol car.

"Not a clue," replied Callahan. "But it must be important."

Daniel and Jane hurried up the steps, through the double glass doors and straight to the elevators. Jane reached for Daniel's hand and squeezed. Ever since Callahan had delivered Alice's dictum, her anxiety level had caused an increasing shortness of breath. They got off on the third floor. Directly across from the elevator was the Office of Children's Services. Alice was waiting in the hallway for them, her hand nervously patting the manila folder she was holding. A broad smile spread across her face as they stepped out of the elevator.

"That boy knows the meaning of ASAP, doesn't he!" gloated Alice. "Come on in."

With a sense of nervous compliance engulfing them, Daniel and Jane obediently followed Alice into her office.

"Please have a seat," Alice said, gesturing to the antiquated steel conference table in the corner of her office. "Can I get you two some water?"

"I don't think I can swallow, Alice. Please, what's this all about?" pleaded Jane.

"I have some very unexpected good news for you two. Flo and I pulled some strings, called in a few favors, and got the fastest background check in Charleston PD's history, thanks to Sergeant Mike Callahan. This is going to need some thought by you two. So, listen carefully, Charleston Memorial Hospital notified me this morning they have a nine-month-old baby, a girl, with a nineteen-year-old white mother with a history of drug use and abandoned by her family. The father is a twenty-year-old Hispanic father in this country illegally. He split when he heard of the pregnancy. The responsibility of raising an infant on her own was too much for the poor girl. She left the infant on the steps of a local Catholic Church. No trace of her was ever found. Take a look," Alice said, sliding the file to Daniel and Jane.

This was the point of no return for many prospective foster parents hoping to eventually adopt. Without opening the file, Alice knew that a racially mixed child with a future of behavioral and medical uncertainties would hardly be anyone's first choice. But if they opened the file and saw the face of a baby girl, blue eyes begging to be held, curled finger outstretched for arms to hold it, hearts would be moved. Hesitantly, Jane reached out for the file. She was too late. Daniel's hand landed on the file. He set it in front of them and without pause opened the file. Jane gave a noticeable gasp. Never had she seen such a beautiful child. Angel-like hair, the consistency of dandelion fuzz, covered her head. The picture captured the deepest, bluest eyes Jane had ever seen. Set against an olive complexion, Jane wanted to reach into the picture and pull the infant into her arms. Moistened eyes were about to release the first of many tears. Daniel carefully traced the infant's hands. He envisioned her grasp as he would set her upright or supporting her first steps. After several moments, Daniel looked up at Alice and asked.

"And your question is?"

Jane's intuitive sense of Daniel's question brought a glowing smile to her face.

"You are approved for foster care right now. If you want, you can take her now, and we'll wait for your decision to adopt or not."

Jane's heart was nearly exploding as she looked at Daniel for some sign of what he wanted to do. Daniel closed the file and pushed it back to Alice. He looked into Jane's eyes, and announced with unwavering confidence, "Yes, we want her now and don't wait to start the adoption process. She's going to be ours."

28
TWO YEARS LATER

If you doubted that the harmonic convergence of the stars could sustain the perfect meld of reality and dreams, Daniel and Jane Kilgore would tell you differently. Since the adoption of their nine-month-old daughter they named Mary, there was a clarity of focus in how the two viewed each other that had not existed previously. Suspecting that Daniel would have preferred a boy, Jane marveled at Daniel as he adapted to the needs and wants of an infant daughter. Tiny hands reaching for that shining, glimmering object never came away empty-handed. Daniel even took to having an extra pair of cheap glasses on him whenever Mary insisted on grabbing for the good pair he was used to. It delighted Jane to no end when she heard her giggles as Daniel would tenderly spread soap suds over her as she reclined in the baby tub. After being dried with an ultrasoft terrycloth towel, Daniel would apply a liberal amount of talcum powder, enough to create a small cloud over her body. Then he dressed her in Jane's predetermined selection of clothes, and present her to Jane, by saying, "My princess to my queen." Jane's heart would swell to the bursting point.

Such displays of attention were not restricted to the home. There was a large artisan food store named "Farm to Table" where Daniel and Jane liked to shop. Jane preferred to cater to local growers while Daniel liked connecting with Ed Popkey, the store owner and fellow Clemson grad. Jane had stopped there one afternoon to pick up a few extra items for dinner as Eddy and Maddy Pinafore were coming over. The storefront had an extended canopy shading multiple displays of fresh produce and a spot for carts. Ed Popkey, the store's manager, stopped Jane as she pulled out a cart to use.

"That husband of yours sure gets a lot of attention when he shops here with the baby," chuckled Popkey.

"How so?" replied Jane, knowing shopping was not one of Daniel's favorite tasks.

"When he comes in, he has Mary in her baby backpack. He'll make his way up each aisle announcing to her what they're looking for. When he finds it, he stops and reads the ingredients out loud to her, careful to emphasize the high fructose sugar content or any other ingredients Mom says is no good for her. Shoppers in the same aisle would crack up because Mary would be sound asleep in her carrier and completely oblivious to his well-intended remarks."

Jane kept this little story to herself to remember whenever she sent Daniel shopping again.

For his part, Daniel had been through the child-rearing stage once before, and though he knew how much Jane had wanted a child, the adage "Anticipation is greater than realization" gave him pause to wonder if having a child would be all it's cracked up to be for Jane. He was not disappointed. There was no need for the baby monitor they kept on the bed stand in their bedroom. Jane had that mysterious maternal alarm system that made electronic devices useless. It would go off whenever the child made the slightest cooing sound in the middle of the night, jolting Jane to an upright position. Dressing her in the morning had its own special flair. Jane wore a front sling to hold Mary. As she laid out each combination of tops and bottoms, there'd be a fashionista dialogue between mother and daughter.

"Now, this white top compliments these pink bottoms, don't ya think?" "Or what do you think about this matching Kelly Green t-shirt and pants?"

But nothing pleased Daniel more than to listen to Jane read to Mary from any of a plethora of children books they had received from family and friends. Jane imbued each character with her own interpretation of the morality of the situation. There were never bad characters, only characters that made wrong choices.

This was the life that had absorbed Daniel and Jane Kilgore for almost three years. They relished the demands of parenthood. Every touch from her tiny hands, every smile from her angelic face, united Daniel and Jane even closer. He loved reliving a wonderful part of his past and the anticipation of shaping a future life. Jane was enthralled with all the hopes and dreams that motherhood brought with it. These last few years neither gave a thought that it wouldn't last forever.

~

"HAVE YOU GOT EVERYTHING LOADED?" JANE ASKED DANIEL AS HE returned from his fourth trip to their Honda Odyssey. He had insisted the Odyssey was the perfect car for them now that they had a child. It had a middle aisle leading to the rear seats which Jane had no problem filling with items she insisted her daughter had to have. Now he wasn't sure. He was wondering if there would be room for his golf clubs and a single suitcase.

"Yes, if you don't find something else Mary can't do without," he replied in mock frustration. His handsome features displayed feigned displeasure.

Realizing he was right, she acquiesced. "Okay, I admit I can overdo the packing, but she's your daughter too. Don't you want her to look her best?" she added.

She had maneuvered him into the obvious and he had no desire to go further. He responded, "Touché!" leaving Jane with a smug smile on her face.

As Eddy and Maddy were Mary's godparents, they had insisted

that the three come to their home in Beaufort to celebrate Eddy's new job. Samantha Callahan had opted for raising a family rather than continue as the acting Director of Magnolia Gardens, a decision that sorely disappointed the Board of Directors, but much pleased her husband, Mike. Maddy had encouraged Eddy to apply for the position. After all, he had more than enough years in the Navy to retire, and his experience in helping disabled veterans seemed a perfect transition to the administrative task of running Magnolia Gardens. Fortunately, the Board of Directors agreed.

"Ready to go!" he said, wolfing down a handful of almonds from a crystal bowl in the kitchen. The bowl had been glued together several times, the result of tiny hands pulling it too close to the edge. Jane hoisted Mary into her arms and with one last prompt to Daniel not to forget the wine they were bringing, headed to the car. Daniel followed with a wine box in hand containing four bottles of Windy Oaks finest Pinot Noir. With the wine secured in the back of the Odyssey, Daniel helped Jane get Mary into her car seat. When he got around to the driver's side, he noticed something about the tire's tread. It was wearing at a severe angle. He ran his hand over the worn pattern only to have the exposed steel core prick his hand. *I should have listened to him*, he thought, when the guy at Randy's Tire told him he needed new tires. The expense of remolding the extra bedroom for Mary seemed a higher priority. It was about a forty-minute drive to Maddy and Eddy's place in Beaufort from their home in Charleston, and Daniel had expected a long dialogue of nonsensical gibberish from his daughter at every passing item of interest to a three-year-old. To his dismay, that's exactly what had happened. Mary had fought the urge to sleep, and Jane was forced to opine on every scene the coastal beaches presented, surfers, parasailers, beachcombers, and the inevitable beach barbequers. Daniel had a chance to enjoy the gorgeous coastline. There were miles of flat white sandy beaches. Within a hundred yards of the water's edge, lines of tall wheat shrubs with lavender blossoms appeared atop small, sandy dunes. The plant's density acted as a barrier against the sand blown inward by the daily sea breeze coming off the Atlantic. Jane looked back at her daughter. The stare lasted several minutes.

"What are you thinking?" Daniel asked.

Jane kissed her fingertip then placed it on Mary's forehead.

"Only that Maddy and Eddy could find the happiness we have with Mary."

"If it's their fate, then they will," mused Daniel, as if he were some Greek Oracle preaching from Mount Olympus.

Fate, tragic or joyous, is inevitable.

❧

IF MARY WAS THE MIRACLE OF A LIFETIME FOR DANIEL AND JANE, EDDY and Maddy's discovery of Dr. Wilhelm Kruger at the Mayo Clinic in Rochester, Minnesota, was theirs. Maddy's longtime eye doctor, Wallace Stuart, had been following Dr. Kruger's research with anti-VEGE inhibitors and macular degeneration in the New England Journal of Medicine. He was confident Kruger's research was the answer to Maddy's prayers. After a video conference between Maddy, Eddy, Dr. Stuart, and Dr. Kruger, it was decided to start a series of Anti-VEGE inhibitor injections designed to improve the vision of those suffering from Macular Degeneration. The results were truly a miracle to Maddy. Within a matter of months, her vision had improved from a 2040 rating of very poor to a 2020 rating of average. It exposed Maddy to the world she used to know and to a man she had grown to love more with every passing day. Eddy was in the garage cleaning his golf clubs. The game had become both therapeutic and challenging to Eddy, and he needed both. Therapeutic because of the exercise and the effects on his mind as he anticipated club selection, shot placement, etc. and the challenge, *can you do this,* to a Navy Seal never goes unanswered. His recent round of par at Hilton Head earned him the One-Armed Golfer of the Year Award from the Professional Golfers Association. He was anxious to show off his prowess to Daniel. He and Maddy were going to watch their goddaughter that night. Daniel and Jane had reservations at the Beaufort Inn for dinner to celebrate three years of parenthood, then a round of golf at the Beaufort Greens the following morning.

The highway wove gently along the coastline in a gradual ascent to Beaufort Heights where Daniel and Jane had planned a celebratory dinner while Eddy and Maddy watched Mary. At the base of the incline was Beaufort Greens, a gated community of upper-class homes built around an eighteen-hole championship rated golf course. Within a couple of hundred yards of the entrance was the four-bedroom, Mediterranean style home of Eddy and Maddy Pinafore. Not one attracted to landscape work, Eddy had instructed the builder to make both the front and back yards maintenance free. Replacing the traditional Bermuda grass lawn were beds of decorative white crystal rocks with random placement of dwarf palmetto and sego palm trees. Rough-hewn wood stained brown trimmed the windows. The red tile roof gave the house an undeniable Spanish flavor. Eddy's only other indulgence was the design of the swimming pool. It was to be four feet deep. There were four sets of steps with close-set handle rails around the pool to facilitate Eddy getting in and out using one leg.

The alarm in the garage sounded indicating someone had used the code to open the gate leading to their house. It was an amenity Eddy took great pleasure in having and hoped he could find the same feature in the new home they would be moving to when he started his new position in three months at Magnolia Gardens. The Honda Odyssey moved slowly around the circle driveway and parked in front of the garage.

As the garage door rose, Eddy stepped out. He had been cleaning his golf clubs in anticipation of their match the next day though the gray clouds forming out to sea made that seem more improbable than possible. "Finally," called out Eddy, as he tossed his cleaning rag on top of his workbench where his golf clubs were neatly arrayed.

"How many times do you think a three-year-old can poop in her diapers in forty-five minutes?" Daniel announced in mock frustration as he exited the car.

Eddy smiled. He and Maddy could only wish they had that problem. Fate played them a different card and so be it. Daniel went to the back seat to help Jane get their daughter out of the car seat. As if some extrasensory perception was at work, Mary had awakened just as they passed through the gated entrance. With the announcement, "We're here, sweetie!" Mary exuberantly hollered, "See Maddy! See Maddy!

"Where's Maddy?" Jane asked as she passed her squiggling, squirming child to Eddy.

"In the kitchen making Mary's favorite cookies, macaroons," replied Eddy, who scooped up the three-year-old with his good arm and began twirling the child in circles. His prosthetic leg provided a stable pivot point. The child arched her head backward yelling, "Faster, faster."

That proclamation caused the child to explode with new excitement, shrieking, "Roons, roons," macaroon in kid speak.

The commotion brought Maddy out the door from the kitchen into the garage. She held one hand behind her back.

"Is my sweet Mary here?" Maddy called out, her eyes roaming about as if she could not see the child a mere ten feet away.

With the excitement of a child running from one Christmas present to another, more eager to tear the wrapping than see what's inside the box, Eddy set the squiggling child down who then ran to Maddy's arms.

"I'm here, auntie," the child screeched.

"Then this must be for you," Maddy responded, opening her hand to the alluring aroma of a freshly baked macaroon cookie.

Foregoing the traditional thank you, the child devoured the cookie in two bites. Swallowing was impossible as she retained as much of the cookie as she could in her pooched-out cheeks to suck out the maximum amount of coconut flavoring.

"You boys can bring in the luggage. Jane and I need to catch up," directed Maddy as she, Jane, and Mary headed into the house.

Maddy had intended to have lunch by the pool, but the warm breeze of mid-morning had given way to a cooler sea breeze. *Surely a sign of an impending storm,* she thought. Jane had moved the rolling toybox she and Eddy kept for their goddaughter into the living room. The sound of countless Legos, parts of several teapot sets, and any number of other toys of interest echoed off the red tile floor with such force both Jane and Maddy grimaced. The pile of toys soon spread over much of the floor in front of the Spanish style coffee table as Mary lost interest in one toy after another as if she was searching for her favorite one.

With the last of the luggage put in the spare bedroom, Eddy and Daniel returned to the living room and joined Maddy and Jane.

"Can I get anyone something to drink?" asked Eddy.

Glancing at his watch, the ever-ready to imbibe Daniel replied, "It's five o'clock somewhere. Let's try that Windy Oaks pinot we brought."

Dutifully, Eddy headed to the kitchen. Jane gave Daniel the evil eye indicating she thought three in the afternoon was a little early to start with alcohol. Realizing he needed to explain, Daniel sought approval by expounding, "Honey, you know how expensive wine will be at the Beaufort Inn. I'm just trying to be frugal."

"Good God, Jane, if you believe that I've got some oceanfront property in Arizona," laughed Maddy.

Eddy thought his friend had made a noble attempt at justification, but even he had to chuckle at its lameness.

∾

As the water from the first drops of rain began flowing down the steep hillside on the coastal highway, the top of a granite rock reflected through the darkness with every burst of lightning. At first, it didn't seem like it was a large rock. Like any one of a million other rocks and stones embedded in the geological layers of time that formed this earth, time would dictate its fate.

29

TO WHAT PURPOSE

The gleeful laughter of Mary was an endless source of pleasure to Maddy. She glanced out from the kitchen island where she was preparing some hors d'oeuvres to accompany their wine. Eddy was sitting on the floor next to the child, dutifully handing her pieces of the jigsaw puzzle she was attempting to complete: *He's so good with children,* Maddy thought, then quickly put that thought out of her mind.

The ding of the oven timer told her the puffed pastries stuffed with brie cheese were done. With mitten in hand, she removed them from the oven and slid them on to a platter. She gathered up the plate with crackers and two different types of hummus along with the pastries and headed to the living room. She set them on the Spanish style coffee table. When Maddy and Eddy had seen it on an antique shopping spree, he was particularly taken with its ornately carved white oak legs and the glass top edged with matching wood trim. The table came with matching end tables that were set against the ends of the couch. He decided he had to have the entire set.

Maddy sat in an easy chair next to one end of the couch. Eddy preferred to stay seated on the floor, engaging little Mary in the construction of some imaginary kingdom the child had envisioned in her mind. The sight reminded her of the gift of life that had been so savagely taken from her decades ago.

"To us," toasted Maddy, raising her glass in the air.

The other three followed, "To us."

The traditional clink of glasses was followed by an inquiring Maddy asking, "So have you two made reservations at the Beaufort Inn? The Inn can be crowded on weekends."

Daniel held up one finger, having just placed one of Maddy's puffed pastries into his mouth. His eyes rolled upwards as the last bit slid across his palate, indicating he had just eaten something divine.

"Absolutely, dinner at six, even arranged for a window table," he responded, as though he had accomplished some extraordinary feat.

Jane let Daniel bask in the glory of the moment rather than remind him of the note she had left lying next to the phone for the past three days, "Remember to get a window table when you call for reservations!"

"Are you sure you don't mind watching Mary? I promise we won't be too late."

"Are you kidding! Does he look like he's being imposed on?" replied Maddy, looking at Eddy. Mary had lost interest in her magic kingdom and was now fascinated with Eddy's prosthetic leg. Her tiny fingers traced over the plastic molded foot, tickling to see if she could get a reaction. Eddy feigned enough laughter that Mary joined him in the revelry.

"Since they're having such a good time, maybe we should take advantage and get ready. I bought a new dress for the occasion," said Jane.

Maddy had always thought Jane's taste in clothing impeccable, so she gleefully responded, "I can't wait to see."

"Take your time," added Eddy, "I'll watch the precious one."

If ever two people deserved children, Eddy and Maddy did, Daniel thought, following his wife into the bedroom.

~

Emerging from the bedroom into the living room, Jane did a slow turn, her arms outstretched like a model at the end of the runway.

"What do you think?" she asked.

Eddy gave a slow, exaggerated wolf whistle. Daniel smiled in agreement. He indeed had a trophy wife. Maddy could not contain her admiration.

"Honey, you look like a movie star!"

Jane smiled. "I asked my hairdresser to do something special and I love it."

The stylist had rolled Jane's brown hair into buns centered above both ears, giving her the look of a glorified Princess Leia. Gold earrings with a matching Cleopatra layered gold necklace reflected upward toward her magnificent emerald green eyes. The off-the-shoulder black dress hung perfectly with only a hint of the few extra pounds she had put on since marrying Daniel. Her five-inch black heels only added to her regal stature. Jane reached out to take little Mary from Eddy.

"Now you be good for Uncle Eddy and Auntie Maddy," Jane ordered while smothering the child with kisses. "Mommy and Daddy will be home later."

Mary giggled in compliance.

Drawn by the aroma of another macaroon cookie Eddy held in his hand and his promise to make a new magic kingdom, Mary abandoned her mother for the pleasure of another macaroon and playing with her nonsensical uncle.

"You guys drive safe," cautioned Eddy, "The rain is coming down pretty good."

To avoid the rain as much as possible, Daniel and Jane exited through the garage, leaving Eddy, Maddy, and Mary waving good-bye.

～

THE 6 PM VIEW FROM THE BEAUFORT INN WOULD NORMALLY HAVE THE setting sun radiating off the gently rolling seas of the Eastern Atlantic. A million stars would begin to appear in the heavens. Swarms of seagulls would be swooping down to the water for an evening meal, and the barking of sea lions could be heard from the rocks below. Tonight, clouds from the unexpected storm working its way down the Eastern seaboard hid the usual magnificent view. The darkness was interrupted with intermittent lightning flashes. The pelting of raindrops against their window caused a macabre uneasiness. Electing to use valet service to avoid getting wet, Daniel pulled under the awning. One of the service attendants, dressed in black pants and a crimson short-waisted coat, hurried to Daniel's side of the car, while the other opened the passenger door for Jane to exit the vehicle.

"Welcome to the Beaufort Inn, sir," he said, as he opened the door for Daniel.

Noticing a half-full parking lot, Daniel queried the attendant, "Slow night tonight?"

Looking skyward, the young man responded, "Yes, sir. This rain seems to have scared people away."

The attendant gave Daniel a gold chit to be used to redeem his car when they were finished dining. Daniel and Jane followed the verdant green awning along the Inn's frontage to the entrance. In keeping with its Southern heritage, a doorman dressed in attire matching the valet attendants opened one of the towering twin doors topped with matching gold carriage lights.

"Welcome to the Inn, sir. Registration is to the left, and the restaurant is to your right. Have a most pleasant evening."

As they stepped through the door, Daniel and Jane were taken with the vintage Civil War ambiance the owners had taken steps to create. A full-size alabaster statue of Robert E. Lee stood in the corner of the foyer. In the opposite corner was the figure of General Nathan Prentice Banks. An arch-shaped front desk of highly polished Cherry wood was lit by an ornate three-tiered gold chandelier. On either end of the front desk were glass display cases containing the field uniforms of an enlisted soldier and an officer. The owners had chosen to use authentic faded uniforms complete with frayed bullet holes and dark smears of spilled blood, all intended to remind visitors of the brutality of war and not the glorification of long past lifestyle.

Behind the desk stood a stately man probably in his sixties. He had white silver hair and wore black horn-rimmed glasses. He wore a white dinner jacket causing Daniel to immediately think of the caricature of the Kentucky Fried Chicken founder, but he wisely thought not to say anything lest he insult the gentleman.

"Good evening, Mr. and Mrs. Kilgore. Welcome to the Beaufort Inn. How may I help you?"

The look of surprise on Daniel's face caused the elderly man to smile.

"The only reservations for 6 o'clock this evening are for a Daniel Kilgore. Your punctuality gave away your identity, I believe. Are you here for the night or to enjoy our fine cuisine.?"

"For dinner only, Andrew," Kilgore replied, noting the gold nameplate on the pocket of his jacket.

Andrew gave a golden bell resting on the desk two sharp taps. Immediately a man appeared. He wore a freshly starched white shirt, black slacks, and a white apron tied firmly behind his back.

"James, this is Mr. Daniel Kilgore and his lovely wife, Jane. They're here for dinner. Please accommodate their every wish." He winked at Daniel. "Captain Pinafore called in advance."

With a polite bow, James said, "Please, follow me."

The dining room had an unusually high dome ceiling covered with a painting of Charleston Bay. Alternately placed along the crown molding above each table were small mini-pendant lights of polished chrome intended more for ambiance than illumination. Plush crimson carpet deadened the sounds of the footsteps of guests and staff. The twenty or so tables were ornately decorated with white tablecloths covered by a thick pane of glass. Each table had matching high back chairs made of polished mahogany covered with a rich, gray fabric. Outlining the back and seat were small curls of gold beaded embroidery. Silverware settings were tightly bound in burgundy cloth napkins and sealed with a small, gold stamp embossed with the letters B.I. A small oil lamp sat mid-table. James deftly pulled out a chair for Jane and then removed the glass chimney from the lamp. Out of nowhere he had a BIC propane lighter in his hand which he used to light the lamp. After placing the chimney on the lamp base, he carefully adjusted the flame for the perfect amount of light. With menus lying at each corner of the table, James asked, "May I get each of you something to drink?"

"I'd love a glass of Pinot Noir, James. By any chance, do you carry the Windy Oaks label?"

James smiled. "Obviously, you have a fine palate. The owners sampled that label at a national wine conference and were so taken with its quality they order a monthly shipment sent from California. Corralitos, I believe, wherever that is."

"I'll have the same," said Daniel.

And so began the celebratory dinner consisting of perfectly chilled salads sprinkled with chunks of blue cheese, with an appetizer of six oysters on the half shell. For the entree, Daniel chose caramelized sea scallops served over risotto with grilled vegetables. Jane selected Clams Casino served in a garlic butter sauce over linguine.

After one poignant period of silence, Jane asked Daniel, "A penny for your thoughts."

Daniel twirled his glass of wine, thoughtfully watching the legs run down the inside of the glass. Raising his glass to Jane, he said, "That we have been so blessed with each other, good friends and Mary. May it last forever."

Jane reached across the table, taking Daniel's hand in hers. Before she could speak, an eruption of thunder and lightning occurred, that along with a flickering of the lights, sent an eerie chill up her spine.

"I hope forever outlasts this storm," she replied, temporarily losing her train of thought.

"How was your meal, Mr. Kilgore?" asked the waiter, whose attentiveness to each phase of their five-star meal Daniel appreciated but found mildly annoying.

"The sea scallops were delicious, James," Daniel replied.

Daniel liked using the waiter's first name. He thought such familiarity an ice breaker between customer and server.

"And your Clams Casino, Mrs. Kilgore?"

"Divine, James, absolutely divine," Jane replied, lightly dabbing the corner of her cheeks with her napkin.

"And the wine?" James added.

"That Windy Oaks Pinot was perfection," answered Jane.

Dutifully, James poured the remaining Pinot into Jane's glass.

"Shall I bring you the dessert menu?"

"I don't think so, James. This rain is only getting worse, and we've got a bit of a drive down the hill."

"I hope to see you again, sir, perhaps when the weather is better," James said, laying the bill discreetly next to Daniel's plate.

Standing under the awning for the valet service to bring them their car, Daniel asked, "I hope this storm didn't ruin your evening? I wanted tonight to be as perfect as the last three years have been for me."

Daniel's words struck deep into Jane's heart. Even during those times when the topic of having a child brought tremendous stress and tension to their marriage, Jane never lost her love for him. With his epiphany about having children, she and Daniel became more one than ever. She placed both hands around his neck and replied, "I've never felt so loved or loved anyone more than you."

Unembarrassed by the arrival of the valet driver, she and Daniel embraced in a prolonged and somewhat sensuous kiss. The driver opened the door for Jane then walked around to the driver's side, handing Daniel the keys.

"Have a wonderful evening," the driver said with a smile alluding to the aftermath of the kiss he had just observed.

Daniel smiled and handed the young man a twenty. Headed down the hill, Daniel and Jane shared a silent moment of thankfulness and gratitude for the path their lives had taken.

～

THE RAIN HAD WASHED AWAY THE SURROUNDING SOIL, COMPLETELY exposing the white granite rock, now no larger than a cantaloupe. It rested about one hundred feet above the coastal cliff highway. It teetered precariously on a tree root before beginning its descent down the cliffside. With every roll, it gained momentum loosening other rocks and soil on the way. The rush of rock and soil served no earthly purpose. The rock existed solely due to ages of geological pressure. A random unexpected rainstorm put it on its current path. A random act of nature serving no purposeful end until it smashed into the driver's side tire of a vehicle headed down the hill. The force exploded the thinly worn tire causing the vehicle to swerve violently toward the road rail. In an instant, the car smashed into the rail and flipped end over end to the jagged rocks below.

30

THE ALPHA - THE OMEGA

Thunderstorms throughout the night made sleep almost impossible for Eddy and Maddy. Little Mary was not bothered in the least by the nocturnal clatter. Eddy had so busied her with games and activities from her play box that when Maddy had called her, the droopy-eyed child had fallen asleep on the living room floor. Eddy straightened up the living room while Maddy took Mary off to bed. Though she had a fiercely independent streak, bedtime was one where Mary treasured the presence of a body next to her. Normally curled up next to one of her parents, Mary would recount what she remembered of the day activities until her speech became mumbled phrases as she fell asleep. With Mary in a deep sleep, Maddy quietly made her way back to the Master bedroom to find Eddy in his own slumberland.

The awakening thunder, coupled with the reflection of the digital numbers on his radio clock around 5:10 a.m., caused Eddy to bolt up in bed. Frustrated at the lack of sleep he was getting, Eddy suddenly realized he had not heard Daniel and Jane return from their evening out. This was not in either one's makeup as they would routinely check to see if Mary would have slept with them or in her own bedroom. A sense of anxiety arose in him. Eddy grabbed his robe off the foot of the bed and walked into the living room. Peering out the living room window, Eddy could see through the drizzling morning fog that Daniel's Odyssey was not parked in the driveway. Now he was really concerned. His movements had awoken Maddy, who was now standing next to him in the living room.

"What's going on, Eddy?" she mumbled as she rubbed her eyes.

"They're not home. The car's not in the driveway. I think something may have happened to them," Eddy responded in a tone that seemed to accentuate his fear was, in fact, a reality.

"Oh, God! Eddy. Not Daniel and Jane!" Maddy clutched at his robe in abject terror at the possible reality of his words.

Maddy started the Mr. Coffee while Eddy turned on the early morning news on the TV careful to keep the volume low so as to not wake little Mary. As they sat on the couch, every bit of hope that they had quickly faded as the TV showed the news channel team on site filming a rescue team haul a white Odyssey over the road rail. Its front left wheel was completely crushed in. As the tow crane settled the vehicle onto the highway, the TV camera panned in on the rear of the car exposing the tragic outcome. The license plate read R Mary. Maddy found herself unable to speak. Her lungs fought for air. She was suffocating on her own inability to breathe. She almost passed out before her paralyzed lungs began to work. Eddy found himself in a kind of out of body experience. *Call the police department, find out what hospital the ambulance is taking them to,* he told the person sitting on the couch next to him, but that person did not respond. Maddy reached deep into her soul. *Was this really what a loving God had in store for her friends? Was Jane to be given the dream of a lifetime only to have it torn from her this way? Daniel was learning to love and be loved by one of God's smallest creatures. Who would extend that love to his child now?*

The ringing of the phone brought Eddy's mind to the situation at hand. He reached for the phone and signaled to Maddy to turn off the TV.

"Yes, this is Alan Pinafore."

Eddy listened carefully to the voice on the other end. He wasn't sure if it was a curse or a blessing.

"Yes, of course. I'm on my way."

Curious as to who had called, Maddy asked, "Who was that?"

"The neurological surgeon at the ER. They found a contact card in Daniel's wallet to call me in case of an emergency. He wants to talk to me."

"About what," asked a more curious Maddy.

"I'm not sure. I'll call you after I hear something."

Eddy hurriedly dressed and headed to Charleston Central about a thirty-minute drive. At the wideout where the highway leveled out, He saw the gathering of police and rescue vehicles, including the tow truck with Daniel's car on it. A road worker was signaling for traffic to slow down. As he drew near Daniel's car, he couldn't help but notice a white granite rock about the size of a volleyball wedged between the top of the wheel and the frame of the vehicle.

∼

IMMEDIATELY UPON ARRIVING AT THE HOSPITAL, PINAFORE WAS DIRECTED to the offices of Dr. Shane Tipton, Head of Neurological Services. Eddy waited impatiently in the small waiting room to be called in. *Come on! You called me. Remember?* The impatience of his thoughts seemed almost audible to him and a huge embarrassment if true. Finally, the door opened. A man entered wearing a blue skull cap. A stethoscope hung around his neck. Wearing casual tan dockers, a white shirt embossed with the Carolina Panthers logo, and casual brown walking shoes, Tipton hardly appeared the renowned neurosurgeon that he was.

"Mr. Pinafore, I'm Doctor Tipton. Please come in."

Eddy followed instructions without saying a word. Tipton's office was unpretentious for a doctor of his stature. The usual licenses and certificates hung on the wall as if to bring authenticity to his presence. Three gray metal chairs formed an arch around a small matching table. After taking one last look at several x-rays and images taken by the ER technicians, Tipton offered his hand to Eddy. He had a firm grip which Eddy appreciated as most people meeting him for the first time shook his hand with timidity because of the loss of his arm.

"Before I get started, may I ask what was your relationship with victims?

"Daniel and his wife, Jane, are my wife's and I best friends. We've known each other for years; in fact, we are Godfather and Godmother to their daughter, Mary."

This news made the burden of what Tipton had to tell Eddy even more difficult. No matter how many times he had done this in the past, it never got any easier. The finality of human life is impossible to deliver without feeling some pain for those who live on.

"I'm not sure how much you know of the accident, so let me start from the beginning. From the initial police report, for some reason undetermined at this time, the driver, a Daniel Kilgore veered off the road and over the road rail. It was nearly a hundred-foot drop to the rocks below. He suffered massive trauma to the chest and head. He did not survive. However, in spite of suffering similar injuries, his wife did survive and by that, I mean she is able to breathe on her own, and she has a strong pulse and heartbeat."

Tipton paused to let Eddy digest this initial phase of his diagnosis. Eddy had been down this road before. At first, you get whatever good news the doctors can muster up. Then they give you the likelihood of what the future really holds. Tipton gave Eddy a different feeling, be it spiritual based or some innate faith in the progress of medicine.

"I'm not going to give you any false hopes of a recovery, Mr. Pinafore. Mrs. Kilgore has several fractures to her spinal column. She appears to be paralyzed from the neck down. She suffered massive facial fractures and broken bones throughout her body. We fixed a lot of those injuries. There appears to be some intermittent brain activity, but until we can reduce the swelling around her brain, we won't really know what we have. We'll have more information over the next several weeks."

"What's ahead of her now?" Eddy asked.

"I'd like to move her to the Neurological Center in Charleston for further study. They have a first-rate staff on hand. Any hope for an improved future will lay in their hands."

Eddy nodded

As Eddy stood up to leave, Tipton said, "I'm going to take good care of her, Mr. Pinfore."

On his way back home, Eddy thought this is not the fate Daniel and Jane deserved. They found in each other a chance for second love. Baby Mary was a different type of second love for Daniel and for Jane. Now this, Daniel gone, and God knows what's ahead for Jane. It was at Daniel's funeral where Eddy found his answer. Daniel's sister, Kristin, felt it was more appropriate to hold a Celebration of Life for Daniel rather than the more intense Catholic Requiem Mass for the Dead since Daniel had ceased attending Catholic Church as a young man. As a member of the Elks, Eddy was able to rent the local Elks Lodge for the service. Maddy thought it better to keep Mary away from the service, so she stayed home with Maddy while Eddy attended the service.

Eddy arrived about twenty minutes prior to the start of the service which was scheduled to start at ten a.m. He was surprised to find the parking lot three-quarters full. The line leading to the hall extended outside and along the sidewalk in from the Elks Hall. The rather nondescript building sat atop a small knoll consisting of about one acre of land. Only the large mosaic on the front of the building of an elk centered in a golden circle gave the building any identity. As Eddy waited in line to enter, he could not help but overhear the endless stories of how Daniel had touched the lives of so many people. After finally getting inside and signing the Guest Book, Eddy walked into the large hall. There were three large easels adorned with pictures of Daniel's life from early childhood through adulthood. Eddy paused in front of each to garner some feeling for Daniel's life before the two had met. Eddy's only contact with Daniel's sister had been through emails following the accident discussing the temporary custody of little Mary. Kristin and her husband were in their sixties and had expressed no desire to take on the responsibility of raising a young child. He thought it better to take a seat than to introduce himself at such an awkward time.

Eddy scanned through the handout given him at the podium where he signed the Guest Book. Kristin began her part by thanking everyone who had come. Then she took a rather abrupt turn from the usual protocol.

"I'm not going to speak of Daniel's life growing up, or the tragedies that fell upon him, that is what the picture boards are for. Instead, I want all who knew Daniel to speak about the impact he had on their lives."

The first to raise was an older man about Daniel's age. His gray hair was trimmed short and neat. The scuff of a silver beard gave him some resemblance to Sean Connery. A deep baritone voice got everyone's attention.

"My name is Dutch Harrison. I first met Daniel in our senior year at Clemson University. I was taking a two-unit elective class in education. Daniel sat next to me. Throughout the semester, Daniel spoke of how he wanted to change the world by teaching children. I was going to be in law enforcement, determined to clean up the world. Over the years Daniel and I kept in touch. At one particular meeting, he asked me if I felt I was having an impact on others by being a police officer. Sadly, I had to answer no. Nobody thanks you when you get to the scene of a crime. All they want to know is what took you so long. You're scrutinized for your use of force by the public, and your fellow officers expect you to back them up with whatever story they concoct to justice their actions. His words to me were, "Why not try teaching?" Change a mind, affect a heart, and you really impact the lives of others."

Looking out across a packed hall, Harrison continued.

"So I did, and I've never looked back. Daniel Kilgore led me and countless hundreds of others to a career in service, in impacting the lives of others. There is no greater legacy."

For well close to an hour, person after person spoke of the effect Daniel had on their lives. The man whose family couldn't afford to buy him a baseball glove as a child, Daniel Kilgore was his benefactor. Another spoke of going on camping trips with the Kilgore's to get away from an abusive father. Eddy was particularly affected by those who spoke of turning to Daniel when they were in high school and struggling with those difficult hormonal teenage periods. The gentle smile and understanding words of Daniel Kilgore provided a light when their world seemed darkest. Many spoke of choosing their career path based on Daniel's favorite phrase, "There is no greater accomplishment in life when to impact the lives of others." Eddy returned home no longer mourning a lost friend but admiring the life his friend had led. As for Jane Kilgore, her life could continue that legacy in the most ironic way.

~

IN THE SIX WEEKS JANE KILGORE SPENT AT THE CHARLESTON Neurological Studies Center, Eddy and Maddy were overwhelmed with an avalanche of things to do. There had been Daniel's funeral arrangements, now insurance issues, notifications to family and friends, and lastly custodial arrangements for Mary. The one that should have been the easiest to deal with turned out to be the most contentious - custody of Mary. The Superior Court Building in Charleston glistened in the heat of the mid-day sun. The sun's rays reflected off the mineral contents embedded in the white granite columns lining the entrance to the courthouse so much that anyone walking up the two dozen steps was forced to look downward to avoid the blinding glare. The air-conditioning system was working overtime to cool the air for those who worked there, and the tempera-ments of those awaiting a decision in some litigious case. Such was the situation for Eddy Pinefore and his wife, Maddy. Bad news seemed to follow Eddy and Maddy when the story of the accident became public knowledge. Some advocacy group from the State Department of Children Services had petitioned the court to have Mary returned to the agency for suitable placement, as the paperwork was worded. Emotionally, Maddy didn't know how much more she and Eddy could take. There was no use relying on the hometown manipulations of Alice Franklin and Florence Abby out of Family Services now. This was the big leagues.

The layout of the court building had three courtrooms on the front side and three more courtrooms along the sides. The backside of the main floor was reserved for court offices. Unfortunately for Eddy and Maddy, they were scheduled for courtroom #3, forcing them to endure a steady parade of litigants coming and going. Of some minor comfort was the fact that the visitor's benches, made of Carolina pine, had extra thick seat cushions making the visitor's wait somewhat more comfortable. However, nothing could dispel the cacophony of sounds made by hundreds of shoes, boots, and canes traversing the black and white marble tiles of the courthouse floor. They echoed with increasing or decreasing intensity depending on the direction of the walker. Maddy kept Mary busy with a variety of toys from a tote bag she had whenever they went out, but her mind was preoccupied with thoughts more foreboding than little Mary's next toy selection. *What if the court decided against their petition to adopt her? What if they could never be anything but custodial representatives?* These thoughts tore at Maddy's heart while generating a flood gate of emotions. Adding to their angst was the fact that that child had started calling them Mommy and Daddy.

The ad nauseam of mindless sounds ended when Flo came out of the courtroom. Her face reflected the anxiety surging through her body, facial muscles tightened, her throat felt dry. She had seen family court decisions rendered in the past that tore families apart, that defied logic only to satisfy some legislative requirement. Her eyes moistened as she contemplated the worse possible outcome.

"We're up next."

Panic surged through Maddy's body. Her body turned rigid. Her eyes scanned back and forth for an escape route in the event they tried to take her Mary. At that moment, she was Mary's mother. The three had decided that Eddy would attend the hearing with Flo, leaving Maddy to babysit Mary. Eddy kissed Maddy saying, "Wish me luck." Echoing her daddy's words, Mary went on a whimsical chant, "Luck, luck, luck, luck."

~

EDDY HAD MORE THAN HIS SHARE OF ANXIETY AS HE FOLLOWED FLO INTO the courtroom and to the plaintiff's table. As they seated themselves at the table, Flo reviewed their paperwork one last time.

"Damn," she whispered. "I sure wish I knew this judge, but he's a stranger to me."

"What's his name?" Eddy replied, surprised that there was anyone in the Family Court Circle that Flo Abby didn't know.

"I can't even pronounce it," said Flo with a major sound of frustration in her voice.

"K..o..t..o..w..s..k..i.. First name John, middle initial A."

Eddy quickly took the paper from Flo. *It can't be true,* Eddy thought. *No way!*

Yes way, he said to himself. John A. Kotowski was the Naval Jag attorney who had handled Eddy's case. Kotowski had always thought Eddy had been screwed over by the Navy. It was the final blow for the idealistic young attorney's Naval career who subsequently had left the Navy for private practice, eventually becoming a Superior Court judge. The judge hadn't forgotten the name Pinefore.

"Ms. Stevens, you'll be representing the state of South Carolina?"

"Yes, your Honor," replied the eager young attorney, newly out of law school.

"And Ms. Abby, you will be handling the interest of Mr. and Mrs. Pinafore?"

"Yes, your Honor," answered Flo, more intrigued than ever by the smiles being exchanged between the judge and her client.

"Then let's begin," sounded the judge.

The young attorney meticulously presented the facts of the case from the state's perspective, case studies supporting the state's position, and prior rulings for the state in similar cases. In a self-destructive move, she included the ages of the plaintiffs and the disabilities involved as mitigating factors.

"Are the ages of the plaintiffs and their disabilities really relevant, counselor?" asked the judge.

"As mitigating factors for potential problems, I think they are, your honor," replied a confident attorney.

Judge Kotowski took his glasses off and wiped them with a white handkerchief.

"Are you familiar with the name Jim Plunkett, Ms. Stevens?" asked the judge.

"No, I'm afraid I'm not," answered the state's attorney, realizing she was being played.

"Mr. Plunkett played football at Stanford University, was a first-round NFL draft choice of the Buffalo Bills, led the Oakland Raiders to two Super Bowl victories, and is in the NFL Hall of Fame. By the way, both his parents were blind."

A sense of confidence began to swell in Florence Abby. New ideas were not always popular with judges, especially if they set a precedent, but then Judge Kotowski was not averse to thinking outside the box.

"If I've read your petition correctly, Ms. Abby, your client is merely requesting to be named a co-parent of the minor child of Daniel and Jane Kilgore. Mr. Kilgore was killed in the same auto accident that left his wife a quadriplegic. She is confined to a bed unable to speak or feed herself, and slips in and out of consciousness, is that correct?"

"Yes, your honor."

"And your request would in no way hinder Mrs. Kilgore from

resuming her maternal responsibilities should some sort of miracle occur."

"Absolutely not, your honor," assured Flo.

When Flo and Eddy exited the courtroom, she gave an exaggerated fist bump to Maddy. Realizing its significance, Maddy let out a triumphant yell of jubilation.

∼

WITH THE MYRIAD OF DETAILS EDDY AND MADDY WERE DEALING WITH, the dreaded call from the Neurological Center was never far from their minds. Maddy had returned from visiting Magnolia Gardens. Everyone from the Board of Directors to the staff on down wanted to know how Jane was doing and if there was anything they could do. Dr. Blaine Williams, the Chief Operating Officer for the Board and a longtime supporter of Jane Kilgore, was particularly interested in a potential placement for Jane. He asked to be updated. Everything seemed to hinge of the final evaluation from Dr. Tipton.

"The Center called, Maddy," Eddy announced on Maddy's return. "They'd like to see us tomorrow at 9 a.m. I arranged for my bother to watch Mary."

An impatient Mary wiggled free from Maddy's arms to run to her toy box. Her life seemed so unaffected by the circumstances at hand. There was only an occasional reference to Jane or Daniel. Eddy and Maddy had decided to redirect any such conversation for later time. Much later would have suited both of them. Both wondered how the meeting would address the uncertain future facing everyone.

∼

DR. TIPTON'S OFFICE AT THE NEUROLOGICAL CENTER WAS AS unpretentious as his office at the hospital, except for the fact it was on the top floor of the eight-story medical complex. The slow ticking of the elevator at each floor caused Maddy to grip Eddy's hand tighter with each passing floor. Directly opposite the elevator door was the receptionist's desk. Remembering his own history with doctors and their prognosis, Eddy felt a sudden urge to leave, avoiding the confrontation of hope and reality. His words sputtered, "Tip...Tipton."

The receptionist looked up.

"I'm sorry, but what did you say?"

He forced the words out. "Doctor Tipton, we're here to see Doctor Tipton."

"May I have your last name, sir?" asked the receptionist.

"Pinafore, Eddy and Maddy Pinafore," the raspy tone in his throat caused Eddy to cough.

Glancing at her computer screen, and thereby verifying their appointment, the receptionist replied, "Please have a seat. I'll let the doctor know you're here."

They had barely taken their seats when a door opened and Tipton appeared.

"Eddy and Maddy, come on in," he smiled. He led them down a short hallway to his office on the right. "Step on in," he said, holding the door open for them.

As a decorator, Maddy thought Tipton was something of a minimalist, to say the least. For one, the office was on the interior with no expansive view. Secondly, there was nothing personal of his on display. No family pictures, no special piece of art, just the obligatory certificates of competencies from various colleges and universities. Maddy couldn't help but comment.

"I would have thought you'd have the office with all the windows. The view is so impressive."

Tipton smiled. "Some of my colleagues prefer their clients to be impressed with the view. I prefer my clients to be impressed with my work."

The jab at the elitists within the medical profession pleased Eddy, who had to deal with that type for years.

"Can I get either of you something to drink?" Tipton asked, as he seated himself at the table with Eddy and Maddy.

Speaking for both, Maddy replied, "No, thank you. I'm more anxious to hear the prognosis for Jane."

The smile on Tipton's face faded, replaced by one that said, *now for the cold hard objective facts.*

"Let me spare you the part where I say what medical research may hold in the future for Jane. In time, fractures to her jaw, orbital bones, both arms and legs, and most of her ribs will heal. However, the multiple fractures to her back have left her completely paralyzed. She has lost the ability to speak, but she is making slow progress using a system of eye blinks, one for yes, two for no, to answer questions. Brain scans indicate some activity, but it's intermittent, at best. Medically, we've done all we can. Time may bring some improvement in audio and visual stimuli. What Jane needs is the best twenty-four-hour care you can afford. Fortunately for you, that's not going to be a problem."

Eddy and Maddy were barely coping with Jane's prognosis when they were told that the best twenty-four-hour care for Jane was not going to be a problem. There were only so many ups and downs their hearts could take.

"What does that mean, Doctor?" Maddy asked.

"Blaine Williams, the COO at Magnolia Gardens, called me recently. He has personally arranged for Jane's placement at Magnolia Gardens. He also told me that you, Eddy, have accepted the position of Executive Director. He was pleased that someone with family ties would be on hand to periodically check on Jane's status. As he told me, Jane was part of their family as well as yours, and family doesn't forget family."

~

"ARE YOU SURE? THEY USUALLY COME HERE FOR LUNCH ON SATURDAYS," answered the attendant into the phone.

"Okay, I'll tell staff they're here."

John Wray was the quintessential "Old Hippie" of the Bellamy

Brothers Country Album only instead of a returnee from Vietnam, it was Desert Storm and two tours in Iraq. He preferred tie-dyed t-shirts and a bandana around his head. The stethoscope around his neck was his only acquiescence to the professional appearance of an RN, which he was. He closed his cell phone and headed down to the last room on the right.

When Eddy had arranged for the transfer from the rehab center, he told the staff at Magnolia Gardens the patient was being admitted as an unidentified female patient, which explained the name tag, Jane Doe. With her head and face covered with bandages, there was little chance anyone would recognize her. Eddy and Maddy wanted to spare her the continual interruption of friends and staff wanting to check on her. Medical charts don't lie, and soon the staff knew who the newly admitted patient was. Her legacy at Magnolia Gardens had not been forgotten by the staff. Many made a point of daily visits to see her if only to reintroduce themselves and say hey. Jane was totally paralyzed, her skin literally clung to her skeletal structure. Her brain struggled to allow her to respond to eye blinks when asked a question. That never dissuaded them from coming. There was an eternal hope that somehow, someday, she might remember, that she might respond. Jane never gave up hope in her residents and the staff was not about to give up on her.

It was a good time to be out on the patio, Wray thought. Cloudy skies deferred some of the mid-day heat from the sun. There was just enough breeze to move the plant life to sway gently back and forth.

"You don't mind if I smoke, do you, Jane?" Wray asked, as if expecting an answer to the absurd.

He missed the single blink of the eye as he lit a Marlborough Lite, deeply inhaled, and exhaled. He believed with all his heart that his patients could hear, sense, or feel in some way when he was talking with them and it didn't matter about what. "My friend, Bob, was a great guy. We were in Iraq together." He stared off into the distance, his eyes moistening. "He never came back." He gently put her hand on his. Proceeding with his story, Wray paid no attention to the Director, his wife, and their daughter, who were walking up the gentle slope from the pond.

Halfway up the slope, Eddy and Maddy paused.

"Is this Jane's fate, Eddy. To sit in that chair, unable to speak, unable to move, people wondering if her brain can tell her anything? For what purpose, Eddy, for what purpose?"

He put his arm over Maddy's shoulders. He knew exactly what she was going through. All that pain, all the operations he had gone through after his failed mission, could not restore Eddy to the man he once was. *Why him?* he had often thought during those years. No amount of counseling seemed to help. After a particularly challenging day helping a vet in his office cope with a recurring dream, his nurse said, "Nice job, Sir. You really helped him." That's when Eddy realized his purpose was to help others. What had happened to him had put him in a position to get help and now to give help.

"Honey, Jane has a new purpose in life. To inspire others to see there is value in human life, no matter the form that life takes. Jane and others like her will bring out the best of humanity in all who work with her. There must always be hope that things can change. Maddy, don't look at what Jane can't do as her fate. Look at those around Jane and see how she's affecting their lives. Think of the goodness she had inspired in others and will continue to do."

John, seeing them approach, digressed from his war story, put out his cigarette, and hollered, "Hey, we're over here."

Looking up, young Mary, not realizing the resident might be asleep, responded, "Hey, John. It's me, Mary."

Young Mary and her father were regular visitors every Friday. Wray had been soon mesmerized by the child's gregarious and outgoing personality.

Equally unattentive to the resident's state, John responded, "Come on up, Mary. I want you to meet a friend of mine."

Mary bolted forward before Eddy could get a hold on her. In the blink of an eye, she was at the wrought iron fence that enclosed the patio. Wray's long arms reached down and swung the child up and over the rail onto the tiled patio. Eddy seemed unconcerned with the scene before him. After all, young Mary had the run of Magnolia Gardens, what with her white custom-made candy stripped uniform she usually wore, helping the staff with whatever make-believe jobs they could come up with for her.

Taking Mary's hand in his, John walked her over to the resident's wheelchair.

Placing her hand on Mary's hand, he said, "Mary, this is my friend, Jane. Jane, this is my friend, Mary."

There was little reaction from Jane except for that oh so subtle repetitive blinking of her eyes.

Not wanting Mary to be concerned with Jane's lack of response, Wray said, "Why don't you sing her a song?"

"From pre-school?" the child asked.

"Sure, that would be fine," replied John.

"Can I use my outside voice?" she asked. "Sometimes, I have to be reminded."

"Sing away," chuckled Wray.

Taking advantage of her outside voice, the tranquilness of the moment was shattered by the shrill voice singing,

"Mary, Mary, quite contrary, how does your garden grow.
With silver bells and cockle shells and pretty maids all in a row."

"Keep going," Wray urged.

"But I don't know anymore," replied a saddened Mary.

"Then just sing it again, Mary," said Wray, giving new confidence to the child.

So she did, over and over again, until Eddy and Maddy reached the patio fence.

"Sweetheart, we can hear you all the way down by the pond. Maybe you could sing just a little softer. We wouldn't want to disturb anyone."

～

Somehow, someway, in that tangled mess of shattered neurological pathways, the unexplainable had occurred. One name, repeated over and over, had echoed through the unresponsive mass of brain matter until it found the anatomically smallest connective tissue that remained. It was faint at best and certainly indiscernible to the outside world, but in the trapped world of her mind it was loud and clear. *Mary..! Mary...!*

EPILOGUE

The *Journey's End*, Book 3 of Michael J. Sullivan's *Forgotten Flowers* series, brings to an emotional climax to the lives of Madeline, her husband, Eddy, and their daughter, Mary. Madeline had been the love of his life and Eddy would be with her to the very end. Their daughter, Tina, would face her own challenges after meeting Ryan Callahan. What is the journey's end for some is the beginning of a journey for others.

ACKNOWLEDGMENTS

Always to my loving wife Ginny for her patience and critical eye to my writing, without which I would accomplish nothing. To Frank Eastland and his staff at Publish Authority for their continual support and encouragement to stretch my imagination and trust in the creative process. To my friend Rob Gordon for his much-needed advice to write so the reader understands what the writer already does.

THE AUTHOR

Michael J Sullivan is the author of the acclaimed *Forgotten Flowers*, among other works. The remarkable reception to this novel inspired him to create the Forgotten Flowers Program, a non-profit organization established to help facilitate youth and adults to regularly visit the elderly ("forgotten flowers") in their homes and assisted living facilities. Michael and his wife Ginny live in Sonora, California.

Find out more about Michael at www.michaeljsullivanbooks.com

A NOTE OF THANKS

Publish Authority

Thank you for reading

If you enjoyed *The Journey Home*, we invite you to leave your honest reviews online and recommend the novel to family and friends.